A FAMILY MADE AT CHRISTMAS

BY
SCARLET WILSON

THEIR MISTLETOE BABY

BY
KARIN BAINE

MILLS &
BOON

Scarlet Wilson wrote her first story aged eight and has never stopped. She's worked in the health service for twenty years, trained as a nurse and a health visitor. Scarlet now works in public health and lives on the West Coast of Scotland, with her fiancé and their two sons. Writing medical romances and contemporary romances is a dream come true for her.

Karin Baine lives in Northern Ireland with her husband, two sons, and her out-of-control notebook collection. Her mother and her grandmother's vast collection of books inspired her love of reading and her dream of becoming a Mills & Boon author. Now she can tell people she has a *proper* job! You can follow Karin on Twitter, @karinbaine1, or visit her website for the latest news—karinbaine.com.

A FAMILY MADE
AT CHRISTMAS

BY
SCARLET WILSON

Published in Great Britain 2017
By Mills & Boon, an imprint of HarperCollins*Publishers*
1 London Bridge Street, London, SE1 9GF

© 2017 Scarlet Wilson

ISBN: 978-0-263-92678-1

Printed and bound in Spain
by CPI, Barcelona

Dear Reader,

It's official! Christmas is my favourite time of year. I can't get enough of it, and what I love more than anything is writing Christmas books. I have to be honest and say that this one is my favourite yet. I *loved* writing about these characters. April and Riley's story jumped off the page at me, and certain scenes—especially the ones with the little boy Finn—made me cry. There are lots of difficult issues in this story, but true love conquers in the end. I hope you love this story as much as I do.

I have lots of traditions with my family and good friends at Christmas, but being a Mills & Boon author has let me develop some new ones. One of which is buying a Christmas bauble from a very famous London store every time I come down to London for the official Mills & Boon Author Lunch. This year I hope to take that number up to seven. I've been buying one since I was first published in 2011 and I'm rapidly running out of colours!

I love to hear from readers, so feel free to contact me via my website, scarlet-wilson.com, or you can find me on Facebook or Twitter.

Merry Christmas!

Love,

Scarlet

This book is dedicated to Sheila Hodgson, my fabulous editor. Thank you for believing in this story and letting me see it through, and thank you for being the best advocate for Medical Romance in the world!

Books by Scarlet Wilson

Mills & Boon Medical Romance

Christmas Miracles in Maternity

A Royal Baby for Christmas

Midwives On-Call at Christmas

A Touch of Christmas Magic

The Doctor She Left Behind
The Doctor's Baby Secret
One Kiss in Tokyo…
The Doctor and the Princess

Mills & Boon Cherish

Maids Under the Mistletoe

Christmas in the Boss's Castle

Visit the Author Profile page
at millsandboon.co.uk for more titles.

CHAPTER ONE

'HURRY UP, RILEY. It's your round.' The hard slap on the shoulder nearly ejected him from his chair. Riley laughed and turned around. Frank Cairney, one of the rehab nurses, was standing with his rucksack on his shoulder. The rest of the team were hovering outside near the door. 'Should I go and hold up the bar for us?'

Riley nodded. 'Just a few notes to finish and I'll be there. Thanks, guys.'

He typed quickly on the electronic record, leaving detailed notes on the plan for Jake Ashford, a soldier injured on duty in Afghanistan and now a resident in the army rehab hospital at Waterloo Court.

It was late afternoon on a Friday. Those who could go home had gone home. But some patients wouldn't be able to go home for some time—Jake was one of those.

Working in the rehab hospital hadn't really been on Riley's career plan. But, due to a family crisis, a fellow colleague hadn't been able to start when he should have, meaning the hospital needed someone to fill in. Riley's surgical experience in orthopaedics had been flagged and his deployment had been delayed on a temporary basis for a few weeks.

But today was his last shift. And truth was he was

relieved. The staff and support team at Waterloo Court were fantastic, as were the world-class rehab services, but Riley liked the pace of emergencies. On Monday he'd be in Sierra Leone, where another outbreak of Ebola seemed to be emerging.

He finished his notes and walked down the corridor to the in-patient beds. He heard the laughter before he saw her familiar frame.

April Henderson had Jake sitting at the side of his bed. Laughing. Really laughing, as if she'd just told him the funniest joke in the world.

Even from here he knew exactly what she was doing—testing Jake's sitting balance. She was one of the best physiotherapists he'd ever worked with.

She was tireless. She was relentless. She was polite. She was professional.

He'd caught himself on more than one occasion watching that blonde ponytail swishing up the corridor in front of him as she made her way between the ninety patients that were housed in the state-of-the-art unit.

But even now—four weeks later—he really didn't know a thing about her.

April was the quietest co-worker he'd ever met. Every conversation, every communication had been about their patients. When he asked her about life, what she was doing at the weekend or anything other than work she just shut down.

He'd asked other staff a few questions about her, but no one really said much. Apparently she wasn't married and hadn't mentioned a boyfriend. The staff here were a mixture of military and civilian. April was civilian. She'd transferred to the new unit at Waterloo Court. The centre dealt with serious musculoskeletal injuries, neurological injuries and complex trauma, including amputees. The brand-new facility was four times bigger than its predecessor. There were gyms, full of cardiovascular and resistance equipment, two swimming pools, a hydrotherapy pool and a specialist centre where artificial limbs were manufactured on-site and individually tailored to the patients' needs.

'Doc?' Jake caught his eye.

Riley crossed the room, holding out his hand. 'I came to say goodbye.' He paused for a second. 'I'm shipping out again tomorrow.' He had to be truthful, but he could see the momentary pang in the young man's eyes. Jake loved the army. Had wanted to serve since he was five. And now, at the grand old age of twenty-three, would be unlikely to ever ship out again.

Jake took Riley's extended hand. 'Good luck, Doc— it's been short and sweet. Where are you headed?'

Riley gave a shrug. 'At the moment, I think it's Africa. But you know how things can change. By the time Monday comes around it could be somewhere else completely.'

He glanced down at April, who was leaning against a stool at the side of the bed. 'Are you coming to the farewell drinks, April?'

It was obvious he'd caught her off guard because two tiny pink spots flared in her cheeks and she stumbled over her words. 'Wh-what? Er...no...sorry. I don't think I'll manage.'

Jake nudged her with one of his dangling feet. 'Oh, go on, April. When was the last time you could tell me a good night out story?'

The pinkness spread. But the shy demeanour vanished instantly. He'd always found that curious about her. April Henderson knew how to engage with her patients. *Really* engage with her patients. Around them she was relaxed, open and even showed the occasional glimmer of fun. But around any of the staff? She was just April.

'I'm not here to tell you night out stories, Jake. I'm here to help get you back on your feet again.' She leaned forward and put her hands on his bare leg. 'But don't think I didn't notice that deliberate kick.' She looked up and gave Jake a wide smile. 'That's great. That's something we can work on.'

With her bright blue eyes, blonde hair and clear skin, April Henderson could be stunning if she wanted to be. But there was never any make-up on her skin, never any new style with her hair. It was almost as if she used her uniform as a shield.

Riley watched the look on Jake's face. For the first time in weeks he saw something that hadn't been there much before. Hope.

It did weird things to his insides. Jake was a young man who should be filled with hope. His whole life was ahead of him. But there was already a good hint that his injury could be limiting. They still didn't have a clear prognosis for him, and that was why April's work was so vital.

He winked at Jake and folded his arms across his chest. 'I'm completely and utterly offended that you won't come to my farewell drinks. Four long weeks here, all those shifts together, and you can't even say goodbye.'

'He's right, April.' Jake nodded. 'It is shocking. Thank goodness you're not actually in the army. At this point you'd be getting a dishonourable discharge.'

For the briefest of seconds there was a flash of panic behind her eyes, quickly followed by the realisation that they were kidding with her.

She raised her eyebrows. Gave her best smile. The one reserved for patients in trouble. Both of them recognised it instantly.

'Uh-oh,' Riley muttered.

April touched Jake's leg. 'Well, just so you know, Jake, now that we've established there's some movement and—' she stood up '—your balance is gradually improving, I think I'll have a whole new plan for you, starting tomorrow.'

Jake groaned as Riley laughed. He couldn't quite work out why April could chat easily with patients but could barely say a word to him on a normal day.

Jake pointed at Riley. 'This is all your fault. You're abandoning me to this wicked, wicked woman. You know she'll work me hard and exhaust me.' He said the words with a twinkle in his eyes.

Riley nodded as he glanced at April. Her blue gaze met his. For the first time since he'd met her, she didn't look away instantly. He smiled. 'You're right, Jake. But I'm leaving you with one of the best physios I've ever met. She'll push you to your absolute limit—exactly what you need. If anyone can get you back on your feet again, it's April Henderson.' He put his hand on Jake's shoulder as he leaned forward to fake whisper in his ear, 'Even if she won't have a drink with me.'

There was something about that bright blue gaze. Even under the harsh hospital lights that seemed to drain the colour from everyone else, April still looked good. The edges of her mouth gave just the slightest hint of turning upwards. It was the first time he'd wished he wasn't leaving.

Jake reached up and grabbed his hand, giving it a shake. 'Thanks, Lieutenant Callaghan. Good luck with your deployment.' There was a tiny waver in his voice. Almost as if he knew the likelihood was he'd never make another deployment himself.

Riley clasped his hand between his. 'I'll look you up again when I come back.' He started towards the door, then glanced over his shoulder and gave a warm smile. 'You too, April.'

Her heart was acting as though she were racing along a beach, rather than sitting at the side of a patient's bed.

Darn it.

Ever since Riley Callaghan had turned up on this ward she'd spent the last four weeks avoiding him. It was everything. The little kink in his dark hair. The smiling green eyes. The cheeky charm. Oh, lots of doctors and servicemen she'd met in the last few years had the talk, the wit, the *lots* of charm.

But she'd had enough to deal with. The diagnosis of her twin sister's ovarian cancer, rapidly followed by her failing treatment, then Mallory's death, had meant that she had found it easier to retreat into herself and seal herself off from the world. Her own genetic testing had floored her. She had decisions to make. Plans for the future.

Her last relationship had been half-hearted. Mallory had got sick and she'd realised quickly that she needed to spend time with her sister. But, since then, the last thing she wanted was a relationship.

After her own testing, she'd spent a day wondering

whether she should just find some random guy, try to get pregnant, have a baby quickly and deal with everything else after.

But those thoughts had only lasted a day. She'd met the surgeon. A date for her surgery would be agreed soon. And she needed to do this part of her life alone.

Then Riley Callaghan had appeared on her ward. All cheeky grins and twinkling eyes. It was the first time in a long time she'd actually been aware of every sense in her body. Her surge of adrenaline. Every rapid heartbeat.

That was the reason she didn't engage in small talk. That was the reason she kept to herself. She couldn't afford to let herself be attracted to a guy at such a crucial point in her life. How did you start that conversation anyway? Oh, you want to go on a date? Great. By the way, in a few months' time I'm going to have my ovaries and fallopian tubes removed and maybe later my breasts. What? You don't want to hang around?

It didn't matter that she'd found herself glancing in Riley's direction every time he'd appeared on the ward. She'd hated the way she'd started stumbling over her words around him, or had trouble looking him in the eye.

But as she watched his retreating back her mouth felt dry. Part of her wanted to grab her jacket and join the rest of the staff for a drink. But then she'd be in a pub, where her inhibitions could lower, and she could encourage the gentle flirtation that could go absolutely nowhere.

She shook her head and turned her attention back to Jake. 'Can we get you more comfortable? I'll work on your new programme and we'll start tomorrow.'

Jake gave her a nod and she helped settle him in a comfortable, specially designed chair for those with spinal injuries.

Her shift was finished but it wouldn't take long to write up her notes and make the adjustments needed for tomorrow. It wasn't as if she had anywhere to go, right?

Half an hour later there were a few voices in the corridor behind her. This was a military hospital. When the Colonel appeared, it was never good news.

All the hairs bristled on her arms. She looked around, wondering who was about to get bad news.

'Ms Henderson?'

She spun around in her chair and jumped to her feet. Her? How? What?

A woman with a pinched face and dark grey coat stood next to the Colonel. She didn't even know that he knew her name.

'Y-yes,' she stumbled.

'We're wondering where Lieutenant Callaghan is.'

Her heart plummeted in her chest. Riley? They had bad news for Riley?

She glanced around. 'He's not here. But I know where he is. Can you give me five minutes? I'll get him for you.'

The Colonel nodded and she rushed past, going to the changing room and grabbing her jacket. If she ran, the pub was only five minutes away.

As soon as she stepped outside she realised just how much the temperature had dipped. It was freezing and it was only the middle of November. As she thudded down the dark path a few snowflakes landed on her cheeks. Snow? Already?

She slowed her run. If spots of rain had turned to

snow, then there was a chance the damp ground would be slippery.

The pub came into view, warm light spilling from its windows. She stopped running completely, her warm breath steaming in the air around her.

She could hear the noise and laughter coming from the pub already. She closed her eyes for a second. She hated that she was about to do this. To walk into a farewell party and pull Riley away for news he probably wouldn't want. Did his family serve in the military? Did he have a brother? She just didn't know. She hadn't allowed herself to have that kind of conversation with Riley.

She pushed open the door to the pub, the heat hitting her instantly. It was busy. She jostled her way through the people, scanning one way then another. It didn't take long to recognise the laugh. She picked Riley's familiar frame out of the crowd and pushed herself towards him. Her work colleagues were picking up glasses and toasting him. She stumbled as she reached him, her hands coming out and landing square on his chest. His hard, muscular chest.

'April?' He looked completely surprised. 'Oh, wow. You made it. That's great.' His arm had automatically gone around her shoulder. He pulled her a little closer to try to talk above the noise in the pub. 'Can I get you something to drink?'

He frowned as he noticed she hadn't even changed out of her uniform.

She looked up into his green eyes. 'Riley, I'm sorry— I'm not here for the drinks.'

He pulled back a little whilst keeping his arm on her shoulder. 'You aren't?'

Her hands were still on his chest. She really didn't want to move them. 'Riley—' she pressed her lips together for a second '—the Colonel is looking for you. He came to the ward.'

She felt every part of his body tense.

'What?' His voice had changed.

She nodded. 'I said I'd come and get you.'

Riley didn't even say goodbye to anyone around him. He just grabbed hold of her hand and pulled her behind him as he jostled his way through the crowd.

The snow was falling as they reached the main door. Riley spun around to face her, worry etched all over his face. 'What did he say? Is it just the Colonel?'

April shook her head. 'He didn't tell me anything. And there's an older woman with him. I didn't recognise her.'

She reached up and touched his arm. It didn't matter that she'd vowed to keep a distance. This was a completely different set of circumstances. This was a work colleague who was likely to receive some bad news. She'd never leave a workmate alone at a time like this. 'Let me come back with you' was all she said.

And, after the longest few seconds, Riley gave a nod.

He started walking quickly but eventually just broke into a run. His brother. It had to be his brother. He was on a training exercise right now somewhere in Scotland, flying out to Afghanistan tomorrow. Accidents happened. As a doctor, he knew that more than most. Unless something had happened to his mum and dad. Could they have had an accident?

He was conscious of the footsteps beside him. The

ones that broke into a gentle run when he did. He'd been surprised by April's appearance earlier—it had made his heart lurch for a few seconds. But it hadn't taken long to notice the paleness of her complexion. The worry in her bright blue eyes. And she was right by his side. Trouble was, right now he couldn't think straight.

By the time he reached the ward area his brain was spinning completely. He slowed down to a walk, took a few deep breaths and tried to put on his professional face. He was a soldier. He could deal with whatever news he was about to receive.

The Colonel ushered him into a room where a woman in a grey coat was sitting with a file in front of her.

April hovered near the door—she didn't seem to know whether to leave or not—and he was kind of glad she was still around.

'Lieutenant Callaghan. Please take a seat.'

He didn't want to sit. In fact, sitting was the last thing he wanted to do. But if it would get this thing over with quicker then he'd do it.

He sat down and glanced at the woman. She leaned across the table towards him. 'Dr Callaghan, my name is Elizabeth Cummings. I'm a social worker.'

He frowned. A social worker? Why did she need to speak to him?

She flicked open her file. 'I understand that this might seem a little unusual. Can I ask, do you know an Isabel Porter?'

He flinched. This was not what he'd been expecting to hear. He glanced at the Colonel. 'Sir, my parents? My brother?'

The Colonel shook his head and gestured back to Ms Cummings. 'No. They're fine. They're absolutely fine. Please, this is something else entirely.'

Riley shifted in his chair. He glanced behind at April. She looked just as confused as he was.

Now he felt uncomfortable. He looked back at the social worker. 'Isabel Porter, from Birmingham?'

The woman nodded.

'Yes, I know Isabel. At least, I did. Around five years ago. Why are you asking me that?'

Ms Cummings gave a nod. 'I see. Dr Callaghan, I'm sorry to tell you that there was an accident a few days ago. Isabel was killed in a road traffic accident.'

It was like a cold prickle down his spine. Nothing about this seemed right. 'Oh, I see. I'm really sorry to hear that. But I don't understand. Why are you telling me?' He looked from one tight face to the other.

Ms Cummings glanced at the Colonel. 'There is an issue we need to discuss. Ms Porter left a will.'

'Isabel had written a will?' Now that did sound weird. Isabel had been a bit chaotic. Their relationship had barely lasted a few months. And they hadn't kept in touch. He hadn't heard from her at all in the last five years. 'Why on earth are you telling me this?'

Ms Cummings slid an envelope across the desk to him. 'Maybe this will help explain things.' She kept talking. 'Obviously there's been a delay. Isabel had no other family. No next of kin, which is probably why she left a will and wrote this letter for you. It takes time to find out if someone has left a will or not.'

Riley glanced at the letter on the table in front of

him. He had no idea what was going on. Nothing about this made sense.

April walked over and put her hand on his shoulder. From the woman who'd seemed so shut off, it was such an unexpected move. But the warm feel of her palm on his shoulder sent a wave of pure comfort through his confused state.

Ms Cummings stared at April for a second then continued. 'It's apparent that your name wasn't on the birth certificate. I'm not quite sure why that was. But because Isabel didn't have you formally named as next of kin, Finn has been in temporary foster care for the last few days.'

Riley shook his head. 'Who?'

She stared at him. 'Finn. Your son.'

For the first time he was glad of the chair. If he hadn't had it, his legs might have made him sway.

'My son?'

Ms Cummings glanced at the Colonel again. 'Yes, Dr Callaghan. That's why I'm here.'

'I have a son?'

She stared at him again. 'Finn. He's five. Isabel never told you?'

He shook his head as his brain just spun. Not a single rational thought would form. 'No. Isabel never told me.'

Ms Cummings pushed the letter towards him again. He noticed it was sealed. The social worker had no idea of the contents. 'Well, maybe that's why she left you the letter.'

Riley looked at the cream envelope in front of him. He picked it up and ripped it open, pulling out a matching cream sheet of paper.

Dear Riley,

I hope you never have to read this. But if you do it's because something's happened. I'm sorry I never told you about Finn. You'd already left for Afghanistan and it just seemed pointless. We already knew our time was over and I didn't need to complicate your life.

I hope I'm not about to spoil things for you. I hope you've managed to meet someone, marry and have a family of your own.

Finn and I have been great. We haven't needed anything at all. He's a funny, quirky little boy and I can see traits of us both in him every single day. I love him more than you can ever know, and I hope you'll feel that way about him too.

He knows who you are. I only had a few pictures, but I put them in his room and told him you worked away and would meet him when he grew up.

Please forgive me, and love my darling boy for both of us.

Isabel

He couldn't speak. He couldn't breathe. His life had just been turned upside down and on its head. He had a child. He had a son.

And he'd never been told. Rage filled his brain, just as April's fingers tightened on his shoulder. She could probably read every word of the letter over his shoulder.

April leaned over and spun the letter around to face the social worker, giving her a few seconds to read it. Her face paled.

Ms Cummings looked at him. 'You didn't even know that Finn existed?'

He shook his head. The firm touch by April was dissipating the rage that was burning inside. Isabel had been quirky. She'd been a little chaotic. This didn't seem completely out of character. He just hadn't had a clue.

'Where is Finn now?' April's voice cut through his thoughts.

Ms Cummings looked up. 'And you are?'

April leaned across and held out her hand. 'I'm April Henderson. I'm a friend and colleague of Dr Callaghan's.' She said the words so easily. A friend. It almost sounded true.

Ms Cummings shuffled some papers. 'Finn's been in temporary foster care in Birmingham.'

Panic started to fill Riley. 'My son is in foster care?' He'd heard about these things. Wasn't foster care bad for kids?

Ms Cummings nodded. 'We have a few things to sort out. As your name isn't on the birth certificate, you may want to arrange a DNA test. However, Ms Porter named you as her son's guardian in her will. Pending a few checks, I'll be happy to release Finn into your custody. You will, of course, be allocated a local social worker to help you with any queries.' She lifted something from her bag. 'As you'll know, in England we have a number of legal procedures. Isabel left everything in trust—via you—for Finn. But probate takes some time. I can only let you have these keys to the house for a day or so—to pick some things up for Finn. Although ultimately it will come to you, the keys have to be returned to the lawyer in the meantime.'

'When do I pick up Finn?'

'Do you have somewhere suitable for him to stay?'

His thoughts went immediately to his temporary army lodgings. He was only supposed to be here four weeks. 'I'm supposed to leave for Sierra Leone on Monday.' The words came out of nowhere.

The Colonel interjected quickly. 'Don't worry. I'll take care of that. You have a family emergency. Your son obviously takes priority here. Do you want me to arrange some other accommodation for you?'

He nodded automatically. He didn't own a property. He had money in the bank but had never got around to buying a place as he'd no idea where he'd eventually end up.

His eyes caught sight of a box in the corner of the room. Red tinsel. It was stuffed full of Christmas decorations. Christmas. It was only six weeks away. His son had lost his mother, six weeks before Christmas.

'I'll give you an address. I can meet you at the foster parents' house tomorrow if that suits.'

'It suits.' The words were automatic.

Ms Cummings gave a nod. 'There's one other thing.'

'What's that?'

She licked her lips. 'As Ms Porter had no other next of kin and you're the only person named in the will, it will be up to you to organise the funeral.'

'What?'

Ms Cummings's eyes narrowed. 'Will that be a problem?'

He shook his head. 'No. Of course not.'

Ms Cummings pushed some papers towards him. 'Here's a copy of the will. A note of Ms Porter's address and her lawyer's address to drop the keys back.

And a copy of the address for the foster family tomorrow. Let's say eleven o'clock?'

Business obviously concluded, she gathered her papers and stood up. Riley glanced at the clock. In the space of ten minutes his life had just turned on its head.

'Do you have a picture?'

She looked startled. 'Of Finn?'

He nodded. Of course of Finn. Who did she think he wanted to see a picture of?

She reopened her file and slid out a small photograph. His mouth dried instantly. It was like a blast from the past. That small innocent face. Thirty years ago that had been him. A whole world he didn't even know existed.

He didn't even speak as the Colonel showed Ms Cummings out.

April had an ache deep inside her belly. This was a whole new Riley Callaghan in front of her right now.

He looked almost broken. She'd spent the last four weeks secretly watching his cheeky grin, positive interactions and boundless energy. There had been a few emergencies on the ward and Riley thought and moved quicker than anyone. He was a great doctor. Happy to help others. And always itching to get on to the next thing.

It was the first time she'd ever seen him slumped. He just seemed stunned.

His hand reached up and crumpled the letter on the table in front of him. She moved instinctively, brushing her fingers against his, pulling the paper from his and smoothing the paper back down.

'Don't. In a few years' time you might want to show that to Finn.'

He stood up so quickly the chair flew back and hit the floor. 'She didn't tell me. She didn't tell me about him.' He flung his hands up. 'How could she do that to me? How could she do that to him?'

April's mouth dried. She didn't know what to say. How on earth could she answer that question?

He started pacing, running his hands through his thick dark hair. 'What do I do? I don't know the first thing about children. I don't know how to be a father. What if he doesn't like me? What if I suck at being a dad?' He threw his hands out again. 'I don't have a house. What do I buy for a five-year-old? What does a five-year-old boy need? And what about my job? Will I still work here? What about school? Does Finn even go to school yet? I move about, all over the place. How can that be good for a kid?'

April took a deep breath. It was clear that every thought in his brain was just tumbling straight out of his mouth. She shook her head and stood in front of him. 'Riley, I don't know. I honestly don't know. But there's a foster mother. She'll probably be able to help. You have keys to the house. Everything that a five-year-old boy needs will be there. And it will probably help Finn if you take his own things to help him settle.'

The light in the office was dimmer than the rest of the hospital. But Riley's hurt green eyes were the thing she could see clearest. She was standing right in front of him. Closer than she'd ever wanted to get.

He closed his eyes for a second then nodded. 'You're right. I know you're right. But my son… Finn…he's been in foster care. Isn't that supposed to be terrible?'

She gave a soft smile. 'I think those days are long gone. Foster carers have to go through a mountain of checks these days. Finn will have been well looked after. But the last few days will probably have been a blur.'

He reached out and took her hand in his. It made her catch her breath. It was so unexpected. And more. He just didn't let it go.

She could almost feel his pain. It was palpable. It was right there in the air between them. Riley Callaghan had just had the legs swept from clean under him. And, to his credit, he was still standing. Just the way she would have expected of him.

'Will you help me, April?' He squeezed her hand.

Fear swept through her. 'What do you mean?'

'I don't know. I don't know anything. Will you help me?'

Help. What did that mean? She was all for supporting a colleague in a difficult situation. But this one was probably bigger than anyone could have expected.

'Please? I'm out of my depth, April. I know that already.' His green eyes were pleading with her. Twisting her insides this way and that.

A child. A little boy had just lost a parent. Finn must be feeling lost. He must feel as if his whole world had just ended.

She met Riley's gaze. 'I'll help where I can,' she said cautiously. 'I can help you with the funeral.'

He frowned. 'You will?'

Mallory. She'd organised every tiny detail of the funeral, even though it had ripped her heart out. Who else knew her twin better than her?

She nodded. 'Let's just say I'm good at funerals.'

And she squeezed his hand back.

CHAPTER TWO

WHAT ON EARTH am I doing?

April spent the whole time on the motorway questioning herself. Riley's hands gripped the steering wheel so tightly his knuckles were white. He'd looked pale this morning. As if he hadn't slept a wink.

By the time the satnav took them into the Birmingham street, the tension was so high she felt as if it could propel the car into the sky. As he killed the engine she leaned over and put one of her hands over his. She really didn't want to touch him. Touching Riley did strange things to her senses, but this wasn't about her. This was about a little boy.

'Stop.'

'What?'

'Just…stop.'

He pulled back his hands and sat back in the seat. 'What are you talking about?'

She could see the tension across his shoulders, reaching up into his jaw.

'You can't go in there like this.'

'What?' The anger that had been simmering beneath the surface was threatening to crack through.

'This is the first time Finn will see you. None of

this is his fault. He's about to meet his dad—someone he's only seen in a photograph before.'

She lifted up her hand as Riley opened his mouth to speak. 'I thought about this last night. I told you I don't have any experience with kids, but what do I think this little boy needs to hear?' She leaned a little closer to him. 'I think he needs to hear his dad loves him. His dad is going to look after him and stay with him. His dad is his family and you'll always be together.'

He frowned and then his face relaxed and he shook his head. 'I know. I know that's exactly what I should say.' He lifted one hand and ran it through his hair. 'I spoke to my brother last night.'

Her stomach twisted. 'Isn't he in Scotland?'

Riley nodded. 'He's on a training exercise. There's supposed to be radio silence. But the Colonel made some arrangements for me. Dan was blown away. Says he can't wait to meet Finn.'

'Good. That's great. At least you know you'll have the support of your family.' Then she tilted her head to the side. Something seemed just a little off. 'What aren't you saying? Did you speak to your mum and dad?'

He shook his head and put one hand back on the steering wheel. 'That's the one thing Dan actually understands. My mum and dad will be great. They'll be overwhelmed. They've always wanted a grandchild. But—'

'But what? Don't you need all the help you can get?'

Riley hesitated. 'My mum…has the best of intentions. I love her. I really do. But she'll want to take over. She'll pick up her life and sweep right down.'

'Ah…and you don't want that?'

Riley smiled. 'Maybe…eventually. But right now I need to get to know Finn. I need to spend some time with him. Like I said, I have no idea about five-year-old boys.'

April shook her head. 'Well, that's a strange thing to say.'

He shrugged. 'Why?'

She lifted her hands. 'Because you've been one. Your brother has been one. You know all you need to know about five-year-old boys.'

He shifted in his seat and pulled his phone from his pocket. 'Look at this.' He opened an app. 'This is what I bought last night.'

She leaned forward to glance at the screen and couldn't help the little laugh that came out. 'A parenting guide? You bought a parenting guide?' She started shaking her head.

'What? I told you. I don't know anything. Anything at all.'

She leaned back against the seat and looked over at him. Riley Callaghan was just about to change before her eyes. The doctor, the soldier and the cheeky charmer was about to take on a whole new role. She admired him for his fear. She admired him for wanting to get to know Finn without letting his mother take over.

Her mouth dried. This was a whole world that she'd never know. She'd already made the decision. She'd never have kids. Her biological clock would never be allowed to tick. When her sister had died it had almost been like watching herself in a mirror. Mallory hadn't had the information that she had. April's genetic testing had only been approved because of Mallory's diagnosis and a look back through the family history. If she ignored the results she would be disrespecting her sister's memory. She could never do that.

But this time of year was especially hard. Her heart gave a little squeeze as she thought of her parents. Before this—before any of this—her mother had always joked she would like a house filled with grandchildren once she retired. But that would never happen now.

And even though her mum and dad fully supported her decision, she knew they had a secret ache for the future life they were losing.

'April?'

Riley's voice pulled her from her thoughts. She gave him a soft smile and wrestled in her pocket for her own phone. She turned it around so he could see her Internet search: *Top ten Christmas toys for five-year-old boys*.

Riley groaned. 'Christmas. It's only six weeks away. I made no plans because I thought I'd be in Sierra Leone. I don't even have a Christmas tree.'

'It's the middle of November. You have time.'

He was staring at her with those bright green eyes. There was silence for a few seconds. She shifted in her seat and brought her hand up to wipe her cheek. 'What is it—do I have something on my face?'

'Why wouldn't you talk to me before?'

She was surprised. 'I did. We spoke about patients all the time.'

He gave a gentle shake of his head. 'But you wouldn't talk to me about anything else.' He paused and continued with his curious stare. 'April, why did you tell me you were good at funerals?'

She could sense his wariness in asking the question. But he'd still asked. He was like this at work too. He always asked patients the difficult questions. Always spoke to the surgeons about the risks and possibilities.

This time he reached out and touched her hand. 'April, did you lose someone? Were you married?'

She closed her eyes for a second. Riley had only been there four weeks. Word obviously hadn't reached him. Then again, the turnover of staff at Waterloo Court could be high. Not everyone knew her background and she preferred it that way.

This wasn't normally something she would share. But she'd just shared a major part of Riley's life. If they'd been on the ward, she would have found a way to dodge the question. But, alone in the confines of the car, there was nowhere to hide. And she didn't want to tell a lie.

'I lost my sister,' she said quietly.

The warmth of his hand was flooding through her system. 'When?'

'Eighteen months ago.'

'Was it an accident?'

She licked her lips. She should have known he would press for more details. This was hard. Probably because she hadn't really shared with anyone before. Probably because she didn't want them to figure out the next step. 'No. It wasn't an accident.' The rest of the words stuck somewhere in the back of her throat. She didn't mention the cancer. She didn't mention the fact they were twins. She didn't mention the genetic tests. These were all things that Riley Callaghan didn't need to know.

By some grace, he didn't ask any more. He didn't ask those details. 'You organised the funeral?'

She nodded. 'She was my sister. My mum and dad were devastated—we all were—but it seemed the one thing I could do that made me feel a little better, a little more in control.' She took a deep breath and met his gaze, trying not to think that his hand was still covering hers. 'So, I can help you with that. If I can find a few of Isabel's friends, talk to some of them, I can make the practical arrangements for you, and you can focus on Finn.'

At the mention of Finn's name again she sensed him tense. 'Riley,' she said warningly.

'What?'

'You're tensing. You're angry. You've been angry the whole drive up here. That's no use. No use at all.' She was talking to him firmly, the way she usually spoke to a patient who was just about ready to give up on their physio.

He snapped. 'What do you expect? I've been cheated out of five years of my son's life. If I'd known about Finn, I would have been there. If Isabel had been involved in an accident, at least my little boy would know he would be with someone who loved and cared about him. He doesn't know any of that. I'm a stranger to him. She did that.'

She shook her head at him. 'Don't you dare.'

'Don't dare what?' He was almost indignant.

She pulled her hand out from under his and pointed her finger at him. 'Don't you dare go in there simmering with resentment at Finn's mother. You're an adult. Deal with it. Deal with the fact that life doesn't always give you the hand of cards that you want. Finn will need you to talk about his mum. If he hears resentment or anger in your voice he'll close off to you. You'll wreck your relationship before it even has a chance to form.'

'I thought you didn't know anything about kids?'

'I don't. But I know enough about people. And so do you. You're a doctor. You deal with families all the time.' She dropped her hand and let her voice soften. 'I know you're angry. And if you are, talk to me. Talk to your brother.' She stared out of the window at the blue sky above them. 'My sister and I used to do a thing.'

'A thing?'

She nodded. 'If either of us was angry or upset—and it happened a lot—we used to hug it out.'

'You what?'

She shrugged. 'Hugging. Physical contact. Scientifically proven to reduce stress and anxiety. To release tension.'

He looked amused. 'You want me to hug it out?'

The expression on his face was incredulous. She unclipped her seat belt and opened her arms. 'Why not? You can't go in there all tense and angry. That doesn't help you. That doesn't help Finn.' She raised her eyebrows. 'And, just so you know, this is a one-time offer.'

His face broke into a smile as he shook his head and unclipped his own belt. 'I must be crazy.'

'I've heard you called worse.'

He leaned forward and wrapped his arms around her. Riley Callaghan knew how to hug. This was no gentle, delicate hug. This was a massive pick-you-up-and-swing-you-round bear hug. Just as well they were in the car.

His emerging stubble brushed against her cheek. The waft of soap and masculinity flooded through her senses. That whole sensation of being held by a man, being comforted by someone who wrapped you in their arms, made her catch her breath. It had been so long. So long since she'd let someone this close.

She was doing this for him. Not for her.

So why did it feel like this?

He couldn't see her face, so she closed her eyes for a few seconds. Letting herself just remember the moment. Feel the heat, the warmth and the comfort.

She'd missed this. Missed this contact more than she'd ever expected to. What she'd done with the best of intentions had turned into something that was kind of overwhelming.

His voice murmured in her ear. 'Thanks, April.'

'No problem,' she replied automatically. Lost in the warm breath near her ear.

After the longest time he pulled back.

'Okay,' he said. 'We're all hugged out.' She could see how nervous he was. 'It's time for me to meet my son.'

In the blink of an eye his life had changed.

He was a father. His first priority was his son.

April was a godsend.

His first sight of Finn, sitting on the edge of his bed in the foster home, ripped his heart clean out of his chest. Finn was his living image. If he'd sat his five-year-old self down next to Finn they would have looked like twins.

He'd never need a DNA test.

He'd wondered about the photo last night—if it was really a good representation of Finn. If they really looked that alike. Now he knew.

The foster carer was possibly the greatest human being he'd ever met. All preconceived ideas were swept out the window in a matter of seconds. She was used to taking kids in crisis situations and was very experienced. She even ran rings around the po-faced Ms Cummings.

She was warm and friendly. She knew Riley and Finn hadn't met before and had already made a little list of things Finn had mentioned in the last few days. That included things from home he wanted, a list of clothing he would need, the contact details of his school and a few names of friends of his mum's.

April stayed in the background, just accepting the lists with a gracious nod and leaving Riley to ask all the questions that he wanted.

It hadn't taken much to notice the slight tremor in Finn's hands. Riley had sat down on the bed next to him and spoke to his son for the first time. He'd never been so terrified in his life. Not when he'd been serving, not when he'd been retrieving military casualties and not when he'd been stranded on a battlefield with virtually no equipment. This was a whole new ball game.

Somehow it felt good that April was there to have his back. She didn't interfere. She just stayed in the background. That hug in the car had done weird things to his mind. Her body pressed against his had sent a quick flash of a few thoughts he'd had about her in the past four weeks. The vanilla scent that had drifted up his nose had taken him to a whole other place. One where April wasn't permanently dressed in her physiotherapist uniform.

Today was the first day he'd seen her in something else. She was wearing a dress. A dress. He hadn't thought of April as a dress sort of girl. It was dark, covered with assorted pink butterflies, finishing just above her knees, which were covered in thick dark tights and knee-high black boots. She'd wrapped a pink scarf around her neck and was wearing a black military-style jacket.

She even looked as if she had a little make-up on. Either that or her lashes were darker than normal and highlighting those blue eyes. He'd never seen April outside the work environment and somehow it felt as if he'd been missing out.

April Henderson looked good. But then he'd always thought that.

And she'd been right. He'd needed to leave his resentment at the door. One look at Finn told him that.

Finn was charming. Polite, well mannered, and the first thing he told him was that he was going to be an astronaut. Riley smiled. He remembered having the same ambition. His little voice shook when he spoke about his mum and Riley wrapped his arm around his shoulder and pulled him close. 'I'm sorry, Finn. I'm sorry about the accident. But I'll look after you now. I'm your dad. I didn't know about you before, but I know about you now.'

He'd pulled Finn up onto his lap. 'If you want to, we'll go and get some of your things. You can bring whatever you want.'

'I can go back home?'

It was like staring into his own green eyes, but these little eyes were laced with uncertainty. Riley tried to keep his voice steady. 'You're going to stay with me now. But your mum's house will stay as it is for now. We can collect your clothes, your toys, some photographs and anything else you want.' He ran his hand over his son's brown hair. Finn had the same little kink in his hair that he did. 'I know some people who will be so happy to meet you. Your uncle Dan has just flown out to Afghanistan. But he's already sent me a message for you. And your gran and granddad will be really happy to meet you too.'

Riley's mouth was running away with him. He could see the tiny tremble in Finn's hands. It made his heart ache. Should he squeeze him harder? He wasn't quite sure.

'I have a gran and granddad?' Finn's eyes widened. 'I never had those before.'

Yes, you did. You just didn't know it.

He resisted the temptation to say the words out loud. 'Well, you do now.'

It wasn't just Finn's hands that were trembling; it was his voice too. Riley had spent his life as a doctor seeing things that affected him deep down. He'd wished a million times he could change things for the patients he worked with. But he'd never wished he could change things more than he did right now. He'd do anything to take away the hurt in Finn's eyes.

Finn looked up shyly across the room, as if he were searching for something. Riley had the oddest sensation.

'Who is the lady?'

Riley shifted on the bed. 'The lady?'

'The pretty one with the blonde hair. Is she your girlfriend?' There was an almost hopeful edge to Finn's voice.

Riley followed Finn's gaze. April was talking quietly with the foster mum, scribbling down a few more notes. He wasn't quite sure what to say.

Something washed over him as he watched the expression on Finn's face. He was right on Riley's knee but it was almost as if he were trying to anchor himself. Finn had spent his whole life brought up by his mum and, from the sound of it, mainly in the company of her friends. His heart squeezed. That was why he was looking at April.

He was used to being with women. Being in the company of a male from this point onwards would be a huge deal for Finn. Riley squeezed his eyes closed for the briefest of seconds as he remembered all the things his mum used to do with him and his brother as kids. Climbing into bed for cuddles, secret cake baking, her patience with homework, and the way one look could let him know that everything would be all right. It was only in the last few years he'd realised that even though she could be overpowering, how central she'd been for him and his brother. Finn had lost that. He'd lost his central point. Could Riley ever hope to become that person for Finn? Or would he always look for a mother figure in his life?

Riley's skin was pale. 'That's April. She's my…friend.' Was she? 'She works with me at the hospital. She's a physiotherapist. She helps people get well again. Sometimes she has to help them walk again.' It seemed the simplest explanation.

Finn frowned. 'If Uncle Dan is in Afghanistan, will you have to go there too?' His voice had a little tremble. 'What will happen to me?'

And, just like that, the thoughts from last night filled his brain again.

He loved his job. He loved the postings. They fired his enthusiasm and ignited his passion. The last four weeks had been fine, but only because he'd known it wouldn't be for long.

His heart twisted in his chest as he said the words he had to out loud. 'It's you and me, Finn. I won't be going away again. I'll be staying here, with you.'

He looked up. April had appeared in the doorway. He could see the expression on her face. She'd heard him in the last few weeks. Being excited about his future plans, talking about all the missions he'd been on.

The Colonel had phoned him this morning. He could stay at Waterloo Court for the next six months. He had temporary family accommodation. This was his life now. Part of him ached. But he pushed it away. He gave April an almost imperceptible nod.

He'd decided. His son would come first. Always.

She could tell he was struggling. And she felt like an intruder, watching two people who were alike in so many ways getting to know each other for the first time.

The visit to the house was the hardest. And she could relate to this. She really could. She'd had to pack up her sister's house and give away some of her belongings. She'd heard other people talk about it in the past, but you could never really appreciate how hard something like this was until you had to do it yourself.

She fingered her necklace as they reached the house. Two intertwined gold hearts. Her parents had given Mallory and April the same thing for their twenty-first birthdays. Mallory had been buried wearing hers.

The first surprise when they reached the house was the tree.

It seemed that Isabel loved Christmas and even though it was only November the tree was already up and covered in decorations.

'We did that last week,' Finn said shakily.

April knelt down and looked at some of the decorations on the tree. She could see instantly they'd been made by a child's hands.

'Will we take some of these too? You made these, didn't you?'

Finn nodded and pointed to a few of them, which April folded into some tissue paper that she found.

She'd done the practical things. She'd found all the clothes and packed them up. She'd helped Finn choose all the toys and books he'd wanted. Then she'd taken a deep breath and thought about all the sentimental things the foster carer had spoken to her about.

'Photos,' she whispered to Riley. 'We need to find some photos for Finn to have of his mum.'

Riley knelt down in front of Finn. 'Should we get some photographs? Pictures of you and Mum we can put in your new bedroom?'

Finn gave a nod and broke into a run. 'This one,' he shouted. 'This is the one I have.'

April glanced at it and her heart gave a little flip. It was a picture of Isabel and Riley together. They were in a pub somewhere. He had his arm around her shoulders and they were looking at each other and laughing. It looked as if it could have been taken yesterday.

It was like a little spear hitting inside her.

Why? She instantly pushed the feeling aside. She'd no right to feel like that. Riley and her weren't anything to each other. Never could be. She wasn't at that point in her life. And he had his hands more than full for the next while.

Riley's face had blanched. The letter had said Finn

had a photograph of his dad; he must not have expected Isabel to be in it too.

April bent down and took the photo frame. 'This is a good photo, Finn. I like it a lot. But let's take some other photographs too. Ones of you and your mum together.'

Finn nodded and darted through to the main living room. April followed his lead and took a photograph from the wall he pointed at, and a calendar from the kitchen that had different photographs of them for every month of the year.

'And the stick!' said Finn. He jumped on top of a chair and found something on a shelf. 'My mum has all our pictures on this!'

Riley gave a nod and put the USB stick in his pocket.

He bent back down. 'Finn, do you want to take anything else?'

Finn hesitated. There was clearly something in his mind.

A wave of something came over April. She'd packed up Finn's bedding to take with him. But after her sister had died, when she'd been packing up the house, she'd collapsed onto the bed at some point and been overwhelmed by the familiar scent from her sister's pillow. She'd sobbed for hours.

She brushed her hand against Riley's. 'I think I know,' she whispered.

She reached out with her other hand and touched Finn's head. 'Should we take some other things of your mum's? How about her pillow, or a blanket that she used? Is there a jumper she loved? Do you want to take something like that?'

Riley squeezed her hand. He must know what this was doing to her. But his look was pure gratitude.

Finn sniffed. So April took his hand and gathered up the things he showed her. He buried his face in his mother's pillow for a few seconds and let out a sob. She couldn't help herself. She gathered the little boy into her arms and just held him. 'I know, honey. I know how hard this is. I'm right here with you. And so is your dad.'

The little body crumpled against hers and a tear slid down her cheek.

This wasn't about her. This wasn't about the family of her own that she'd never have. This was about a little boy who was desperately sad. But somehow it felt about both.

Riley seemed choked too. They gathered up the rest of the belongings and he walked Finn out to the car.

'Wait,' she said. Something had just struck her. She pulled out her phone. 'Let's get a picture of the two of you together.'

Finn looked up at his dad. 'Can we?'

Riley seemed surprised at the question. He knelt down and wrapped his arm around Finn's shoulder. 'Absolutely. I'd love a picture of us both together.'

She knew she should capture it. A first picture of father and son together. But the smile Riley plastered on his face didn't quite reach his eyes. They were still full of worry. As for Finn? He just looked a little nervous. As if he didn't quite know what would come next.

She snapped a few. 'Perfect,' she said.

Riley strapped Finn into the car. As she walked around to her side of the car, he pulled her hand and stopped her, spinning her around to face him.

'April, I just wanted to say something.'

Her heartbeat quickened. It was starting to get dark. Collecting the things had taken a little longer than expected. It had been such a big day. One she'd never expected to be part of.

Today was a Saturday. She might have gone into work for a few hours—even though she wasn't on duty. She'd planned on working with Jake today, but when she'd phoned and left a message for him he'd been absolutely fine. The only other thing she would have done was pick up a few things for dinner.

As it was cold she might even have stayed in her pyjamas all day and watched Christmas movies on TV. Part of her knew that if life had gone as planned, she would probably have had a little pang about not going to Riley's drinks last night. She would have had a twinge of regret that she wouldn't see him again. But part of that would have been reassuring.

It would have left her clear to lock away the attraction she'd been trying to ignore for the last four weeks. She could have parcelled it up in a box like a Christmas present and stored it away in a cupboard. That would have been so much simpler than any of this.

Before she had time to think, Riley slid his hand behind her waist and pulled her towards him, resting his forehead against hers.

It was so up close and personal. They were at the back of the car. Finn couldn't see them. The temperature had dropped; their warm breath was visible in the cold air.

A wave of emotions swept through her. She'd seen a whole other side of Riley Callaghan today. There had already been a glimmer of attraction. Now, she'd seen him at his most exposed. She'd been there when he'd got the news about Finn, then met his child for the first time. It felt too big. Too much. More than she could handle right now.

Finn was adorable. He pulled at every heartstring she had. In a way she knew that she'd picked up some things that Riley might have missed. Riley would be a good father; he just had to get to know his little boy first.

Her heart flipped over. That parent relationship. The one she'd never have. The one she'd never even allowed herself to think about since she'd made her decision. For a few seconds today she'd felt…something. Even if it was only tiny. That urge to reach out to help a child in need. She pressed her lips together and tried to push all the emotions away.

She had to think about the surgery. She had to think about preparing herself. She didn't need her heart tangled up in this mess. She had to keep it somewhere safe.

She hadn't moved. His head was still pressed against hers.

'Thank you,' he whispered. 'Thank you for coming here with me today.'

She gulped and pulled back.

'You're a colleague. No problem.' Her hand brushed against a piece of paper she'd pushed into her pocket. 'I think it's best if you and Finn have some time to yourselves now. I've got a couple of numbers of friends from Isabel's phone book. I'll talk to them to get an idea of what she would have liked. They might want to help with the arrangements.'

A frown furrowed Riley's brow. 'That would be great, thank you.' The words were pleasant but the look on his face told her something different. It was almost as if she'd just abandoned him on a cross-country hike with no provisions.

And he didn't say another word until he dropped her back at her house.

CHAPTER THREE

THE THING ABOUT life throwing you a curveball meant that you didn't always get things right. Finn was the easiest and best part of it all. Riley had heard children were resilient and Finn was still hesitant around him.

But they'd set up his room the way he wanted, hung up his clothes and established a little routine. When he'd heard Finn crying in bed one night, he'd just gone in, wrapped his arms around him and lay with him until he stopped.

He now knew that Finn hated peas, liked chicken in all forms, was also partial to sausages and tomato ketchup, and loved a kids' TV show with spacemen. He had seven DVDs of it and Riley had watched them all with him.

The whirlwind that was Riley's mother was a whole other matter. Thank goodness he hadn't seen her in the flesh when he'd told her about Finn. He was pretty sure she'd had a heart attack at the other end of the phone. Of course she was driving right down. She wanted to meet her grandchild straight away. She'd asked a million questions that Riley didn't know the answers to.

Eventually he'd told her a white lie. He told her that the social worker had recommended that he and Finn spend the first week together on their own to get used to each other. Not to overwhelm him with things. In fact, the social worker had recommended routine as soon as possible. So he'd registered Finn at school and taken him in to say hello. The headmistress had been great, suggesting he bring Finn in for a few hours in the first instance to let him find his feet.

Riley had finally managed to placate his mother by sending the picture that April had taken of them both together. She'd cried at that point. But at least it had given him some time.

What he couldn't work out right now was how to be around April.

Since they'd picked up Finn together, she'd retreated right into herself again. She'd spoken to him about a few funeral arrangements she'd helped put together after talking to Isabel's friends. She'd asked him to speak to Finn about a few things too. But that was it.

No closeness. No real glimmer of friendship.

Maybe it was his fault? If she'd planned her sister's funeral, had she had to deal with other things too? Maybe empty her house, or deal with all her financial affairs. She'd seemed so knowledgeable in Isabel's house—a place he'd felt entirely uncomfortable. She'd seemed to know exactly what Finn needed—even though she said she had no more experience of children than he had. The visit might have revived memories for her that he hadn't considered. Was it any wonder she was keeping her distance?

The rest of the staff had been great. They'd been surprised he was still there. But the news had spread quickly, and everyone was supportive.

Finn had asked to stay at school today until lunchtime. That meant he had three hours. Hours best spent in the hospital.

He'd barely got across the doorway before someone gave him a shout. April.

'Dr Callaghan? Can you come and assess Robert Black for me, please?' He could see the concern on her face straight away.

He nodded and walked over quickly. Robert had been caught in an explosion. His spinal injury was severe and he was currently in neurogenic shock. This was always a crucial time for patients. Neurogenic shock happened in almost half of patients with a spinal injury above T6 in the first twenty-four hours and didn't go away for between one to three weeks. Patients in neurogenic shock needed continual assessment of their circulation, senses and breathing abilities. Neurogenic shock could lead to organ failure.

Robert Black's blood pressure was low, his heart rate bradycardic. His limbs were flaccid, his skin warm and flushed due to the vasodilation caused by the neurogenic shock.

Riley signalled to the nurse. 'Connie, can you get me some atropine?'

She nodded and handed him a vial from the emergency trolley. April moved automatically to the head of the bed to keep assessing Robert's breathing. The staff here were used to emergencies and good at recognising the symptoms.

Riley kept his voice calm and even as he flushed the atropine through the Venflon in Robert's arm. 'Robert, I'm just giving you something to speed up your heart rate a little. I'm also going to give you something to help your blood pressure.'

He nodded at Connie again. 'Get me some dopamine.' He turned to April. 'Can you put some oxygen on for me, please?'

April nodded and slipped the mask over Robert's face, lowering her head to the bed to monitor the rise and fall of his chest and keeping her eyes on the numbers on the oximeter.

Teamwork was crucial. Neurogenic shock was difficult. It was different from spinal shock or the most common type of shock with injuries—hypovolemic—and had to be treated differently. Often patients could have a respiratory arrest.

Right on cue, April waved her hand. 'Can we call an anaesthetist?'

'No time,' said Riley as he finished administering the dopamine and moved to the head of the bed. It only took a few seconds to tilt Robert's head back, using the laryngoscope to insert an endotracheal tube.

He glanced towards the doorway. 'We need to transfer him to high dependency. Does anyone know if they have a bed?'

April took his cue and ran over to the phone. Riley kept bagging the patient. At this stage, Robert needed to be ventilated. He could only pray this was a temporary setback.

Robert's regular doctor appeared at the door. His eyes widened. 'What the—?'

He stopped himself and held open the ward doors. 'High dependency?'

April put the phone down and nodded. 'They'll be waiting.'

He moved over and grabbed a side of the bed. Between the other doctor, April and the nurse, the transfer was smooth. Riley concentrated on the airway, bagging the whole way, then setting up the ventilators and pressures when they arrived.

'Need anything else?' he asked his colleague.

The doctor shook his head. 'I take it he had just had a rapid deterioration?'

Riley nodded. 'April was working with him. She picked up on it straight away.'

'Thank goodness. This could have been a disaster.'

Riley gave a thoughtful nod and stared back towards the door. April had stopped in the corridor. He gave a brief smile. 'Give me a page if you need any help.'

The other doctor nodded and he headed out into the corridor.

April was dressed in her usual attire of the physios, white tunic and navy trousers, with her hair pulled back in a ponytail. She had her eyes closed and was resting her head and body against the wall.

He touched her arm and her eyes jerked open. 'April, are you okay?'

Their eyes connected for a few moments. Hers were bluer than ever. Maybe it was the bright hospital lights. Or maybe it was the fact he was noticing so much more about her. April had always looked away quickly before, but this time she didn't. This time it felt as if there was more to their gaze.

But she pulled her arm away. 'Of course, I'm fine.' She gave her head a little shake. 'I just got a fright when Robert deteriorated so quickly.'

He nodded. As a doctor, he was used to dealing with emergencies, but other staff didn't have the same exposure as he did. Quite often they did a debrief after things like this.

'Come with me.'

Her eyes widened. 'What?' She shook her head fiercely. 'No, I've got work to do. I need to get back to the ward.'

'Actually, you don't.'

She glared at him and folded her arms across her chest. 'I can't.'

He spoke firmly. 'You can. Get your jacket. I have to pick up Finn at twelve. But we have time for a coffee before I go get him.'

April shifted on her feet. 'I have work to do.'

'You must be due a break, and we need a chance to debrief—to talk about what just happened. We usually do it as a team after any emergency. Let's take some time out.'

She hesitated and took a few breaths. He gestured towards the locker room. 'Go and get your jacket.' He wasn't going to let this go. There was something in that glance. Some kind of connection.

She gave the briefest nod then disappeared for a few seconds while his stomach gave a little roll.

No getting away from it. April Henderson had definitely been avoiding him. He just had to figure out why.

Her hands were still shaking as she opened her locker and grabbed her jacket. The canteen and coffee shop were across the main courtyard. She slid her hands into her puffy winter jacket. Riley was waiting for her at the door.

This was nothing. It was a simple chat. A debrief. She had heard of them before—she'd just never needed one.

So why was her stomach flip flopping around?

She'd spent the last few days avoiding Riley. She'd done the things she'd been asked to do. The funeral arrangements were sorted. She'd arranged the undertaker, the church, the minister and the plot at the cemetery. According to Isabel's friends, she'd been a little unconventional. One had offered to speak. Another had offered to say a poem. She just had to find out what Riley would think appropriate for Finn. She figured he'd want to give Finn the chance to say goodbye to his mum. She just wasn't quite sure how a kid did that.

She lifted her bag. All the paperwork and arrangements were inside. She just had to hand them over.

Riley was holding the door open. Large flakes of snow were falling outside. Even though it was still morning, the sky had a grey tinge.

They started walking across the courtyard. 'Coffee shop or canteen?'

April shrugged. 'Either.'

'How hungry are you? Do you want an early lunch?'

She shook her head.

'Then coffee shop it is.'

They walked over to the coffee shop and he held the door for her again. 'Take a seat. I'll get the coffee.'

She sat down on a red fabric sofa next to the lit fire. There was a garland above the fireplace and red tinsel adorning the walls. November. Another place with decorations. The music being piped around the room was a medley of Christmas songs. She smiled. This would have driven Mallory crazy. She used to say that Christmas seemed to begin as soon as Halloween had finished.

A few minutes later Riley appeared, carrying a tray.

She looked up as she shrugged her way out of her jacket. The heat from the fire was already reaching her.

He smiled as he set down the two tall latte glasses filled with hot chocolate, with whipped cream and marshmallows spilling over the edges. A plate with shortbread Christmas trees followed.

She looked up. 'Really?'

His eyes twinkled. 'Why not? I love Christmas.'

There was something about that smile. Something about that twinkle in his eye. It had always been there before, and it was part of the reason she'd avoided him. Riley Callaghan was too easy to like. He was almost infectious.

She was surprised. 'You do? So do I.'

'At last.' He smiled. 'Something we have in common.'

She frowned. 'I imagined you were always away for Christmas.'

He looked amused. 'You think about me?' He couldn't hide the cheeky gleam in his eyes. Then he shrugged. 'A lot of the time I am. But here's the thing…' He leaned across the table as if he were going to whisper to her.

She followed his lead and bowed her head next to his as his face lit up with a wicked grin. 'Many other places in the world do Christmas too. Sometimes in forty degrees. And if they don't? Well, I can always take it with me.'

She sat back and shook her head, pointing her finger on the table. 'Well, I don't want a sunny Christmas or to be anywhere else. I like Christmas *here*. I like tacky Christmas songs. I *really* like it when it snows. I like Advent calendars, Christmas cards and—' she winked at him '—I really like Christmas food.'

She spooned some of the cream into her mouth.

'So do I,' he said cheekily as he dug his spoon into her cream instead of his.

'Hey!'

She gave his hand a playful slap. 'Watch out, Riley. I bite, you know.'

His gaze met hers for a few seconds. He didn't speak. Just kept staring at her. As if he were contemplating a whole host of things to say. A whole type of discussion she just couldn't think about right now.

She broke their gaze and dug her spoon back into the cream.

'About today,' he started. She looked up. Work. This felt like safe territory.

'You did everything right. There is always a risk of sudden deterioration in patients with neurogenic shock. It can happen at any point. You picked it up well.'

She sighed and leaned her head on her hand. The teasing and fun had finished, but that was fine. This was what they really should be talking about. 'But he's ventilated now. That can't be good.'

Riley nodded. 'It's not great. It is a deterioration. Now, we need to monitor carefully in case he's going into organ failure. He might not.'

She met his gaze. She felt sad. His emerald-green eyes were saying a whole lot of things that they weren't discussing out loud. They both knew that things for Robert might not be good.

He leaned across and touched her hand. 'You did everything you should.'

She stared down at his blunt cut fingernails. She should pull her hand back. Jerk it away. She wanted to. But somehow after the events earlier she wanted a few seconds of comfort.

She looked up again. 'How is Finn?' It was the question she should have asked immediately. It didn't matter she was trying to step back and detach herself from the situation. She'd spent the last few days worrying about the little guy.

Riley took a long slow breath. 'He's not happy, but he's not sad. He's getting there. He's met some school friends and the teacher says he's fitting in well. They're going to do some bereavement work at school with him because it's still all so new.' He stirred his hot chocolate. 'He was crying in bed the other night.'

Her heart squeezed in her chest. 'What did you do?'

He pressed his lips together. 'I thought about it for about ten seconds. Then I climbed in next to him and just held him. What else could I do? I hate that he's sad. I hate that this has happened to him. I know the upheaval must be awful. And my learning curve is steep.'

'What have you done?'

A smile crept onto his lips. 'Well, my fridge and freezer are now stocked with child-friendly foods. I never knew there were so many yogurts. Potatoes have to be mashed. Raisins have to be a particular brand and he'll only eat Pink Lady apples.'

April smiled as she spooned marshmallows into her hot chocolate. 'But that all sounds good. It sounds as though he's settling.'

Riley nodded. 'We've put up the pictures you brought from the house. It's weird. Seeing Isabel all around me.'

He dropped his head and stopped speaking.

Something inside her lurched. A horrible feeling. Envy. Why on earth was she feeling that? It was so misplaced. So wrong. But it was definitely there. Maybe there had been more to the relationship than she'd initially thought. 'So...do you miss her?'

He sighed; the pained expression on his face said it all. 'That's just it, April. I didn't really know her that well. We only went out for a couple of months. I don't have a million nice tales I can tell Finn about his mum. I don't have a lot of memories. She was nice.' He shrugged his shoulders. 'How awful is that? That's about as much as I have to say about her. Finn deserves more than that.'

She licked her lips for a second. She could see what he wasn't saying. 'You're still angry.'

He pulled a face. 'Inside, I am. But I hope I don't show that around Finn. It's just when I turn around Isabel seems to be staring me in the face.' He ran his fingers through his hair. 'And the family housing. It's not ideal. You probably already know that. I need to find a place for us. A home.'

The way he said those words sent a little pang through her. Riley wanted to make a home with his son. Would she ever get to make a home with someone? Would anyone want to be in a relationship with a girl who could always have a cancer risk hanging over her head, and couldn't have a family? It wouldn't exactly make for a winning profile on a dating website. She cringed at the thought of it and focused back on Riley.

'You can't just jump out and buy the first thing you see.'

'Can't I? Why not? I can get a mortgage. I have enough money in the bank.'

'But you don't know if you'll always be here. Another move might not be good for Finn.'

'But what if it's a permanent move?'

Riley Callaghan. Here permanently. Working together every day. She'd need to see his smiling face. Avoid his cheeky grins. Four weeks had been manageable—there had been an end date in sight. But for ever? How could she lock away the attraction she felt for him for ever?

She leaned back in her chair. 'It's a lot to think about.' She glanced at the glass in front of her. 'This must be a million calories. You—' she wagged her finger at him '—are a bad influence.'

He leaned forward. 'Just call it a bribe.'

He had that grin on his face again. The one he used time and time again on the ward when he wanted to talk someone into something.

She pointed at the shortbread Christmas trees. 'Am I going to need one of these?'

He pushed the whole plate before her and clasped his hands on the table. It seemed such a formal stance for Riley she almost laughed.

'Thing is,' he started seriously, 'I appreciate all the arrangements you've made for me. I know doing something like that really goes above and beyond.' He pointed at the hot chocolate and shortbread. 'And these don't count for that.' He waved his hand. 'I'll get you something more appropriate.' He leaned a little closer across the table. 'But there's something else.'

She shook her head and ignored the 'more appropriate' comment. Riley Callaghan was trying to sweet-talk her. 'Don't build it up, Riley. Just hit me with it.'

He did. 'Finn.'

She narrowed her gaze. 'What about Finn?'

He sighed. 'I haven't had that conversation yet—the

one about the funeral. And I was hoping you might help me do it.'

She sat back again. But Riley kept going. 'I'm still taking baby steps here. I don't want to do anything wrong. And I could ask my mother, but then—' he shook his head '—that would just open the floodgates for her to bulldoze all over us.'

'Has your mother met Finn yet?'

He shook his head. 'I'm holding her at bay. I've told her the social worker advised to give him a few days to settle.'

She opened her mouth. 'You what?'

He held up his hand. 'You haven't met my mother—yet. Don't judge.'

She folded her arms across her chest. 'What exactly is it you want me to do, Riley? I'm not sure I should be getting involved. This is really something you and Finn should work through together.'

'I'm scared.'

He said the words right out of the blue.

And she couldn't catch her breath.

'What if I make a mess of this, April? Do I say Finn's too young to be at a funeral and everything should go on without him, or do I insist he attends when he really isn't ready for it? Do I ask him what he wants to do? At five, how can he even know?'

Anguish and pain were written all over his face. She understood. What had happened on the ward today had just helped open the door for him. He wasn't grieving for Isabel. He was grieving for his son.

'I get that you're scared, Riley. But this is your son. I think you need to have this conversation with him.'

He didn't look any better. He turned a shortbread tree over and over in his hands before finally looking up through dark lashes and meeting her gaze. 'He's been asking for you.'

'What?'

'Finn. He's asked where you were. I think because we brought him back together he's expected to see you again.'

She gulped. The kid was five. He was confused. It wasn't such a strange thought to have. 'I don't want to give him any mixed messages.'

'What mixed messages? Aren't we friends, April?'

She didn't speak. Her brain was flooded with memories of her hands against his chest, his forehead next to hers. All things she didn't need to remember. But they were annoying; they seemed to have seared their way into her brain and cemented themselves there.

She locked gazes with Riley. He'd asked if they were friends.

No. They weren't. Being around Riley was making her feel things she didn't want to. Didn't need to. Life was hard right now. She was clear about her decision. She knew what her next steps would be. Getting involved with anyone would confuse things. They might want to talk. They might have an opinion. Somehow, already, she knew Riley would have an opinion. And she wasn't ready for any of that. After Christmas her ovaries and fallopian tubes would be removed. It wasn't a complete and utter guarantee that she would remain cancer-free, but when the odds were against her it was as good as it could be.

The image of Finn's face clouded her thoughts. He was so like Riley.

It still made her ache. She was trying to stay so strong. But being around a kid as adorable as Finn had made all those children she would never have suddenly feel so real. All those grandkids her mum and dad would never have to entertain. She couldn't help but pine for the life that would never be hers. She stared down at the shortbread Christmas tree. And Christmas made it seem just that little bit harder—because Christmas should be all about family.

She sucked in a breath. How dare she feel sorry for herself right now? The person she should be thinking about was Finn.

She met Riley's gaze. Somehow he knew just when to keep quiet.

She took a deep breath. 'I'll come over tomorrow. I still haven't arranged the flowers. I'll ask Finn if he knows what his mum's favourites were. Maybe if he can help pick something it will help that conversation get started.' She pointed to the pile of paperwork. 'The minister at the church is pretty modern. I told him I'd get back to him about music. If there is a particular song that Finn likes, maybe that's the one to use? I asked Isabel's friends. But they all had different ideas.'

Riley nodded. 'Thank you. I mean that.'

She gave him a smile. 'It's okay.'

'Is it? Until a few days ago we'd never really had a proper conversation. You always seemed to avoid me. When I saw you come into the pub the other night I thought…' His voice tailed off.

'You thought what?'

He shrugged. 'I thought you might actually have come in to have a farewell drink. I thought you might have found it in your heart to be nice to me for five minutes.'

He was teasing her. She knew that. But his words seemed to strike a bit of a nerve. She had the feeling some of it might come from a little deeper.

And there was that little twisting feeling again. He might as well sell corkscrews from the way his words, his looks and his touch affected her.

'I like to keep focused at work. These patients, they've been through enough. They need our full attention. They deserve it.'

He shook his head. 'Oh, no. Don't give me that. You engage perfectly with all the patients. It's only me that gets the cold shoulder; don't think I didn't notice.'

There was a surge of heat into her cheeks. 'Maybe you're just hard to be around, Riley?'

She knew it was a deflection, and as he folded his arms and narrowed his gaze she also knew he wasn't about to let her off.

'So what is it? Why no chat? Why no friendly banter? You seem to do it enough with the patients.'

'Maybe I just don't like to mix work with pleasure.'

As soon as the words left her mouth she realised her mistake.

His eyes gleamed. 'Oh, so I could be pleasure, could I?'

She shook her head and waved her hand. 'Don't be ridiculous. Anyway, you servicemen, you come and go so often. You were only supposed to be covering for four weeks. It's exhausting having to befriend new staff all the time. Sometimes I just don't have the energy.'

His grin had spread from one ear to the other. It was clear he wasn't listening any more. 'So I'm exhausting, am I? I kinda like that.'

'I didn't say that.'

He nodded firmly. 'You did.'

She sighed in exasperation. 'It's not all about you, Riley.'

She didn't mean it quite to come out like that. But if he heard he didn't react badly. The smile was still plastered across his face. He must have thought she was joking with him.

If only that were true. Her heart gave a little squeeze.

If only she could have a different life. If only she could have a different gene pool. But that would mean that she and Mallory would never have existed—and she wouldn't have spent more than twenty years with a sister she'd both hated at times and adored. Sisterly love could never really be matched. And the bottom line was: she couldn't change her genes. She just had to find a way to manage her risk. For her, right now, that meant finding a way to live her life. She swallowed the huge lump in her throat. No matter what little strings were tugging at her heart right now, it was best to ignore them. Best to stay focused on what she could manage.

He glanced at his watch. 'I'm sorry to cut and run but I need to go and get Finn. I don't want to be late.' He pulled his jacket from the back of the chair. 'Thank you for your help with Finn. I mean it.' Then he gave her a cheeky wink. 'But it looks like I'm here to stay. Better get used to having me around.'

He disappeared out of the door into the snow as her heart gave a lurch.

Riley Callaghan here on a permanent basis.

This could be trouble.

CHAPTER FOUR

IN A WAY, the funeral went so much better than he ever could have expected.

The horrible conversation with Finn had turned out much easier than he could have hoped for. When April had come over to chat to Finn about flowers, Finn had asked outright if she would come to the funeral too.

It seemed that the thought of not being there hadn't even occurred to Finn.

Isabel's friends and workmates turned out in force. They all wore bright colours and sang along to the pop song that Finn had picked for his mum.

He was thankful they'd all attended. The decision to bury Isabel here instead of Birmingham had been a difficult one. But Riley and Finn would be the ones who tended her grave, and he didn't want to have to travel every time Finn wanted to visit.

April stayed steadily in the background. Finn had drawn her a picture of the flowers his mum liked best and, even though it was nearing the end of November, the church was full of orange gerbera daisies. The room felt bright. And Finn's little hand had gripped his the whole time.

He felt oddly detached about it all. He'd organised

a funeral tea afterwards but only vaguely recognised a few of Isabel's friends, even though they all made a point of coming and speaking to Finn. The little guy seemed overwhelmed. April looked even more uncomfortable.

He crossed the room, Finn's hand still in his. He glanced down at Finn. 'I think we've probably stayed long enough. I was thinking we could do something together with Finn right now.'

He could tell she was hesitant but Finn had perked up at the suggestion. 'Can we go and pick a spaceman film?'

He looked at her again. She was pale in the black dress with her blonde hair tied back. The outfit had a severity to it that just didn't seem quite right for April. They'd discussed wearing something bright like Isabel's friends, but somehow it didn't feel quite right for them. April had found a brooch with a bright orange gerbera that matched the church flowers and pinned it to her dress. Riley had relented and worn a bright orange tie with his dark suit. Even though they'd asked Finn if he wanted to wear one of his superhero T-shirts he'd shaken his head; he'd wanted to wear a suit like his dad's.

Riley had been choked. He'd love to wear matching clothes with his son—just not like this. Everything about this was hard. He was questioning every decision he made.

He almost gave a shout when April gave a sigh of relief. 'Let me get my coat,' she said.

As they walked along the icy street together Finn reached out to hold April's hand too. Riley was glad of the cold, fresh air. Finn hadn't said much at all during the service. He'd placed a bunch of orange flowers by the grave and shed a few tears while Riley held him in his arms.

It had been exhausting. Smiling politely and shaking hands with people he really didn't know—all of whom he knew were looking him up and down and wondering about his suitability to bring up Finn.

He'd had a stand-up fight with his mother about attending the funeral. She wanted to offer 'support' to her grandchild. But Riley had been insistent that the event was already too overwhelming for Finn. He'd been clear that she needed to wait a few days. Finn needed some space.

He would be starting full days at school next week and Riley had suggested his mum and dad come down to meet him then. He hadn't told her that Finn had video-chatted with his uncle Dan a few nights ago. It was obvious that Dan was smitten by his nephew straight away, and Finn with him, but Dan being away was actually easier. More manageable.

'Who is your favourite spaceman?' Finn asked April out of the blue.

She looked surprised and he could see her searching her brain. 'Well, it would have to be the one that I met.'

Finn stopped walking, his mouth hanging open. 'You've met a spaceman?'

She nodded. 'I went on holiday to Florida once and visited NASA. I got to have lunch with a spaceman. It was great.'

Finn's eyes were wide. 'Really? Dad, can we do that?'

Riley smiled. He was still getting used to being called Dad. First few times, he'd looked around to make sure it was really him that was being spoken to.

He gave a sort of nod. 'We haven't had a chance to talk about holidays yet. But it's always something we could consider.'

'Could we, Dad, could we?' The excitement on Finn's wide-eyed face made his heart swell. Right now he was tempted to promise the world to Finn, but he wasn't sure that was the best idea. He wanted his son to grow up to appreciate people, things and places. He was still trying to figure out everything in his head.

And that included the woman walking at the other side of his son.

April had been quiet most of the day. She'd agreed to come because Finn had asked her to. Riley wasn't sure she would have come on his invitation alone.

Although he'd been curious about April before, he hadn't pursued things. He'd been due to leave. But that hadn't stopped him trying to engage her constantly in conversation and trying to find out a little more about her.

Her face was serious. She'd told him she was good at funerals. She'd said she'd lost her sister but hadn't elaborated. Had today brought back some bad memories for her?

He was still curious about April. She was fantastic with patients. She'd been supportive to him in the most horrible set of circumstances. Even now, she was holding his son's hand. April Henderson had a good heart. Why didn't she let anyone get close to her?

They walked onto the main street and into one of the local shops. Finn raced over to the large display of DVDs. Riley put his hands in his pockets. 'Are you ready for this?'

She raised her eyebrows. 'You think I can't handle a little sci-fi?'

He gave a playful shrug. 'I thought you might be more of a romance girl.'

'Oh, no.' She shook her head straight away, even though her gaze was locked directly with his. A smile danced across her lips as she brushed past him to join Finn. 'What I don't know about *Star Wars*, *Star Trek* and Buzz Lightyear isn't worth knowing,' she whispered into his ear.

He grinned. Another tiny piece of information about April Henderson. He was just going to keep chipping away at that armour she'd constructed around herself.

After a hard day for him and Finn, April was the brightest light on the horizon. And he'd never been so happy that she was there.

Two hours later Finn was fast asleep against April's shoulder. He might even have been drooling a little. The credits of the sci-fi movie were rolling on the screen. The room had grown dark and it was almost as if Riley read her mind as he crossed the room and flicked the switch on a lamp.

She wasn't quite sure how she'd managed to end up here. She hadn't intended to. But when Finn had asked her to come back she didn't have the heart to say no. Meaning that right now she had a five-year-old draped halfway across her, snoring.

Riley glanced towards her legs. As she'd sat on the sofa with Finn her dress had crept up a little more than it should. She tried to wiggle her dress down but it was nigh impossible with Finn's weight on top of her.

'April, can I get you something else a little more comfortable to wear?'

She almost laughed. It sounded like the old adage, *Do you want to slip into something more comfortable?*

He must have caught the expression on her face. 'I have scrubs,' he said quickly.

'Scrubs would be great,' she said. The black dress had been perfect for a funeral, but as the day had progressed it had started to feel more restrictive.

He disappeared for a second and set down a pale blue set of scrubs next to her, leaning over and adjusting Finn's position to free her up.

She pushed herself from the sofa and looked around. 'Bathroom this way?' she asked.

Riley nodded and she walked through to the hall. It was a typical army house. Adequate. But not perfect. As she wiggled out of her dress in the cramped bathroom she understood why he'd immediately thought about getting a place of his own. Everything in the house was bland. It would be difficult to put a stamp on the place and give it a family feel. It didn't really feel like a home.

By the time she came out of the bathroom, Riley was in the kitchen. 'I thought I'd make us some dinner,' he said simply.

She opened her mouth to refuse straight away, then stopped. Would it really be so bad to share a meal with him? It had been a big day. For him, and for Finn. And, truth be told, for her too. It was the first funeral she'd been to since her sister's. It didn't help that Isabel had only been five years older than Mallory. Mallory's funeral had been full of young people too. And, while it was comforting, there was also a terrible irony about it. Some people were cheated out of the life they should live. If she was honest, she didn't really want to be alone right now.

'Can I help?'

Riley pulled a face. 'That depends.'

'On what?'

'On how fussy you are. I can make lasagne, spaghetti bolognaise or chilli chicken. That's as far as I can go.'

'Three things? I'm impressed. My speciality is chicken or sausage casserole.'

He laughed. 'Okay then, which of the five—' he opened his fridge '—no, sorry, four—I've no sausages—do you want to go for?'

April leaned her head on her hand. She was tired. It had been a long day. And it had been a long time since she'd had a conversation like this. A guy actually offering to make her dinner.

'I think I'm brave enough to try your lasagne. Do I get to watch the chef at work?'

He smiled. 'Sure you do. I'll even give you wine. But, just so you know, I'm a bit of a messy cook.'

He pulled two wine glasses out of the cupboard, held them up to the light and squinted at them. 'I'm just checking that they're clean. I moved in such a rush that I literally just walked from the flat to this house with things in my arms.'

She shook her head. 'Riley Callaghan. So far, you've told me that you only have three recipes, you're messy, and now I'm questioning your housekeeping skills.' She shook her head. 'If this were online dating, you wouldn't get a "like".'

He went into another cupboard and brought out two bottles. 'But I have wine! So I win. Now, white or red?'

'I guess for lasagne it should probably be red but I fancy white. Is that okay?'

He opened the bottle and poured the wine, then started pulling ingredients from the fridge.

She took a sip of the wine and relaxed back a little into the chair. 'I'll cut you a deal. You let me pick dinner—' she raised her eyebrows '—from a limited menu, of course, and you let me pick the wine. How about I do the clearing up?'

He tipped the mince into a pan to start browning it, giving her a wink from the corner of his eye. 'My plan has worked.'

April glanced back through to the living room at the little sleeping boy. 'Will Finn eat this?'

Riley followed her glance. 'Probably not. I'll give him it first, but have some chicken on standby in case he doesn't like it.' He leaned against the doorjamb as the mince began to sizzle in the pan. 'I wonder if he'll wake up at all. It's been a big day.' He picked up his glass and took a sip of his wine. 'Thanks for being there.'

She shrugged. 'It's fine. He's a cute kid.'

She could see the pride on his face. Riley was rapidly turning into a doting dad. He moved back into the kitchen and started chopping an onion.

He was methodical. He added the herbs and tomatoes, then made a quick white sauce. Five minutes later he'd layered up the mix with lasagne sheets, sprinkled with cheese and put it in the oven.

She nodded. 'I'm impressed. You never struck me as the organised type.'

He sat down opposite her. 'I didn't? What's that supposed to mean?' He wrinkled his brow. 'Am I supposed to be offended right now? Because if I am, I'm just too tired.'

She shook her head. 'For the last four weeks you've been racing about the place doing one hundred things at once. The unit isn't normally like that.'

He pulled a face. 'I know.' He sat back a little and looked at her carefully. 'I've been used to working at a frantic pace. I need to step down a gear and get more perspective.'

'Can you actually do that?' she asked softly.

He sighed. 'I hate the way you do that.'

'What?'

He lifted his hand towards her. 'You ask the questions that I don't really want to answer.' He turned his head into the living room again. 'The answer to the question has to be yes. And you can see why. I have to change things. I have to be a father to Finn. I'm all he's got.'

'But…?'

He groaned and leaned forward, putting his head on the table. His real thoughts were written all over him. She touched his dark hair. 'You weren't born to be a rehab doctor, Riley. You want to be where the action is. But if you're going to have Finn on a permanent basis that will be impossible.'

He looked up a little as she shifted her hand, his bright green eyes peeking out from underneath dark lashes. 'I love him. I love him already. Finn comes first.'

She bent forward, her head almost touching his. 'You're allowed to say it, Riley. But maybe just to me. You're allowed to say that this life change gives you twinges of regret.' She licked her lips. 'Maybe I understand that a bit more than most.'

And she did. She was inches away from a guy a few years ago she would have flirted with, enjoyed his company and maybe even dated. There might even have been more possibilities that right now she didn't even dare think about.

His face crumpled and he put his head in his hands for a second. He kept his eyes closed as he spoke. 'Last week I thought I was going on a tour of Sierra Leone. I was looking forward to it. It might sound strange but I love the overseas tours. Always have.' He opened his eyes slowly. 'But last week I didn't know I had a son to come home to. My whole life has changed in the blink of an eye. I'm not sure I was ready for it.'

She spoke carefully, sliding her hand across the table and letting her fingers intertwine with his. 'Promise me that you'll only ever talk to me about this. Don't let Finn know. You've had the legs swept from under you. Mallory and I used to call that being cannonballed. It will take a while to get your head around things. To work out what is best, for you and for him. You can do this, Riley. I know you can.'

He looked at their connected fingers. 'I'd never take out how I'm feeling on Finn. You must know that.'

'I do,' she said simply. 'But I want you to know that it's okay to feel like that. It's complicated. If you're having a bad day you can call me.'

They were touching. Having their fingers intertwined was so much more personal than a brush of the hand. And it was sending a weird stream of little pulses up her arm. Under the bright kitchen lights there was nowhere to hide. Those bright green eyes were even more startling. Last time she'd seen something that green, she and Mallory had been taking a photo of the emerald-tinged sea in Zante at Shipwreck Beach. It was still one of her favourite ever pictures.

The little lines around his eyes gave him character, made her know that he'd seen and done things she never would. There was so much to like about Riley Callaghan, meaning there were so many more reasons to push him away.

So why wasn't she?

He looked at her, the barest hint of a smile quirking his lips. 'You mean you're going to give me your number?'

She frowned. 'Didn't I already when I was helping with the funeral arrangements?'

His fingers tightened around hers. 'Ah, but that was different. That was for practical reasons. This—' his smile broadened '—this sounds like almost *giving* a guy your number.'

She shook her head and pulled her hand back, surprised by how much she didn't want to. 'Don't get the wrong idea, mister.' She picked up her glass. 'You're supplying the wine and—' she nodded towards the oven '—the food. I'm a practical girl; I'm only nice as long as you're feeding me.'

Riley laughed. 'Oh, I have plenty of wine. As long as you're happy with a limited menu, we can be friends for ever.'

Something warm spread through her. It was like the kind of thing kids said to each other. The kind of thing she and Mallory used to say. Her fingers went automatically to her neck. To the pendant their parents had given both girls on their twenty-first birthdays.

Two golden hearts linked together. Touching it made her feel closer to her sister. Touching it made her feel that sometimes Mallory wasn't quite as far away as reality told her.

'What's that? It's pretty.' Riley noticed her movement straight away.

She hesitated before letting her fingers fall away to reveal what she was touching. 'It was a gift from my parents.' She didn't add the rest.

Her brain started working overtime. What would Mallory have thought of Riley Callaghan? They'd generally had different taste in men. But somehow she knew Mallory would have loved this guy. It was both a comfort and a regret, that her sister wasn't here to meet him.

Riley leaned his head on his hands and gave her a curious stare. 'Are you going to tell me anything about yourself, April?'

She caught her breath. She hadn't expected him to be so direct. 'What do you mean?'

He counted off on his fingers. 'Well, I know you're a physio. I know you're a good physio—a great one. I'm not quite sure what age you are. Or where you live, although I know it's close. I know you had a sister. And you like spacemen.' He gave her a smile. 'But that's about it.'

She couldn't help but be defensive. 'What exactly do you think you're entitled to know about me?'

He stood up, his wooden chair scraping on the kitchen floor as he turned around, grabbed a tea towel and pulled the steaming-hot lasagne from the oven.

He didn't speak as he handed her a plate, some cutlery and a serving spatula. He didn't seem fazed by her briskness at all; in fact, it almost felt as if he was teasing her now. He sat down opposite and folded his hands on the table. 'I don't *think* I'm entitled to know anything. But I'd *like* it if you shared.' He even grinned. 'For example, my mum and dad are up north. My mother can best be described in terms of weather elements—she goes from snowstorm, sandstorm, whirlwind and tornado. My brother Dan is serving in the army. He's twenty-seven and can't wait to meet Finn. He probably is at the same stage of maturity.'

She wanted to smile. She really did. The waft of the enticing lasagne was winding its way across the table to her. He made everything sound so reasonable. But sharing wasn't the place she wanted to be right now. Sharing about her sister would mean sharing about the disease, and the follow-on questions about genetics. And surgery.

Inside, a little part of her shrivelled up and died. The whole reason she wasn't in a relationship right now was to give herself space to get this part of her life sorted. To not have to explain her thoughts or decisions to another person.

But a tiny part of her also recognised that she'd never actually been in a relationship where she would have been able to have that kind of serious conversation. Perhaps that was why she was trying to wrap Riley Callaghan up and stick him in a box somewhere in her brain before he let loose thoughts she wasn't ready for.

Thoughts like the ones where those perfectly formed lips were on hers.

She choked as Riley started to dish out the lasagne.

He still didn't speak. Just handed her the dish with a raise of his eyebrows.

This guy was too good at this.

'Maybe there's just not much to tell. I'm twenty-seven too. I've worked here for the last eighteen months. Before that I was in a general hospital, specialising in chronic injuries. And before that I did a year with kids who had cystic fibrosis. I've moved around to get a variety of experience.'

Not strictly true. She'd moved to the general hospital to be closer to Mallory when she'd got her diagnosis. And she'd moved to Waterloo Court after Mallory died because she couldn't face all the sympathy and questions from her colleagues. It was easier to be in a place where people didn't know your history.

'Are your mum and dad still around?'

She nodded. 'They moved up to Scotland just over a year ago. My nana was starting to get frail and they wanted to be closer to her.'

Her family felt as if it were falling apart. They'd lost one daughter and knew there was a possibility they could lose the other. And every time she looked at them she could see the pain in their eyes—that this was genetic. A time bomb that no one could have known about—at least not until fairly recently. But their pain had also affected her own decision. Would she want to risk passing faulty genes on to her own child? No. No way. Not when she saw the pain it could cause.

'Do you visit?'

She nodded. 'I visit a lot. Well, whenever I get time.' She looked up from the lasagne. 'I can't believe how good this is. Who taught you how to make it?'

He smiled. 'It's a secret.' His eyes were twinkling.

Was it a woman? She felt a tiny stab of envy.

He topped up her wine glass. 'I worked with an Italian doctor in an infectious disease unit for a while. He gave me his grandma's recipe.'

She kept eating. 'Well, I hate to say it, but it might even beat my sausage casserole.' She glanced through to the living room. 'Do you want a hand to wrestle Finn into his pyjamas? I don't think he's going to wake up now.'

Riley followed her gaze as he kept eating. 'In a minute. Darn it—jammies. I need to put them on the list.'

'Finn doesn't have pyjamas?'

He shook his head. 'He does, but I think he might just have taken a little stretch. Either that or I've shrunk them in the wash. I'll need to get him some new ones.' He looked around the plain kitchen. 'And I need to get some decorations too. I don't even own a Christmas tree. I'm not even sure where to buy one around here.'

'There's a place just a few miles out of town—that's if you want a real one, of course. They can be a little messy, but they smell great.'

'Will you show me?'

She paused. She wanted to say no. She should say no. But a little bit inside of her wanted to say yes. Riley Callaghan was messing with her mind.

'I can give you directions.'

'I didn't ask for directions.' His fork was poised in mid-air and he was looking at her pointedly.

She licked her lips. It didn't matter she'd had plenty of wine; all of a sudden her mouth felt very dry. 'Why don't we just play it by ear? I've got some plans in the next few days. If you let me know when you're going I can see if I'm free.'

His eyes narrowed for a moment. He was a doctor. He could recognise a deflected question easily. It was second nature. But Riley was gracious enough not to push.

They finished dinner and she washed up while he prepared Finn's room. It only took a few minutes to wiggle Finn into his pyjamas, and then Riley carried him up to bed.

She couldn't help but follow him up the stairs as he laid Finn down in his bed adorned with a spaceman duvet. He whispered in his son's ear, put a kiss on his forehead and switched on the nightlight that illuminated stars on the ceiling.

'Oh, wow,' whispered April. 'That's fantastic.' She smiled at him in the dim light. 'I think I want one.'

He raised his eyebrows as he walked back to the doorway, his shoulder touching hers as he bent to whisper, 'I hate to break it to you, but you'll have to sweet-talk my mother. She sent it down yesterday for Finn and I've no idea where she got it.'

April watched the circling stars on the ceiling. It was almost magical. Hypnotic. And by the time she stopped watching she'd forgotten about how close she was to Riley. She could smell his aftershave. Smell the soap powder from the soft T-shirt he'd changed into when they'd got home. Her eyes fixed on the rise and fall of his chest, then the soft pulse at the base of his neck. She was suddenly conscious that the scrubs she was wearing were thin. Thin enough to probably see the outline of her black matching underwear beneath the pale blue fabric.

All of a sudden it felt as though a part of life that was so far out of reach was right before her eyes. A gorgeous man, a beautiful child—things she couldn't even contemplate. Things that seemed so far away and unobtainable. When she and Mallory had been young they'd always joked about who would marry first, and being each other's bridesmaids. They'd both taken it for granted that those things would naturally happen. Right now, she had to concentrate on surgery. Getting through that, gaining a little confidence again and getting some normality back to her life. Pursuing anything with Riley Callaghan wasn't possible. It wasn't fair to her. It wasn't fair to him. It especially wasn't fair to a little boy whose whole world had just been turned upside down.

In the dim light Riley's hand lifted oh-so-slowly towards her. 'April—'

She turned swiftly and walked out of the room, her breath catching somewhere in the back of her throat. She needed to go. She needed to get out of there.

She rushed down the stairs and picked up the bag with her dress in it and her black coat. 'It's getting late. I need to get home. Thanks for dinner.' She said the words far too brightly.

Riley was at her back, but his hands were in his pockets and his eyes were downcast. 'Yeah. No problem. Thanks for coming today. I appreciate it.'

She nodded as she slipped her arms into her jacket and headed for the door. 'Say goodnight to Finn for me. See you at work tomorrow.'

Riley gave the briefest of nods as she hurried out the door. It didn't matter how quickly she walked, she could sense his eyes searing into her back the whole way, as the smell of his aftershave still lingered around her.

He watched as she hurried away like a scalded cat. What had he done? He hadn't *actually* touched her. Yes, he'd meant to. Yes, he'd wanted to.

His lips were still tingling from the fact he'd wanted to kiss her. To let his lips connect with hers. Right now, he almost felt cheated.

But it was clear that something else was going on.

There was a reason he'd been curious about April Henderson. It wasn't the good figure, the blonde hair and cute smile. It was *her*. The way she engaged with the patients. The way he could tell sometimes she was considering things, trying to do what was best. She'd captured his attention in a way he'd never really been caught before.

She'd relaxed a little around him tonight. When she'd been with Finn she'd been happy. She was so good around Finn. He seemed to almost sparkle when he was with her they connected so well.

And it wasn't just Finn. Riley wasn't imagining things. There was definitely something in the air between them. Even though she was trying her best to ignore it.

He should probably ignore it too. Finn was his priority. Christmas was coming. His son was about to face his first Christmas without his mother, but Riley was about to spend the first Christmas with his son.

He wasn't even sure how to mark the occasion. He should be overjoyed and happy, but in the circumstances it wasn't appropriate.

There were obvious times when Finn's childhood innocence shone through. He spoke about his mum. He cried at times. But children possessed a resilience that adults couldn't quite comprehend. And he seemed to be settling in to his new house, his new surroundings.

But for Riley there was something else. Finn seemed to light up around April. It seemed he'd spent much of his five years around women, so that didn't seem so unusual.

What was unusual was the way it made Riley's heart skip a beat.

Or two.

He sighed and closed the door. It was just the wrong time. He still had to work out his career plans. His house plans.

His life plans.

It was best that he do it alone.

CHAPTER FIVE

WORK FELT STRANGE. April had spent most of the last few days glancing over her shoulder in an attempt to try to stay out of Riley's way.

What might have happened if she'd stayed longer the other night? It annoyed her that there was almost an ache inside at the mere thought of it. By the time she'd got home that night she'd been resolute. It was best not to get involved with Riley and Finn Callaghan. Things would get busy anyhow. They would forget about her. Riley's parents would visit and Christmas plans would start to be made. She could fade into the background and take care of herself for now.

So why had she spent the last few days with her stomach doing flip flops?

Lucy, the staff nurse in the ward, was waiting for her when she arrived. 'Hi, April. You here to see John Burns?'

April nodded. John had been wounded in action and after a few weeks with an extremely damaged lower leg and a persistent infection they'd taken the decision to perform an amputation. 'How's he doing?'

Lucy pushed his notes over. 'Riley's spent quite a bit of time with him this morning. He's had a lot of phantom pain. He had some analgesia about two hours ago, so he should be fit for you to see.'

She nodded and walked down the corridor towards John's room. She could hear the laughter before she reached the room and her footsteps faltered. Riley. This was where he'd been hiding out. From the way Lucy had spoken she'd assumed that Riley had already left.

She screwed up her face. She couldn't avoid this. It was her job. Physiotherapy was essential for John's recovery and for his confidence. She'd just have to keep her professional face in place.

She fixed on a smile and walked into the room. 'Good morning, John. How are you doing today?'

Riley was sitting on an easy chair in the corner of the room. He looked comfortable. Too comfortable. She gave him a glance. 'We don't want you distracting us, Dr Callaghan. John and I have some work to do.'

John was sitting up on the bed. He waved his hand. 'No, it's fine. Riley wanted to stay to make sure I'm good to go with the painkillers he's given me.' John shook his head. 'I just can't get my head around this phantom pain stuff. How can I feel something that just isn't there?'

April took a deep breath. Riley hadn't spoken; he was just watching her with those green eyes. She turned her full attention to John as she sat beside his bed. 'You're right. It is difficult to understand. And we still don't really know why it happens. Scientists think that the sensations come from the spinal cord and brain. The imprint of the leg has always been there, so it's almost like the brain keeps hold of it.' She licked her lips. 'You're not alone, John. Lots of patients experience phantom pain after this kind of operation. It's our job to manage that pain for you. So you need to tell me if anything we do today is too uncomfortable.'

John let out a sigh. 'I just want to get back on my feet as soon as possible.' Then he realised the irony of his statement. He let out a hollow laugh. 'Well, at least one of them.' He met April's gaze. 'I just want to get some normality back. The last few months have been terrible. I want to be able to do things for myself.'

April nodded in appreciation. John's mobility had been badly affected by his damaged and infected limb; that had been part of the decision for the amputation. 'And we'll get you there, John. We will.'

She looked at his position. 'How has lying flat worked out for you?'

The first essential procedure for patients who'd had an amputation was to lie flat for at least an hour each day. This helped straighten the hip as much as possible. Any risk of hips tightening could make it more difficult to walk with a prosthesis.

John gave a nod. 'That's been okay.'

She gave him a smile. 'So how do you feel about hitting the gym with me today?'

He grinned. 'I thought you'd never ask. Music to my ears.'

She wheeled in the chair that was parked in the corridor outside, taking care to help him change position and ease into it. Riley stood up.

She gave him a tight smile. 'I take it you have other patients to see? I can leave a report for you about how John does in the gym.'

But it seemed that the more she tried to brush off Riley, the more determined he became. And the most annoying thing about that was how casual he was about it. He didn't act offended. He didn't appear to be angry. He just seemed determined to hang around.

She pushed John down the corridor to the state-of-the-art gym. It was specially designed for patients with spinal cord injuries and amputations. April turned towards Riley. If he was going to hang around, she might as well use him.

'I've looked over John's wound and think it's looking good. Good enough to take part in a walking trial. What do you think?'

Riley nodded. 'It's healing well. No problems. I think it would be useful to see how John manages.'

April gave a nod and took the chair closer to the parallel walking bars. She turned around and picked up what she'd left in preparation for today's session. 'We're going to try one of these,' she said, smiling as she watched the expression on John's face.

'What on earth is that?'

She kept smiling. 'It's called a pam aid. Pneumatic Post-Amputation Mobility Aid. It's basically an inflatable leg. It helps reduce the swelling around your stump and helps you walk again. We need to assess your muscle strength and standing tolerance.' She raised her eyebrows. 'And the big one—your balance.' She gestured behind her. 'We always start with the parallel bars.'

John frowned. 'Can't you just give me one of those prosthetic limbs and let me get on with it?'

Riley stood up alongside as April started to make adjustments to John's stump-shrinker compression sock. 'If you manage well with your walking trial over the next few days then we'll make arrangements to have you fitted with a prosthetic limb. But it has to be made just for you. And we have to wait until your wound is completely healed and any residual swelling has gone down.'

John gave a nod. 'Then let's get started. I want to be out of this wheelchair as soon as I can be.'

It was almost like being under the microscope. Even though she knew Riley was there to observe John, every move she made, every conversation that she started felt a little forced. She hadn't even been this self-conscious when she was a student and was being assessed.

Riley, on the other hand, seemed completely at ease. He cracked jokes with John and kept him distracted while April got things ready.

But she was conscious of the way he watched. It was annoying. Her emotions were heightened.

Eventually she stopped keeping the false smile on her face. 'Are you going to do something to actually help?'

Riley's brow furrowed with a deep frown. Now, finally, he looked annoyed. He glanced around the gym as he positioned himself next to John. 'What would you like me to do?'

April pulled herself into professional mode. It was the safest place to be. Then she wouldn't notice those eyes. Then she wouldn't focus on the fresh smell stretching across the room towards her.

She didn't even look at him. She waved her hand. 'I'll stay on one side of John. You stay on the other.'

She bent forward in front of John. 'First time standing on your own can be difficult. I'm going to let you push yourself up—it's best if you can get a sense of your own balance without us taking your weight. Don't worry. If it's too painful, we can help you sit back down, and we're on either side; we won't let you fall.'

John nodded. Guys who'd served always had a grim determination about every task. They didn't like to fail at anything and John was no different. He placed a hand on either parallel bar and pulled himself up sharply. April kept her hands off but close by, ready to catch him if he swayed. There was a kind of groan. Weight bearing on a stump for the first time would be sending a whole new range of sensations about John's body. She didn't look up at Riley. He had adopted a similar position to herself, ready to take the strain of John's weight if it were necessary.

After around thirty seconds, John's breathing started to slow a little. 'Okay,' he said gruffly. 'It's not exactly comfortable, but it's bearable.' He turned his head to April. 'Do I get to walk in this thing?'

She nodded. 'Only a few steps at a time. I'm going to pull the wheelchair behind us so it's handy if you need it.'

John shook his head. 'No way. I'm going to make it to the end of these bars.'

She smiled. Somehow she didn't doubt he would.

Riley leaned forward. 'John, just remember. This isn't a military operation. Your wound is healing well. But parts will still hurt. We need to be able to judge how much analgesia you need to be able to take part in your physical therapy. If we give you too much, you could do yourself harm. Push your body to do things it's not quite ready for.'

'Do people normally make it to the end of the bars?' John asked April.

She held up her hands. 'Some people can't weight

bear at all the first time. Some people can stand for a few minutes; others manage a few steps. We're all individuals, John. And this is the first day. Your first steps. Let's just take it as it comes.'

He nodded, his hands gripping tightly to the bars, his knuckles blanching.

She could see Riley noticing the same things that she was. Why was he even here? This was her job. Doctors rarely visited the gym. They usually only appeared if their presence was requested.

Suddenly, there was a pang in her stomach and she caught her breath. That had been a few times today. She hoped she wasn't coming down with something.

John took a step forward with his affected leg. She pressed her lips together for the next stage. It was just as she expected. He had his weight on the amputated limb for the briefest of seconds before his weight fell back on his good leg.

That was entirely normal. It was hard for the body to adjust. It was hard for the brain to make sense of the changes. John was starting to sweat. It was amazing how much work just a few steps could take. She stayed right next to him. As did Riley.

It took another ten minutes to reach the end of the parallel bars. By the time John had finished he was thankful to sink back down into the wheelchair. April put her hands on his shoulders. 'Well done, John. That was great.' She walked around to the front to release the pam aid. 'Ideally, we'll do a bit of work in the gym three times a day.' She looked at Riley. 'Dr Callaghan will have a conversation with you about what works best analgesia-wise for you. The more regularly we can get you down to the gym, the more quickly your body and brain will adjust. The nurses will also do regular checks of your wound to make sure there are no problems.'

John gave an exhausted sigh. 'Any chance of a coffee?'

She laughed. 'Absolutely.' She set the pam aid aside. 'I'll take you back down to the ward and we'll set a programme for tomorrow.'

John looked over at Riley. 'She's a hard taskmaster.'

Riley's voice wasn't as relaxed as it had been earlier. 'She is. But it's the only way to get you back on your feet.'

He pushed his hands into his pockets as April finished tidying up. His pager sounded and he glanced at it. The expression on his face changed.

'Sorry, need to go.' He'd already started striding down the corridor in front of them when he turned around and looked back. 'John, I'll be back to talk to you later.'

April watched his retreating back. Part of her wanted to ask what was wrong. Part of her knew it was none of her business.

Could something be wrong with Finn?

She tried to push things out of her mind. She had a patient to look after. She had work to do. But, as they reached John's room, he said the words she'd dreaded. 'Isn't Ballyclair the local school?'

She nodded.

'Thought so. That's what his pager said. Hope his kid is okay.'

Her footsteps faltered as she took the final steps towards the chair in John's room. 'Oops, sorry!' she said brightly as she bent down to put on the brake. Her heart was thudding against her chest. She moved automatically, helping John into the other chair.

This was none of her business. None of her business at all.

So why did she want to pull her mobile from her pocket and phone Riley right now?

One of the nurses stuck her head around the door. 'April, are you free? I'm wondering if I could steal you to do some chest physio on someone who is sounding a little crackly?'

She nodded straight away. Work—that was what she had to do. That was what she should be concentrating on. She smiled at John. 'Can we coordinate our diaries for around two p.m. and we can go back to the gym again?'

John put his hand on his chin. 'Let me think. There's the afternoon movie. Or the browsing of the dating websites. But I think I can fit you in.'

She laughed and put her hand on his shoulder. 'You did good this morning. Let's keep working hard. See you in a while.'

Her fingers brushed against her phone again and she pulled them from her pocket.

None of her business.

She gritted her teeth and kept walking.

He was trying to be rational. But the words 'Finn's been hurt' had sent a deep-rooted fear through him that he'd never experienced before. His legs had just started walking to the car even with the phone still pressed to his ear.

Apparently it was 'just a little head-knock'. When was any head injury 'just a little head-knock'? Finn had slid in the school playground, fallen backwards, cracked his head on the concrete and been knocked out for a few seconds.

His car was eating up the road in front of him. Finn's school was only a ten-minute drive from the hospital but right now it felt like a million miles away.

His mum and dad had come down for the weekend to meet Finn. He'd told April that his mum was like a whirlwind—truth was she'd been more like a tornado. She'd taken over everything. Cooking. Cleaning. Every conversation with Finn. His dad had been much more thoughtful. But Riley could tell that his father just wanted a chance to have five minutes to sit down with his grandson.

It hadn't helped that his mother kept bursting into tears every now and then. Finn had just seemed a little bewildered by it all. He'd finally whispered to Riley, 'I've never had a gran before,' as he'd watched Riley's mum talk and cook at a hundred miles an hour. Riley had given him a hug.

It had all been exhausting. His mother hadn't wanted to leave, and Riley had been forced to tell her quite pointedly that he needed some time with his son. Right now, he was regretting that decision. What if he needed some help with Finn?

His eyes narrowed as he noticed the traffic slowing in front of him on the motorway. He'd come this way to save a few minutes and to stop wasting time at a hundred sets of traffic lights in the town. Seemed like it hadn't been the best plan.

His foot hit the brake as it became clear that things were much worse than he could ever imagine. Smoke was directly ahead. The cars in front had stopped, but it was clear the accident had only happened around thirty seconds before.

Riley's stomach clenched. Two cars, both totally smashed, facing each other and blocking the motorway completely.

For the first time in his life he was completely torn. His doctor instincts told him to get out of the car and start helping. But his newly honed parental instincts told him to find a way to Finn.

He gulped and looked behind him. It only took a few minutes for the motorway to back up completely. There was no exit nearby. There was no way out of here.

He pulled his phone from his pocket as he climbed out of the car. Someone else had already jumped out and ran to the smoking cars. For the first time he regretted sending his mother back home after her weekend meeting Finn. There was only one other natural person to phone in a situation like this. He pressed her name on the screen as he opened the boot of his car and grabbed the emergency kit that he always kept there.

There was only one other person he'd trust with Finn.

April's stomach plummeted when she saw who was calling. 'Riley? What's wrong? Is it Finn? Is he okay?'

His voice was eerily calm. But she could hear some shouting in the background. 'April? There's an accident on the motorway. I can't get off. And I need to help. The school phoned. Can you get Finn? Can you check he's okay? He's had a head injury. He was knocked out. Don't come this way. You'll have to drive through the town. Check his reactions. Check his pupils. If he's nauseous or sleepy take him to hospital.'

April was stunned. It took a few seconds to find some words.

'Of…of course. Of course I'll get Finn. No problem. Riley, are you okay?'

She could almost physically feel his pause. 'I'm fine. I have to go and help. Just take care of Finn.'

She stared at the phone. Her hand had the slightest shake. April moved into automatic pilot. She wasn't sure if Riley had spoken to anyone when he'd left, so she followed procedures and spoke to her boss, making arrangements for someone to cover her workload, and then left a message for Riley's boss. Waterloo Court was a real family-friendly place. No one had problems about her leaving. It only took fifteen minutes to drive through town and reach the school.

Finn was sitting at the office as she arrived, looking a little pale-faced. He didn't seem surprised to see her as she rushed over to sit next to him and give him a hug.

The head teacher looked at her in surprise. She held out her hand in a way that only a head teacher could. 'I'm Mrs Banks. I don't believe we've met. I was expecting Dr Callaghan.'

April nearly opened her mouth to speak, then had a wave of realisation. She pointed through the doors. 'Can we speak in there, please?' She didn't wait for a reply before she whispered in Finn's ear, 'I'll be just a second, honey.'

Once they'd walked through the doors she held out her hand to the head teacher. 'Apologies. I'm April Henderson. I'm a colleague of Dr Callaghan. He's stuck at a road accident on the motorway. I didn't want to say that in front of Finn, since he lost his mother in an accident.'

The head teacher gave a nod of acknowledgement and shook April's hand. 'Of course. I understand. But we have a problem.'

'We do?'

She nodded. 'I'm afraid Dr Callaghan hasn't named you as an emergency contact. It means I can't let you take Finn away.'

'Oh.' It was all she could say. Her brain filled with distant memories of conversations with colleagues over the years about making things safer for kids at school. Of course they wouldn't just hand Finn over to anyone. But that hadn't even occurred to her on the way there. It must not have occurred to Riley either. They were both treading waters unknown.

'I take it Riley didn't manage to call you and tell you I was coming?' Why did she even ask that? Of course not. She shook her head. 'He's treating people at the accident scene.'

The head teacher gave her best sympathetic look. 'Well, I'm sorry. But we have good reasons for our rules. Until we hear from Dr Callaghan, we can't let you leave with Finn.'

April glanced through the glass panel in the door, where Finn was so white he seemed transparent. She took a deep breath. 'Let me keep trying to get hold of Riley while I keep an eye on Finn.'

Riley surveyed the scene. Two cars—both had their bonnets completed crumpled, one had its side doors crushed inwards. He ran towards the cars, checking in one, then the other. Another man was talking to a lady in the first car.

'I'm Riley Callaghan, a doctor.'

The guy looked up. 'I'm Phil—just Phil. I know a little first aid but that's it.'

Riley gave a nod and took a quick look in the car. It was an elderly couple. The man was unconscious, the woman making a few groans. Both looked trapped by the crumpled front end of the car. Riley tried to pull the door open nearest to him. After a few attempts he put his foot up to get more leverage. The door opened but not completely. He put his hand in and felt for a pulse, watching the rise and fall of the man's chest. He grabbed some gloves from his back pocket—life had taught him to permanently have them handy. He then put his hand down the non-existent footwell. He fumbled around. There was no way to see clearly, but after a few seconds he found a pulse at one ankle, but couldn't get to the other. He pulled out his hand; unsurprisingly the glove was covered in blood. He pulled it off and found another. 'How's she doing?' he asked Phil.

Phil pulled a face. 'I'm not sure.'

Riley was around the car in an instant. 'Mind if I have a look?'

Phil stepped out of the way. Riley was keeping calm; his main aim was to have assessed the occupants of both cars in as short a time as possible. He'd take it from there.

He checked the woman's pulse. She was terribly pale, but that might be her normal colour. He checked her breathing; it was erratic and he put his hand gently at her chest. She'd broken some ribs. He was sure of it. And it could be that one had pierced her lung. He did a quick check of her legs. One was definitely broken; he suspected both tib and fib. The second seemed okay.

'Stay with her,' he said. 'I'm going to check the other car.'

He crossed quickly to the other car. There was a man of a similar age to him, coughing, with a little blood running down his forehead. The airbag had deployed and the air was still a little clouded around him. The man was clearly dazed. In between coughs he spluttered, 'Aaron. How's Aaron?'

Riley felt his heart plummet. He looked into the back of the car. A little boy—around two—was strapped into a car seat. He yanked at the rear car door, pulling it with all his might. It was stiff. Part of the door was buckled, but after some tugging he finally pulled it free. The little boy greeted him with a big smile. He started babbling and wiggling his legs.

Riley's actions were automatic. This car already had smoke coming from the engine. He reached and unclipped the little guy, grabbing him with both hands and pulling him out. He leaned Aaron towards his father. He would never have thought to do something like that before. But he could see that in amongst his confused state the man's first thoughts had been for his son.

Finn. As held the little body next to his, all he could think about was Finn. Was he okay? Had April got to him yet? He should be with him. Not here.

Not stuck at a roadside.

'Aaron looks good; the car seat has kept him protected.' He glanced anxiously at the man as his head slumped forward a little. It was obvious he was still completely dazed. 'What's your name?'

'Ben,' came the mumbled reply.

'Well, Ben, I'm going to hand Aaron over to someone else to keep an eye on him and get him somewhere safe. We need to think about getting you out of this car.'

A woman had appeared from one of the cars stranded in the traffic jam. She arrived just as he turned around. He moved away from the cars. 'Can you hold this little guy for a second?' She held out her hands and Riley thrust Aaron into them. 'Wait a second,' he commanded and he gave Aaron a quick check over. No apparent injuries. Breathing fine. Moving all limbs. No abrasions. He pulled his pen torch from his back pocket, choking back a gulp. He'd meant to use this on Finn. He quickly checked Aaron's pupils. Both equal and reacting to light.

He looked at the woman. 'This is Aaron. Everything looks fine but can you take him over to the side of the road and keep an eye on him for now?'

She nodded quickly, seeming relieved to be of some help. 'No problem.' She started chatting to Aaron as she walked away. Riley's phone rang.

April.

He actually thought he might be sick. Something must be wrong with Finn. It must be something terrible. A subdural haematoma? Skull fracture? Intracranial bleeding? His hand fumbled with the phone. 'April? What's wrong?'

'Riley. Are you okay? Finn looks fine. But the school won't let me take him home. They say they need permission.'

Relief flooded through him, rapidly followed by frustration. 'Let me speak to them.' He turned back to the car. The smoke looked a little worse. He needed to get Aaron's dad out of there.

A stern voice appeared on the phone. 'Dr Callaghan?

Mrs Banks, head teacher. I'm afraid you haven't listed Ms Henderson as an emergency contact for Finn. We really need you to sign some paperwork so that, like today, we can release Finn into her care.'

He was instantly annoyed. He knew why Mrs Banks was saying all this, but it felt like a reprimand for an unruly child. As he stood, flames started licking from the silver car holding Aaron's dad. 'Damn it!' He started running back towards the car. He tucked the phone under his chin, put his foot on the car and started pulling at the driver's door with all his might. 'Come on!' he yelled in frustration at the door.

'What?' came a squeak from the phone.

'Mrs Banks,' he said between yanks at the door. 'I'm trying to pull a guy from a burning car. You—' he stopped and pulled again '—have my permission to—' every muscle in his arms was starting to ache '—release Finn into April's custody.' He pushed the phone away from his ear and shouted to some guys who were talking near the front of the traffic jam. 'Can you give me some help over here?' He could feel the heat from the flames near the bare skin on his arms. He pushed the phone back to his ear. 'Could you do that, please?'

He pushed the phone back into his pocket, not bothering to wait for a reply. April was there. She'd seen Finn. She'd said he was okay. Maybe his definition of okay was different from hers, but he had to have faith in his colleague. Had April worked with kids before? Hadn't she mentioned something about kids with cystic fibrosis? Maybe she knew more than he thought.

Three men ran over; one joined him, two tried the opposite side of the car. Why hadn't he thought of that?

The man's hands squished over his at the handle.

'Now,' he grunted at Riley as the two of them pulled in unison. His hands were nearly crushed beneath the guy's vice-like grip but the extra strength gave him what he needed. The car door was finally prised open and they both landed on the ground.

Riley picked himself up and leaned in to check on Ben just as the flames shot up towards the sky. The two men on the other side of the car yelled and leapt backwards. Riley reached forward to check Ben's legs weren't trapped. He knew the rules. A casualty should never be moved from a vehicle without a neck collar in place to protect them.

But threat of imminent death from fire took priority over all the normal rules.

He gestured to the other guy. 'Give me a hand getting him out of here.' There was a sound of sirens in the distance. The other guy looked at the flames. Riley could see the doubt on his face but, to his credit, the guy stood up and came forward. Together, they half pulled, half lifted Ben out of the car, looping arms around his waist and carrying him over to the side of the road.

Ben winced in pain as Riley touched his leg. Riley glanced around. His emergency bag was lying on the ground next to the first car. He ran and picked it up, pulling a swab out to stem the bleeding from Ben's forehead.

He shouted over to Phil, whom he'd left at the side of the first car. 'How's everything?'

Phil looked anxious. 'Her lips look a bit blue,' he shouted back.

Riley looked up. He could see the blue flashing lights now and the sirens were getting louder. The police cars and ambulances were trying to weave their way through the traffic. They would still be a few minutes.

He ran over to the car to check both patients again. A quick glance at the man showed he still hadn't regained consciousness. But his pulse was strong and he was breathing easily. The leg injuries remained but it was likely that he'd need to be cut out of the car. There wasn't much Riley could do for him at the side of the road. He turned his attention back to the woman. He spoke quietly. Her handbag was behind the seat, so he checked her details. 'Elizabeth? Mrs Bennett?' She gave a nod. 'I'm Riley. I'm a doctor. There's an ambulance coming soon.' He put his fingers on her pulse again. It was faster and more thready than before. 'Are you having difficulty breathing?'

She nodded again. He glanced at Phil at the other side of the car. 'Take a run towards the ambulance. Tell them we have a pneumo—' He changed his mind about the language. 'Tell them a possible punctured lung. Tell them I need some oxygen.'

Phil nodded and took off. The cars were doing their best to get out of the way of the police cars and ambulances but there was virtually no room to manoeuvre.

Riley was frustrated. He hated the fact he had little or no equipment. From her colour, Mrs Bennett had either a collapsed lung or a blood-filled one. Both needed rapid treatment. But there was nothing he could do right now. He held her hand and spoke quietly to her, trying to ascertain if she had family and if there was someone to contact, in case she became too unwell to communicate. The thud of boots behind him made him look up. The familiar green overalls of a paramedic. He was carrying as much equipment as he could. His eyes fixed on the car that was now firmly alight.

'Tell me no one is in that?'

Riley shook his head. 'Man and a little boy, both at the side of the road. They'll need to be checked but—' he nodded to the car '—Mr and Mrs Bennett look as if they need attention first.'

The paramedic nodded. 'Eric' was his reply. 'What we got?' He handed over the oxygen cylinder.

'Lieutenant Riley Callaghan, a doctor at Waterloo Court.' He leaned forward. 'Elizabeth, I'm just going to slip an oxygen mask over your face.' He did that quickly. 'Mr and Mrs Bennett. Mr Bennett has been unconscious since I got here. I think he has a fractured tib and fib in the footwell. His pulse has been strong and his breathing fine. Mrs Bennett, I think, may have had some damage from the seat belt and I don't know about her pelvis. She also looks like she has a tib and fib fracture. I think she may have fractured a few ribs and punctured a lung.'

A female paramedic arrived too, shaking her head. 'Still can't get the ambulances through. Where do you want me?'

Eric signalled to the side of the road where Aaron and his dad were sitting and she nodded and ran over. Eric ripped open the large pack he'd brought with him. 'Right, Doc, let's get to work.'

CHAPTER SIX

FINN WAS SLEEPING NOW. April wasn't quite sure what Riley had said to Mrs Banks on the phone, but Finn had been released into her care with a few mutterings of 'exceptional circumstances'.

After she'd realised she didn't have a key to Riley's place, she'd made a quick trip to the shops to let Finn pick something for dinner then brought him back to her flat.

Thank goodness for the TV. There was a whole host of kids' TV channels she'd never known about or watched, but Finn could tell her exactly where to find them. She'd checked him over as best she could and, apart from being a little pale and not wanting to eat much, he seemed fine. As soon as he'd eaten a little dinner, he'd fallen asleep, lying on the sofa with a cover over him.

Part of her had been nervous. Hadn't Riley said something about sleepiness being a sign of head injury? But her gut instincts told her that Finn was simply exhausted. It was after seven; she wasn't sure when he normally went to bed.

She walked through to the kitchen to make herself a

drink but when she came back through Finn was awake again with his nose pressed up against the window.

'Hey,' she said gently as she crossed the room and put an arm on his shoulder. 'What are you looking at?'

It took her a second or two to realise his shoulders were shaking a little. She knelt down beside him so she could see his face. 'Finn? What's wrong?'

'I… I heard someone shouting. I heard someone shouting my name…' His voice stalled for a second.

April glanced outside. There was a family directly under her window, laughing and carrying on in the light dusting of snow outside. The woman shouted at the little boy and girl. 'Finn, Jessie, come over here.'

Finn started to shake next to her. 'I thought it was my mum,' he gasped. 'I thought it was her.'

Her actions were instinctive. She gathered the little body as Finn's legs collapsed under him and he started to sob. She pulled him in towards her shoulder and stood up, clutching him tightly. Normally she would have thought a five-year-old might be too big to carry like a toddler. But there was nothing else she could do right now. Finn needed her and she would never let him down.

She rubbed his back as he sobbed and whispered in his ear. 'I'm so sorry, honey. I'm so sorry that your mum isn't here.'

His words came out in gasps. 'I… I…miss…her.'

Tears started to flow down her face. She walked over to the sofa and sat down, keeping Finn firmly in her arms. 'I know you do. Of course you do. And I know that your mum wishes she was still here with you.'

He curled in her arms, pulling up his knees and resting his head on her chest. 'I want my mum.'

She rocked back and forward. His pain was so raw. So real. She wanted to reach out and grab it. To take it away for him. No child should have to go through this.

She stroked his hair. 'It's not the same. But I had a sister who died not long ago. I know how hard it is when you lose someone you love very much. And it is hard, Finn. I won't tell you lies. You'll miss your mum every single day. And while it's really horrible right now, and you'll think about her all the time, I promise that at some point it won't be quite as bad as it is now.'

Finn shook his head. 'I just want her back. I just want to go home.'

It was almost like a fist reaching inside and twisting around her heart.

She kept rocking. 'I know you do, honey. But you're going to have a new home with your dad. He loves you. He loves you just as much as your mum does. It just takes a little getting used to. For him too.' She gave a little sigh and tried to find the right words. Were there even right words?

'Mum used to do this,' whispered the little voice.

April froze mid-rock.

She'd only done what came naturally. She wasn't trying to be a mum to Finn. She was just doing what she thought she should.

Finn's hand crept up and his finger wound in her hair. Now, it was her turn to almost shake. 'Can we stay like this till I fall asleep?' came the tired voice.

Her brain was screaming silent messages at her. *No! Too close.*

Her body started to rock again, but she couldn't say the words out loud. It was almost like being on automatic pilot. And even though her movements were steady her thoughts weren't.

She was overstepping the mark. This was wrong. It was Riley's job to comfort his son—not hers. She couldn't let Finn rely on her. That would be wrong. That would be *so* wrong. Particularly when she didn't know what might lie ahead.

Finn's little heart had already been broken once. It was bad enough for a child to experience that once. If things developed…

She pushed the thoughts straight from her head. No. They wouldn't. She couldn't let them. It wasn't good for her. And it really wasn't good for Finn.

Her brain buzzed as she kept rocking until the little finger released its grip on her hair and Finn's head sagged to the side.

Moving carefully, she positioned him on the sofa with a blanket on top as she stood on the other side of the room, leaning against the wall and breathing heavily.

She hadn't meant for this to happen. She was getting too close. She was feeling too much.

A few extra tears slid down her cheeks. She had to get a hold of herself.

But it wasn't how he felt about her that was hardest. It was how she felt about him, and Riley.

For her, they were a perfect combination at a completely imperfect time. A guy who made her heart beat quicker with just one glance, and a little boy with so much love to give.

Her heart ached. She just wasn't ready for this. Not right now.

There was a gentle knock at the door. It startled

her and she took a few deep breaths, pushing her hair back from her face and wiping her eyes before she pulled it open.

Riley looked exhausted. He was still wearing his pale blue scrubs from work. They were rumpled and had a number of stains that she really didn't want to question.

'How's Finn?' He almost pushed past her in his rush to get through the door.

She shook her head and stepped completely aside. 'He's fine. He's just tired.' She pointed towards the sofa. She hesitated for a second. 'He had some dinner and he's sleeping now. But he was a little upset earlier.'

'He was? Is he sick?'

Riley turned towards her and she could instantly see his panic. She held up her hand in front of him. 'No, he's not sick. His pupils are equal and reactive. I gave him some kiddie paracetamol that I bought at the pharmacy. Yes, he felt a bit queasy for a while, but was fine after I'd fed him.' She took a deep breath. She was being automatically defensive because she wasn't that experienced with kids. Looking after kids with cystic fibrosis had been a whole different ball game. But she could imagine how Riley must have felt, thinking there was something wrong with Finn and he couldn't get there.

He crossed the room in a few strides and knelt down in front of the sofa. She watched as he gently stroked Finn's hair and whispered to him. 'Hey, buddy, sorry I was so long. I've missed you.'

The truth of every word that he said was etched on his face, and she turned away as tears sprang to her eyes.

This guy was doing crazy things to her heart. His love. His connection to his child. That overwhelming parental urge that she'd never felt—and would never feel.

Or would she? When she'd seen Riley's name on the phone screen today her heart had been in her mouth. She'd been immediately worried about Finn. Seeing him, and knowing he was okay, had relieved her concerns instantly. Spending time with him this afternoon had been a pleasure—even though he'd been a little cranky.

His every move, every gesture had reminded her of Riley. Being with Finn today had made her realise that even though she'd made her decision about the future she still had the ability to love a child as if it were her own.

That had almost seemed like something so far out of her reach she hadn't even thought about it that much.

She'd been focused on making the decision and getting her surgery out of the way before she gave herself a chance to regroup and think about what the future might hold.

But the guy who was currently leaning forward, showing every element of being a doting dad, was wrapping her emotions up in knots and her interaction with Finn earlier had exposed her to some overwhelming feelings.

After a minute he came over and stood next to her. 'What happened?'

She sucked in a breath. All of a sudden she didn't really want to tell him. He was Finn's father. He had a right to know his child had been upset. But she couldn't quite extricate her own feelings from all of this. Not without revealing them to Riley.

She gave her head a shake. 'He misses his mum. He heard a woman outside call his name—her son must be called Finn too. For a few seconds I think he thought it was his mum and he got upset and was crying.'

Riley ran his fingers through his hair and shook his head. On top of the exhaustion that was already there, he almost looked broken. 'How do I deal with this, April? What do I do?'

She gulped at the pleading tone to his words. She wanted to wrap her hands around his neck and pull him close.

This was a conversation she couldn't have. She just couldn't.

Not the way she felt right now. He had no idea what she was preparing herself for. She turned and walked into the kitchen. She had to try to distance herself from this. She couldn't let Finn see her as some sort of mother figure. She couldn't let this potential relationship with Riley develop any further.

She kept her voice steady as she flicked on the kettle. 'You just be his dad, Riley. That's all you can do.'

She looked at the pained expression on his face and the sag of his shoulders. She'd never seen him look so tired. It was time to try to change the subject. 'What happened?' she asked.

He paused for a second and gave her a quizzical glance. She could almost see the words forming on his lips to ask her why she was pulling away, but in the end he gave a brief shake of his head. 'There was another RTA at another part of town. Turned out A&E also have a sickness bug. I had to travel with one of the patients in the ambulance. When I got there...' He let his voice trail off.

She nodded. 'You couldn't leave. You had to stay and help.'

He sighed. 'I'm a doctor; what else could I do? They didn't have enough staff to deal with two major RTAs. By the time I could hitch a lift back to the scene of the accident to pick up my car half the day had just gone. I'm sorry, April.'

She put her hand on his arm. 'It's fine. Really.'

He wrinkled his nose and squinted back at Finn. 'What is he wearing?'

April shrugged. 'He couldn't lie around in his school uniform. I gave him a T-shirt to wear. He picked it. It's a superhero one. He said it was better than the one with pink sequins.'

They'd laughed about it. Finn had been impressed with her variety of superhero T-shirts. He'd been even more impressed by her collection of superhero socks, especially when she'd whispered, 'I think these are mostly for boys. But girls need superheroes too. And I always have cold feet. So I need *lots* of socks.'

Riley smiled, shook his head and followed her into the kitchen. He looked around. 'Nice flat. Have you lived here long?'

She shook her head. 'Just since I took the job at Waterloo Court.' She held up her hands in the glossy black kitchen. 'It was brand new when I bought it, and already finished, so I didn't have much say. Hence, the wooden floors throughout and the black kitchen.' She shrugged. 'I think they do up most new places the same these days. White walls, white bathrooms and very little personality.'

He pointed towards a large cardboard box tucked in the corner of the kitchen. 'What's that?'

She lifted a cup out of the cupboard. 'Oh, that's the Christmas tree. I just pulled it down from the loft last night. I have a little loft space because I'm the top floor flat. It's good. I'm secretly a hoarder, so I can hide all my junk up there.'

Riley stood up and lifted the edge of the cardboard box. His eyebrows shot up. 'A black Christmas tree? I thought you loved Christmas? This seems kinda weird.'

She smiled. 'Yeah, well. It fitted with the flat. It has purple baubles, though. I'm sure Finn will approve.' She wagged her finger. 'And, believe me, you have no idea just how many other Christmas decorations I actually have. Now, tea or coffee?' She held up both in her hands.

'What, no wine?'

She shook her head. 'Not on a school night. It seems like there's no dinner either. I bought something for Finn but forgot about myself. I can make you chicken nuggets if you want? Or cheese on toast.'

Riley let out a groan. 'Coffee, please. Just black since you don't have a fancy cappuccino maker. And I'd kill for some cheese on toast.'

She smiled as she opened the grill. 'I'm glad you appreciate my cooking talents.'

It only took a few minutes to start toasting the bread under the grill and to grate some cheese. Riley nursed his coffee as he watched.

'How was the accident? Was everyone okay?'

He sighed. 'Hopefully, yes. There was an elderly couple. The man has a broken tibia and fibula. He was pinned in the car and I waited until the fire brigade could cut him out. He was unconscious while I was there, but came around when he got transferred into the ambulance. The woman had a pneumothorax and a fractured tib and fib too. She needed a chest tube when she reached A&E and then had to go to emergency theatre. It took about three hours for the anaesthetist to agree to take her. The other two were a father and son. The little boy was unharmed and the father just had a head lac, and some burns from the airbag.'

'What happened?'

He shook his head. 'Apparently a deer ran across the road. Who knows where it came from.'

April turned around and bent down to watch the cheese on toast as it started to bubble. A few seconds later she slid the grill pan out and lifted the toast onto plates.

Riley was watching her carefully as she sat down opposite him. She could tell straight away that something was bothering him.

'Thank you,' he said. 'Thank you for picking up Finn and looking after him.' His bright green eyes were fixed on hers with an intensity she hadn't expected.

'No problem.' She looked at the cheese on toast. He hadn't started eating yet.

She could see his tongue pressed into the side of his cheek, as if he were contemplating saying something.

'What?'

He met her gaze with those green eyes. 'I didn't have anyone else to call.'

She shifted in her chair. 'So?'

He was still nursing the coffee cup in his hand. 'That's just it. I didn't have someone else to call for Finn.'

She wasn't quite sure where this was going but her

skin prickled. 'But you called me, I picked him up, everything was fine.'

He shook his head. 'But it's not right. Finn should have more family than me. I should have more people around him.'

Her stomach started to churn. 'But you have your mum and dad. Didn't you say your mum wanted to move closer?'

He ran his fingers through his hair. She took a bite of her cheese on toast. She wasn't going to wait any longer.

'That's just it. I made a decision today.'

Uh-oh. This sounded serious. She swallowed quickly. 'What?'

He shook his head. 'I can't leave Finn. I just can't. Today, when I couldn't get to him, it made me re-evaluate everything. I'm going to speak to the Colonel. He's arranged things for me on a temporary basis. But I need to plan ahead.'

She gave a slow nod. 'You got a fright, Riley. That's understandable. It was unusual circumstances.' She gave him a smile. 'It's your first time in this situation as a dad. It will feel different.'

Riley was staring at his cheese on toast. It was as if it were easier to look at that than to look at April. 'Being a doctor, being in the army. It's all been about me. That has to stop. That has to change. I can't take an overseas posting again. Those days are gone. What happened if I was in Sierra Leone and Finn took ill? Who would take care of him?'

April had been about to take another bite and she froze, not quite sure where he was going next. Was he about to suggest her?

Please don't suggest me.

But Riley shook his head again. 'No. That's it. I'm done. I have to look for something else. Something that will suit Finn.'

She frowned, part of her brain so mixed up about this whole conversation. 'It doesn't matter what you do, Riley. There will always be days when you're not available. Maybe you just need to set up some kind of contingency plan?'

'Maybe I just need to have a look at my life and wonder how I got here.'

His tone had changed and she jerked her head up.

'What does that mean?'

'What kind of guy am I, that a girl I went out with for two months fell pregnant and didn't feel the urge to let me know? She didn't even seem to want my name on the birth certificate. No financial support. Nothing.'

These thoughts had already shot through her brain. But she shook her head. 'I can't speak for Isabel. I have no idea what she was thinking about. But she did leave a will. And she named you as the person to have Finn. If she thought so badly of you, she would never have done that.'

'Maybe she didn't have any other options? Isabel didn't have siblings, and her mum and dad were dead.' He said the words bitterly.

But April could think a bit clearer. 'No. She did have other options. One of her friends at the funeral said they'd offered to take Finn if something had happened. They'd had a drunken conversation once. But apparently Isabel said she'd made plans for Finn and she knew it was the right thing. She did have confidence in you, Riley. Even if you never had that conversation.'

There was silence for a few seconds. Then he kept going. 'April, how well do we know each other?'

He was jumping all over the place. She was going from confused to bewildered. 'Well…not very.' She hated saying that. It seemed odd. She'd been there when he'd found out about his child. She'd gone with him to his first meeting with his son. And now today, she'd been the person to cradle and hold Finn while he'd cried about his mother.

He set down the cup and drummed his fingers on the table. 'That's just it. How well did I know Isabel?'

She choked. 'Somehow I don't think it's the same thing.'

He gave the slightest shake of his head. 'But it is. What am I going to be able to tell Finn about his mum? I hear what you're saying but it still seems unreal. Why didn't she tell me about Finn? Did she think I was some kind of deadbeat? Some kind of unreliable guy that wouldn't pull his weight?'

She didn't even know how to start to answer that question. She shook her head gently. 'Maybe she was just an independent woman. Maybe getting pregnant was accidental; maybe it wasn't. Maybe she'd reached a stage in her life where she wanted to have a child and didn't want any complications.'

His gaze completely narrowed. He looked horrified. 'A complication? That's what I am? I'm his father!' His voice had risen in pitch and she shook her head and glanced through to Finn's sleeping form on the sofa.

'Shh. I know that. You're asking me to make guesses about someone I never even met. How can I do that? I have no idea what was going through Isabel's mind. How can I?' She took a deep breath. 'Somehow I don't think she'd write you off as a deadbeat. You're a doctor, Riley. It's hardly a deadbeat career. But maybe she thought if she told you that you might be angry with her. You said you were focused on your career. Maybe she knew that?'

He ran his fingers through his hair and closed his eyes. 'But I've missed five years of my son's life. I've missed so much. I didn't hear his first word. I didn't see his first steps.' He shook his head again. 'I wasn't bad to Isabel. Why wouldn't she tell me?'

April ran her tongue along her lips. She could see his anguish. See how distraught he was about all this. The tiny fleeting thought she'd had a few months back entered her mind again. She'd considered going out and trying to get pregnant. It had been the briefest thought. A moment of madness. She could have done to some random stranger what Isabel had done to Riley.

'I have no idea about any of this, Riley. It's horrible. I know that. But this isn't about you. This is about Finn. You have to put all this aside. You can't let Finn know that you're angry at his mother. You can't let him see this resentment. Isabel obviously didn't need financial support from you.' She paused; something he'd said had just struck her. 'Your name—it isn't on Finn's birth certificate, is it?'

There was a real sadness, a weariness about him. 'No. I had a discussion with the social worker. The will was clear. That's why Finn is with me. But if I want to get my name on his birth certificate, there will need to be a DNA test and it will go through court. It's just a formality. But it will also help if I want to change Finn's name. Right now he's still Finn Porter. He should be Finn Callaghan.' He pushed the coffee cup away from him. 'This is such a mess, April. I want to do every-thing right. But I can't make up for five lost years. And the truth is I'm never going to get over that.'

She ached for him—she really did. Riley was a good man. The kind of man she'd spent part of her life searching for. But now that she'd found him?

It wasn't the right time. For either of them. And that made her sad. If she blinked she could imagine meeting him five years ago—when Isabel had. Before she'd known about her genetic heritage, before she'd lost her sister. When the world had still looked bright and shiny. Riley would have fitted in well.

If Finn was their child, would she have told him?

Of course she would have. She knew that with cer-tainty.

But today she'd been overwhelmed by her motherly feelings towards Finn. They'd made her realise exactly what she was missing. Exactly what she would never be. And she wasn't ready for that. Not right now.

'You have to stop thinking about what you've lost, Riley.' She reached across the table and let her fingers brush against his. 'You have to start thinking about what you've gained. And that's the best little boy in the world.' She licked her lips again and prayed her voice wouldn't shake. Because she meant that—she truly did. 'Some people don't ever get that far. They never get that chance, no matter how much they want it. Count your blessings.'

He looked up sharply, his gaze melding with hers. She knew she'd revealed part of herself that she hadn't meant to. It was only words. And she hadn't actually told him anything. But Riley was a doctor. A good doc-tor. He would pick up on the words she wasn't saying.

He spoke carefully. 'You're right. Of course you're right. If someone had told me a few weeks ago how much my life could change...' His voice tailed off as he looked through at Finn.

Her heart swelled against her chest. A few weeks ago she would have said that Riley Callaghan was a cheeky charmer—a flirt, with good looks to match. It was part of the reason she'd kept her distance. She didn't want the pull; she didn't want the attraction. She had enough going on in her life.

But there was so much more to him. He was changing before her eyes. Watching him take these first few steps as a parent was enlightening. It was revealing more and more of the man to her. Was she really prepared for this?

'I need to sort things out. I need to make plans. Get things in place.' His voice cut through her thoughts.

She gave him a smile but his face was serious. 'And that starts with you, April.'

'What?' She sat forward in her chair.

He gestured towards her. 'You did me an enormous favour today. And there's always a chance I might ask it of you again. If that's okay with you, of course.'

She nodded automatically before she really had time to think about it. Her brain was screaming *No* at her. But her heart had overruled her head in milliseconds.

Caution still niggled at her. Once she agreed a surgery date she'd be in hospital for a few days. She might not be able to drive for a few weeks after. She chose her words carefully. 'Do you really think that's a good idea? It's really important right now that you and Finn get a chance to bond. I think me being around could complicate matters.' She was trying to steal herself away in the easiest way possible.

Riley didn't seem to pick up on her cautionary words.

He held up his hands and looked around. 'I'm only asking you to be a second contact for Finn in case of emergency. Situations like today are unlikely to happen again. I just need a second number. You can do that, can't you? I think it's most important for Finn right now to be around people he can trust. Isn't it?'

She swallowed. When he said it out loud it made perfect sense. If she argued now it would make her look petty and small, and it might mean that Riley would ask more difficult questions. She gave a brief nod. 'Okay, fine. You've got my number. You can use it.'

He smiled. 'Perfect, thank you.' Then he looked around. 'Since I'm trusting you with my son, I think we should get to know each other a little better. I've never been in here before. I only knew where you live because you came with me to pick up Finn. I feel as if I'm doing this all back to front.'

She shook her head. 'What are you talking about?'

'Okay. Tell me something about yourself. You picked up Finn today because you were the one person I could think of to phone—to trust with my child. But are we really even friends?'

Her stomach coiled. He was right. How well did they really know each other? What kind of movies did he like? What kind of food? Instinctively she felt as if Riley needed a giant bear hug. A simple show of affection because he'd had a bad day and was feeling so confused about things. That was the kind of thing you would do for a loved one—or for a friend.

But there was a prickliness to him. An edge. As if he just didn't know where he was in this life.

She recognised it because she'd worn it herself for so long.

It was almost like staring into a mirror and it made her heart flip over. Because, no matter how hard she tried to convince herself, she didn't think of Riley as a friend. It felt like so much more.

'I... I...think we're friends,' she said hesitantly, almost as if she were trying the word out for size. Why was that? Was it because saying she was Riley's 'friend' out loud didn't seem quite adequate?

He gave a nod. 'I would say so too. But we have gaps. We have bits missing.' He gave the tiniest wince. He already knew she hadn't talked about her sister much. Was he going to try to push her to talk more?

But he didn't. He just held up his hand towards her. 'Tell me something—' he paused '—not related to work. For example—' he frowned, as if trying to think of something himself '—tell me something most people wouldn't know about you. Like when I was a kid—' he put his hand on his chest and looked a bit sheepish '—I caused a panic on a beach once by saying I'd seen a shark. Truth was, I didn't want to swim in the sea but didn't want my brother to know.'

Her mouth fell open. 'What?' She wrinkled her brow and leaned forward. 'Riley Callaghan, were you scared?'

He winked. 'My lips are sealed. I'll never tell. Now, your turn.'

She racked her brain for something equally odd. It was hard being put on the spot. After a few seconds something came to mind. 'Okay, I once tried to steal a chocolate bar from a shop. But I chickened out when my sister saw me.'

From the expression on his face that was the last thing he'd expected. He leaned forward. 'You? Really?'

Now she felt ridiculous. Where on earth had that come from?

She just nodded.

'Why?'

She threw up her hands. 'I don't know. I just wanted it, I suppose.'

Riley shook his head. 'What age were you?' He wasn't going to let this go.

'Five,' she snapped.

Now, he laughed. 'Okay, that was random...and unexpected.' His hand crept towards the now cold cheese on toast. 'Tell me about your sister?'

Her skin prickled. 'What about her?'

'Let's start with her name.'

She wanted to change the subject. Her brain started thinking of random questions to throw at him.

Who was the first girl you slept with? was the one that danced around inside her head. But she didn't want to ask that. She didn't want to *know* that.

She imagined herself pulling on her big-girl pants.

'Mallory' was what she finally said.

He looked thoughtful. 'April and Mallory. Nice names, quite unusual.'

She nodded. 'My mother thought so. She picked April and my dad picked Mallory.'

'Ah, so they took turns? Interesting.'

She opened her mouth to say no. Then stopped. She hadn't told him Mallory was her twin. And she didn't want to. Not when she could guess where this conversation might lead.

'So you said that Mallory died eighteen months ago. I'm sorry. What happened?'

This was the second time he'd asked her. She tried not to let her voice shake, but she certainly couldn't meet his gaze. 'Mallory had cancer.'

'Oh. That's terrible. What kind?'

He hadn't missed a beat. She squeezed her eyes closed, just for a millisecond. He couldn't know the rest of what was going on in her head. He couldn't know the connections.

'Ovarian cancer,' she said quickly. 'She was unlucky.'

He pulled back a little. 'She was young.'

'Lots of people die young. It's a fact of life. Look at Isabel.'

It was a little bit cruel to turn it back around. But she needed to. She didn't want to have this conversation at all.

All it was doing was reinforcing the gulf that was between them. How far apart they really were.

The dreams of motherhood she'd felt earlier while looking at Finn? She had to push them away for now. Her stomach gave another twinge.

That was a few times that had happened now. What if it was...*something*?

It was as if the temperature had just plummeted in her flat to freezing. One hand went automatically to her arm, rubbing up and down.

She was being ridiculous. It was nothing. Surgery was to be scheduled in the New Year. She always experienced painful periods. She often experienced ovulation pain too. It was just that. It must be.

Riley tilted his head and looked at her curiously—maybe even with a little disappointment. 'I guess you're right. It's still sad. For all parties.'

'I know.' It was a blunt response. But she just didn't want to go down this road.

He sucked in a deep breath. 'I'm going to be staying. I'm going to be staying at Waterloo Court for now and thinking about other options. We could be working together for a long time.'

His hands pressed together for a second on the table. Then he seemed to regain his focus. 'How do you feel about that?'

He wasn't looking at her. Her heart missed a beat, then started doing somersaults in her chest. Part of her was praying he wasn't about to suggest something more between them, part of her wishing that he would.

'What do you mean?' Her mouth seemed to go into overdrive. 'That will be fine. You staying is what's best for Finn. It will give you a chance to get to know each other more.' She held up her hands casually. 'And work? That's just work.' She narrowed her gaze. 'We get on well at work, don't we?'

He looked a bit amused. 'I just wondered what you'd say.' He gave her a playful wink. 'Unless I'm buying you hot chocolate you seem to avoid me. Now that you're my emergency contact for Finn…' He let his voice tail off as he kept smiling at her. 'Thank you for saying yes. It means a lot. He knows you. He trusts you. *I* trust you.'

She blinked. It almost felt like diving off one of those high Greek cliffs over the perfect sea. That sensational plummet. There was nothing romantic about this. No promises or intentions. But there seemed to be a huge amount of unspoken words hanging in the air between them.

She'd thought he was attractive from the start. She'd deliberately tried to keep him at arm's length. And her instincts had been right, because being around Riley Callaghan was tougher than she had ever imagined.

Just being in his company made her wonder about the brush of his skin next to hers. It sparked memories of the hug—that she'd initiated—and the reminder of what it was like to be close to someone.

She missed it. But it felt amplified around Riley. Because his company was so much more appealing than anyone else's.

And it was ridiculous, but an icy glove had just wrapped around her heart. After her feelings earlier around Finn it all seemed too much.

Her mouth was dry. She stood up, picking up her plate and cup. 'It's fine, providing I'm free and available.'

He smiled. 'Planning any month-long holidays in the near future?'

She shrugged. 'You never know. Things can come up.'

She kept her back to him and started washing up. The *I trust you* statement wasn't giving her the warm glow it probably should. And this wasn't about Finn. None of this was about Finn.

This was about her and how mixed up she was about everything.

This was about the fact that for the first time in a long time she'd started to feel attraction and a pull towards another human being. And it wasn't just that it didn't fit in with her plans.

This was all about Finn. Just like it should be. The only reason Riley was staying in one place now was because of the unexpected arrival of Finn.

He wouldn't have stayed here for her. No, he would have been on that plane to Sierra Leone, probably with a sigh of relief and a smile on his face. Riley Callaghan would just have been a doctor she'd briefly worked with at some point.

But was that really what she wanted?

Riley appeared at her side with his cup and plate. It seemed he'd managed to eat the cold cheese on toast after all. 'I'll take Finn home now,' he said quickly. 'Thanks for looking after him. I appreciate it. How about I pick you up on Saturday and you can help us pick a Christmas tree? I think it would be good for him. He's already said he wants you to come with us.' He let out a short laugh and looked at her cardboard box. 'Maybe you want to trade yours in? Or buy some new decorations for your hidden stash?'

He had no idea. No idea of the crazy thoughts that had just pinged about her head and her heart. She moved into self-protection mode. She could do this. She could make completely inane conversation. She could find a way to make a suitable excuse.

'Oh, I'm not sure. I was going to do some Christmas shopping. Try and get a head start on things.'

Riley had already walked through to the main room. 'Well, that's perfect. You love Christmas. I love Christmas,' he said easily. 'You can do your shopping at the garden centre.'

For a second she was stunned. She hadn't quite been ready for that one.

He pulled his jacket over Finn, picked him up and walked over to the front door. 'See you later,' he said as he opened the door and walked out into the foyer.

April was a bit stunned. Her plan was to say no. Her plan was to create some distance between herself and Riley.

She closed her door and sagged against it.

She was becoming more confused by the second.

He'd almost said something. He'd almost hinted to her that maybe they should reconsider their relationship. What relationship? He wasn't even capable of having a relationship. At least, that was what Isabel must have assumed since she hadn't even told him about his son. He was still struggling with that.

It was just, for a few minutes today, he'd looked at April sitting across the table from him and been overwhelmed by the sadness in her eyes. That was why he'd pressed her. That was why he'd been quite pointed.

He liked her. He more than liked her. If he was being truthful, he might actually care. She was a good person. She was the only person he'd considered when he'd realised he couldn't get to Finn.

But even before Finn, even before he'd realised the enormity of being a dad, there had still been something about April. He could remember, as clear as day, that overwhelming lift he'd felt when she'd appeared in the pub and he'd thought, for just a second, she might actually have come to see him.

And she had. Just not in the way he had hoped for.

When he watched her with Finn it was like a little clenched-up part of him just started to unfurl.

He knew he should only concentrate on his son. Finn had lost the person that he knew best. Riley was playing rapid catch-up. And sometimes feeling like a poor replacement.

But April was constantly around the edges of his thoughts. And she had a shell of her own. He knew that. He could tell. She was doing her best to keep him at arm's length.

It was almost as if they were doing a dance around each other. He liked her. She liked him. Sometimes when their gazes connected he could see the sparks fly. Other times he could almost see her retreat into herself.

And she'd hinted at something today. As if she might be going somewhere in the future. At least that was what he thought. Was she considering another job? Would that mean she wouldn't be around?

That thought sent a wave of cool air over his skin.

He just didn't know what to do next.

The more time he spent with April Henderson, the more time he *wanted* to spend with her. She was infectious. And being in her company made him happy. Made Finn happy. He wanted to act on the pull between them—but did she?

He already knew he wouldn't sleep tonight. He'd be too busy watching over his son. It didn't matter that, as a doctor, he would say it wasn't necessary. Right now he wasn't a doctor; he was a parent.

He also knew that April was going to haunt his thoughts tonight.

He'd watched her try to make an excuse for Saturday but he'd already decided he wouldn't listen.

Chipping away at April Henderson's armour was helping him chip away at his own. He just wasn't quite sure where it would lead.

CHAPTER SEVEN

EVEN THOUGH IT was early afternoon, the sky was already darkening and the lights from the garden centre twinkled in greeting to them. Finn pressed his nose up against the window of the car, sending steamy breaths up that smoked his view. 'Is this where we get the Christmas tree?'

April nodded. She'd spent the last few days trying to make up an excuse not to be around Finn and Riley—each of them more pathetic than the one before. Her stomach had been in a permanent knot for the last few days. Finally, she'd realised it was almost like being a teenager going on a first date. Mallory used to tease her relentlessly about it. April had nearly always been sick before a first date, whereas Mallory had walked about the house singing.

And as soon as she'd had that thought, she knew she was going to go.

She smiled at Finn. 'They have lots to choose from. You'll find the perfect one.'

Riley opened the door of the car for Finn so he could climb out. The car park was busy; a group of children were crowded around the outside display—Santa's sleigh being pulled by reindeers.

'Look!' gasped Finn as he wriggled free of Riley's grasp and ran over to lean on the barrier. He stretched to touch the carved wooden reindeers. The largest one was just out of his reach. April looked around and gave him a bump up, so his fingertips could brush against the roughened wood. 'I touched him!' Finn squealed excitedly. 'I touched Rudolph!' April laughed as she let him down. Sure enough, someone in the garden centre had painted the nose of this reindeer bright red. Finn pulled her down towards him and whispered in her ear, his eyes sparkling, 'Are these the real reindeers? Do they come to life on Christmas Eve so they can deliver all the presents?'

April glanced conspiratorially around her. 'What do you think?' she whispered back. Finn's smile spread from ear to ear. Riley was standing behind them with his hands in his pockets.

'Come on, you guys. Let's go pick a tree.'

April nodded; she slipped her hand into Finn's and he took it without question. As they walked through the main entrance she gestured to a blacked-out area to the left. 'All the neon trees are in here. The real trees are on the other side. I wasn't quite sure what you would want.'

Riley bent down to Finn. 'Should we take a look at them all?'

Finn nodded excitedly. The area was encased by a giant black tent and, as soon as they pushed the curtain aside, Finn gasped. The tent was full of trees, all different sizes, all pre-lit, some multi-coloured, others with just white lights. Some of the lights were programmed, twinkling intermittently, or staying bright the whole time. Finn walked slowly from one tree to the other, stopping in front of one tree that was covered in bright blue lights. 'I like this one, Dad,' he breathed.

Riley glanced at April, then bent forward and lifted the price tag. His face gave a twisted look. He turned the tag towards her and mouthed, 'How much?'

She laughed. 'Come on, Finn.' She gave his hand a tug. 'Let's look at them all before we make a decision.'

They walked out of the tent, past all the rope lights for decorating the front of houses, and an array of illuminated parcels, Santas and white reindeers. The back of the tent led out into the middle of the garden centre, with tinsel and tree decorations as far as the eye could see.

Riley blinked. He turned and put his hand on April's waist. 'Boy, Christmas is really a big production, isn't it?'

'And you want to buy a house?' she quipped. 'By the time we leave here, you won't be able to afford a house.'

The decorations were all organised by colour. Finn made his way over to the red ones, his little fingers touching everything that was hanging on the wall in front of him. April laughed at Riley flinching every time Finn stretched for something delicate-looking. 'Let him look,' she said quietly. 'It's part of the fun.'

Riley rolled his eyes. 'I can see me leaving here with an enormous bill and not a single thing to show for it.'

She shook her head. 'Don't worry; they're used to children.'

They spent nearly an hour, Finn running between the coloured displays then back into the tented area. Finally, April pointed to outside. 'Do you want to go and see the real Christmas trees?'

Finn nodded and slipped his hand into hers. Her

heart swelled. It was ridiculous—it didn't mean anything. But the warmth of that little hand in hers sent a whole wave of emotions circling around her body.

Riley held the door and they headed outside. In the space of an hour, the last elements of light had gone, leaving the perfect backdrop for viewing the real Christmas trees, which were planted in lines and all currently topped with a dusting of snow.

April sucked in a breath. 'Well, this is definitely the place to pick a Christmas tree.'

Riley brushed against her. 'I think you could be right.'

Finn's hand slipped from hers and he ran yelling down the middle of the path. 'This is great!' he shouted, holding out his hands to brush against the trees.

'Eek!' April took off after him and swept her arms around him. 'Watch out—you might damage some of the trees. And you've not picked your own yet.'

He looked a little disappointed, his head turning from side to side. 'But how do you pick a tree?' He wrinkled his nose. 'What's the strange smell?'

Riley laughed. 'It's all the trees. Haven't you had a real one before?'

Finn shook his head, so Riley knelt down in front of him. 'Well, now is the time to decide. Do you want a light-up tree from inside, or a real one from outside?'

Finn looked confused. 'Does the real one go in the garden, or go in the house?'

'It goes in the house.'

He touched the nearest tree. 'But if we pick one of these does that mean our Christmas tree has no lights?'

Riley shook his head. 'We just buy some lights separately. We need to buy some Christmas baubles too.'

Finn looked thoughtful. He started to walk in amongst the row of trees again. April and Riley exchanged glances and followed him around. There were plenty of other families at the garden centre picking Christmas trees. April realised that people would assume the same about them—that they were a family. Her heart gave a squeeze as she realised how much she'd wished for something like this.

Riley was confusing. It was clear he was trying his best with Finn. It was clear he was learning along the way. And so was she.

She couldn't work out in her head how she felt about all this. She'd been attracted to Riley from the start, but he was only there for a short time and she hadn't been in a place to begin a relationship.

Now, he was staying. And she wasn't entirely sure how happy he was about it. It was clear he loved his son. But his career plans had just been halted abruptly.

And the constant lingering looks made her wonder what else there could be between them. Riley was flirtatious. He hadn't mentioned any significant long-term relationships in the past. Who knew what he'd want in the future?

She hadn't even revealed her health issues to him. It was quite likely that Riley might see his future with more children in it. That couldn't happen with her.

She had surgery to go through. There would always be that threat of cancer somewhere in the background.

That could be true for a lot of people. She was well aware that one in three adults in the UK would develop cancer at some point in their lives. But, even with surgery, chances were her odds would be higher.

The long and short of it was that she was a risk.

Finn had already lost a parent. Was it fair she might even consider being a part of his life—even as a friend?

As for Riley... She squeezed her eyes closed for a second. Finn was running around a Christmas tree now. He seemed to have picked his favourite. And Riley was joining in and chasing him around.

Her heart ached. She liked this man far more than she should. He was a charmer. Last thing he needed in his life was a woman with a potential ticking cancer and no ability to have children.

There was a real pang deep inside as she watched Finn. Another woman was standing to her side with a small curly-haired girl, and her stomach swollen. April turned away quickly. She didn't want to get emotional. Since she'd made her decision about the surgery it seemed as if the world was full of pregnant women.

It felt as if the number of female staff she worked with who'd announced they were pregnant recently had doubled. It could be that there was something in the air. Or it could be that she was noticing more, and becoming more sensitive to it.

She gritted her teeth. Her decision would give her a better chance at *life*. A life she should embrace. A life she would live on behalf of herself, and her sister.

'Okay?' Riley came up behind her, his breath visible in the cold air, his cheeks tinged red and his eyes shining. He caught the expression on her face. 'What's wrong?'

She shook her head. 'Nothing. Nothing at all. Are you done?'

He gestured with his hand towards the tree Finn was still dancing around. 'We've picked our tree. I've spoken to the sales guy. They'll deliver it. We just need to pick some decorations.'

For a second she thought she might have to paste a smile on her face. But she didn't. The warm feeling of being around Riley and Finn was spreading through her stomach and up towards other parts.

'Great. Let's get back inside.' She rubbed her hands together.

Riley looked down and closed his hands over hers, rubbing them with his own. 'Are you cold? Sorry, I didn't think.'

The gentle heat from his hands was so personal. So unexpected. He smiled as he did it for a few seconds. 'I should buy you some gloves.' He pulled his hands away and turned back to Finn. 'Come on, Finn. April's getting cold. Come and pick some lights.'

Finn turned at his father's shout and ran straight to them. 'What colour? What colour will we get?'

Riley slid his hand around Finn's shoulders. 'Well, you get to pick. I don't have any decorations yet, so you can pick your favourite.'

She followed them back into the darkened area. The lights twinkled all around them. It wasn't just lights. There was a whole array of illuminated animals at their feet, and a whole Christmas village on a table too. April wandered over. She knew as soon as Riley was at her back as she could smell his woody aftershave. 'What are you looking at?' he whispered.

She bent down to get a closer look. 'This village. I just love it. Look, there's a schoolroom. A bakery. Santa's workshop. A church. A shop. There's even a skating rink.'

Riley was right behind her and, instead of stepping

around her, he just slid his hand forward, brushing against her hip as he turned one of the price tags over. His cheek was almost touching hers. 'They're not too expensive.' Then he gave a low laugh. 'That's if you only buy one. If you buy the whole village...'

She laughed too, leaning back a little, her body coming into direct contact with his. Neither moved. It was as if both of them just paused, and sucked in a breath.

After the longest time Riley spoke, his warm breath at her neck. 'Which is your favourite?'

She looked over the village again. There were tiny characters in every scene, packages on shelves, mounds of snow at doorways, each one gently lit. Everything was so detailed. She sighed. 'I don't know. I think I love them all. I want the whole village.'

She reached down and picked up the toyshop. 'This is like the kind of thing where you could buy one every year, build up your collection and keep them for ever.'

He was smiling at her, only inches from her face. He reached and brushed a strand of hair away from her eyes, his hand covering hers as she held the shop. 'So how about you let me buy you your first one? As a thank you,' he added, 'for coming here with us today.'

The twinkling lights were behind them, but even though his face was in shadow his green eyes seemed brighter than ever. And they were focused totally on her.

She held her breath. Her hand itched to reach up and touch his dark hair that glistened with moisture from the snow outside. His cheeks were tinged with pink. Those green eyes were still, just locked with hers, and as she watched he licked his lips. Every nerve in her body was on fire. Every sense on overload.

He reached up again, this time his finger touching her cheek. 'Let me do something for you, April.'

The rush of emotion tumbled through her in waves. When was the last time someone had spoken to her like that? When was the last time she'd wanted someone to get this close? It felt like for ever. It felt like a whole lifetime ago.

A lifetime before her sister's vague symptoms. Shock diagnosis. Frantic treatment attempts. And the life just slowly draining from her body.

He made the smallest move. His cheek touched hers as his lips brushed against her ear. 'A toyshop. Along with the superhero T-shirts, I think you might secretly be a *Peter Pan* kind of girl.'

She could sense he was smiling.

Her eyes were closed, the toyshop held in front of her chest. She turned towards him just as his head pulled back from her ear.

Every part of her literally ached. Ached for his lips to touch hers.

Then, before she had time to think any more, his lips brushed against hers. The sensation was just as sweet as she'd imagined. Every bit as magical.

His hand tangled in her hair as the gentlest pressure increased.

She wanted this. She wanted this more than she'd ever imagined.

But just this—the slightest kiss—put her sensations into overload. Every part of her brain fired. She was starting something she might not be able to continue. She was taking what could not be hers. She was kissing a man she hadn't been entirely truthful with.

She trembled as the feelings threatened to overwhelm her and her eyes filled with tears. She pulled back.

Riley rested his head against hers. 'April? What's wrong? Did I do something wrong?'

She shook her head quickly. 'No. Of course you didn't.'

'But—' he started.

She placed her hand on his chest and gave him a regretful smile. Everything about the kiss had been right.

And everything about the kiss had been wrong.

'It's just not the right time,' she said as she looked around.

For a brief second she could see the flash of confusion, but then he glanced around and gave a nod.

Her heart squeezed in her chest. He thought she meant here, in the garden centre, was the wrong time. But she meant so much more than that.

Riley looked around and spotted Finn racing around a Christmas tree. He gave an approving smile and dropped to his knees, looking under the table and emerging with a box in his hand. 'Look. The toyshop. You can take it home.'

She felt a pang inside.

Home. She wasn't quite sure what that meant for her any more.

Her flat had seemed so empty the other night after Finn and Riley had left. Her footsteps had echoed around the place. She'd never noticed that before.

Before it had been her haven. Her quiet place. Now, she was just conscious of the fact it had seemed so full with the two of them in it.

'Dad! I want these ones!' Both of them jerked at the

sound of Finn's voice. He'd found blue twinkling stars wrapped around one of the trees.

Riley nodded in approval. He gave her a wink. 'Come on then. We've got more shopping to do.'

He walked off towards Finn and her stomach clenched. Riley had the box with the toyshop tucked under his arm. He was going to buy it for her.

As a thank you.

But when she'd thought about buying a piece of the village every year, she'd never really imagined just doing it for herself. She'd imagined it with a family around her.

Finn squealed as his dad threw him up in the air. 'April, I've picked the blue ones! Come and see.'

Her lips tingled. Riley's aftershave still filled her senses.

She glanced around. Christmas surrounded her. Both the best and worst time of year for some people. She could almost hear Mallory's voice in her head urging her on.

One kiss. That was all it had been. But she wanted so much more.

Right now, it just didn't feel honest, and she hated that more than anything. She licked her lips and looked around.

Was it wrong to want to enjoy this time with Riley and Finn? Was it wrong to join in with their celebrations? Mallory was whispering in her ear again. *Go on.*

Riley caught her eye. 'Okay?' he mouthed.

She nodded and walked over to join them. It was time to stop brooding about things and start enjoying life. 'Come on, guys.' She looked at the toyshop box and the Christmas lights. 'Oh, no, we're not finished yet. Someone grab a basket. We're going to shop till we drop.'

CHAPTER EIGHT

PLANS SEEMED TO be bursting from his head. Riley was buzzing. He couldn't wait to find April and tell her.

For the first time since all this had happened, things seemed to be falling into place.

He'd kissed her. He'd finally kissed her and it just felt so right. And all he could think about was kissing her again.

Okay, so she'd pulled back. Maybe April was more private than most. Maybe she didn't like being kissed in a public place. But that was okay. He could handle that. He could deal with that.

As long as he could kiss her again.

And even though he was currently bursting with excitement there was a tiny part of him that wondered if there could be something else—something else going on with April. He was sure it wasn't another man. April would never have let their spark and attraction grow if there was another man in the background.

She still hadn't really talked that much about her sister. Maybe it was just Christmas and the time of year? It just felt as if there was something he couldn't quite put his finger on yet. But he had to give her space. If he wanted to have some kind of relationship with April, he had to trust her to tell him the things he needed to know. Right now he should be concentrating on Finn.

His mother had stopped calling ten times a day. April had shown him a Top Ten list of Christmas toys for boys and it had been the biggest blessing in disguise. Finn seemed to like a whole range of things, so he'd handed the list over to his mother and asked her to track down what she could.

She'd been delighted. It had been a brilliant idea and he could hug April for it. Gran was over the moon to have a task related to her grandson and was tackling the list like a seasoned pro.

Finn seemed to be settling well. The crying at night had stopped after the first week. He was still wistful at times, and Riley encouraged him to talk about his mum as often as he liked.

Riley was finally making peace with the pictures of Isabel around the place. April had been right. It was good for Finn and that was what mattered. And, if all went to plan, they would have a place to permanently call home soon.

Work was still something he had to sort out, but he had plans for that too.

But he still didn't really have plans in his head for April.

He liked her. He more than liked her. He wanted to move things on. As soon as he set foot on the ward in the morning, the first thing he did was look for the swing of her blonde ponytail. Last night he'd nearly texted her around five or six times. He'd had to dial back in and only text twice. And it was all nonsense. Nothing that couldn't wait until the next time he saw her. But that had just seemed too far away.

If the phone buzzed and the screen lit up with her name he could feel the smile on his face before he'd even pressed the phone to his ear.

And it was ridiculous. Because sometimes it was actually about work.

He knew he should only be concentrating on Finn. Of course he should be. But there was something about April Henderson. The way she sometimes caught his gaze and gave him a quiet smile. The expression on her face when they'd been in the garden centre and she'd looked at all the Christmas decorations. But, more importantly, it was how he *felt* around her. It had been a long time since his heart had skipped a few beats at the sight of a woman. It had been a long time since he'd met someone he'd felt a real connection to. But even though it had been the briefest kiss, even though they hadn't really acted yet on the growing bond between them, Riley knew that at some stage he would take things further.

He knew there was more. Her sister had died of ovarian cancer. That must have been tough. It must have been a shock for her family. Maybe she was just quiet right now because it was the lead-up to Christmas. Tomorrow would be the first day of December. Finn would get to open the first door on his Advent calendar, though Riley was almost sure it wouldn't last that long.

In the meantime, Riley had to find April. He wanted to share his news. Maybe when she knew for sure that he and Finn planned on staying around it might take them to the next stage. He'd told her he was staying, but she'd looked as if she hadn't really been convinced.

His plans had changed. He'd found what he had

been looking for, but the funny thing was, when he'd
seen the house he hadn't just imagined Finn and himself being in it. If someone had told him this a few
months ago, that he could see himself staying in one
place and settling down, he wouldn't have believed
them. But April was making those plans seem real.
They weren't even dating yet. But he planned on rem-
edying that soon.

Maybe proving he planned on staying around could
be the key to opening her heart.

'Come here—I want to show you something.'

April looked over her shoulder. No one else was
around. 'Are you talking to me?' She couldn't stop
the little pang she felt as soon as she heard his voice.

Riley glanced around. 'Who else would I be talking
to? Here—' he spun the laptop around '—look at this.'

She bent down to see what he'd pulled up. Her eyebrows shot up. 'A house?'

He nodded. The excitement was written all over his
face as his fingers moved over the keyboard.

She wasn't quite sure what to say. 'But Finn has just
moved here. You can't want to move him again?' She'd
phrased it as a question, but she hoped he'd get the hint.

He looked at her in surprise. 'But where we're staying is only temporary. It won't do. Not long-term.'

She licked her lips. 'So…your long-term is here?'

He shrugged. 'I told you it was. Where else would
it be?'

This was going to take longer than she'd thought.
She hitched her hip up onto the desk. 'Have you spoken to the Colonel?'

He shook his head. 'But I did try and get an appointment. Why?'

She wasn't part of the forces but had been here long enough to know how things usually worked. 'I thought he just let you stay here as a temporary measure? Won't you maybe have to change regiment or posting to get a permanent headquarters?'

What she really wanted to say was, *Are you crazy for considering buying a house right now?*

But she didn't. She kept her thoughts in her head. Riley flicked through the pictures. It was a large grey Georgian sandstone semi. The house was full of character. Original doors, large sash windows with internal shutters. A huge fireplace. A large drawing room, separate dining room and a smaller room at the back they could make into a snug. A kitchen that had been renovated with a Belfast sink. Two bathrooms. The wide entranceway and sweeping staircase gave her a pang of envy. Long-term, she'd always wanted to own a house like this. The bedrooms. Three of them. And a large garden at the back of the house—big enough for a kid to play football in.

Riley couldn't stop smiling and she wasn't quite sure what to say. It was ideal—a family home and something like that seemed so far out of her grasp right now.

She could almost picture the perfect woman who'd be standing next to him in a few years with a new baby in a pram to complete the family. And that hurt in a way she could never have imagined.

'It's for sale, but I could temporarily rent it for a few months—try it out for size—with a view to buying it. It's even in the right catchment area for Finn's school.' He gave her a nudge with his elbow. 'See? I'm learning.'

He was. Riley was getting the hang of things quicker than she'd given him credit for. He had no idea about the fact she could barely breathe right now.

Since when had she started having such irrational thoughts?

'When could you start renting?' she managed to ask.

'This week,' he answered quickly. 'The owner has moved to Japan. He just really wants someone to either buy the house or move in and take care of it.'

April thudded backwards in her seat. She still wasn't sure what to say. Riley hadn't seemed to notice. He was either too excited or too swept up in the idea to figure out she'd stopped talking.

He sat back too. 'So, if I sign the agreement tomorrow, Finn and I can move in the next few days.' He pointed at some of the décor. 'It maybe isn't perfect but it's in good condition. I can give the place a lick of paint. That's all it really needs.'

The thoughts jumbling around in April's mind started to sort themselves into some kind of order. Practical things. That was what she could think of. At least they were the kind of things she could say out loud. 'You'll need furniture. You don't have a sofa or a dining room table. Or beds. It's only a few weeks until Christmas. Riley, do you have any idea how much stuff you'll need?' She started to shake her head.

The smile had faded a little. 'Well, just the stuff you've said. A sofa, a table and some beds. What else is there?'

April leaned forward and pulled a piece of paper from the printer. 'Here, let me get you started.' She wrote down the things they'd just mentioned, then started adding more. 'Cushions, cutlery, dishes, lamps, towels, bedding…' She frowned and turned the computer towards her. 'What comes with the kitchen? Do you need a washer, dryer and fridge freezer?'

Riley looked pale. 'You're beginning to sound like my mother.'

'Does your mother think you need a reality check?' She sighed and put down the pen. 'What happens if they move your base?'

He pressed his lips together and looked around. 'I might not be in the army much longer.'

'What?' She couldn't help it—she said the word much louder than she meant to.

'Shh—' he put his finger to his lips '—I haven't decided yet. I've just started to look into other options.'

'Like what?' A strange feeling was spreading through her. Like any serviceman, there was always a chance he would get moved. But she hadn't expected him to consider other options like this.

'I've looked at a few things. I could go into one of the training schemes at the local general hospital. I have a lot of experience. The most natural places would be accident and emergency, general surgery or orthopaedics.' He held up his hands. 'I could even look into infectious diseases, but the nearest place for that is around thirty miles away. Or…' His voice tailed off.

'Or what?' She was incredulous. When had he had a chance to think about any of this—his career plans or the house?

'I could think about training as a GP. It takes a year, and would have better hours for me.'

'You could still work here.' Where had that come

from? And even she could hear the edge of desperation in her voice. 'Not all the staff here are service personnel. There's a mix of NHS and army personnel throughout Waterloo Court.'

He met her gaze. It was the first time since they'd sat down. 'I don't know if rehab is for me, April.'

It was like a spear into her heart. She gulped. He wasn't talking directly about her, but he might as well have. This was the place she'd chosen to work. This was the career path she wanted. It didn't matter that only a few weeks ago she'd known in her heart that he wasn't really a rehab doctor. It was all right for her to think those things. It felt entirely different when *he* said them to her.

It was almost as if Riley was saying it wasn't good enough for him.

She stood up, letting the chair roll away behind her. 'Well, I guess that's all up to you, isn't it? I have patients to see in the other ward. Good luck.'

She stalked off, picking up her blue coat and shoving her arms into it, all the while trying to figure out why she really just wanted to cry.

Riley stared at April's retreating back. He wasn't quite sure what he'd just done.

He was only being honest. What was so wrong with that?

But part of him was uncomfortable. He hadn't meant to say anything that offended. But he was disappointed. He'd thought she'd be excited for him. Thought she might suggest talking over career plans with him. Maybe even suggest dinner. Instead she'd acted as if he'd just said he had the most infectious disease on the planet and made a run for it.

He shook his head. Since when had he got so bad at all the woman stuff?

Riley had never had problems getting dates. Never had problems with dating for a few months at a time. He might have had the odd few issues when he'd broken things off. But that had all been about his career. He didn't want long-term when he knew he was going to be away for months at a time.

He hadn't even got to the date stage with April.

Though there was no denying that was where he'd like to go.

In fact, he'd like to go a whole lot further.

He sighed, leaned back and put his hands behind his head.

What was he doing?

Was he crazy? She was gorgeous. She was fun when she wanted to be. She was sexy. She was sweet. She was great with Finn. But, most importantly, he'd found himself gravitating towards her more and more. He wasn't imagining things. There was a definite tug between them. April Henderson had well and truly buried her way under his skin.

And up until a few seconds ago that had made him happy.

For too long he'd focused his life on his job. Training as a doctor had taken all his energy; serving in the army had helped him focus. Moving around every six months had meant he was constantly meeting new faces and always learning to adapt. The medical situations were frequently frantic. Setting up in emergency situations was exhausting, and the long hours were draining. But for a long time Riley had thrived in that environment. He'd frequently been praised for his clinical care and cool head in a storm.

Thinking about a new career path was daunting. But since finding out about Finn he was just so anxious to get things right.

April pushed the door open, letting an icy blast sweep past him as she vanished out into the snow, and his heart gave a little tug. He liked her. He *more* than liked her. And that was so different from being attracted to her. At least it was in his head. Because that was the way he'd lived his life for the last twelve years.

So many things were changing. Was he changing too?

Finn flashed into his head. His laugh, his smile, the way he said the word *Dad*. All his energy right now should be focused on the little boy who needed him most. He didn't have room for anything else. But when he closed his eyes for a second Finn's face was replaced by the hurt expression on April's.

In an ideal world he would have liked it if she'd told him she loved the house and thought it was perfect. His stomach coiled. Perfect for whom?

'Stuff it!' he said out loud as he grabbed his jacket from the chair beside him.

The snow had picked up as he ran outside. The other ward was based on the other side of the courtyard, but right now he couldn't even see that.

He stopped. April hadn't made it to the other ward. She was standing in the middle of the courtyard, snow falling all around her. His footsteps slowed as he pulled on his jacket and walked over to her.

It was bitter cold. The snow was falling in thick

flakes all around them. April had her hands at her throat, fingering her necklace, with hot, angry tears spilling down her face.

He cringed. No. He'd made her cry. And he didn't even really understand why.

'April? What's wrong? What is it?' He put his hands on her upper arms.

She tried to shake him off but he stayed firm. She shook her head. 'Nothing. Everything. I don't know!'

Her hair had loosened from her bobble and was straggling around her face. She looked so hurt. So desperate. This couldn't just be about him.

He took in a deep breath of the icy air. 'Talk to me, April. I'm right here. Just talk to me.'

She was shaking. She was actually shaking. He looked from side to side. 'Let's get inside. Let's get somewhere warm.'

She shook her head again. 'No. I don't want to. I need air. I need fresh air. I need to think straight.'

'What do you need to think about, April?'

This was killing him. He could see how upset she was, how much pain she was in. But he couldn't understand it.

'The house,' she breathed.

'You don't like the house?' He was confused.

Tears were still spilling down her cheeks. 'I love it.'

Now it was Riley who shook his head. 'April, you have to help me out here. I don't understand what's wrong. I don't understand what you're so upset about.' His insides were churning.

His grip tightened on her arms. 'Why won't you talk to me? Why do you keep pushing me away?'

Her face crumpled and he couldn't stop the stream

of thoughts in his head. 'Is it me? Is it Finn? Don't you like being around kids?'

She shook her head.

Exasperation was building.

'April, you're gorgeous. And even though you try to pretend you're not, you're a people person. Why don't you have a husband? Why isn't there a boyfriend? I bet you could have a string of dates if you wanted.' Now he'd started he couldn't stop. 'And don't tell me you're not interested.' He moved over to her so he was only inches from her face. 'I see it, April. I sense it. We don't need electricity for Christmas lights. There's enough between us to light up the whole house—a whole street. What's happened to you, April? What's happened that you won't let anyone get close to you? What's happened that you won't let *me* get close to you?'

She shook her head. He could sense her frustration. It almost equalled his. But she just seemed so determined to keep him shut out. 'Don't ask. Just don't. I don't want to talk about it.' The blue of her coat seemed to make her eyes even brighter. It didn't matter how cold it was out here, or how cold she pretended her heart was, he wouldn't move away from her. He couldn't move away from her. He'd never felt so connected to—and yet so far away from—someone.

He couldn't hide the wave of concern that swept over him, feeling instantly protective towards her. 'Are you hurt? Has someone done something to you?'

He reached up and touched her cheek. 'April? Tell me—I want to help you.'

She blinked. Several heavy snowflakes had landed on her eyelashes. Those blue eyes fixed on his. He'd never seen anyone look so beautiful. So vulnerable. So exquisite.

The urge that had been simmering beneath the surface since the first time he'd seen her, the one that had spent the last few weeks threatening to bubble over at any point, just couldn't stay hidden any more. Riley had always been an action kind of guy.

She wouldn't speak to him. She wouldn't tell him what was wrong and that meant he didn't know how to support her—what to say to make things better.

But sometimes actions spoke louder than words.

'April,' he whispered, 'please tell me you don't have a husband, fiancé or boyfriend hidden away somewhere.'

Her eyes widened. She shook her head. 'No. Why?'

'Because I have to do this again. I have to show you how I feel about you.'

He bent his head and kissed her. Her lips were cold. Her cheeks were cold. But it only took a few seconds to heat them up. April tasted exactly the way he remembered. Sweet. Pure. Exciting. Like a world of possibilities. And the perfect fit for him.

At first she didn't move. Then her lips gradually opened, her head tilting to allow their mouths to meld against each other.

He couldn't remember ever feeling a kiss like this. The tingles. The flip flops in his stomach. His hand slid from her soft cheek, tangling through her messy hair and anchoring at the back of her head. Her hands moved too. Sliding up around his neck. Her body moved closer to his.

It didn't matter that they were both covered by thick jackets. He could still feel her curves against his, sense the tilt of her hips towards him as her light floral scent drifted up around them.

In a way, being out in the snow was the perfect place for this kiss. They both loved Christmas. And there was nothing more Christmassy than snow.

Their kiss was deepening. It was almost as if he couldn't get close enough to her. To get enough of April Henderson. His brain was going to a million different places right now. Of course he wanted to know what was really going on with April. But kissing her had just seemed like the right thing to do.

The only thing that made sense to him. Her cold nose touched his cheek and he laughed, their lips finally parting. But he didn't want to part. And it seemed neither did she.

They stood for a few seconds with their foreheads pressing together as the snow continued to fall all around them. Their warm breath instantly steamed in the freezing air.

Riley couldn't help but smile. 'Should I apologise for kissing you?'

'Don't you dare' was the prompt reply, but after a second she gave a little shudder.

'What's wrong? Are you cold?'

She pulled back a little. 'I'm sorry, Riley. I can't do this.'

She was saying the words, but he could see the look in her eyes. It was almost as if she felt she *had* to say it, instead of wanting to say it.

'Why, April? Why can't you do this? This is the second time I've kissed you and the second time you've pulled back.'

She bit her lip. She lifted her hand to her necklace again. What was it about that charm?

'Is this about Finn?' Guilt started to swamp him. He was just coming to terms with being a father. His head was telling him he had to concentrate all his time and energy on that. And he would. Finn needed stability. Riley knew that. But April? She was just… April. How could he ignore what was happening between them?

She shook her head firmly. Sadness almost emanated from her pores. 'Oh, no. This could never be about Finn.' Tears glazed her eyes. 'He's perfect, Riley. He just is.'

'So what is it, then?'

She pulled a face. 'I'm going to say the corniest thing in the world. But, right now, it's just so true.'

He didn't speak. This was confusing him more by the second.

'It's not you, Riley. It's me.'

He let out an exasperated gasp. 'Oh, no. I'm not taking that.'

'There's so much you don't know.'

'Then tell me.' His voice was firm.

She was staring at him with those big blue eyes. 'My si-sister died,' she stuttered.

He stopped. It seemed an odd thing to say. 'I know that,' he said steadily. 'And I know this time of year is hard for everyone.'

She shook her head. 'My *twin* sister died.' Her hand was clasped around that charm.

It took him a few seconds. 'Your twin sister?'

She nodded.

'Identical twin?'

She nodded again.

It was cold out here—freezing. But Riley had the horrible sensation that he'd just been plunged into icy depths. Ovarian cancer. That was what she'd said Mallory died from. She'd mentioned she was young. She'd used the term 'unlucky'.

Twins. How much did he know about twins? How similar were their genes? Something clicked in his head. Her necklace. Two hearts linked together. He felt a wave of panic. 'April, do you have cancer?'

She shook her head. 'No. Well, I don't think so. Not yet.'

Her voice sounded detached.

Thoughts were flooding through his brain. He'd seen the reports. It might not be his speciality but he couldn't miss the headlines from a few years ago about the famous actress. They were making discoveries about cancer all the time. But this was the one that had been given the most news coverage. 'April, do you have the gene?'

She let out a sob and he pulled her towards him. His brain was doing overtime. Trying to remember everything he'd ever heard. He could already guess that her statistics wouldn't be great.

There were thick flakes of snow on her blue coat. The outside of her was freezing. But he didn't care. He could feel her trembling against him. He hugged her even tighter and bent his lips to her ear. 'There's things that can be done. Have you seen someone? Have you spoken to a counsellor?'

Her words were low. 'I've done all that. I know my chances. My surgery will happen in the New Year.'

He pulled back, surprised, and put both hands on

her face. He couldn't believe she'd been helping him so much while going through something like this.

'January? April, I had no idea. I'm so sorry. Why didn't you tell me?'

Another tear slid down her face. 'How do I tell someone that? How do I say, *Nice to meet you, but I'm a carrier of a potentially deadly gene, I'm going for surgery soon and I won't be able to have children.* I'm never going to get to be a mum. And maybe I won't even be here. The surgery isn't a guarantee. I might still go on and develop cancer at some stage. And yes, I have looked at all my options. It's all I've thought about for months.'

He lifted his thumb and wiped away her warm tear. He couldn't even begin to comprehend what she'd been going through. He'd been so focused on himself, and on Finn. He hadn't really left room for anything else. He hated himself right now. He'd known there was something he couldn't put his finger on. He should have pressed her. He should have pushed harder and let her share the burden, let her talk things over.

Her head was against his chest. 'I'm sorry. I didn't want to tell you. I didn't want to tell anyone. I need to get this over with. I need to have my surgery, get out the other side, then see what comes next. I just needed some time. I just needed a chance to—'

He pulled her back again. 'A chance to what? To be alone?' He shook his head. 'You don't need to do that. You don't need to be on your own, April.'

She sucked in a deep breath as she pulled herself free of his grasp. But he wasn't quite ready to let her go. He put his hands on her shoulders. 'But I do, Riley. This is hard. This—' she held up her hand '—whatever it could be, it just isn't the right time.' She met his gaze. 'And it isn't for you either. You have Finn to think of. You have to concentrate on him.'

'I know I do,' he had to stop himself from snapping. 'But Finn likes you. I like you. I don't want this to go away, April. I want to see what *this* is. I want to know.'

Her lips were trembling. She lifted her hand and put it over his. 'We both work in the medical profession. Let's be clear about this. I think I'm well right now. I hope I'm well. But until I have my surgery, and until I have my pathology report, we just don't know. What if I'm not okay? What if I'm riddled with cancer? You've just introduced me to Finn. He's lost his mum. He's a five-year-old kid who just had to stand at his mother's funeral. What kind of person would I be if I didn't consider Finn here?'

It was like a fist closing around Riley's heart. Protect. That should be his first parental responsibility. As much as he hated every word, she was making sense.

'I could be in an accident tomorrow, just like Isabel was.' They were the first words that came into his brain. He knew they sounded desperate. But that was how he was feeling right now.

She shook her head. 'I know that. But it's a cop-out. You need to give me some space. You need to spend time with Finn and leave me out of the equation.' She tipped back her head and let out an ironic laugh. 'I knew from the first second that I saw you that you'd be trouble. I tried so hard to stay out of your way—and it almost worked.'

Something swelled inside his chest. 'You did? You deliberately kept away from me?'

'Of course I did.' She was smiling as she shook her head.

'Darn it. I thought my spider sense had stopped working. I thought you didn't like me at all.' The pathetic thing was that her words gave his male sensibilities a real sense of pride. He hadn't imagined things. She'd felt the attraction as much as he had.

Her hand was still over his and he gave her shoulders a squeeze. His stomach was churning. He didn't know enough about this condition. He only knew the bare basics and statistics he'd heard in casual conversations with other professionals. All of a sudden he wanted to know so much more.

'I don't want you to be alone through all of this, April. Let me be your friend.'

Her voice was shaky. 'I don't even know if we should do that.'

'Why?'

She winced. 'Riley, you're buying a house. A beautiful family home. In a few years, once you and Finn are settled, you'll want to fill that house with more children. I can already see what a good dad you are. It's a steep learning curve. But you're getting there. And you will thrive doing this, Riley. You will.'

'And?' He didn't get where she was going with this.

Another tear slid down her face. 'And once I have the surgery, my ovaries are removed. My fallopian tubes are gone. I can't have kids of my own. I can't have kids with you. The option is gone. And I'm not going to change my mind about this. The disease is such a silent killer they haven't really found any reliable way to monitor for it yet. I can't live with a perpetual cancer cloud over my head. I won't. But I also

don't want to take the chance of children away from
you. Finn should have the chance to have brothers and
sisters. At some point you'll want to fill that house with
children, Riley, and I can't do that with you.'

He shook his head. 'You…we don't know any of
that yet. And you must have thought about this. There's
other ways to have kids. You must have considered that
in your future.'

She pressed her hand over her heart. 'There is.
And that's the option for me.' She lifted her hand and
pressed it against his chest. 'But it doesn't have to be
the option for you.'

There was so much swirling around in his head right
now. He'd just had the best kiss of his life. A kiss that
seemed perfect. A kiss that told him everything he
thought he needed to know.

And now it seemed that kiss could result in a life he
couldn't quite add up in his head. Finn had been a big
enough shock. Families and kids had always seemed
in his distant future. Filling a house with kids seemed
a bit Neanderthal, but was he really willing to write
all that off after a kiss? And what if April was sick or
did get sick? What could that do to Finn? How much
could one kid take?

April must have read all the confusion on his face.
It was like watching a shield come down. A protective barrier.

'Concentrate on Christmas. Concentrate on Finn.'
Her voice sounded tight.

He reached up to touch her cheek again but she
stepped back. Her hair was coated with snow. She must
be freezing right now. And even though his brain was

telling him to take some time, to think about things, his heart was telling him something else entirely.

'And give me a little space at work,' she added.

His mouth opened to respond. He didn't want to give her space. But she held up her hand. 'Please, Riley.' She pressed her lips together. 'Now, I have work to do.'

She turned and headed off through the heavily falling snow to the other ward.

And left his broken heart somewhere out in the snow.

CHAPTER NINE

IT HAD FELT like the longest day in the world. She'd held it together as long as she could but as April walked into her flat and turned on the side lamp she felt exhaustion overwhelm her.

The mask she'd worn all day on her face finally slipped and the pent-up tears started to fall again.

Her Christmas tree was in the corner of the room. It was black with purple baubles and lights. When she'd bought it a few years ago black trees had been very avant-garde. But those days were long gone, and now it just felt a bit pretentious.

She sagged down onto the sofa. She'd loved this flat since she'd bought it after getting the job at Waterloo Court. But as she sat in the dimly lit room, watching the flickering purple lights and staring out into the dark night outside, for the first time it seemed so empty.

She'd always unconsciously smiled when she got back home. She'd felt warmth walking into her own place. She quite liked staying on her own. It was nice not to have to wrestle the duvet off someone else, or fight over the remote control.

Or was it?

A tear prickled in the corner of her eye. She'd been

a twin. She *was* a twin. Mallory had been an integral part of her. When they'd reached their teenage years both had chosen separate university and career paths. Both had created their own circle of friends. But they'd still had each other.

That teenage resentment which had flared for around five minutes had rapidly disappeared. They'd started to appreciate each other more. Their university campuses had been two hundred miles apart but April had spent more time speaking to her sister on the phone than they'd spoken in the last few years sharing a room at home.

There were still mornings when she woke and, for a few brief seconds, she thought her sister was still alive. Then realisation hit all over again.

She couldn't pick up the phone and hear Mallory's voice at the other end. She couldn't hear about her latest date. The latest fight at work.

Mallory had left this life as she'd entered. With April by her side.

April had climbed into the hospice bed alongside her sister and just held her as her mother and father had sat on either side.

April wiped the tear from her eye. She rested her head back against the sofa. If only she could talk to her sister about the genetic tests. The surgery. The family that she'd always hoped for but would now never have.

Today, everything she'd kept tightly locked inside, everything she hadn't talked about to anyone but her parents, had come bubbling to the surface.

Her finger touched her lips and she closed her eyes.

That kiss. For a few moments, a few seconds, things had been perfect.

Life had been what it should be.

The gorgeous, sexy guy who had flirted with her and teased her, tangled his way around her heart, had kissed her in a way that had made every single part of her feel alive again.

Every nerve ending had sparked, lit up by the sensation of his lips on hers. It was better than she'd ever even imagined. And she might have imagined quite a bit.

But it had broken her heart more than she ever could have contemplated.

Her actions felt selfish. But she wasn't being selfish.

She didn't want to make promises to Riley that she couldn't keep. She had to be upfront. She had to be honest. She didn't want to form a relationship with the gorgeous man and little boy that could ultimately hurt them all.

She wanted him to be happy. She wanted Finn to be happy.

But ever since she'd met him she'd been so confused. Living in her own little box had seemed to simplify things for her. Gene testing. Decision. Surgery.

Then…

She pulled her knees up to her chest and hugged them tight.

She'd never felt so alone.

First Mallory. Then Riley. Now Finn.

Her stomach twinged again and she rubbed it to ease the pain.

Her mind was as foggy as the weather outside. And she just couldn't see a way through.

* * *

Finn was sleeping by seven o'clock. He'd said school was busy and he was tired.

Riley was distracted. He couldn't concentrate. His mind had been full of what April had told him.

He set up his computer and began researching.

He read and read and read. Everything he could find out about BRCA1 and BRCA2. Finding out the risks for twins was much more difficult. There was limited research.

BRCA1 genetic mutation was scary. April had mentioned something about a strong family history and, considering her sister had already died, he had to assume there had been some other ovarian cancer cases in her family too. There was also the added risk of breast cancers—although she hadn't mentioned that. At least for breast cancer, there was an evidence-based screening programme that could pick up early signs. Ovarian cancer was much more difficult.

The hours just seemed to meld together, his concentration only broken by some mumbles from Finn's room. He walked through. Finn seemed restless and Riley sat at the edge of the bed and stroked his hair. 'Hey, little guy, it's okay. Go back to sleep.'

'Dad,' came the muffled voice. He smiled at that. It warmed his heart. There would always be that tiny sense of resentment that he hadn't seen Finn get to this stage. When his mother had visited she'd voiced her opinion about Isabel's decision over and over once Finn had gone to bed. And he did understand, but it also made him appreciate how unhelpful that was.

'Is April here?'

Riley was jerked from his thoughts. He lowered his head down next to Finn's. 'What?'

Finn still looked as if he were sleeping. 'I miss April,' he murmured.

It was as if the little voice tugged directly on his heart. 'I miss her too' was his immediate response. He'd seen her today. He'd kissed her today. He'd held her today. And she'd revealed the deepest, darkest secret that she'd been keeping for so long.

It felt as if he'd failed her. Completely and utterly failed her.

The conversation kept playing back in his head but each time with different scenarios. He'd said something different; he'd done something different. He'd told her how much she meant to him. He'd told her he wanted to help her through all this.

His stomach curled again as he looked at his sleeping son. He was so peaceful. So settled. This might be the honeymoon period. The social worker had told him that Isabel's death could affect him in a whole host of different ways that might manifest over time.

He squeezed his eyes closed. What if the surgery wasn't soon enough for April? What if she was already sick and just didn't know it yet?

His hand kept stroking Finn's head. He felt physically sick now. Her risk of particular cancers was still higher. Getting rid of her ovaries and fallopian tubes would not be the all-clear. But it would reduce her risk of dying of ovarian cancer by eighty per cent. That was massive. After surgery, it would be about learning to manage the risks.

He wanted to be by her side. He didn't want her to go through any of this alone.

But what about his son?

He would be making a decision that could leave his son vulnerable. They could both put their hearts on the line, loving someone who could possibly be sick at some point.

It was a risk he was willing to take for himself, but could he really do that for his son?

He sighed and lay down next to Finn. There wasn't a parenting book in the world that would cover this one.

CHAPTER TEN

'Is that our new house?' Finn's voice echoed from the back of the car as they pulled up outside.

Riley wanted to smile. He did. Even from here he had a good feeling about this place. 'Yes, it is.'

Finn waved something from the back of the car. 'We still have to give this to April, Dad.'

Riley nodded. Finn had made a card at school for April yesterday. It had melted his heart and he just wasn't sure what to do with it.

'No problem. We'll do that later.'

He glanced down at the keys in his hand as his mobile sounded.

His mother had organised things with military precision. The sofa, beds, TV, fridge freezer, washing machine and dryer were all arriving in the next few hours. Money just seemed to have haemorrhaged from his bank account in the last few days. He looked down at the message. It seemed that the engineer would be here in the next hour to connect the Internet and cable TV.

He jumped out of the car and unclipped Finn's seat belt. 'Come on, little guy. Let's go pick a bedroom.'

The rest of the car was jam-packed with bedding,

towels and kitchen paraphernalia. He hadn't even started trying to get their clothes together.

Finn skipped up the path. This was odd. In his head he'd sort of imagined April being next to them when this happened. The key turned easily in the lock and he pushed the door open.

He'd rented this place without even setting foot in it. But it seemed his instincts had been spot on. People always said you knew within thirty seconds if a house was for you or not; Riley didn't need that long.

They walked from room to room. After army housing the space just seemed enormous. Two people could never fill this place.

His stomach rolled. April's eyes appeared in his head. The sorrow in them when she'd mentioned this place and how she could imagine it filled in the future.

But although he could see it in a few years, filled with his touches and decorated the way he wanted, he couldn't imagine the anonymous wife that April could, or the nameless children. The only person he could see here was April.

She'd avoided him the last few days. He knew that. Of course he knew that. And even though she'd insisted he give her some space, his heart wouldn't really let him comply. He'd sent her a text. And left a phone message. Just saying he was thinking about her. Because he was. And Finn was too. Even if she didn't want to know that right now.

He didn't like this distance between them. Every cell in his body told him that it was wrong. But he wanted to respect her request. He didn't want to force himself and Finn on her if that wasn't something she could cope with right now.

Because this wasn't all about him.

The thought sent a memory shooting through him. April, saying almost those exact words to him when they'd sat in the coffee shop together. He hadn't understood at the time. He'd still been at that jokey, flirty stage then. It seemed like a lifetime ago.

Then there had been that kiss in the garden centre. The one where she'd told him it wasn't the right time.

She hadn't been talking about the garden centre at all. She'd been talking about now. Now was not the right time for April. Now he understood—even if he didn't really agree.

Finn ran up the stairs, darting from room to room. 'This one—no, this one. No, this one!'

Riley smiled. Finn could have any room he wanted. He walked through to the dining room that looked out over the back garden. A football goal—that was what he could put out there for Finn. The garden was much longer than he'd anticipated. A lawnmower—he'd need to get one. Something he'd never owned and never even considered. Thank goodness it was winter and the grass wasn't growing. The whole place was covered in snow and ice; it looked like something from a kid's book.

Somehow things just didn't feel right. He'd imagined April somewhere in this picture. But she'd made it clear she wasn't ready for that—and he was trying so hard to respect her wishes right now.

He sighed and turned back to the living room. The large sash windows with internal shutters were exactly what he'd expected in a house like this. His mother had even ordered blinds for the windows, but they wouldn't arrive until tomorrow.

His mother was doing better than he'd anticipated.

He knew she wanted to be here—he knew she wanted to smother Finn. But, for once, she was listening. And giving her a range of tasks to do that would benefit Finn seemed to have played to her strengths. He was starting to appreciate her tenaciousness in a way he'd never imagined.

The previous owner had left a pile of wood next to the fireplace. It made him laugh as the 'living flame' fire was actually gas. He walked over and bent down to light it. It didn't matter that it was the middle of the day and the house was warm enough already. He needed some more heat. He wanted the place to seem more cosy. Because right now the emptiness echoed around him.

A white van with green writing pulled up outside. He smiled. Perfect. The most ridiculous thing to do first in the new house. He couldn't have planned it better.

'Finn, come on down! The Christmas tree is here,' he shouted. He'd persuaded the garden centre to delay their delivery until they arrived at the house. Sure enough, the guys were already bringing the boxes with the decorations to the door.

Finn squealed and ran down the stairs, throwing the front door wide to the world and letting the icy-cold air blast in around them.

Riley gave a nod to the delivery guys. 'Welcome to the mad house,' he said.

This was going to be a long, long day.

It was later than she expected. But the last few days April hadn't been in a hurry to get home from work. So she'd taken a few of the patients down to the gym

for an extra session after dinner. They'd started an im-
promptu game of wheelchair basketball and she'd been
dumped out of her chair on at least three occasions.

She knew she was safe. Riley wasn't working today.
This was the day he got the keys to the house. The place
that he and Finn would call home.

She wanted to be happy for him. It was a gorgeous
house. A perfect place. Her own flat paled in comparison. And she hated that, because she used to love it.

Her stomach gave yet another twinge as she righted
the chair and shook herself down. 'That's it for me,
guys. You've finished me.'

They laughed. The camaraderie in here was one of
the best parts of the job. Everyone looking out for each
other. She was sure if she shared with her colleagues
her plans for surgery they would be more than supportive. Of course they would. But it was coming up
to Christmas. She didn't want to have those kinds of
chats. Maybe in the New Year when she knew her surgery date she'd start to tell a few people.

The guys left and she finished tidying up the gym
before turning the lights out, grabbing her coat and
heading for home.

The snow seemed to be heavier yet again. She pulled
her hat down over her ears and fastened the top button on her coat.

Her stomach growled. Food. There was little in the
fridge. Maybe she should get a takeaway? She groaned.
She'd forgotten her purse today. She'd have to go home
first and pick it up.

As she pushed her front door open, she almost trod
on an envelope that was bright red with squiggly writing on the front. She picked it up. *ApRiL*. Her heart

lurched. It was obviously a child's writing, a mixture of upper- and lower-case letters, and she could almost imagine Finn's tongue sticking out at the side of his mouth as he'd tried his hardest at writing. It couldn't possibly be from anyone else.

She blinked back tears as she pulled the handmade card out of the envelope. There were a few things stuck on the card. A silver foil star. A green, badly cut out tree along with something else in yellow she couldn't quite distinguish. Baubles were drawn at the edges of the tree in red pencil, and another wiggly blue pencil line snaked up the tree, representing the lights or the tinsel. Her heart gave a tug as she remembered the blue lights that he'd picked.

She opened the card.

To my fiend.
Love Finn

She laughed. She couldn't help it. She loved the fact he'd missed the R.

It was beautiful. It was sorrowful. She could imagine how long he'd taken to make this for her. But it was also joyful. She hugged the card against her chest, wishing it was both Riley and Finn.

She blinked back the tears as she walked over to her shelf and put Finn's Christmas card in front of all the others. It had pride of place for her. She wanted to look at it and remind herself what could be out there when she was ready.

Her stomach growled loudly again and she grabbed her purse, which was lying on her sofa. The walk to the main street only took a few minutes.

She loved the winter time—especially when the pavements were glistening and the trees were dusted with snow. The lamp posts glowed orange, bathing the rest of the street in a warm hue. Even though it was after seven, the hustle and bustle of Christmas shopping was alive and well on the high street. All of the shops had started opening late, enticing people to shop more and more.

Some of the takeaways already had queues but her eyes were drawn to the soft yellow lights from the old church. She smiled. From here it looked like the church from the Christmas village in the garden centre. There were sandwich boards on the pavement outside. *Christmas Cheer Dinner.* She'd forgotten about that.

She rubbed her hands together as she glanced at the queue outside the pizza shop. She'd been introduced to the Christmas Cheer Dinner last year by a colleague. The church members chose one night to make a proper Christmas dinner that everyone could attend and pay what they wished. It was really a charity fundraiser, allowing them to use the proceeds from that night to make an actual Christmas dinner for those in the homeless hostels on Christmas Day. She'd planned on eating at home, alone. It might be nice to eat amongst some other people and donate to the cause.

Her feet carried her into the church hall automatically. She smiled at a few familiar faces and joined the queue of people waiting for dinner. There was a choir from the local school singing some carols in a corner of the room, with a few playing instruments. She couldn't help but smile. Christmas was always all about the kids. The biggest tree she'd ever seen was in another corner, adorned with red and gold decorations, and small tea lights were on the window ledges beneath the stained-glass windows, sending streams of red, blue and green across the room.

The line moved quickly and she soon had a plate with a steaming-hot Christmas dinner and she stuffed a few notes into the collection pot next to the cutlery.

She looked around. There was a low hum of chatter amongst the people already eating dinner. Most of the tables were full, with only a few spaces here and there. The lights at the food dispensary were bright, but the lights in the hall were dim; the tables had flickering candles lining them, creating a more Christmas-like atmosphere.

She walked over to the table nearest the choir. It would be nice to hear the children sing as she ate.

'April!' came the shout.

She recognised the voice instantly. Finn was in the front line of the choir—how had she missed that cheeky face?—and he looked as proud as Punch dressed in his uniform of grey trousers and a red jumper. 'There's a space next to Dad. You can see me!'

April gulped and looked to where an excited Finn was pointing. Riley glanced up from his plate of turkey and gave her a half-smile and shrug. He'd texted and left her a message a few days ago but she hadn't responded. She'd spent the last two days timing her visits to wards to ensure they didn't coincide with his. But she couldn't keep doing this.

Her heart gave a lurch as she sat down next to him.

'Sorry,' he murmured.

'It's fine,' she said, giving Finn a wave. 'I had no idea he was singing with the choir.'

'Neither had I,' sighed Riley. 'I found the note in his

school bag about five minutes after the last delivery guy left.' He gave a wry smile. 'Remind me in future that I need to check the school bag every day. There were four notes in there.'

April smiled as she tried not to look into those green eyes. It had only been a few days and she missed them—no matter how much she'd tried not to.

She picked up her knife and fork. 'I'd forgotten about the Christmas Cheer Dinner. I came last year too. Couldn't eat for about three days after it because the portions here are huge.' She glanced sideways. Riley's eyes were locked on hers.

'How are you?' he said quietly.

She broke their gaze and looked down at her food. 'I'm fine,' she said automatically. She paused. 'Thank you for the card. It was lovely. It was so thoughtful.' She looked up at Finn, who automatically gave her another wave.

'He missed you.' Riley's voice was hoarse. 'I miss you too.'

As she stared at her dinner her appetite started to leave her. She moved her knife and fork; it would be a shame to waste this lovely dinner. She didn't want to get upset. She'd come in here tonight because it felt like the right place to be. She wanted to help the charitable cause, and she wanted to surround herself with people who loved Christmas as much as she did.

She started eating. People around them were chatting easily. The kids started another song. One of the helpers came around and filled up all their glasses.

The words *I miss you both too* reverberated around her brain. She really, really wanted to say them. It felt honest to say them. But something still stopped her.

'How was the house move?' she asked quickly.

For a second it seemed as if Riley's face fell, as if he'd been waiting for her to say something else. But he gave a brief nod. 'Exhausting. I didn't know I could plumb in a washing machine, but apparently I can. I had to go and knock on a neighbour's door to get him to help me lift the TV onto the wall.'

'You bought one of those giant TVs?' She was smiling. She couldn't help it.

'Of course I did.' He gestured towards Finn. 'The cable and Internet guy arrived this morning. It's the first time I've ever paid for cable TV in my life. I was living in hope of endless nights of watching the sports channels, but it seems Finn has other plans entirely.'

She swallowed her food. 'He found the cartoon channels, didn't he?'

Riley raised his eyebrows and nodded, folding his arms across his chest. 'Boy, did he. Do you have any idea how many kids' TV channels there are?'

She laughed. 'Oh, yes. I had an introduction the other night. We should compare lists.'

He met her smile. 'We should, shouldn't we?'

Their gazes meshed again. It was almost as if the world fell silent around them. The hum of voices blocked out. It was just him. And her. In the flickering candle-light.

Riley. The guy who had well and truly captured her heart. She couldn't deny it a second longer. She hadn't meant to fall in love. She absolutely hadn't. But it seemed that fate had other ideas for her.

And it wasn't just Riley she'd fallen in love with. It was Finn too. They were a package deal.

She'd never hated her genes more than she hated

them now. Not even when they'd stolen her sister from her. The thought made her catch her breath.

She wanted to move on with her life. She wanted to feel as if she could plan for the future. Her fingers actually itched to pull her phone from her pocket and demand a surgery date right now. Once she'd had the surgery she might feel as if she could take stock. To sit down with Riley and talk about the possibility of a future together—if he still wanted that.

She'd seen the fleeting worry on his face when she'd mentioned Finn the other day. Maybe that worry had planted seeds and grown? If it had, there was nothing she could do. She'd never do anything to hurt Riley and Finn.

But, if that was the case, why was he telling her that he missed her?

She couldn't pull her gaze away from his. She wanted to stay right here, in this moment, for the rest of her life.

It was like being in a bubble. A place where no one was under threat of being sick. Christmas was captured, Finn was happy and there was time just for the two of them. Why couldn't she just stay here?

Riley's hand closed over hers, sending a wave of tingles up her arm. 'This won't ever go away, will it?' she breathed, half questioning, half hopeful.

He lifted one hand and put it behind her head, pulling her closer to him. 'I don't want it to,' he whispered as his lips met hers.

It didn't matter that they were in the middle of the church hall. It didn't matter that people were on either side of them. It was just the simplest and sweetest of kisses. Nothing more. Nothing less. But it filled her with a warmer glow than any fire or candle could.

The music changed around them, a more modern tune bellowing from the speakers. Riley pulled back, smiling. 'Since when is "Jingle Bell Rock" a Christmas carol?' he asked.

She laughed and put her head on his shoulder, just taking a few seconds to breathe in his scent and remind herself what she was doing. Their little bubble had vanished. But she didn't mind. The kids had all been handed out tambourines and were banging away to their own beat. Riley pulled out his phone to video Finn for his mum. 'If I send her this it will keep her happy. She's coming down in a few days to apparently "sort the house out". I might come and hide at yours.'

He slid his arm around her shoulders as they watched Finn and his classmates singing. Tears glistened in her eyes. 'He's doing so well, Riley. He really is.'

'He'll do even better if he thinks you'll be around,' Riley replied. 'We both will.' He sounded so determined. So sure.

Her heart skipped a few beats. This was what she wanted. It had just seemed so far away. So impossible right now.

She closed her eyes for a second and sent a silent prayer upwards.

Please let this be for real. Please.

CHAPTER ELEVEN

EVERYTHING FELT GOOD. Everything felt right.

It didn't matter that the house was still organised chaos. It didn't matter that he'd spent twenty minutes this morning trying to find one of Finn's school shoes. All that mattered was that he finally felt as if things were on the right track with April.

He'd made a few more casual enquiries about jobs. It seemed that the GP track would be the most viable for him, and the more he considered it, the more interested he became. All the clinics that he'd ever done in settings overseas had been walk-ins. It meant he'd had to deal with a wide range of different issues—a bit like GPs did here. Sure, there had been a whole host of area-specific complications, but it wouldn't be as big a jump as he'd first thought.

Finn had been so animated last night. He'd been so happy that April had watched him sing with the choir and when he'd finished she'd made a fuss of him. She hadn't gone home with them last night, but they'd walked her back to her flat and she'd given them both a kiss on the cheek.

It might not have seemed like enough. But it was enough for right now.

He looked around the ward again. April hadn't appeared yet today. He glanced at his watch. It was coming up to lunchtime. She must be at the other ward. He would go and find her and see if he could interest her in some lunch.

April hadn't walked home last night—she'd glided. At least that was what it felt like. When she'd finally gone to bed she thought it was just nervous excitement that meant she couldn't sleep. It didn't take long to realise it was more than that.

For the last few weeks she'd had weird occasional grumblings in her stomach. Sometimes it felt like indigestion, leaving her feeling nauseous and sick. She was used to having painful periods. Her doctor had put her on the oral contraceptive pill to help reduce her risk of ovarian cancer and also to help with her painful periods. But the period pain had continued. But this type of pain felt different.

She'd shifted around in bed all night, finally getting up to take some painkillers, then getting up an hour later to try to drink some tea.

It hadn't helped. She'd finally pulled on her uniform and gone into work as normal. But as the morning progressed, so did her pain.

John Burns had even commented on her colour as she worked with him. 'Hope you're not coming down with something. Last thing I need is a sickness bug. You're a terrible colour.'

She'd made her excuses and left, going to the ladies' bathroom and retching in the sink.

Her skin broke out in beads of sweat. But the beads of sweat were cold. She shivered as the pain swept through her abdomen again. She ran into the cubicle and sat down, bolting the door.

The sweating wouldn't stop. She could feel it running between her shoulder blades. But it was the waves of pain that were worse.

She put her head against the side of the cubicle as she doubled over in pain. Horror swept through her. Her stomach felt rigid.

Mallory's had been bloated. But she'd had a whole host of other symptoms. Unusual bleeding. Nausea. Pain in her abdomen, pelvis, back and legs. Indigestion. And a complete and utter feeling of exhaustion.

Now, she thought she might be sick again. Her stomach wasn't bloated. She hadn't had any strange bleeding, or pain in her back or legs. But she had felt nauseous a number of times over the last few weeks. There had also been niggling pains—nothing like today, of course.

But now she felt gripped with panic. She'd been so distracted these last few weeks. All because of Riley and Finn. They'd captured her attention. Made her less vigilant.

She'd had a few tiny thoughts when she'd felt the niggles of pain. But she'd been used to painful periods and just put it down to that. She hadn't been tired, or bloated, so it had seemed over the top to start panicking.

But right now she'd never felt pain like it.

She should never have kissed Riley. She should never have started to feel attached to Finn. What if she was sick? Riley had enough to cope with, learning to be a father. Finn didn't need someone to enter his life, then leave him alone again. He was just a kid.

He didn't deserve that. A hot, angry tear spilled down her cheek.

She pushed herself up and opened the cubicle door again.

This was a hospital. It might not have an accident and emergency department, but it had enough doctors that someone would be able to take a look at her.

She tried to straighten up, but her abdomen didn't really agree.

Catching sight of herself in the mirror didn't help. There were black circles under her eyes, only highlighted by the paleness of her skin.

She opened the door back into the corridor.

Riley was standing directly opposite, talking to someone in the corridor and showing them his phone. 'The pictures are great—the house looks fabulous.' The nurse smiled and gave him a nudge. 'And big. I take it at some point you'll be planning on using all those rooms?'

April froze and Riley gave a casual response. 'Yeah... maybe.'

She already knew it was time to walk away. She didn't want Riley and Finn to see her sick. But that? That was just the extra push that she needed.

Riley looked up. 'Hey, there you are. I've been looking for you. Want to go and get some lunch?'

She shook her head and did her best to walk in the opposite direction. She didn't even want to have this conversation. Her brain was so mixed up. Last night she'd been so happy. Things that had seemed out of her reach were right in front of her. She should have known it was too good to be true.

Why should she get to live the life that Mallory

didn't? They'd come into this world together—maybe they should have gone out of it together.

Her head was swimming. She couldn't think straight. Irrational thoughts were filling her head.

'Hey—' Riley stepped in front of her '—is something wrong?'

He seemed to blur in her vision. His voice seemed far away, even though he was right in front of her. 'Go away, Riley. Go away. This isn't going to work. It was never going to work. I asked you to give me some space.' She stopped. The wave of pain made her want to double over again.

'April—' this time his voice was directly in her ear '—April, what's wrong?'

She shook her head. She couldn't do this. If she was ill, she didn't want Riley to feel as if he had to be around her. There was enough going on in his life. He didn't need a sick girlfriend, and she couldn't bear for him to see her the way her sister had ended up. A shadow of her former self, weak, emaciated, in constant pain and finally wishing her life away. It had broken April's heart. It had broken her mum's and dad's hearts. She didn't want him to stay with her out of duty or some kind of responsibility.

But, more importantly, she didn't want him to stay with her out of love.

That would break her heart as much as his and Finn's.

She had to walk away. She had to be strong and determined.

She pulled herself straight, willing herself to forget the waves of pain just for a few seconds.

'I'm sorry, Riley. We should never have got involved.

It was wrong of me. It was wrong of you. Finn needs your full attention.' She took a deep breath. 'And I'm not sure if I could ever love someone else's son the way I should.' She hated those words. Every single one of them was a lie. But pushing Riley away now was so much more important than him feeling indebted to her when she finally got the diagnosis she was dreading.

Why hadn't her last lot of bloods shown the CA125 antigen? Why hadn't she acted sooner? Why had she wasted time?

Right now she was angry with herself. But she still cared about Riley and Finn. She didn't want them to have to take this path with her.

Riley's face was pale. 'April, what on earth are you talking about? What's changed between now and last night? Have I missed something?'

'No,' she answered abruptly. 'But I have. Let's just leave it. Let's just not take things any further.'

She was trying her absolute best to hold things together. She could see the hurt in his eyes. She knew this was really what neither of them wanted.

He grabbed hold of her arm. 'Wait a minute. You don't mean this.'

She met his gaze. 'You were just a distraction for me, Riley. A chance to not think about things. And, let's face it, I was just a distraction for you too. I can't give you what you want. We both know that.' She couldn't pretend that she hadn't heard those words he'd just said to the nurse.

Confusion swept over his face. He looked as if she'd just punched him in the chest. 'Finn,' he stuttered. 'You think you can't love Finn?' The cruel words had obviously stuck in his head. He looked shell-shocked.

'No. I can't.'

She pushed past him. She had to get out of here. She had to get away from him and find someone who could help her get to the bottom of this pain.

She walked as quickly as she could, her whole body shaking. Riley would hate her now, almost as much as she hated herself.

Maybe that was for the best.

She pushed open the door to the courtyard. The cold wind took the breath from her body just as another wave of pain hit.

The last thing she remembered was the white snow coming up to greet her.

Riley was stunned. At first he'd thought April was unwell. Her colour was terrible and she'd looked in pain.

But maybe he'd imagined it? Because when she looked directly into his eyes and told him she'd made a mistake and she couldn't love Finn it had felt like a knife stabbing through his heart.

This wasn't the woman that he knew. This wasn't the caring, compassionate and supportive woman that he'd spent time with over the last few weeks. The woman who had stolen his heart and helped him reassess his life. Nothing about this felt right. He loved her. He just hadn't told her that yet.

And it looked as if he wouldn't be telling her that now.

How on earth could he be with someone who proclaimed they didn't have the ability to love his son?

They were a package. Nothing would come between them. He couldn't let it.

His feet were rooted to the spot as she walked away.

Finn. He had to focus on Finn. Maybe he just hadn't taken the time to get to know April properly. He'd been so caught up in being a good father to Finn, and acting on the attraction between them both, that he hadn't really taken time to step back and think about the future.

His breath caught in his throat. That was a lie. He *had* thought about the future. He'd contemplated the words that April had said to him about the possibility of being sick. He'd sat next to Finn and wondered if he should take things forward.

Guilt swept over him. Of course he had. But surely it was his duty to Finn to consider these things and how they might affect him? Was that really why he hadn't told April that he loved her?

It didn't matter that he'd pushed those thoughts aside. It didn't matter that even though he'd still been worried, the thought of not having April in their lives had seemed like a much more difficult concept than dealing with the fact she could get sick.

The truth was any one of them could get sick. Riley, Finn or April. Life was about taking risks. Taking the safe route could mean that he and Finn would miss out on so much more.

That was what he'd believed. That was what he'd thought after a long and sleepless night.

So why hadn't he just told her? That he and Finn wanted April in their lives full stop.

'Help!' The shout came from down the corridor. Riley started running. It was one of the domestic staff—

she was holding the door open to the courtyard. Two
of the nurses came running from the other direction.
And then he saw her.

April. Her body crumpled in the snow.

And he didn't think he could breathe again.

CHAPTER TWELVE

EVERYTHING WAS WHITE. Everything was too white.

Fear gripped her. Was this it?

Then she heard a noise. A shuffle of feet.

She turned her head. A nurse gave her a smile as she pressed a button and made a BP cuff inflate around April's arm. April grimaced. She'd seen this done a hundred times but she hadn't realised it made your arm feel as if it were going to fall off.

After a few uncomfortable minutes the cuff released. She looked around. She didn't recognise this place. 'Where am I?'

'Arlington General.' The nurse gave her another smile. 'I think you managed to give your work colleagues quite a fright. They've all been camped outside.' She checked the monitor once more. 'I'm going to go and tell the surgeon you're awake. He'll want to come and chat to you.' The nurse went to leave then pointed to something on the bedside table. 'Oh, someone left a present for you.' She gave an amused smile. 'Apparently it's very important.'

The nurse seemed relaxed as she left the room. April tried to move in bed, letting out a yelp. Her right side was still sore, but this was a different kind of pain.

Had the surgeon removed her ovary? She let her

hand slip under the covers to feel her abdomen. She had some kind of dressing on her right side. Why would he remove one, and not the other? Surely it was better to do both at once?

She looked from side to side. Her mouth was dry and she couldn't see any water. There was a buzzer at the side of the bed but she didn't want to press it. The nurse had just been in; surely she would come back soon?

Her eyes fell on the parcel. She frowned. It didn't have the neatest wrapping she'd ever seen. But at least it was close enough to reach.

Yip. It looked like recycled wrapped paper, along with half a roll of sticky tape. She peeled away at a small piece of the paper that had managed to escape the sticky tape frenzy. It was something soft—very soft—and pink that was inside.

Now she was intrigued. What on earth was that?

There was a noise at the door.

She looked up. Riley. He was nervously hanging around the door. He looked pale. He looked as if he might have been crying.

Tears welled in her eyes. What she really wanted was a bear hug. But she couldn't ask for that. She wanted to hug it out like she and Mallory used to.

'The surgeon is coming,' she said hoarsely. 'I'm not sure that you should be here.'

He glanced over his shoulder and stepped inside. 'I know that. But I had to see you. I had to know if you were okay.'

She pressed her hand on her stomach. 'I don't know, Riley. I have no idea if I'm okay.'

He nodded and hovered around the side of the bed. 'They wouldn't tell me anything. I mean, of course they wouldn't tell me anything. I know they've phoned your mum and dad. They're on their way.'

'They are?' Now she was scared. She was truly scared. They'd be coming down from Scotland in snowy weather. It probably wasn't the best idea, but if they were on their way, surely it only meant one thing.

The paper from the present crinkled in her other hand as it tightened around the parcel.

Riley glanced at the door again. 'It's from Finn. He said you needed it. He said it was important.' She looked down. She had no idea what it was.

'Riley, I...'

'Stop.' He moved forward and grabbed hold of her hand. 'I don't want you to talk. I just want you to listen.' She'd never seen him look so pale. 'I don't care what the surgeon tells you. Well, of course I care. But it won't change how I feel, and it won't change what I want to do.' He took a deep breath and paused. 'What I want *us* to do.'

She didn't even get a chance to respond.

'You're part of me, April. Whether you want to be or not. I know you said you need space. I know you said the timing isn't good for you. I didn't expect to find out I was a father and meet the woman I want to marry all in the space of a few weeks.' He held up one hand as he said the words. 'But too late. It's happened. And it's good. It's great. I can't pretend that it's anything else. I should have told you the other night. I should have told you at the Christmas Dinner. I don't know why I didn't. But I love you, April. Finn and I love you. Yes, things may be hard at times. Yes, we might take some time to get used to being a family. But I didn't believe you when you said you can't love Finn. I've seen it, April.

I've seen it in your eyes. It's in every action you take, every move you make around him. You're good for him. And you're good for me.' He stopped talking for a second to catch his breath. 'Don't push us away. Don't. I am choosing to be part of your life. I am choosing for us to be part of your future. Whatever happens next, I want to be by your side. All you have to do is say yes.'

She couldn't breathe. How could this be happening? Didn't he know what could lie ahead?

'You can't, Riley. You can't hang around. It's not fair.'

His voice became strong. 'What's not fair is meeting someone that you love and not being able to be with them. I want this, April.' He held up his hands. 'Whatever this may be, I want it.'

Tears pooled in her eyes.

He leaned closer. 'Tell me. Tell me if you love me and Finn. Be honest. If you don't, I can walk away. But I still won't leave you alone. I'll still be your friend. I'll still be around. But look me in the eye and tell me you don't feel the same way that I do.'

She felt her heart swell in her chest. Those green eyes were fixed straight on her. She could see the sincerity. She could see the strength. It was right there before her. His hand was still on hers. But he wasn't gripping her tightly. He was holding her gently, letting his thumb nuzzle into her palm.

She blinked back tears. 'I do love you, Riley. And of course I love Finn. But I just don't feel I've any right to. Not when I don't know what lies ahead.'

He bent forward and kissed her on the forehead then looked at their hands. 'Your hand in mine, April.

That's the way we go forward. That's the way it's supposed to be.'

There was a noise at the door behind them. The surgeon cleared his throat and walked in. 'Everything okay in here?'

April nodded. Her mouth couldn't be any drier. She just wanted this part over with.

But as she waited to hear him speak she realised he didn't look the way she'd expected. He seemed almost jolly. The nurse came in too, holding a glass of water in her hand that she set on the bedside table.

He waved his hand. 'Chris Potter. I was the surgeon on call. You gave us quite a scare, lady.'

April swallowed. 'I did?'

He nodded and pointed to Riley. 'Okay to discuss things in front of your friend?'

Riley's grip tightened around her hand. 'Her fiancé,' he said quickly.

What? He'd just said what?

The surgeon didn't notice her surprise. He just carried on. 'It seems that you have quite a high pain threshold. Most people would have been at their GP's days ago with a grumbling appendix. You must have tolerated that for quite a few weeks. Unfortunately, you're one of the few that has gone on to develop acute appendicitis. Your appendix actually ruptured and you currently have peritonitis. You'll need to stay with us a few days for IV antibiotics. We need to ensure there's no chance of sepsis.'

It was like having an out-of-body experience. April was tempted to turn around to see if he was talking to someone else. Trouble was, she already knew the only thing behind her was a wall. There were no other patients in this room.

'My appendix?' she said quietly. Her brain was trying to process. And it was struggling. She hadn't imagined anything so…so—ordinary. Her mind had immediately gone to the worst-case scenario. There hadn't been room for anything else.

'Her appendix?' Riley said the words like a shout of joy. Then he must have realised how it looked and he tried to look serious again. 'So, that's it. Nothing else?'

The surgeon narrowed his eyes for a second, then nodded. 'I've seen your notes, Ms Henderson. I'm assuming you thought it might be something else?'

She nodded weakly.

He shook his head. 'Had we known about the grumbling appendix, then your gynaecologist and I could have arranged to do surgery together. Unfortunately, as it was an emergency, we didn't have your consent for any other procedure and your gynaecologist was unavailable. I'm afraid your other surgery will have to be scheduled as planned in the New Year. Another anaesthetic isn't ideal, but I didn't have any other option.'

'But…but you didn't notice anything suspicious?'

The surgeon sighed. It was obvious he understood her question. 'I'm not a gynaecologist. I'm a general surgeon, so it's not my speciality. But no, at the time, on the right side I didn't notice anything of concern. Nothing obvious, at least.'

It was amazing, the temporary relief she felt. Of course she knew things happened at a cellular level, but even the simple words 'nothing obvious' were almost like a balm. That, and the hand firmly connected to hers.

The surgeon gave a nod. 'So, at least another twenty-four hours of IV antibiotics. Then we can discharge you home on oral. I think you'll still be sore for a few days and, as I know you're a physio, I'd recommend you stay off work for at least six to eight weeks.' He raised his eyebrows. 'I know you healthcare personnel. Itchy feet. Always want to go back too soon.' He gave them both a wink. 'But those transverse abdominal muscles take a while to heal properly. I'm sure you both know that.'

He picked up her case notes and left. The nurse with him gave them a smile. 'I'll give you some time alone. April, your mum phoned. They're stuck in traffic but should be here in around an hour.' She picked up the observation chart and left too.

For a few seconds neither of them spoke. It was as if they were still trying to take the news in—to process it.

Riley's hand squeezed hers again. 'When can we breathe again?' he whispered.

She laughed, instantly regretting it as her stomach muscles spasmed in protest. She didn't quite know what to say. 'I guess now would be good,' she finally said.

Riley didn't hesitate. He leaned over the bed and gathered April firmly but gently, slipping his arms under her shoulders and hugging her loosely.

She was taken aback, but after a second slid her arms around his neck and whispered in his ear, 'What are we doing?'

He pulled back with a smile, resting his forehead against hers. 'We're doing something that a good friend taught me. And we're doing it in honour of someone else. We're hugging it out.'

Her eyes instantly filled with tears. 'Oh.' Now she

really was lost for words. He'd remembered. He'd re-membered the one thing she always did with her sister.

He moved and the paper on the gift crackled—it had been caught between them.

Riley picked it up. 'You haven't managed to open this yet. I think you should or I know a little guy who'll be immensely offended.'

She nodded, pulling at the paper again to try to uncover what the pink fluffy thing was. It took some tugging, finally revealing her prize. She pulled it free. 'Bed socks?' she asked in surprise.

Riley nodded. 'Finn said you have cold feet. He was very insistent.' He raised his eyebrows. 'I'm beginning to wonder if my son knows you better than I do.'

She laughed as she shook her head, struck that Finn had remembered. Then she frowned. 'You had bed socks?'

He shook his head. 'No, I had money. I just had to hand it over to Finn and let him spend it in a shop on the way here.'

She tried to push herself up the bed. 'Finn is here too?'

Riley nodded. 'Of course he is. Where else would he be?' He met her gaze again. 'We're family,' he said simply.

A tear slid down her cheek. Riley was proving again and again that he meant what he said. He was here. And she knew he'd still be here if she'd had a bad diagnosis instead of a good one.

Why was she trying to walk away from the two men who'd captured her heart?

She licked her lips and he lifted a glass of water

with a straw, almost as if he'd read her mind. 'Here, the nurse left this for you. Take a sip.'

She took a sip of the water and closed her hand over his. 'We need to talk.'

He raised his eyebrows. 'Why do I feel as if I'm about to get into trouble?'

She smiled. 'Oh, because you are.'

He perched at the edge of the bed. 'Hit me with it.'

'You called yourself something when the surgeon was in. I don't think we've had a chance to talk about it.'

He nodded. 'Fiancé.' Then he bit his lip.

Riley Callaghan was actually nervous. It was the moment that she actually loved him most.

'I know it's soon. We can have a long engagement if you want. We can wait until after your surgery, and make sure that Finn is doing well, before we plan the wedding.' He squeezed her hand. 'But I want to let you know that this is it. This is it for me and Finn. We're yours, April Henderson. A package deal. And we'd like you to join our package. I love you, April. What do you say?'

She swallowed as a million thoughts swamped her head. Her heart so wanted to say yes. But she was still nervous.

'They think I'm clear, Riley. But what if I'm not? What if they find something—maybe not now, but later? What then, Riley? I don't want to put you in that position. I don't want to do that to you, or to Finn.'

Riley ran his fingers through his hair. 'How many times, April? How many times do you need me to tell you that I love you? That I accept the risks along with you. No one knows how long they have in this life. You don't know that, and neither do I. But I do know who I love, and who I want to spend the time I have on this earth with. That's you, April. It will only ever be you.'

She gulped as her eyes filled with tears.

He leaned his face close to hers. She could see every part of his green eyes. 'Tell me that you don't love me. Tell me that you don't love Finn. Tell me that you don't wonder about the life we could all have together.'

'Of course I do, Riley,' she whispered. She couldn't lie. Not when he was looking at her like that. Not when his love seemed to envelop every part of her.

He slid his hand into hers. 'We have a life. Let's live it, April. Let's live it together. You, me and Finn. This Christmas will be hard for Finn. But let's get through it together. You, me and him. Let's start something new. Let's create some memories together. As a family.'

She hesitated for the briefest of seconds as her heart swelled.

His eyes widened. 'Is that a yes?' Then he muttered under his breath, 'Please let that be a yes.'

She gave the surest nod she'd ever given. 'It's a yes,' she managed before his lips met hers.

EPILOGUE

IT HAD TAKEN HOURS, but Finn was finally sleeping. He'd crept back downstairs four times, asking if Santa had been yet, and each time Riley and April had laughed and chased him back upstairs.

But she'd just checked. He was now slightly snoring in bed, wearing his superhero onesie.

'At last,' groaned Riley as they flopped down on the sofa in front of the flickering fire. The tree with blue lights was in front of the main window, decorated with a mishmash of coloured baubles and topped with a golden star. April thought it was the most magnificent tree she'd ever seen. The decorations that they'd brought from Isabel's house had joined the new ones on the tree. It was just the way it should be—a mixture of the past and the present.

It had been a big day. She'd lived here since her discharge from hospital. Riley had insisted, and it had felt right. But today Finn had experienced a bit of a meltdown. She'd found him crying in the morning as the whole momentum of Christmas just seemed to overwhelm him. 'I miss my mum,' he'd whispered.

'I know, honey,' she'd said as she hugged him. 'I

miss my sister too. But I think I know something we can do today that will help.'

Riley had been in complete agreement and they'd all gone shopping together in order to find something appropriate for Finn to take to his mother's grave. In the end he'd picked an ornament in the shape of a robin with a bright red breast. It was perfect. And they'd taken him to the cemetery and let him talk to his mother for a while and leave her the gift.

His mood had seemed easier after that, and April had gone and bought flowers to leave at her sister's grave too. 'We need to make this a tradition,' Riley had said quietly in her ear. 'Not a sad one for Christmas Eve, more like a chance to take five minutes to acknowledge the people who aren't here and are missed.'

And she agreed completely. It was something they would do together every year.

Now, it was finally time to relax. The presents were wrapped and under the tree, along with a tray with carrots, milk and mince pie for Santa. 'Better remember to eat that or there will be questions asked in the morning.'

April sighed. 'I've never been fond of carrots. Maybe we can hide it back in the fridge?'

Riley looked a bit odd. He stood up and walked over and picked up the little tray. 'I think Finn counted them earlier; we'd get found out.'

He sat back down on the sofa next to her and put the tray on her lap. He then knelt under the tree and added a couple of small red parcels. April tilted her head and looked at the tray. 'I think in future years, if I'm consuming what's on the tray for Santa, we'll have to negotiate its contents.'

'What does that mean?'

She grinned. 'It means that I think Santa might pre-
fer a glass of wine and some chocolate cake.'

He nodded slowly. 'Why don't we just take things
as they are right now?' He nudged her. 'Open your
presents.'

She lifted the first one and tugged at the gold ribbon around the red glossy paper. She let out a gasp. It
was the most perfect Christmas ornament she'd ever
seen. A replica of her necklace. Two golden hearts
joined together.

'Where on earth did you get this?' Her voice cracked
slightly.

He smiled. 'I got it made for you. Do you like it?'

She nodded as she tried not to cry. 'I think it's perfect,' she sniffed.

He nudged her again. 'Open the next one.'

She smiled. 'I thought I was supposed to wait until
Santa visited?'

He sighed. 'I'm far too impatient to wait for Santa.'

She pulled the ribbon on the second present. The
paper fell away to reveal the church from the Christmas
village. She felt her heart swell in her chest.

'I bought it for you after the Christmas Cheer Dinner. I wanted to remember how perfect that night was.
And I thought we could add it to our collection.'

She hugged him. The way he said *our collection*
just seemed perfect.

His face looked serious for a second. 'Now, other
traditions. It's time to eat the contents of the Christmas tray.'

She looked at him strangely and picked up the mince
pie, taking a nibble. He kept watching her with those

green eyes. When she finally finished she licked her fingers then picked up the carrot with her other hand. 'So what am I supposed to do with this?'

The carrot gave a wobble in mid-air then fell apart, one part bouncing onto the floor, the other part staying in her hand with something glistening at its core.

'What...?' she said as she turned it towards her.

She wasn't seeing things. There, somehow stuck inside the carrot, was a gold band and a rather large sparkly diamond. She turned back. Riley was sitting with the biggest grin on his face.

'Oh,' he said quickly. 'This is my cue to move.' And he did, moving off the sofa and onto the floor in front of her.

He took the carrot from her hand and gave the ring a little tug. 'Just so you know, the story is that Finn thinks Rudolph will leave the ring for you once he finds it.'

'He will?' She was mesmerised. She hadn't expected it at all. Sure, he'd called himself her fiancé in the hospital. But he'd talked about next year, after her surgery was completed, for making future plans.

Riley held it out towards her. The diamond caught the flickering light from the yellow flames of the fire, sending streams of light around the room. 'April, I love you with my whole heart. Even though you tried to avoid me, time and time again, I felt the pull from the first time we met. I know I haven't sorted out my job yet. I know we've still to get through your surgery. But I can't imagine a future with anyone but you. I don't *want* to have a future with anyone but you. I know it's soon. I know some people might think we are crazy. But will you marry us, April?'

Her heart gave a pitter-patter against her chest. Could she ask for any more?

She bent forward and slid her hands up around his neck. 'Now, this is what I call a proposal.'

He pulled her down onto his knee. 'Can I take that as a yes?'

She put her lips on his. 'You absolutely can.'

And there it was. The best Christmas *ever*.

* * * * *

*If you enjoyed this story, check out
these other great reads from Scarlet Wilson*

*THE DOCTOR AND THE PRINCESS
A ROYAL BABY FOR CHRISTMAS
ONE KISS IN TOKYO...
THE DOCTOR'S BABY SECRET*

All available now!

THEIR
MISTLETOE
BABY

BY
KARIN BAINE

MILLS & BOON

Published in Great Britain 2017
By Mills & Boon, an imprint of HarperCollins*Publishers*
1 London Bridge Street, London, SE1 9GF

© 2017 Karin Baine

ISBN: 978-0-263-92678-1

Printed and bound in Spain
by CPI, Barcelona

Dear Reader,

Writing a Christmas book has been a dream come true for me. I am one of those people, like Freya, who still wants to believe in the magic of the festive season. My mum made it such a special time of the year that I never did want to grow up. Even when I left home and had children of my own she still managed to wrap up a slice of that nostalgia in a parcel of sweets, books and pyjamas for me to open on Christmas morning.

For us, the day was always about family. Even though she and my gran are gone now, the rest of us still get together for the traditional board games and obligatory game of bingo after we've stuffed ourselves with turkey sandwiches and chocolate.

Lucas is my Grinch, who doesn't understand that warm, fuzzy feeling of having family around at Christmas because he's never experienced it. Of course Freya and I have worked extra hard to show him how special it can be. And what better place is there to start than on a trip to see Santa Claus in Lapland?

Let's just hope it turns out better than *our* family visit there, with a toddler who hated the cold and has no memory of the trip at all…

Merry Christmas!

Karin xx

For my wonderful mum, who created the magic,
and my boys William and Alexander,
who still let me pretend it exists.

Thanks to Laura, Julia and Chellie
for helping me write the best Christmas story I could.

Books by Karin Baine

Mills & Boon Medical Romance

Paddington Children's Hospital

Falling for the Foster Mum

French Fling to Forever
A Kiss to Change Her Life
The Doctor's Forbidden Fling
The Courage to Love Her Army Doc
Reforming the Playboy

Visit the Author Profile page at millsandboon.co.uk.

PROLOGUE

THIS WAS GOING to be the best Christmas ever. Freya was going to make sure of it. She heard Lucas turning his key in the front door and hoped the smell of her home cooking would put a smile back on his face.

'I'm in the kitchen,' she called, thankful she'd had the day off to make up for their earlier tiff.

Lucas hadn't been in the best of moods lately, which surely hadn't been helped by having to work Christmas Eve or her mistake of bringing up obviously delicate subjects when he was overworked and overtired. Not that she'd expected the idea of having a baby to be so controversial for a doctor who'd chosen to specialise in paediatric care and was so great with his young patients.

They'd never discussed starting a family. Freya had simply assumed Lucas would be as keen as she was, but his negative reaction to the idea this morning had told a different story. He'd surprised her by storming off to the hospital, slamming the door behind him when she'd mentioned feeling broody recently. In hindsight, she had put him on the spot by asking when they could start thinking about babies when he was obviously under a lot of pressure already and not in the right head space to become a father yet.

They could discuss it properly later so they were both clear on the long-term plans for this relationship.

As Lucas strode into the kitchen, still wearing the same scowl he'd had for days now, Freya conceded it probably wasn't good timing anyway when marriage already seemed far from the fairy tale she'd always imagined. Her spirits sank a little as that dream of having a family of her own seemed further away than ever. Lucas's recent mood swings were even making her slightly regret the pact she'd made with him that they would spend the holidays together, just the two of them. This would be her first year not sharing it with her tinsel-loving, Christmas-aholic parents, made more difficult by the fact her new husband didn't appear to share her enthusiasm for the season either.

The more Freya tried to make it special for them, the more detached Lucas seemed to become, but she was determined to make Christmas, and their marriage, a success. She'd lost too much already to let it all slip through her hands again.

'You've been busy.' Lucas leaned up against the refrigerator and gave the baked goods lining the kitchen counter a cursory glance before he continued scrolling through his phone.

If Freya was honest, it wasn't the amorous reunion she'd been hoping for where they would both admit they'd been in the wrong and engage in some wild kitchen make-up sex so they could move on and enjoy the rest of Christmas.

She'd heard passion sometimes went off the boil when you got married but she hadn't expected it after only a few months. They should still be in that can't-wait-to-rip-each-other's-clothes-off honeymoon stage, which was why she was worried she wasn't living up to his wifely expectations. Her mother had always seemed to juggle her nursing career and her home life perfectly and she couldn't help but wonder if this blip in their love life had somehow been down to her. After all, she didn't have a good record for keeping men interested. All she wanted to do was make this first Christmas together special for him.

'The turkey's almost done if you want some. I always love Christmas Eve at home, with the smell of the turkey cooking and getting to sample some before dinner on the big day. I've made my own stuffing too, just the way my mum always did. Maybe I'll get to pass on the family tradition someday too.' It slipped out before she realised and she tensed, waiting for another heated reminder she was alone in her enthusiasm for a large brood to fill her house at Christmas.

'I'm not really hungry. Maybe later.' Luckily, Lucas appeared oblivious to her slip of the tongue, his phone still monopolising his attention. Freya told herself such was the nature of being married to a paediatric consultant—he was always in demand—but there was a niggling doubt something else was behind his recent distraction. Especially when there'd been a few occasions he'd seemed to end calls abruptly when she'd walked into the room.

'I made gingerbread men too. You know Christmas isn't Christmas without creating a cloned army of little dudes capable of breaking your teeth on the one day of the year a dentist is impossible to get hold of. I thought you could help me decorate them later in time for Santa Claus stopping by.' The ironic nod to her childlike obsession with the season had been an attempt to make him laugh but Lucas simply rolled his eyes as though it was a chore she was forcing him to perform, the joke lost on him. Freya made the excuse to herself that he was probably exhausted after his shift because it was less painful than believing he'd tired of her already.

'Great. I...er...think I'll go take a shower first.' He walked out of the kitchen, batting away the paper garlands she'd hung from the ceiling with his free hand, as if they were nothing but a nuisance.

That was exactly how she didn't want him to see her—as if she was nothing more than a pretty decoration he could do without cluttering up his life—but even when he wasn't working he came to bed late and rose early, so they spent little time together as a couple these days. Married life was new to them both but she would do whatever it took to make this work. This was her chance to have the family she'd always wanted and she wasn't going to fail a second time.

Lucas closed his eyes and let the water wash his tears away where no one could see them. As a newlywed spending his first Christmas with his beautiful wife this should have been the happiest time of his life. Yet he couldn't seem to get excited about their future when his past had come back to haunt him so vividly.

He couldn't begin to think of starting a family now when he was still reeling from the news of his father's death. The impact of losing the only parent he'd known had been greater than he'd ever imagined but not because he was grieving the loss of the man who'd raised him. His sorrow was for the childhood he'd been denied and the one he'd suffered instead. The one he now couldn't escape in his head and that wouldn't let him enjoy married life in peace.

Everything he had worked so hard to achieve seemed like a lie now that he was forced to face who he really was behind the career and success he'd built for himself. It wouldn't be fair to bring a baby into existence when he was struggling to hold his own together. He could never hope to give a child a happy, secure home now when his world felt as though it was crashing down around him.

Lucas scrubbed away his self-pity and shut off the shower. None of this was fair on Freya. A normal husband would've told his wife his estranged father had finally succumbed to liver disease and had someone to endure the funeral with him. He would have given her the reason he was so against the idea of bringing a baby into the middle of his personal turmoil—he was afraid of becoming his father's son and ruining another childhood. Except his relationship with his father had been so toxic he hadn't wanted the ugliness of it to taint her. Freya was so idealistic about their marriage and how the next phase of their life together should play out he didn't want to destroy that rosy vision with the disturbing reality behind his.

He should've known it would take more than time and distance to truly escape the man's clutches.

When Lucas had received the call about his father's passing, he'd been forced to think about the man he'd been and had instantly been transported to a time he'd done his best to forget. Now, every time he closed his eyes he was overwhelmed by memories he'd tried to suppress, until even his waking moments were dominated by dark thoughts and a need to escape them.

Freya was the only one saving him from total despair but he was drowning in his own misery and now, more than ever, she was drifting just out of reach as she fussed around, trying to make his house the home he'd never had.

Her talk of babies and family was only natural when he'd never spoken out against it but these past days had reminded him it was an impossible ask. Whilst his mind raged with the fear and injustice of his youth, he could never be the husband, or potential father, Freya assumed she'd married.

By the time he'd changed and come back downstairs she was plating up an early Christmas dinner for him to sample, but as much as he wanted to play along with this game of make-believe, the level of effort she'd gone to to try to please him only served to remind him of everything he'd missed out on. He could no longer force himself to fit into this kind of cosy Christmas scene since his father had managed to crash in and destroy the illusion. It was too late for him to find any enjoyment in it now. At this moment he didn't think he'd find joy in anything ever again.

'I thought we could each open an early present from under the tree. We always used to have a Christmas Eve present at home. Usually pyjamas.' Freya sat down at the opposite end of the dinner table still bubbling with excitement as though she expected Father Christmas to drop down the chimney any second. He'd never had any such delusions as a child or a grown-up.

'Sounds good.' If he'd known that was a thing he would've done a little more retail preparation to make her happy but this was all new to him. He'd never given much thought to gift giving other than a token gesture but the pile of presents she'd assembled beneath the tree would rival any window display on Edinburgh's Royal Mile.

'I know we'd planned a quiet day, but I thought maybe, if it's okay with you, we could drive over to my mum and dad's after lunch tomorrow. We've hardly seen them since the wedding.'

'I thought we were supposed to be spending it on our own?' Lucas's knife and fork clattered to the floor along with his stomach, the last of his appetite quickly disappearing. The last thing he wanted to do was spend the day with her seemingly perfect family when he'd just buried the only sorry excuse for a parent he'd ever had.

'I know. I just thought it might be nice to see them and break up the day a little...'

In that second he could see the disappointment in her big brown eyes that he wasn't enough to make her happy. Christmas was a symbol of everything that was important to her—family. The one thing he'd learned to live without but which was everything to her.

Freya loved being with her parents, couldn't wait to be one herself, and he didn't want to be that dark shadow hanging over either her life or their child's, at any time of the year. What if he turned out like his father, unable to show any emotion other than hate? He was already on that path, distancing himself from his wife's love in the present to focus on the bitterness of his past. She deserved better than a man who wasn't strong enough to separate himself from a frightened little boy intimidated by his father.

Lucas rose from the table with a quiet acceptance he was no longer the man she'd agreed to marry and spend the rest of her life with, even if she wouldn't admit it. Their love might be physically keeping them together but it would ultimately tear them apart inside, forcing this relationship to work when they both wanted, needed, such different things.

'I'm sorry, Freya. I can't do this any more.' The words were ripped from his aching heart, leaving a hole in his chest he knew would never heal.

He couldn't be responsible for anyone else's life when he wasn't sure he wanted his own any more. It was getting too damn difficult to imagine a time when he would no longer be in pain and he didn't want the same for Freya or the child she expected them to raise in this mess.

This was the only way to save them both, even though it might seem like intolerable cruelty tonight. It was painful now but hopefully, with time, Freya would realise it was the right thing for him to do. She was young and idealistic, with the kind of open heart that would help her find love again, where his had been flawed from the start. He'd never been able to fully give himself to her or the relationship when he'd been holding back the truth about his parentage.

'Lucas? I'm sorry... We don't have to go if you don't want to... Lucas?'

He got as far as the door before he heard her quickening footsteps behind him in the hallway but he daren't look back. His knees were already weak, his chest so unbearably tight that he couldn't even trust himself to speak without collapsing to the floor.

Leaving was the best present he could think of to give her. She could still have all those things she wanted, just with someone else. He'd be a lost cause for ever when he was walking away from the best thing that would ever happen to him but he should never have expected to have everything he'd ever wanted.

His father had been right all along. He was a useless waste of space.

CHAPTER ONE

Ten months later

FREYA ADJUSTED THE jingle bells on her hat, straightened her elf ears and pulled up her stripy stockings. Christmas was supposed to be the most wonderful time of the year and she was determined to make sure of it for the kids of Princes Street Children's Hospital. It didn't matter a jot it was only October when they were on their way to Lapland to see the beloved man in the red suit. While she was there she'd make sure to remind him he owed her big style for last year.

'Feeling Christmassy yet?' Gillian, her nursing colleague from the emergency department and fellow elf for the weekend, came to join her at the front of the plane to welcome on board the excited children and volunteers along with the flight staff.

'I'm doing my best.' It was difficult to get into the spirit since everything she'd once loved about this time of year now reminded her of her husband walking out of their marriage and the worst period of her life. However, this wasn't about her, so she plastered on the jolliest smile she could muster and handed out candy canes with a 'Merry Christmas!' to the special group of sick children the hospital had chosen for the charity trip.

'Well, you certainly look the part.' Gillian gave a little wolf whistle that had Freya tugging on the furry white hem of her green velvet dress.

'I knew it was too short. That's what happens when you're forced to shop in the kids' department.' Everything in the costume store had swamped her petite frame but she guessed her height was the reason she'd been chosen to be one of Santa's helpers in the first place. Well, that and her extensive nursing experience, which made her a vital part of this group.

Without a very skilled medical team these poorly children would never get to leave Edinburgh. Such was the seriousness of some of their conditions there were a few of them who rarely left the hospital. That was why this trip was so magical, so important to the families and to her when she saw many of them time and time again in the emergency department. She would simply have to set aside her own heartache and loneliness around the season to make this memorable for everyone.

'You look gorgeous. With any luck you might even catch the eye of a reindeer herder over here and decide not to come back.'

Freya was forced to bite her lip until the young passengers were out of earshot. There was no room for disappointment or disillusionment on this trip and her love life definitely fell into those categories.

'Men are definitely off my wish list for the foreseeable future. I barely survived the last one. All I want for Christmas is to forget about Lucas Brodie and remind myself I'm Freya Darrow—the woman who is Christmas personified, not some sad and lonely divor-

cee who spent last year crying into her eggnog.' So they
weren't officially divorced, but since she hadn't seen
Lucas again from the moment he'd walked out on her,
Freya had eventually had to accept the marriage was
over. She'd reverted back to her maiden name when
she'd decided to rid all traces of him from her life
once and for all.

In those heady days of their intense romance, she
supposed they'd never taken the time to find out about
each other beyond who they'd become as a couple. So
physically wrapped up in each other and the idea of
being together to care about anything else, they'd left
no space for her to confide in him about the loss she'd
suffered as a teenager or for him to share his apparently opposing views on starting a family. During the
early days of their marriage she'd been so happy she
hadn't wanted to spoil anything by reopening the old
wounds of her past, naively believing everything would
simply fall into place.

Then, when Lucas's moods had become unpredictable, she'd been afraid to upset either of them any more
by bringing up the issue, unaware that while she'd been
making plans for a family he had already been plotting
an escape route. He'd given up on them before even
admitting there'd been a problem; without even trying
to resolve whatever issue which had been so great he'd
seen no other option rather than to leave. It made her
doubt if the strength of her feelings for him and invest-
ment in their relationship had ever been reciprocated.

'I'm glad to see you back to your old self but, ah,
there is something about Lucas I should probably tell
you...'

'I don't want to know. I'm only thinking happy

thoughts this weekend.' Freya refused to let further mention of him steal what little there was left of her enthusiasm for the season and shoved the end of a candy cane in her mouth for a peppermint sugar hit. The rumours Lucas was back, working in their sister hospital across the city, had reached her ears too but she didn't want to think about it. Not now when she was just starting to pull her own life back together.

It wasn't so long ago she'd spent Christmas making tearful phone calls around hospitals and friends, trying to find out if he was even still alive. There'd been several days of sheer panic and disbelief before she'd heard he'd gone on sick leave from work and didn't want to be contacted. Apparently that had included her. To this day she still didn't know if there'd been someone else, or if her talk of starting a family had made him have serious second thoughts about spending the rest of his life with her. He hadn't done her the courtesy of ever explaining himself. Not that it would change what had happened now when she was finally trying to move on.

There was no way she'd let memories of her absentee husband spoil things now after she'd spent the week overdosing on schmaltzy Christmas films and hot chocolate in an attempt to recapture her love of the season again. This trip to the Arctic Circle was just what she needed to restore her faith in human nature and awaken her inner child. Plus it was a bonus to embrace every tacky, glittery bauble associated with the spectacle Lucas had despised so much.

'Merry Christmas,' Freya repeated to every little soul as they were helped on board, ashamed she was even thinking about herself today. This was a break from reality for all of them. Even the parents and siblings left at home would enjoy some respite themselves this weekend with a getaway in the Scottish countryside funded by the charity. It made a change for everyone whose lives normally revolved around hospital appointments and stress.

'Is Santa here yet?' A particularly eager young man ran down the aisle in search of the man in red.

'I told you, Sam, we see Santa at the *end* of the trip. Try not to get yourself over-excited before we even leave Scotland.' The volunteer assigned to him followed down the aisle, clutching an asthma inhaler in her hand.

'Someone's keen.' Freya loved the enthusiasm, even though it was a tad premature. They had a whole itinerary to keep tiny spirits up until they reached Santa's grotto deep in the winter wonderland of the Finnish forests. The excitement was catching already and she couldn't help but hope for a little magic herself by the end of the weekend. A memory swipe of her ill-advised workplace romance and an embarrassingly short marriage should do it. Failing that, she was a sucker for cuddly toys.

'His mum said he's been looking forward to this for weeks.' Young Sam and his aide took their seats and Freya could almost feel the sense of relief as well as expectation from everyone. This was an escape into fantasy and a chance for them all simply to be children again.

'Oh, to be that young and carefree again,' Freya whispered after them, hankering for the life she'd had before a runaway husband had left her so jaded and cynical.

'I really think you should know…' Gillian tried

again to force the shadow of Lucas over the proceedings and she was wondering if her friend was trying to tell her he'd been spotted with another woman. After such a lengthy separation it was really none of Freya's business who Lucas might have hooked up with in the interim, or who he might see in the future, but the pain was still too raw for her to find out for sure. It had made it impossible to go and confront him at work when she'd heard he was back. She couldn't face seeing him, knowing he was happier without her, when she'd been broken into a thousand pieces without him. His reluctance to come to her and explain his whereabouts for these past months said everything about his complete disregard for her feelings.

'I think that's everyone on board now. We should find our seats for take-off. Once we're safely up in the air and the captain gives us the go-ahead we can organise the in-flight entertainment.' With virtual fingers in her ears, she put her head down and took her seat near the front of the plane, which was thankfully on the opposite side from Gillian's. She didn't want to spend the next few hours listening to a running commentary on her ex's exploits since he'd returned from the wilderness. Left with no other choice, Gillian huffed out a breath and buckled herself in across the aisle.

The lovely smiley member of the cabin crew who'd helped them decorate the inside of the plane with tinsel patted Freya on the knee to get her attention. 'We're just waiting for one more to arrive. Then we'll close the doors and really get this party started.'

'Of course. We wouldn't be going very far without the doctor, would we?' She prayed there wasn't some sort of medical emergency holding up the very man who'd be coordinating the children's medical care. They'd already had one of the non-medical volunteers pull out, leaving them short-handed. As lead nurse she'd agreed to supervise two of the children herself but they really couldn't do without the doctor.

'They've just called from the departure gate to say he's on his way now.'

At least the delay meant she could take a breather for a little while before she had to face her next challenge. Take-off was the one part of the flight experience she never enjoyed. That moment when the plane left solid ground and the world grew ever smaller beneath her was always a nail-biter.

She settled back in her seat and attempted to relax. From the moment they were up in the air until the time they landed back in Scotland, there wouldn't be much time for her to rest.

'Ladies and gentlemen, we have our last passenger on board, so we can close the cabin doors and prepare for take-off.' The announcement was made as a windswept figure dashed on board and received a round of applause and a chorus of cheers.

Not from Freya. She was dumbstruck. Too traumatised to even remember how to breathe.

Lucas.

Here.

Now.

Unless she was having some sort of sugar-induced hallucination, he'd just stepped onto the plane.

'Sorry I'm late. Car trouble.' The late arrival shook the rain from his thick blond hair. Freya blinked as the water droplets showered over her and she was forced to face the fact her ex-husband was *actually* here. Not only that, he had the nerve to smile and breathe as though he'd never crashed her whole world around her.

She turned, open-mouthed, towards Gillian, who simply shrugged and mumbled, 'I tried to tell you.'

'Not hard enough,' Freya hissed. This couldn't be happening. She had no desire to see him or talk to him, not since it had become apparent he'd abandoned her and their marital home, and now he was here, gate-crashing her weekend away? That was cruel even by his standards.

'The doctor who was supposed to be travelling with us took ill. I only found out myself this morning that Lucas had been drafted in to take his place.'

'That still gave you time to tell me.' Now the doors were locked, she was shut in this very small, very public space with him. It wasn't the ideal place to face him for the first time in nearly a year when her emotions were bubbling so close to the surface they could very well blow out the doors of this aircraft. She was already hyperventilating; each gasping, shallow breath making it a possibility she might just pass out. That really would be the sour cherry on top of this mess.

'I didn't want to upset you or force you to back out. I'm sorry you've been put in this position. I know it's not fair on you, but we need you here.' Gillian wasn't the kind to employ emotional blackmail to get what she wanted and Freya knew she'd only done what she thought was best in the circumstances. If she had been aware Lucas was going to be part of this, she might never have made it on board the plane herself and that would have put the entire trip in jeopardy. It didn't make the prospect of spending enforced time with him any more palatable, though.

'It should've been my decision to make,' she grumbled, letting Gillian off the hook and directing her annoyance at the person who deserved it most. Lucas.

This volcano of bubbling emotion inside her was exactly the reason she hadn't wanted any contact with him. It was difficult to restrain herself from getting up and punching him in the face for running out on her the way he had or squaring up to him and demanding answers she probably wasn't ready to hear. Neither option would settle her again now when the mere sight of him was still enough to make her heart beat a little faster. Memories, good and bad, flooded back so quickly, so intensely she had to forgo her candy cane to reach for the little paper bag in the seat pocket to breathe into.

In.

Their first kiss on a night out with colleagues after weeks of working side by side when he'd been called in for cover in Princes Street and she'd been trying to ignore the growing attraction.

She'd never anticipated any sort of workplace romance, especially when he'd only been at the hospital on a temporary contract. That hadn't seemed the ideal basis for any long-term relationship, and she wasn't the type of woman who would ever find satisfaction in a fling, but he'd been so kind and attentive, to her and his patients, he'd eventually become the exception to her rule. Her gamble in letting her heart rule her head again seemed to have paid off since they'd kept dating long after his posting had finished, but she was still paying the price for her mistake now.

Out.

Lucas on one knee, promising he'd love her for ever and making her believe this time an engagement would mean marriage and a family and everything that had been taken from her in the past.

She'd made no secret of the fact she wanted the same kind of special relationship her parents had one day and had thought he'd understood how sacred marriage was to her, not something to ever be taken lightly. The proposal, over a candlelit dinner at his place, had been perfect because it had been a private moment between the two of them, somewhere she hadn't felt under pressure. The homely, romantic gesture had held more meaning to her than a scripted display of bravado in front of a crowd, and he'd made her believe he held the same values. Only to toss her aside when he'd grown tired of married life all too soon.

In.

Their wedding day, when she'd been on top of the world and had truly believed they'd be together for ever.

It had been a small church wedding since Lucas had had no family he'd wished to invite to the service. He'd looked so handsome, and had seemed so utterly devoted to her during their vows to one another, he would've rivalled any fairy-tale prince. During their first dance as husband and wife at the reception she would've even sworn he'd had tears in his eyes, but the adoration hadn't lasted.

Out.

The last image she had of him, walking out the front door only months later and breaking her heart in two.

That dream of her picture-perfect family had vanished along with him that day. He hadn't loved her enough to even work at their marriage, never mind raise babies with her. She guessed he'd decided somewhere along the way he hadn't wanted to follow that traditional love, marriage, kids route after all.

There'd been several self-centred men in her life since her first teenage infatuation, who'd run out on her when faced with the ultimate responsibility, but none of them had hurt her as much as Lucas because he was the one she'd never stopped loving.

The bag inflated and deflated in time with her shallow breaths.

'If you'll just take your seat, Doctor, we'll be on our way.'

Freya could hear the admiration in the young attendant's voice and an eerie sense of calm descended upon her. She'd been that naive girl once, dazzled by the handsome consultant with the pale blue eyes and the great smile. It had taken a lot longer for her to trust him with her heart. She'd mistakenly believed such a strong, reliable force in the workplace would make him the man who would be there for her when she needed him the most in her personal life too. The kind of man who wanted to settle down and would find contentment with a wife and a couple of kids. How wrong she'd been.

This past year had toughened her up and hopefully made her immune to those superficial charms now she knew he wasn't the man she'd thought he was behind the handsome facade. Lucas was no better than the first man who'd betrayed her trust. Perhaps even worse because he'd broken his vows as well as her heart.

She crumpled up the paper bag with much more force than was probably necessary and shoved it back in the pocket until she could dispose of it properly.

The one consolation she had in watching another woman fawn over him was seeing the smile fall from his lips as he made his way down the plane and spotted her sitting in the aisle seat.

'Freya?' He swallowed hard and Freya found some satisfaction that he didn't appear any more comfortable than she was with the situation. Even if this had been some sort of set-up to force her to talk to him, the reality might've actually made him face up to his actions. Nothing Lucas could say now would change what he'd done but dealing with the consequences might make him think twice about treating someone else with such scant consideration.

It didn't make the idea of spending the weekend in his company any more palatable.

'Lucas. You were the last person I expected to see,' she said through gritted teeth, hoping the disapproval was radiating off her. He was completely out of order, ambushing her like this, but it wasn't the time or place for a screaming showdown. No matter how tightly her fists were clenched or how raw her throat was with the effort of holding back tears and the urge to ask, *'Why?'* He didn't get to ruin any more of her life.

'I was asked to cover at the last minute…and I thought…' He was standing in the middle of the aisle, creating a bit of a spectacle as he blustered around her, attempting to squeeze his carry-on luggage in the overhead locker as the cabin crew tried to chivvy him to his seat.

'What? That this would make a good surprise?' If he was any good at reading body language, her folded arms and scowl should have told him otherwise. The fact that he'd chosen to play out this painful reunion in front of passengers and colleagues made matters worse. The one saving grace was that everyone else was so caught up in their own excitement the general ruckus on the plane should be drowning out this awkward conversation.

He ought to be on his knees again, begging her for forgiveness this time.

'Doctor, I really need you to take your seat as quickly as possible so we don't miss our flight slot.' The flight attendant flashed a warning through her too-bright, teeth-baring smile as she slammed the locker shut and ushered him to the seat in front of Freya's.

She gulped in a deep breath as he turned away from her and released her from the hypnotic trance of those too-easy-to-get-lost-in blue eyes. These months of tears and heartbreak hadn't managed to eradicate the strongest of all the emotions she felt for Lucas—love—and she hated herself for it as much as she wanted to hate him. She'd never asked for their relationship to end and it seemed her feelings hadn't diminished any over time. If she'd stopped loving him at any point during their separation it wouldn't hurt so much to see him again and be reminded of everything she'd lost.

This weekend was going to test her personally as well as professionally and turn her into a prisoner of her own emotions because absolutely nothing was going to spoil the magic for these children. Not even the unresolved issues of her marriage breakdown.

Lucas collapsed into his seat, the sight of Freya after all this time hitting him with the unexpected force of a runaway sleigh, even though he'd known she'd be here.

'Your seat belt, sir.' He was admonished by another member of the cabin crew as they completed their safety checks and waited with increasing agitation for him to buckle up.

'Sorry. So sorry.' He wanted to stamp the word in bold black ink on his forehead so Freya could see it too because he was seemingly incapable of vocalising his regret for the way he'd left things between them now they were face-to-face.

It had been nearly a year since they'd last seen each other, yet her obvious pain, and his shameful guilt, felt as fresh as if they'd only just broken up.

When he'd realised her name was on the staff list he'd had second thoughts about volunteering for this position, knowing a confrontation was inevitable. After all, she'd loved him every bit as much as he'd loved her before he'd abruptly ended their marriage. In the end, he'd realised he had to man up and face her so they could both have closure on that very difficult time in their lives. It wasn't going to be easy to initiate a conversation about the possibility of divorce but a legal end to their relationship was the next logical step if she was ever going to be truly free of him and have the fresh start she deserved. He'd intended to broach the subject with her at some point on this trip when they could talk more freely and once she'd got used to the idea of seeing him again.

Except when he'd been planning his return to the world, he hadn't filtered any residual emotions into the equation.

The sight of her again had unexpectedly choked him up, reminding him in that instant of everything he'd lost to his illness. It was his friend Peter who'd salvaged his career and liaised with the hospital during his sick leave but, ashamed of his weakness, he'd begged Peter not to reveal anything to Freya.

He'd had to jump through hoops with the hospital board to prove he'd recovered and get his job back, with numerous meetings and assessments with occupational health and the GMC before he'd been deemed fit enough to work. His colleagues and the senior consultants had supported his return, and now he was building up his hours at the hospital again, he'd managed to resurrect his career, but he'd known he'd never be able to win his wife back.

Seeing her again only increased that ache in his chest and suggested he wasn't ready to let her go just yet even when setting her free for good was the best thing he could do for her. So much time had passed he'd imagined they would both be glad to escape any ties to one another and he hadn't been prepared for the reaction of either of them upon seeing each other again.

His kind and gentle wife looked as though she wanted to physically hurt him. He'd always been able to read her because she never made any attempt to hide her feelings. Unlike him, who'd kept his secrets and emotions bottled up until he'd imploded from the stress of holding it all back and destroyed everything he'd ever loved.

Those almond-shaped eyes had flashed with wild fire when they'd lit upon him, full of anger and hurt. Arms folded as she'd confronted him, there'd been a hardness to her he'd never encountered before. Lucas wasn't naive or egotistical enough to have expected she'd welcome him with open arms but part of Freya's charm had always been her warm personality. It was a shock to the system to see her changed so much and it made him realise how much time had passed between them. It also made him question how much of that change was down to him.

In his mixed-up head he'd believed that by leaving her he was doing what was best, so he didn't drag her into that dark pit of despair with him. When his conscience did prick at the thought of her tear-stained face staring after him, he'd convinced himself she would've found someone else to replace him by now. That somehow leaving had been a selfless act on his part and she'd be cosied up with another man, planning the family she'd always wanted and he hadn't been convinced he could give her.

The reality was very different, of course, and made him see his actions through her eyes for the first time since he'd turned his back and left her to deal with the fallout alone. They'd been so in love but he'd shut her out to the point of ignoring her pain in favour of his own.

Even without her clipped tone and abrupt manner with him, Lucas could see the distress he'd caused in her defensive body language and it broke his heart. With the clarity of his recovery it was obvious now that walking away hadn't been the answer; he'd only caused them both further agony. At the time what had been left of his pride had decreed that he protect his new wife from the responsibility of knowing about his childhood and subsequent illness. It hadn't been her job to fix him. He'd had to fix himself. Now he was realising the extent of what that decision had cost him and Freya.

The plane rumbled down the runway and he instinctively reached back to give her hand a reassuring squeeze. He knew how much she hated this part of the flight.

'Are you okay?' He peered around the back of his seat to see her sitting bolt upright, her eyes wide with fear.

'I'm fine,' she snapped, and snatched away from his grip as though she'd been burned.

On their honeymoon she'd dug her nails so deeply into the armrest he'd thought she'd never let go as he'd tried to prise her off again, but she was letting him know now without doubt he'd given up that right to touch or comfort her any more. She was his wife in name only now and that was entirely his fault.

The tension in her body and her instant recoil was a stark contrast to the effect he used to have on her. That slightest touch brought back the torturous sights and sounds of their honeymoon and beyond, when she'd once melted beneath his touch. They'd been happy for a time, in love and in lust, and he wished it had never come to this when she'd rather suffer a panic attack alone than accept his help.

There was a long way to go to get her to hear him out and he had the distinct impression that if it wasn't for the people surrounding them she would tell him exactly what she thought of him without stopping for breath. There was a long list of his failings but he'd never been as aware of them as he was now when his sweet wife could barely control the rage she felt towards him. If he thought it would give either of them any satisfaction, or in any way make up for how he'd treated her, he'd offer himself up as a punch bag right now.

He mightn't have thought this through properly but

he remained hopeful this weekend would provide an opportunity for him to explain himself and smooth the way for a talk about the next step. That was all he could ask and yet it was more than he probably deserved from her.

He listened to the *oohs* and *aahs* of the children as the plane soared upward and the city lights blazing through the dark morning gradually disappeared beneath the clouds. The minute they reached cruising height and the seat-belt light went out, the plane became a hive of activity again as people left their seats.

'So, ladies and gentlemen, boys and girls, who's looking forward to meeting Santa Claus?' The intercom crackled with the enthusiastic tone of a non-crew member and a quick glance confirmed it was the other elf he'd seen on board. Freya was on her feet too but she was handing out sheets of paper to the whooping passengers.

'We thought we'd get everybody warmed up with a few Christmas carols, so elf Freya is handing out some song sheets to everyone. If anyone wants to come up and sing a song or tell a joke while we wait, you're very welcome.'

Lucas managed to block out the tones of tuneless childish warbling and recycled jokes because his attention was totally focused on Freya as she made her way through the cabin. That bright smile shone for everyone she spoke to and he held his breath, waiting for his turn; to feel her warmth upon him once again. Of course, it didn't happen. When she reached him the light dimmed in her eyes and the smile faltered.

'You're looking well, Freya.' It was the best he could come up with to fill the awkwardness of the moment but he meant every word of it. The passing of time hadn't diminished her beauty, or the effect it had on him. He still felt like the luckiest man in the world that she'd ever agreed to be his wife, and the stupidest for letting her go.

She turned to move on without saying a word but it had been so long since they'd been this close he couldn't help himself trying to prolong the moment.

'You've cut your hair.' The short, messy bob suited her fine features but he'd always loved her long chestnut-brown hair.

'I needed a change,' she said flatly, suggesting again there'd been more than physical alterations occurring in his absence.

His stomach rolled at the thought he'd been the cause of that sudden edginess to her when she'd always been such a bubbly, loving individual and his actions had hardened her heart the way his father's self-destructive behaviour had his. He knew what a long, painful process it was to get over that kind of damage and what it cost along the way. Not something he would ever have wished for Freya to go through, and exactly the reason he'd walked away in the first place.

'I am sorry. For everything.' Characteristically, he'd remained in denial until crisis point, when he'd been forced to witness the emotional effects of the damage he'd caused first-hand. While he had no desire to embarrass her in front of anyone here, it would be remiss of him not to acknowledge the wrong he'd done her, and if she chose not to speak to him after this flight at least he would know he'd made the apology and meant it.

'Perhaps you'd give us a song, Doctor? I'm sure the children would love it.' There was that smile again but there was no trace of friendliness in the way she'd bunched up the leftover song sheets in her fist. She was rejecting the apology as obviously as she could without drawing attention from the others because she would know taking part was the last thing he'd want to do.

Their marriage might've been short-lived but they'd been together long enough for Freya to know that this Christmas merriment was out of Lucas's comfort zone. Her enthusiasm for the season had been difficult to live with when he'd hated everything about it. The over-the-top glitter and expense was always a reminder of the childhood he'd been denied and the only reason he'd agreed to step in before he knew Freya was involved had been to ensure these kids had the happy memories he didn't.

'I…er…have a lot of paperwork to catch up on.' It wasn't a complete lie. As the emergency replacement for the usual medical coordinator, he'd been handed the itinerary at the last minute. Although he'd done his best to get acquainted with the case notes of the children who'd be under his care so there wasn't any room for error and he was fully prepared for any eventuality. Not that anything could've prepared him for this tense exchange but he deserved every bit of the hard time she was giving him.

'Well, don't let me take up any more of your time.' She made a move to leave but there was such resignation in her tone he didn't want her to think he'd ever dismissed her, or everything they'd ever had, as easily as it may have seemed.

He reached out to touch her arm but she flinched away from him again as though he'd given her an electric shock. A reminder of those early days when they'd been avoiding their growing attraction in the workplace, where every brush against each other had held so much meaning. The most obvious difference now was that she wasn't looking at him with undisguised desire, more like murderous intent.

'Don't be like this, Freya. I really am sorry…' If he'd been in her shoes he knew he'd probably never be able to forgive him either, but how could they ever resolve matters if she refused to be anywhere near him? Expecting a truce here was a big ask but eventually she might accept he was trying to make the best out of a bad situation. Perhaps a divorce would get that anger at him out of her system once and for all.

'If you'll excuse me, we have a very busy schedule ahead of us today and I wouldn't want to let people down.' Freya cut off his attempt to apologise again and put some distance between them, leaving the scent of cinnamon and peppermint lingering in her wake. She launched into the first rendition of an old Christmas classic, encouraging everyone else to join in and handing out percussion instruments to the youngest members of the party.

To everyone else sitting on this plane Freya was the life and soul of the party, bringing festive cheer to those who needed it most, but Lucas could see the brave face she was trying to put on. She refused to make eye contact with him again for the duration of the fun and games on board to pass the time for the children and he knew that determination not to let them down was because she'd been there. She'd been on the receiving end of bitter disappointment and broken dreams and it was all down to him.

His journey to recovery had come at Freya's expense

and he couldn't fully move on from the past when it wasn't only his father who'd left a legacy of unhappiness behind. Unlike the man who'd made his life hell, he wouldn't be able to live with himself if he didn't try to fix things. Although he hadn't been able to provide Freya with the husband and family she needed or deserved, there was one thing he could give her that might go some way to making up for his behaviour. An explanation.

It wasn't going to be easy to open up about the demons that had driven him away or to get her to speak to him long enough to do so, but he owed it to her to try. Perhaps this visit to Father Christmas could give them both the gift they needed most—peace of mind.

CHAPTER TWO

'YOU LOOK LOVELY and cosy in there.' Freya was helping to dress the two little girls she'd been assigned for the duration of the trip in the ski gear and snow boots which had been waiting for the group at the other end of the flight.

It was daylight now and the quick peek they'd had from the plane at the snowy landscape had made them all keen to get out and explore but the subzero temperature meant they needed to be suitably dressed before they could venture outside. With the nature of the conditions a lot of the children were suffering it was doubly important they were all wrapped up against the elements.

Freya had changed out of her elf outfit and into her more suitable snowflake-adorned sweater and warm trousers before they'd left the airport. Even trussed up like the Abominable Snowman in this lurid pink ski suit she felt more comfortable; zipped in and covered up and hopefully protected from the penetrating stare of her ex-husband.

It had never entered her head that she would be forced to face him on this trip but she'd been even more disturbed by the flutter of her pulse every time he looked at her. Something that had happened all too frequently during the flight for her comfort. She felt his eyes burning into the back of her head now, watching her with the intensity of a man who had something he needed to get off his chest. Whatever it was, she didn't want to hear it. Whether he wanted to salve his conscience and finally unload the reason behind his mysterious disappearance, or he was eventually attempting to claim back half of everything that was rightfully his, she wasn't going to do this in front of an audience.

Freya had been over every imaginable scenario in her head since he'd left her—from another woman to some sort of post-wedding jitters that had seen him running for the hills. In the end, it boiled down to the same thing—Lucas hadn't wanted to be with her any more and no amount of talking now could repair her shattered heart. Despite the thermal layers of clothes she couldn't help but shiver every time she thought of him reaching out to take her hand on take-off. The part of her that, apparently, hadn't endured enough humiliation wanted to believe it was more than some residual body memory making him reach out to reassure her. That, irrespective of everything, he still cared about her the way she obviously still cared for him. The wounded Freya, still recovering from her injuries, reminded her it wasn't possible given the way they'd parted and it wasn't healthy to hold out any hope otherwise. Such a weakness in her armour left her vulnerable to another attack on her heart.

'Where did my fingers go?' Five-year-old Hope waved her hand at Freya and pulled her back into the present fantasyland. She was one of several here with type one diabetes, which meant constant monitoring of her blood-sugar levels, to avoid highs and lows, and her activity levels. It left no room for daydreaming paediatric nurses.

'They're in there all snuggled together keeping warm. These are called mittens and all of Santa's visitors have to wear them so Jack Frost doesn't nip those little fingers.' She adjusted the mittens so Hope's thumbs made it into their own holes and gave her a bit more freedom of movement.

'Scarlett too?' She grabbed hold of Freya's other charge for the weekend, the look of concern for her friend's naked fingers clearly etched on her cherubic face.

At least it would make her job easier over the weekend if the two little girls were bonding and not pining for any siblings at home.

'Yes, Scarlett too.' Freya tugged another pair of mittens on, and with their matching cerise ski suits and woolly hats, they could've passed for sisters, twins even.

Her heart lurched at the sight of the two precious bundles whose lives had been entrusted to her for the duration of the trip by their parents. It was a great responsibility but also a huge privilege to be able to give them a taste of a normal childhood. She'd look after them as if they were her own. If things had worked out differently, the way she'd planned her life with Lucas, they could've been making this trip to see Santa with their own little ones.

That space in her heart echoed with sorrow as that image of her, Lucas and the babies she'd imagined they would have flashed into her head. She'd had so much love to give, ready to start their very own family, and he'd ripped it all away from her, leaving her with nothing. Looking after other people's precious babes was as close as she'd ever get to that mothering side again because she knew she'd never trust another man enough to ever start her own family now.

'So, this is Hope and Scarlett? Hi, girls. My name is Lucas and I'm going to be helping Freya look after you. If there's anything you need you just come to one of us, okay?' Lucas had managed to appear beside her without tripping her inner alarm warning and she bristled at having him so close, intruding on the moment. It didn't help when he was wearing a black beanie hat and electric-blue ski suit and looking like someone ready to have fun instead of a professional heartbreaker.

'Okay,' the girls chorused, nodding their heads, no doubt charmed already by the handsome doctor. He had that effect on people.

'It's time to get on the bus.' She ushered the girls out towards the waiting transportation that was going to take them on the first leg of their journey with more urgency now that he'd arrived on the scene.

That first blast of cold air was a shock to the system and she shooed the little ones up the bus steps so they didn't hang about outside any longer than was necessary.

'I only wanted to make sure you had Scarlett's anti-epilepsy drugs and Hope's insulin at hand. I'm checking off everyone's medication before we head out.' Lucas flipped through the paperwork he'd been studying on the flight as he'd avoided all the on-board activities, and unexpected heat burned Freya's cheeks at the mistaken belief his attention had been solely for her. Of course he'd be preoccupied with the treatment all of these children needed while they were here. It was his job to coordinate everything so they could travel safely. She would never question his professionalism. It was his cavalier attitude to his marital status she had an issue with.

'Yes, I have the AEDs, insulin and the times they've to be administered.' When it came to the care of her patients she took her job equally as seriously. She'd checked and double-checked everything these girls needed for the duration of this trip and wasn't leaving anything to chance. Although neither epilepsy nor diabetes were the sort of conditions that necessarily ran to a schedule.

'Good.' He gave her a curt nod before moving along the line to converse with the other medical members of the team. It was easier to deal with him when he was in doctor mode because it reminded her of the days when they'd been able to work together before chemistry and emotions had got in the way. If he maintained this detached manner and avoided any further mention over their shared past she was more likely to hold back the tears and the urge to slap him.

Freya stepped on board the bus with renewed fire in her belly. She'd survived the loss of her baby in her teens and had made it through this last year of absolute hell, so she knew she could get through anything.

'Look at the big snowmen!' Hope and Scarlett had their faces squished up against the bus windows, pointing at the sights along the way, and Freya had to admit she was every bit as impressed by the ten-foot-high figures greeting them on arrival at the clearing where they were to begin their activities.

They'd made a quick stop to check in at their accommodation first, leaving all unnecessary baggage except the medical equipment they needed and an estranged husband she suddenly couldn't seem to shake off, and now she was ready to go exploring.

'Isn't it wonderful?' With the falling snow, frosted pine trees and the marshmallow landscape waiting for the first footsteps to break the surface, this place was exactly what she needed to compensate for last year's miserable time.

The trio was so engrossed by their surroundings that they were last to leave the bus and found the others were already lined up, waiting for the reindeer sleighs to take them through the magical forest, when they stepped outside.

Lucas was waiting to speak to her at the back of the line. 'They can only take two at a time.'

'Well, how's that going to work for us?' The girls were clutching both of her hands and there was no way she could leave one behind or expect them to go without her.

'I've volunteered to take one of the girls with me. It's not a problem.'

Maybe not to him but as it seemed the volunteers had all been allocated already to accompany the children along with the medical staff, and she didn't want them to miss out, she had no other option than to accept his solution to the problem.

'Fine. You go on ahead with Scarlett and I'll follow with Hope.' At least the moment wouldn't be totally ruined if she wasn't expected to snuggle up beside him. Sleigh rides in the snow were supposed to be fun and romantic and definitely not something to be shared with a soon-to-be ex-husband.

In contrast, Scarlett was only too eager to climb onto

the wooden frame with Lucas, and Freya was able to breathe a little easier once they'd begun their journey deep into the woods without her.

'Our turn next.' She gave Hope's hand a squeeze and exchanged cheesy grins with her as their ride arrived.

The figure leading the reindeer towards them was dressed in the bright red and blue, embroidered traditional costume of the area, adding to the wonder of it all. The reindeer was a magnificent beast, his harness the same colourful fabric of his master, and his majestic antlers dusted with snow. He was so awe-inspiring he could've stepped straight out of one of those sentimental movies her mum insisted on watching every year.

'Can I stroke him?' Hope whispered, bubbling with delight at meeting what she probably imagined was one of Father Christmas's faithful servants.

The handler nodded and gave them the go-ahead to get the most from this experience. Freya let Hope pet his muzzle first but she didn't get in the sleigh until she'd had her chance to touch the soft brown fur herself. It was the kind of quiet, contemplative moment that gave her a pang of regret she didn't have a child of her own to share it with. She often imagined what her baby would've looked like if it had survived, but it didn't matter how much she tortured herself—she would never know. The need to be a mother again had almost consumed her when she and Lucas had married, she had been so desperate to fill that hole in her heart. This guardianship was as close as she'd get when she'd been let down one too many times by those who'd promised to be there for her.

If her first fiancé hadn't run out on her when he'd found out she was pregnant at eighteen, she might never

have had the miscarriage. Although she would never
know the cause for sure, the stress of having to face
life as a single mother straight out of high school had
been overwhelming at the time and would surely have
contributed to the tragedy. It was only nursing and the
thought she might still become a parent someday, with
a man who actually loved her, that had got her through
her grief. To have history repeat itself and her husband
abandon her and that dream of motherhood had been
a bereavement all over again. She was reminded of it
every time she looked at him.

'Can he really fly?' Hope's excited chatter about the
reindeer was a welcome interruption to her journey
into self-pity but also a further reminder of everything
she'd lost and now would probably never experience.
She wouldn't be part of that parent and child club that
got to take part in those simple pleasures of storytelling
or leaving snacks out for Santa Claus and his magical
reindeer on Christmas Eve. Freya's parents had made
the whole time so special for her she'd always looked
forward to doing the same for her own children. As
though re-creating that world of make-believe would
somehow bring back the magic she'd lost along with
her precious baby on that cold December night. Now,
with that last hope taken from her, there seemed very
little reason for her to celebrate that time of year at all.

'Only on Christmas Eve, I'm afraid, and with the help
of very special fairy dust the elves add to their food.'
Freya stopped herself from sliding back too far into her
heartache for Hope's sake and took her seat for the big
adventure. Everything seemed a lot more fun when you
still believed in the magic.

The sleigh ride turned out to be a leisurely journey,

and though the temperature dropped the deeper they travelled into the woods, they remained toasty warm under the warm woollen blanket covering their laps.

A sudden flash of movement through the trees caused Hope to cry out, 'Look! It's Scarlett and Dr Lucas!'

Sure enough, every now and again she caught a glimpse of the other two members of the party, grinning and waving frantically at them as they passed on the other side of the track. She couldn't help but wave back with the same enthusiasm as the others. As long as Lucas didn't read anything more into it than her joining in the fun, they'd get through this. She hadn't forgiven him anything and doubted she ever would.

When they came to the end of the trail, the others, including Lucas and his tiny new sidekick, had formed a semicircle around the staff member nominated as event coordinator and were listening intently to his instructions.

'We have a few activities on offer for you today. If you would like to start at alternate stations and make your way around it will be easier for everyone to have their turn. You will find bathroom facilities in the small building behind us along with a seating area for anyone who finds they want a break or needs to get indoors to warm up. We have storytelling in the tepee tent, there are husky sleigh rides, snowmobiles for the more adventurous among us and, of course, the cookout over the campfire where you'll be able to fill your bellies.'

'I know which one I'm looking forward to.' Lucas managed to raise a few laughs from the adults, his easygoing nature making it easy for people to like him, but Freya didn't want to be one of them. She wanted to maintain an emotional detachment from him until this trip was over and she could really let loose about how she felt.

'Let me guess—we need to go in pairs?' She cursed herself for being so slow off the bus and putting herself in this position again.

'Is that going to be a problem?' He cocked his head to one side, the picture of innocence. Once upon a time that playfulness would've made her laugh, or swoon, but now that kind of teasing simply set her teeth on edge. They weren't friends, and they certainly weren't lovers entitled to flirt. It was deliberate goading.

'Do you want me to swap?' Gillian sidled up to her with the little boy she'd been tasked with minding clinging to her, and butted in on the conversation, her face a mask of concern.

'No, it wouldn't be fair on the kids to cause any upheaval now when we've all bonded. Honestly, it's no problem at all,' Freya reassured her friend, even though they all knew that being tied to her ex for the rest of this weekend was going to test her patience severely.

Lucas had never intended to be so actively involved when he'd assumed this role. He'd simply volunteered as a favour to his colleague with the added bonus of boosting his profile again and showing any doubters he was still the same doctor he'd been before his illness had stripped him of everything. That was before he'd discovered his ex-wife was part of the medical team.

He could easily have switched with someone else then, just as he could've swapped with one of the volunteers now, or gone on ahead and let her catch up, but he hadn't been able to resist the chance to spend some time with her again when presented with the opportunity. It was the same fascination and wanting her company he'd had when he'd first laid eyes on her and he'd made any excuse to see her inside and outside work.

It had been tough enough convincing himself he no longer loved Freya when they'd been separated but it was nigh on impossible having seen her again. These past months he'd had his legion of demons to keep him company but now he was free, he realised how much he missed being with Freya. That notion of completely severing all ties now seemed like extra punishment rather than a new beginning.

He'd kept himself busy, trying to reclaim his life and focusing on work, but she'd been very much a part of that life and it was difficult to let go. Especially when the woman he loved wasn't even attempting to disguise her contempt for him. He couldn't blame her when to all intents and purposes he'd walked out of their marriage without a second glance. She wasn't to know he'd spent the best part of a year simply trying to survive the trauma of his past or that her determination to start a family as soon as possible had terrified him. His fear about becoming his father had robbed her of a chance at motherhood too.

It was only now, seeing that haunted expression in her eyes every time she looked at him, he realised she'd suffered as he had. She needed to enjoy this trip as much as the children and rediscover some of that innocence he'd stolen from her, and she couldn't do that when he was here, reminding her what he'd done. He wanted to make amends so she could leave all of that obvious anger and hurt behind and enjoy the rest of her life without any bitterness holding her back. If she would let him close enough to explain the reason behind his departure she might learn to forgive him, even if he'd made it impossible for her to love him again.

'So, Scarlett, where do you want to start?' His little pink-cheeked companion was waiting patiently by his side for more adventures and he wasn't about to discard his responsibilities in the pursuit of salvaging his conscience.

'Can we do that?' She pointed towards the hill of snow where the wooden toboggans were perched, waiting for passengers.

'I think we can manage that, can't we, Freya?' There was less of a queue for the more traditional idea of fun compared to the exciting husky rides and the snowmobiles. He was glad they wouldn't have much of an audience when sledding would be a first for him too. At least it would break them all in gently before the more adventurous pursuits began.

Freya eyed the small hill, and him warily, her arched eyebrow disappearing beneath her cream woolly bobble hat. She was equally as cute in her layers of thermal outerwear as she'd been in her sexy elf costume but she was definitely still rebelling against the notion of being in close proximity to him.

'Do I have a choice?' she muttered, for his benefit alone, as the girls ran ahead as fast as their little legs could wade through the deep snow.

'Always.' He might want her to give him the time of day but he wouldn't force her to be with him if the idea was so distasteful.

'Really?' She didn't have to say any more than that for him to realise he hadn't actually given her a choice when it came to ending their marriage but she didn't wait for him to apologise for it. He knew her reluctance was nothing to do with the activity and everything to do with him but apparently she'd decided to see this through regardless of his presence since she was off, trudging up the hill behind the girls.

Once they were all at the top of the hill they separated into pairs again, having deemed it safer for them to accompany the girls rather than let them sled on their own. The air was colder up here and even the inside of his nose felt as though it was beginning to freeze. He didn't want the girls exposed to the elements any more than necessary.

'How about a race?' It seemed a straightforward run down the hill, no obstacles, trees or dips to worry about, so even the most inexperienced riders could manage the route with relative ease.

'Yay!' Scarlett and Hope were jumping up and down so vigorously he had to quieten them down again in case the excitement became too much for either of them.

Freya didn't fight him on this one, probably because her nose was getting redder by the second too and this was the quickest way back down the hill. They took the reins in their respective toboggans with the girls tucked securely in front and the bags containing their medication stowed safely with them.

'On your marks…'

'Get set…'

'Go!' the four of them chorused as they tipped over the brow of the hill.

The wind whipped at his face as they sped into the snowy abyss but he barely noticed, lost in the exhilaration of it all and being that carefree kid he'd never been before. The shrieks of laughter around him only added to the enjoyment, with even the sound of his own echoing back at him from the forest.

He couldn't say which of them finished first because for him it had become more about that sense of pure freedom of speeding down the hill rather than the race itself.

'That was amazing!' There was a moment when Freya was actually smiling at him as they came to rest, her face glowing with excitement in a brief unguarded moment, making him yearn for more. It brought back memories of their early dates, having fun together when they hadn't had a care in the world. He wanted her to look at him the way she used to, without that constant suspicion.

'It reminds me of the time we did that obstacle race for charity. Do you remember? We slid the whole way to the bottom of the hill in the pouring rain.' They'd laughed the whole way down and Freya's gung-ho attitude to the whole course had impressed him. He'd fallen in love with her that day as she'd tackled rope ladders and crawled under tarpaulins with a grin on her face and dirt in her hair. Her *joie de vivre* had been irresistible and he'd known then he didn't want to be without her. He still didn't.

'I've never seen so much mud in my life.' Her sweet laugh was almost as much of a surprise now as it had been then. Even though she'd been covered from head to toe she'd found only humour in the situation, which had made her utterly adorable.

'And they wouldn't let us on the bus back until we'd been hosed down.' There was another part to that story that wasn't suitable for present company but he saw the rush of blood to her cheeks and knew she was also thinking of the steamy shower they'd taken together later at his place afterwards.

'At least we'll stay nice and dry today.' She got out of the toboggan and dusted down her clothes, the moment over.

'I can't believe we've never done that before.' He helped the girls back to their feet, wondering how different things could've been between him and Freya. There was a reason they'd never gone sledding or done any of this fun festive stuff together. He'd been too caught up in his past to make new, more pleasant memories associated with the season. If anything, he'd gone on to make matters worse. He'd left her at Christmas and he could see the very second she remembered it too as she turned away from him, back towards their two charges, who were tossing handfuls of ploughed snow at each other.

'Hands up who wants to go get some hot chocolate.'

'Me!' Gloves and voices shot up into the air at once, including Lucas's. He could do with a little warmth when the atmosphere between the adults was becoming frostier by the second.

They trekked back towards the others, where he did a quick check to make sure the activity hadn't had any impact on Hope's blood-sugar level before they had their warm drinks and hot dogs. He was making a note of everything she ate and drank today so they could adjust her insulin accordingly later.

Once he'd had his fill, Lucas left them keeping warm by the fire so he could check on the others. When he was satisfied there were no medical emergencies and everyone else was enjoying their day, he made it back in time for toasting marshmallows over the fire.

'Here, you can help.' Freya handed him two of the wooden sticks with marshmallows skewered on the end. Even though he knew it was to save the girls from getting their hands too close to the open fire, he wanted to see it as a truce of sorts where she no longer saw him as the enemy.

'How do you know when they're done?' he asked, holding the sticks tentatively over the fire as the heat seared through his gloves.

When there was no answer forthcoming, he looked up to see Freya tilt her head to one side, amusement dancing with the reflection of the flickering flames in her eyes. 'Are you serious?'

'I just want to make sure I get it right for the girls,' he said with a huff.

This was beyond the realms of his usual out-of-hours leisure pursuits, not that he had many these days. Sledding or toasting marshmallows hadn't been part of his childhood reality or on any syllabus when he'd had his head buried in medical books to escape the horrors of it. He certainly hadn't much call, or want, to do it since.

'You just want a light golden colour. Don't let it burn and make sure they're cooled down enough before you try to eat them.' She stopped teasing and seemed to thaw a little towards him as she coaxed him through the basic skills of marshmallow toasting.

Perhaps it was her caring nature that made her willing to help him out but he wanted to believe it was because she could see he was still the old Lucas at heart. The one who'd never meant to hurt her. The one she used to love. He longed for them both to break free from the memory of that broken man he'd become at the end of their marriage.

'These are really good.' Along with the others he tucked into the gooey white molten goodness with gusto and did his best to lick off the sticky sweetness coating his lips so he didn't waste a morsel or a second of this experience. This could be the last time she let him this close to her again.

'You missed a bit.' She pulled off her mitten and brushed the corner of his mouth with the soft pad of her thumb.

It was an innocent gesture but the moment she touched him his whole body sparked to life, every nerve ending tingling with awareness. As though he'd been dormant for too long, a soulless creature waiting for her to initiate that contact, that bolt of electricity, to awaken him from his slumber.

'Thanks.' He locked his eyes on hers and he saw a brief flare of desire before she blinked it away. They might only have been married a short while but he knew his wife well enough to recognise that look. It was the same flicker of interest he'd found so hard to resist when they'd first started working together and he still didn't want to. He could see that same internal fight against it in her eyes too and hope flared in his chest along with desire.

The most he thought he could ask from her was forgiveness so he could start his new life over, never imagining the one good thing from his past might still be available to him. He'd simply accepted that he'd hurt her too much to ever go back. If she did still harbour feelings for him somewhere beyond that tough shell she'd cocooned herself in, it conflicted more than ever with his original plan for a permanent split. It brought them straight back to square one, where he knew walking away was best for her but when the time came would inflict more suffering on them both.

'They're very messy girls, aren't they?' She fussed around the girls, wiping their mouths and hands in what he figured was an attempt to undermine the significance of the moment they'd had. It didn't work when he could see how flustered she was and she could barely look in his direction. She'd never been very good at disguising her feelings for him, which was what had made him break his rule about dating work colleagues in the first place.

'We'll have to do that again over the weekend.' He wasn't just talking about the sweet treat. If they went back to Scotland without resolving what had happened they'd both be doomed to wallow in their misery for the rest of their days. They needed another moment together; a chance to reconnect properly where he could make amends and finally give them the closure they needed.

'I doubt we'll find the time.' Freya didn't know if he meant toasting marshmallows, talking about their early days together, or another brief moment when she forgot everything except how much she wished they were still together, but all of those scenarios were too dangerous to repeat.

When he was joining in with the kids, doing things he'd apparently never done before, it was too easy to forget they'd been apart for so long. The sight of him so youthful, so carefree took her back to the time when they'd enjoyed each other's company to the exclusion of everything else. It was painful to watch at times when she was no closer to understanding what had brought the sudden change in him and turned him into the distant man who'd eventually walked out on her.

Perhaps she should've confronted him the second she'd heard about his reappearance back into society but she'd worried it might just tip her over the edge of sanity. She'd barely held it together after realising he wasn't coming back to her but she'd also been afraid the sight of him again would prove too painful, that her feelings for him would remain the same despite what he'd done. She'd been afraid of this.

It was vital for her well-being to focus on everything his betrayal had cost her—her marriage, her trust and her chance of baby-filled happiness—instead of attraction and naivety, which had blinded her to danger too often. The only thing she needed from him was a reason for destroying the life she'd planned for them, and nothing more.

She moved the girls on towards the storyteller in the tent so they were safely back in company. With his wooden staff and flowing purple robes he could've been some mystical shaman from the Middle Ages, but the girls were more fascinated than afraid. They edged ever closer to listen to his Christmas tales, leaving the adults in the cold, and she could see Lucas glancing back at the campfire, and most likely the marshmallows, with longing.

'Have you honestly never done any of this sort of thing before? Not even at school?' Freya couldn't quite get her head around the notion a grown man hadn't experienced any of these basic pleasures in life. She knew he'd struggled with her idea of fun at Christmas but he'd never opened up to tell her why. Every time she'd tried to ask him what it was that troubled him so much about it, he'd shut down the conversation and pushed her away. Until living under the same roof had become unbearable.

'Nope.' He still wasn't giving anything away and made her want to shake the information out of him. She'd only ever wanted to understand him and it hurt that he'd never been able to trust her with the sort of personal information a wife should've known—the history of ex-loves and family and all of those experiences that formed a person.

Of course, she hadn't been able to share some important events in her own life but that was because she'd tried to bury them in order to create a future with him. Lucas had given little information about himself and she wasn't convinced it had been in order to benefit their relationship.

Looking back, anytime she'd enquired about his life pre-medical school he'd always distracted her with a kiss, or more. Infatuated as she had been, she had always given in to temptation instead of pushing the subject. Later, towards the end of their relationship, he hadn't bothered to employ any such tactics and had simply refused to answer any questions, that ever-present scowl declaring the matter off limits.

It rankled now that she'd been too blinded by love to see the obvious flaws in their marriage when he'd insisted on erecting that barrier. She'd been so desperate to create the perfect family she'd ignored the first signs of discord and had ploughed ahead with her obsession for a child at all costs. Her blinkered naivety and his insular behaviour had ensured they would never have succeeded as a couple. Yet, even though he was still refusing to be drawn on his personal history, there was something different about him. That willingness to participate in activities beyond his comfort zone had been distinctly lacking during their last time together and her temper was rising at the injustice of it all.

'So what's changed?' Her blunt questioning was directly in line with her sudden desire to uncover the facts. This new Lucas was embracing all the clichés he'd professed to despise when they'd been together and she'd been the one to bear the brunt of his dark moods because of it. It was only natural she should want to know who, or what, had brought about this new attitude. Even if the thought of someone taking her place, sharing a deeper bond with her husband than she apparently had, made her want to weep. At the time she would've done anything to save her marriage, if only she'd been given the chance.

'I came here for the kids. Every child deserves at least one happy time in their lives to look back on.' As a round of applause sounded for the storyteller Lucas bent down to receive a running hug from the returning Scarlett and Hope. There was such a haunted expression on his face it reached that mothering instinct deep inside her and she had to catch the sob in her throat before she embarrassed them all.

It occurred to her then that his own upbringing remained somewhat of a mystery to her. His mother had left home when he was very little, and he had no siblings—he'd revealed that much in the early days, when they'd been getting to know each other—but when it had come to mention of his father, he'd changed the subject, or distracted her, every time. When Lucas had refused to even invite him to their

wedding she'd just assumed it had been a strained relationship. Watching him interact with the children
now and replaying his words made her question what
kind of childhood he'd actually had.

It was a sobering thought to realise she'd never
really known who her husband was beyond the man
he'd become. Even more so to discover she still wanted
to find out.

CHAPTER THREE

FREYA WAS NUMB and not just from the wind and ice sprayed in her face after they'd travelled the snowy plains at high speed on the snowmobiles. Her smile was frozen on for the girls' sakes, but though she was saying and doing all the right things so they didn't know anything was amiss, her head and heart were scrambled, trying to come to terms with a very different Lucas from the last one she'd seen.

He certainly seemed keen to remind her about the good times they'd had together, sending her emotions into a dizzying jumble as she tried to protect herself by recalling those agonising last days of their marriage. When he was smiling at her or playing with the children it was easy to forget they were no longer together. Unless he'd had that chip on his shoulder surgically removed she didn't know what had caused the change in him, which made his past behaviour seem even more erratic in comparison. Despite the nights she'd spent cursing the man's name she found herself clinging to the hope there was something behind it other than being single again. If she had more information to explain the state of his mind then and now she might be able to look back on these past months in a completely different light.

There'd been that one moment when he'd opened the door to his past and let her have the briefest glimpse inside. Unfortunately, she'd been shut out from gathering any more info of a personal nature once he'd thrown himself back into his role of medical supervisor and children's entertainer as they'd continued their day of adventure.

'What did you think was the most fun today?' he asked everybody as they piled on the bus at the end of the day.

'The huskies.'

'Tobogganing.'

'Building snowmen.'

Everyone clearly had their own favourite activity of the day but they all had that same joyful expression as they animatedly swapped stories of their adventures. Apart from Scarlett, who was asleep on Lucas's shoulder, and Hope, who was gently snoring in the seat next to Freya. Exhaustion had finally claimed them. She didn't know if he was using the sleeping child as some sort of buffer to keep her away as he made his way down the stationary bus to his seat but he didn't appear to be in a hurry to discard the little girl dribbling over his shoulder. He'd always had a special rapport with the kids he treated. He was very comfortable in their company and never, ever talked down to them. It was one of the many reasons patients and families loved him and one of the reasons she'd known he would've made a wonderful father.

'What about you, Dr Lucas? What was your favourite thing?' One of the children turned the question back on him and Freya watched and listened for the reply as intently as the tiny interviewer.

She hadn't managed to coax him into enjoying any of the family Christmas traditions she'd been so keen to uphold but she'd seen a whole new side to him today. He'd really thrown himself into the part of Santa's little helper but she couldn't help but wonder if it had been solely for the children's benefit. After all, he'd proved to be a good actor before when she'd believed they had been happily married, only to have him leave her at the worst possible time of the year.

'Um… I have to say it was toasting marshmallows over the fire.' He caught her eye for a split second and the heat of that moment warmed her chilled bones as she recalled that moment when she'd touched him again.

A few days ago, if someone had told her she'd meet up with her ex-husband the only physical contact she would've imagined making had been a swift kick somewhere delicate as payback for the hurt he'd caused her. Not tenderly brushing melted marshmallow from his lips as though they were still together with that spark between them very much alive. She didn't enjoy that hitch in her breath as they connected over the heads of the children filing past because it drew attention to those lingering feelings she apparently still had for him. After everything he'd done and the time they'd had apart, he shouldn't be able to have any effect on her other than the need to hate him. More than that, it left her open for more pain from someone who clearly hadn't loved her enough to stay with her.

Curiosity and a need to salve her own conscience over the end of their marriage might be pushing her towards him for more answers but she'd have to remain wary of getting too close. She wouldn't survive falling for him a second time.

Roll on tomorrow when they were on a plane back to reality and their now very separate lives.

The duo of snow-dusted log cabins welcoming them home for the night was a Christmas card come to life. The orange glow spilling out from the windows into the dark night definitely made Freya want to kick off her boots at the door and take a place by the fireplace inside. Which was exactly what she would do when the children had been fed, the necessary medication administered and everyone readied for bed.

'Thank goodness they got caterers in. That's all I can say.' Freya handed the last plate to Lucas to dry and drained the soapy water out of the sink.

'I know. I'm shattered.' Gillian opened the cupboards to put away the now clean dishes as their efficient production line rid all traces of the group dinner. The hot buffet provided by the hotel to the larger cabin on their return had saved them a lot of extra work but the trio had volunteered for washing-up duty once everyone had taken their fill.

'There wasn't much left over, which means we don't have to worry about any picky eaters not getting enough nutrition. I think everyone worked up quite an appetite out there today.' Lucas folded the tea towel and set it neatly on the counter. He'd always been tidy and not one of those men who insisted on leaving wet towels on the floor or a general trail of mess behind him. With more than a hint of sadness Freya realised he'd never expected her to pick up after him as though she were some sort of replacement parent, had never needed her to look after him. The single life probably suited him better than marriage.

'Now we just have to entertain them for a while until they're finally worn out,' Gillian said with the waning enthusiasm of someone whose energy had deserted her before the evening programme.

'There are a stack of board games for those who want to play, and I have a Christmas CD for a good old sing-along before bed.' It was coming to that time of the evening when they were going to split into their gender-specific groups for bedtime and, tired though she was, Freya wasn't ready for the day to be over. There'd been a truce of sorts between her and Lucas but she couldn't promise tomorrow would be the same once she'd had the night to dwell on events.

'I brought some things that might help pass the time too.' Lucas cleared his throat, and though it wasn't a surprise he'd be opposed to the singing idea, she and Gillian were stunned into silence with the idea he'd come up with an alternative.

'If you can get everybody assembled around the table, I'll pop over to the other cabin to grab my supplies.' Without giving them a chance to quiz him about what exactly he had in mind, he disappeared into the night and left them no choice but to follow his instruction.

As they gathered the group together, Freya had some reservations about whether or not he was going to deliver something to match the kids' excitement. Or if he would even come back at all. Her residual trust issues were sufficient that she was only able to relax when he kept his word and did eventually return, carrying supplies.

'Arts and crafts?' she enquired as he unloaded packages onto the table.

'A little something I made earlier.' He looked so pleased with himself it was impossible not to trust he might have something pretty cool up his sleeve after all.

'Gingerbread men?' Gillian was the first to inspect the pre-cut cardboard shapes, her discovery drawing Freya's attention sharply.

'I thought we could have some fun decorating them.' Sure enough, he provided glue sticks and coloured felt pens to everyone waiting eagerly around the table. Bright buttons and tubes of glitter soon followed, along with a selection of googly eyes to add some personality to the 2D characters.

'What a great idea.' Such a great idea, Gillian was soon abandoning Freya to get stuck in herself.

'It really was very thoughtful of you.' She had to acknowledge what he'd done when there was so much meaning to her personally behind the ordinarily simple gesture.

Not only did this signify he'd thought ahead for the children, disproving her earlier theory that this change in him could be an act, but perhaps also showing an attempt to make up for snubbing the activity last Christmas. He would've known how much this one small act of kindness would mean to her and damn it if the sight of naked gingerbread men and buttons didn't bring a tear to her eye.

'I know it's not the same as decorating freshly baked gingerbread but I thought this was something we could all enjoy instead of leaving out anyone with special dietary requirements. I'm sorry you missed out last year.' He left her in no doubt that he'd been thinking about her as much as the children before going to lend a helping hand to those who couldn't quite manage on their own.

Freya was mesmerised by the picture of him in the middle of the children, concentrating on producing a smiling symbol of everything he'd once despised. It was both heart-warming and heartbreaking to watch when it was all she'd ever wanted for him as much as for herself. They might've been doing this with children of their own if they'd stuck things out a little longer, but they would never know for sure and it certainly wouldn't help her sanity to keep imagining the family that didn't exist.

Lucas glanced up and caught her watching him, but instead of looking away, embarrassed by the attention, he held her gaze and offered a poignant half-smile in return. The regret over what they'd lost was there in his sad blue eyes as much as it was in her flip-flopping stomach. Perhaps if they'd worked harder on their marriage they could've eventually found this level of contentment together.

'Can I have a drink? I'm really thirsty.' Hope tugged on Freya's jumper and helped break the meaningful eye contact that was already putting her in danger of falling for Lucas's charm offensive a second time.

One day back in his company and she was already in turmoil. Another twenty-four hours and she dreaded to think what more havoc he might wreak on her bewildered heart.

'Sure. Have you finished colouring?' Freya ushered the more deserving cause for her attention towards the kitchen area to pour her a glass of water.

'Uh-huh. I'm going to take it home for my mummy. I don't feel well.'

Freya knelt down to take a closer look at the little girl. 'You are a little pale. We should go and check your blood sugar, sweetheart, just to make sure you're okay.'

'I want to go to bed,' Hope whined, at the prospect of the finger-prick test, but it really was important they check her levels before they let her sleep.

It had been a long day and there was always a risk of hyperglycaemia with the increased physical activity and change in routine for her. If left untreated, high blood sugar could lead to a medical emergency—ketoacidosis, a lack of insulin, or dehydration. Her sudden thirst and tiredness were symptoms Freya would not take a risk of ignoring.

'I know, and you will, as soon as we do a quick test.' She took Hope's hand and ushered her towards the door, stopping briefly to have a quiet word with Lucas on the way.

'Could you please keep Hope's gingerbread man safe for her? She's feeling quite thirsty all of a sudden, and tired.' There was no need to panic the others but it was enough information to galvanise the medical lead on this trip.

As she led Hope towards the dorm she could hear Lucas making arrangements for someone else to watch over Scarlett and making his excuses to leave.

Freya helped Hope get ready for bed, made sure her hands were clean and the BM machine was calibrated before she attempted to draw a sample of blood.

'I'm just going to check your blood-sugar level to calculate how much insulin I might need to give you to make sure you feel better. This will be all over in a second.' Even though she went through this every day, it was important Freya reminded her whimpering patient what she was doing and why they were doing it as she pricked her finger.

'You are such a brave girl. I'm sure Father Christmas is going to have a special present for you tomorrow.'

Freya squeezed the tip of her finger until there was enough blood to drip onto the testing strip.

'Are you done yet?' Hope squirmed on the bed next to her as Freya inserted the test strip into the handheld device for analysis.

'Almost. I just need you to hold this on your finger for me.' Freya pressed a cotton ball onto the skin to prevent further bleeding while she disposed of the lancet into the sharps bin.

Unfortunately, the results were, as she suspected, high enough to give cause for concern.

'Knock. Knock.' Lucas gave a courtesy tap on the door before he walked in anyway.

'Hey.' Freya handed him the blood analysis and shifted on the bed to make room for him. After all, he was the doctor in charge and not merely the man she was afraid of being too close to again.

She saw the clench of his teeth with the unfavourable result but he quickly resumed his perfect bedside manner for the little girl trying to burrow down under her bed sheets.

'I know you're tired and out of sorts, Hope, but you know we only want to keep you safe. Right?'

She nodded solemnly.

'Good girl. We can't let you sleep just yet but... I did bring a very special book to read to you before bedtime.' He produced a colourful, sparkly hardboard book from his medical bag, along with her notes and her insulin.

Freya tried to sneak a glance at the title—something about a very forgetful elf—as she tidied away Hope's discarded clothes and tried to suppress a grin. He really had planned ahead.

She folded the small pair of waterproof trousers over her arm, only for a torrent of half-eaten food and sweet wrappers to fall from the pockets onto the floor.

'What on earth—?'

Both adults stared at the evidence of a serious food binge before turning to the tiny culprit currently hugging her knees on the bed.

'Hope? Did you eat all this extra food when we weren't looking?' Lucas kept his voice soft enough not to spook Hope any further while Freya collected the remnants of Hope's ill-gotten gains from the floor. Some of the food had obviously been pocketed from the buffet at dinner but the chocolate-bar wrappers looked suspiciously like the ones she'd seen some of the other children with earlier.

Hope hugged her knees tighter and hid her face with her hair.

'You're not in trouble. We just need to know if that's what's making your poorly.' Freya threw the rubbish in the bin. She'd take it with her to dispose of later so as not to leave further temptation behind.

There was an almost imperceptible nod and Freya brushed the child's hair from her eyes so they could see her properly. Hope nodded again.

'Thank you for telling us. It's very important we know what you've eaten today so we can work out what medicine to give you.' Lucas remained very calm, even though he must've been as concerned as Freya to discover the extra food consumption, which meant they would have to adjust the dose of insulin to be administered. By not overreacting to this slip-up, it prevented Hope from getting further stressed, which wouldn't have helped matters.

They were going to be in for a long night of monitoring her condition to make sure no medical emergency arose as a result of her little rebellion. It was only natural a child would want to help themselves to sweets and treats they weren't usually allowed but in Hope's case it could cause much more than a stomach ache. They had to point out the importance of sticking to the rules without scaring her too much.

Lecture over, Lucas afforded Freya another moment of his attention. 'I can stay here with Hope through the night if you'd like. I'll give her her insulin and I'm happy to pull up a chair for the night if you want to see to Scarlett. We have a book to read anyway, don't we, Hope?' Lucas distracted Hope away from the night ahead of blood tests and injections with the shiny promise of his one-to-one attention. He'd honed that diversionary skill to perfection but at least he was using it for the greater good on this occasion.

'Are you sure?' She knew they couldn't both stay here when they had the responsibility of Scarlett's condition and medication to supervise too, but she hadn't expected such a display of magnanimity from him.

'Of course. You get some sleep and I'll see you in the morning.'

Freya stepped out of the bedroom and took a deep, shaky breath to recover some of the composure she was threatening to lose as he started reading to his captivated audience. This warm, caring side of him was exactly why she'd fallen in love with him. It was lovely to see this grown man relaxed and giving his time to comfort a child, but it also made her wonder why he hadn't been able to extend that compassion to her for the duration of their marriage.

Freya woke early and, after checking on the girls, made her way into the kitchen to make a cup of coffee. She'd been so physically and mentally drained she'd fallen asleep in her clothes but it hadn't been a peaceful slumber by any means. Her thoughts had been with her husband in the other room; dreams of the perfect Christmas they should've had together and memories of the painful reality. Most disturbing of all had been the erotic nature their reunion had taken in her subconscious until she'd woken, breathless and a tad frustrated. At least she'd managed to resist tucking a blanket around him as an excuse to touch the real version when she'd peeked into the room and found him sleeping in one of the hard kitchen chairs.

She poured herself a strong shot of caffeine and carried it into the lounge area. It was still dark outside but she was comforted by the sound of the fire still crackling in the hearth. Without the trappings of modern life out here in the wilds and the constant hum of technology around her there was a peacefulness she'd usually welcome before the start of what could prove to be another long day. She pulled the warm wool blanket off the sofa and tucked it around her feet, sipped her drink and watched the flames flicker in the fireplace but she just couldn't seem to relax. It was only when Lucas walked into the room that she realised it was because she'd been on tenterhooks, waiting to see him again.

This was more than anxiety creeping through her body at the prospect of finally finding out what had prompted their separation in the first place. She found she was actually looking forward to being in his company again. Regardless of how things had ended between them, switching her feelings off for him hadn't been as straightforward as she'd imagined.

Even now her pulse fluttered as he walked into the living room the same way it used to when they'd crossed paths at work. When she had been unable to help the attraction to him but had known it was trouble waiting to happen. Some things never changed.

There was a moment as he walked into the open-plan dining room/living room when he seemed to be looking for someone, or something. Vanity and that unwavering ache in her heart wanted it to be her.

'Oh...er...hi. You're up early.' He did a double take as he spotted her on the sofa and his relaxed smile when he saw her appeared to prove her fancy correct.

'Sorry—did I wake you? I was trying to be quiet.'

'Not at all. I smelt the coffee.' He sniffed the air, hot on the scent of his same beverage of choice.

'There's plenty in the pot.' She pointed him in the right direction while she took a moment to appreciate his rumpled clothes and tousled hair. It was doubtful he'd had any more of a restful sleep than she had but he looked good on it. *Damn him.*

'How's Scarlett?' He came to sit with her and it took a second for the implication of that to sink in. They were going to spend more enforced time together, alone and uninterrupted. As much as they probably needed to, the prospect made her wish she'd had a nip of whisky in her coffee to fortify her for the inevitable rehashing of events.

'She was fast asleep in seconds. No problems at all.' It was the truth, even if she felt a little guilty about probably having an easier night than he'd had.

'Good. Good. Hope's last blood-sugar check was normal, so she was able to get some rest in the end too.'

Now that they'd established both of their patients were healthy and safe, tense anticipation seemed to fill the sudden conversational void between them. There was never going to be a better opportunity for them this weekend to work out their issues in private, if either of them were ready for it.

Although if his apparent disregard for her feelings had remained unchanged from their last days together, she doubted he'd have come down and risked spending time alone with her. He knew her well enough to know she'd want answers now more than ever.

As torturous as this would be, she needed to understand the reasons behind the failure of the relationship so she could either learn from her mistakes or point the finger of blame somewhere other than at the mirror. There was no point in letting this fester and spoil another Christmas for both of them.

Any other man probably should've been cringing at the idea of having an in-depth conversation with his ex about what had led to their break-up. Not least because of her initial, understandable reaction to seeing him on the plane for the first time. Instead, Lucas had found himself restlessly wishing the night away so he could finally clear the air with Freya.

He knew they'd had a breakthrough in their frosty

relationship with her apparent acceptance of his apology and their prolonged eye contact over his craft project. Hope suddenly taking ill had been the much-needed antidote to letting Freya get too far into his system again, though he'd have preferred a less stressful alternative for all of their sakes. Now they were alone together there was so much he needed to say to her, he didn't know where to begin.

He drained his still-hot coffee, taking the top layer of skin from the roof of his mouth, and walked over to rinse his cup in the sink, stalling for time in the hope appropriate words would somehow form in his mouth during the short trip back to his seat.

'They did a good job with the decorations, didn't they?' He flicked one of the silver baubles carefully hung on the tree in the corner of the room.

Freya nodded. 'It looks lovely. Very well-coordinated.'

She was being very diplomatic in the face of his epic procrastination. He knew her taste ran more towards colourful and as gaudy as possible. The twinkling white fairy lights and fragile decorations strung around the real Christmas tree were very pretty but a far cry from her eclectic collection of tat, which leaned more towards sentimentality than any aesthetic purpose. He'd heard her call this kind of sparse display as cold and clinical before and it wouldn't fit in with her penchant for chubby sugar plum fairies and handmade ornaments she hoarded from local craft fairs.

'I imagine it's a dream come true for you too, being in the midst of all this.' He gestured towards the garlands and stockings adorning the fireplace, which were more homely and in keeping with her style of storybook decor.

She shrugged her shoulders. 'Once upon a time it would've been. I'm finding it doesn't quite hold the same appeal for me any more.'

There was no need for her to point the finger of blame at him for that; the weight of guilt was already crushing him at the apathy she'd apparently developed towards the season. The disease that was his father had claimed another victim and he was sick to the stomach he'd been an accessory to the murder of her Christmas spirit.

'I'm sorry to hear that. You were always so…involved.' He'd never intended to take that childlike enthusiasm away from her. She'd always been so full of life, full of fun, he'd never imagined he would've been capable of draining that out of her. There were a lot of things he hadn't thought through properly during that period, his mind so twisted with rage and grief. It was only now that black cloud had dissipated he was starting to see things more clearly and realise what he'd lost in the process.

'I know you hated all of the fuss. Well, you'll be pleased to know I've cut back considerably on my tinsel addiction since then.' She made an attempt at humour but Lucas didn't find anything remotely funny in what she was telling him. It had irritated him when he'd been expected to live in Santa's grotto day after day for an entire month but that didn't mean he was happy to find he might have made her as cynical as he was about the season.

'I guess I just didn't understand it. We didn't really go in for the whole magical fairy-tale scene in our house.' That almost made him snort out loud at the thought of his inebriated father thinking of anything other than his next drink. There had been no stockings hung by the fire or milk and cookies left out for Santa. He'd been lucky if there had been any food in the house at all. It was difficult to get caught up in the wonder of it all as an adult when he hadn't experienced it as a child.

'That's a shame. Some of my best childhood memories are of Christmas, even if recent ones have proved more painful.' She left him in no doubt he was the reason she didn't feel like celebrating any more. It hadn't been a calculated move and it was typical that his father had managed to cause maximum damage with optimum timing.

'I never meant to hurt you. I just—'

'Couldn't do it any more? You said. It didn't make it any easier for me, though. I couldn't eat, couldn't sleep. I couldn't even tell my parents you'd left me for the longest time. I didn't know for sure that's what had happened until I'd exhausted all other possibilities and I got word you'd taken leave from the hospital. You didn't even take your clothes. They're still hanging in the wardrobe. Were you that desperate to get away from me, Lucas?' It was the little hiccup catching his name that finally smashed through his defences and forced him to face up to what he'd done.

'It wasn't like that, Freya.' It was all he could offer to soothe her from a distance without ripping his chest open and letting the trapped crows of his personal anguish beat their wings in flight.

'I suppose it's done now. A broken heart can't ever be truly mended, can it? Slapped back together and held together with sticky tape maybe, so a person can keep on living even though there are days she doesn't want to, but not *fixed*.'

He could hear the irreparable damage he'd left in his

wake in her clipped words. Perhaps he wasn't so different from his father after all. In an attempt to avoid becoming a clone of the man who'd ruined his life by walking away, he'd done the complete opposite. He could hear that pain reflected in every word and hitch in her breath and he didn't want to burden her with any more misery than he already had.

'I honestly thought you'd be better off without me.'

'Why? What did I do to make you think that? Where did you go? Why didn't you let me know you weren't dead?' She launched a volley of questions at him that she'd probably been saving for months.

He couldn't answer any of them without making things worse and adding more to his guilt quota. It had never occurred to him that she might've believed him dead, only that he'd failed her. 'I went to Peter's—'

'Peter? Your best man? The guy who swore he didn't know where you were when I was sobbing down the phone?' She wasn't the only one he'd ticked off with that stunt. Peter hadn't spoken to him the rest of the day after that one.

'I made him lie to you. I needed space.' He tried to picture those early days, which had passed in a blur when he'd never made it out of bed, never said a word, yet Peter had insisted on bringing him food and water and keeping him in the land of the living.

The heart-wrenching gasp he pulled from her chest told of the devastation he'd caused by not letting that person be her, but he hadn't wanted her to see that image of him curled up in the foetal position, weeping like a babe.

'"In sickness and in health. Till death do us part." We made the vows, Lucas. I, for one, intended to keep them.' She was scolding him, yet she was so sincere he wanted to believe it would've been enough to get through it together. For the first time in his life, when he'd really needed someone to lean on, he'd had someone who would love him unconditionally and give him everything he'd ever wanted, pride had muscled its way in and robbed him of the gift. He'd been blind to that fact until she'd come back into his life and made him see what he was missing.

'I did too, at the time, but things change.'

'What things?' Freya threw up her hands and he knew that given half a chance she would have them around his throat. The only reason he was being so obtuse was the same one he'd used when he'd left her—to save her from the darkness that had claimed him. The least he could give her was the reassurance she'd in no way been at fault.

'Me. You know I wasn't the same man you met. Maybe I just wasn't cut out for marriage but that honestly wasn't a reflection of you. You've got a lot of Christmases ahead of you. Don't let what happened between us spoil them all for you.' He didn't want the legacy to continue. Someday she would have a family of her own and he didn't want to be responsible for ruining anyone else's childhood. That was exactly why he'd left their marriage when he'd been at his lowest point and had needed his wife more than ever. She'd deserved someone who wouldn't taint her rosy view of the world.

'I'm trying.' She made a mocking toast with her coffee before gulping it down as though it really had the special powers she'd always claimed.

It was a shame his word wasn't enough for her any

more but that was his own fault. He wouldn't be able to give her an adequate explanation without digging deep into his past, so he could only hope a strong woman like Freya wouldn't have her spirits dampened for long. Unlike him, she didn't tend to dwell on the negative aspects of life. At least, she hadn't in the past. A year apart had already changed her so much he wasn't sure he knew anything about her any more.

'What was the whole deal with the over-the-top festivities anyway? I've never seen anyone tinsel-bomb a house the way you did. I don't think there was an inch of that house devoid of glitter.' A month of cheesy festive tunes and barely being able to see the football on the TV because of the stuffed woodland animals strategically placed around it had bugged him no end. However, he couldn't imagine the house in December without all the palaver. It was simply one of her quirks, which anyone other than a miserable Grinch like him would've found adorable.

She took on that faraway look in her eyes she'd always had when it had come to her favourite time of the year and he was pleased that his Mrs Christmas Fairy, as he'd nicknamed her, hadn't totally lost her mojo.

'No matter how tough things were financially, Mum and Dad always made such a big deal of it. I don't ever remember feeling as though I was missing out because it was just such a warm, cosy feeling of us being together as a family. Sorry—you probably don't want to hear that.' She shook away that glimpse of the old Freya and replaced it with the jaded wife she'd become during his absence who was afraid to express her enjoyment of it all.

Had he really been the dark cloud hovering over the

holidays? He thought back to that Christmas together, when he'd frowned at her whimsy. Yes, he'd virtually beaten her into submission with his cynicism and that guilt wasn't going to be easy to live with any more than being the victim of someone else's rage.

'I wouldn't ever want to take that away from you. You're very lucky to have had such a wonderful family.' If he'd had a mum who'd stuck around or a father capable of loving his son, he knew he'd have an entirely different take on the subject. As it was, the only feelings he connected with any supposed family celebrations were ones of disappointment and fear. Not only had the needs and wishes of a little boy been frequently ignored in favour of the demon drink but it had inevitably led to an outburst of violent temper.

'You never told me anything about your father.' Freya pulled the heavy woollen blanket up towards her chin, cocooning herself in comfort, and he wondered if that was what Christmas had become for her—a comfort blanket she could wrap herself up in once a year. And he'd whipped it away, leaving her exposed to the harsh elements of reality. He sighed and nodded, resigned to the fact he'd have to go some way to sharing the gory details of his past if it would help her understand his actions and rediscover her joy.

'He wasn't worth talking about.' Lucas shrugged, wishing he had been able to dismiss all thoughts of him as easily as he made out. The reason he'd never wanted to discuss his father was because talking meant remembering and that hurt too damn much. He'd spent his adult life trying to block out all thoughts of that time. That hadn't worked out very well for him in the end when the suppressed emotions had all spectacularly erupted at once.

'Wasn't?' She picked up on that minute detail straight away.

In the time-honoured tradition of denial he could've pretended it was a slip of the tongue. It was even less of her business now that they were no longer together. Except if he ever hoped to start building bridges with Freya he knew it had to start with the truth. At least, as much of it he was comfortable sharing with her.

'He died. Last year. Just before Christmas.'

Lucas watched her facial expressions as she ran the gamut of emotions that information brought to the surface—shock, horror, sympathy, and finally the realisation of what that timing meant.

Suddenly he couldn't bear to watch any more. He didn't want to confront this here and now where they were doing their best to make childhood dreams come true, not relive old nightmares. This unburdening of his soul wasn't as liberating as he'd imagined when he could feel her gaze burrowing into his skin, willing him to give more of himself.

'You should have told me,' Freya said softly, reaching across to rest her hand on his knee, but that sympathy was exactly what he hadn't wanted from her. He'd no wish to see pity in her eyes every time she looked at him. He wanted her to see him as the strong man he'd been when they'd met and not the shell he'd become as a result of his father's reign of tyranny.

'It wouldn't have changed anything. I simply wasn't ready to settle down. I could've handled things differently, though, and I am sorry for the way things ended between us. Just know it wasn't because of anything you'd done. That's entirely on me. Don't forget that. Now, I think it's time for me to go check in with the boys and grab a couple of hours' sleep while I still can.' He got to his feet suddenly keen to reclaim that distance between them before he was pushed to dig for a deeper explanation. That panic was already rising in his chest with the mere mention of his dad and he didn't want to trigger the nightmares or the panic attacks by reliving the horror again. It needed to end here. All of it. Including whatever misguided notion his sleep-deprived mind had conjured up about trying to win Freya back.

The cold wind swirled in as Lucas opened the door, its icy fingers reaching in to grab Freya. Not even the blazing logs in the hearth could keep the chill from her bones and she huddled deeper into her blanket. Lucas's father had died and he hadn't told her. That said everything about the state their marriage had been in when he hadn't trusted her enough to confide in her and she'd never suspected he might've been grieving.

She knew what it was to mourn such a huge loss and how that sorrow was able to sneak up and steal your very breath in a moment of weakness. The searing raw pain was enough to make anyone want to walk away from it all and start over. That was exactly what she'd done by throwing herself into her nursing career when she'd lost her baby, never speaking of her little angel again. She hadn't even told Lucas because she'd never wanted him to think a baby of theirs would ever simply be to replace the one she'd lost. These secrets kept from one another had surely contributed to the break-down of their relationship.

The timing left her questioning if his erratic behaviour could've been attributed to grief as well as the apparent lack of communication in their marriage.

Unfortunately, Lucas had reverted to type and shut her out again.

She jumped up from the couch with her comforter wrapped around her and ran after him. He was already knee-deep in the snow between the two cabins by the time she opened the door. As she ran out onto the wooden porch with only her thermal socks on her feet, it wasn't long before they started to turn numb but she wasn't going to let him go a second time without being given the chance to say her piece.

'I would've been there if you'd let me, Lucas,' she shouted, her voice carrying easily across the still, pre-dawn air. Even though their relationship was over, it was important he know that.

It stopped him in his tracks and the words hung between them, crystallising along with the tears on her cheeks as she waited for his response—an acknowledgement that he knew he wasn't alone in the world.

She watched as his head slumped forward, could see the wisps of his breathy sigh take flight into the frozen skies. The snow crunched beneath his feet as he slowly turned to face her.

'I know,' he said with a trembling smile and the glint of tears in his eyes, but it didn't stop him from walking away again.

He might have finally opened up a fraction about what had been going on behind the scenes at that difficult period but it hadn't eased that empty ache in her chest for the husband she'd lost or the family she'd never have. This early morning confessional hadn't changed anything—her marriage was still over. She still wasn't enough to make him happy.

CHAPTER FOUR

'THERE'S PAPER AND colouring pencils for you to draw Santa a picture of what you would like for Christmas, or I could write the list for you if you want?' Lucas made sure Scarlett had everything she needed at hand to complete her task as she took her seat at the wooden counter with the others.

The post office in Santa's Village was a hub of activity as kids and adults alike sent postcards home to their families as souvenirs and penned notes to the man they'd all come to visit. Lucas had never written a letter to Santa in his life and he wasn't about to start as an adult, but he was happy to write a few words on the back of a picture postcard for Scarlett's family as a memento. The address would be in her emergency contact details.

He jotted down the details of what they'd done so far and that they were excited about seeing Santa—a lie on his part but he would be happy once it was all over and he could go home—and got Scarlett to scrawl her name on the bottom before he handed it to a post-office elf. A glance across the table confirmed Freya was still engrossed in helping Hope, reaching for the glitter glue and showing no signs of leaving anytime soon. The tiny specks of silver dust glistening on her cheeks and hands gave him hope she'd recaptured a tiny bit of her inner child on this trip.

He'd hardly been able to look at her today for the same reason he'd been unable to respond appropriately to her after baring his soul. He had been afraid he'd break again as emotions had begun to overwhelm him. Freya had been the one person in his life who'd loved him unconditionally and he'd let go of her anyway. Regret was steadily eroding what was left of his much-needed defences but it wouldn't be good for either of them to let those old feelings for one another resurface when he knew he'd never deserved her love and would only ever bring her more misery.

The pile of picturesque postcards caught his eye, in particular the image of the forest at night with the Northern Lights casting an eerie green glow over the snowscape. It made him immediately think of Freya. She'd always talked with such reverence about seeing the lights one day, as if they held some sort of magical powers. It would be a shame if they went home without her wish coming true, and even if they did witness the phenomenon, the cold temperatures were known to freeze camera screens, so she mightn't even get to capture the event. He wanted her to have a small memento and at the same time give her some sort of explanation in writing because he hadn't made a very good job of delivering it in person so far.

Faced with the blank side of the card it was difficult to come up with the words to both fill it and adequately express what he needed to say. Plus, he didn't exactly want his personal life to be coffee-break gossip in the post room. He took the coward's way out and started with the address—the home he was supposed to be sharing with his wife.

I'm sorry.

He could've left it at that but he'd said it a lot over the past twenty-four hours and it hadn't made a difference either to his conscience or Freya's pained expression every time she looked at him.

I always loved you, never wanted to hurt you, but I could never be the family man you need me to be. You deserve better.
Lucas xx

There seemed no need to mention the mental illness that had cost them their marriage when it was obvious they were going to go their separate ways again on their return. Even without his grief and depression keeping them apart, that basic conflict would remain—he couldn't imagine being part of the happy little family she wanted. He was a successful doctor because he'd studied hard and followed the lead of his mentors but he'd never had a role model to show him how to be a parent. It wasn't the kind of responsibility he would accept and hope for the best when he was a casualty himself of that selfish attitude towards parenting.

It was his fault their marriage was over but using the gory details of his trauma as an explanation now would inflict the very pain on Freya he'd been trying to avoid and only make her want to *understand* more. That was the kind of woman she was. One hint of what he'd been through and she'd already cried for him and tried to fix everything. For both of their sakes he needed to sever the ties, not strengthen them.

He handed the postcard over the counter, picture side up, hoping the elves either couldn't read English or were too discreet to judge the contents.

As he waited for the others to finish up so they could travel the final leg of the journey, there was one area of his life that suddenly became clearer. He'd put off making a decision about his temporary lodgings at Pete's because that had been easier than committing to change, but he could see now they all needed to move on. Remaining static would only prolong his grief for the life he could never have.

Even with the prospect of seeing Santa Claus in person it took some wrangling to get everyone to leave the warmth of the post-office room to go outside again. As soon as he had everyone lined up, one distracted child would invariably wander off.

'Sam, we've finished colouring in now. Can you come back and join the others. Please?' He wasn't averse to begging if it meant they could start the wagons rolling again.

Sam huffed back into line with his arms folded across his chest and a scowl creasing his forehead, just as a streak of pink took off running around the table. Lucas didn't know if it was over-excitement or being homesick that had set them off today. Whatever it was, it left him in no doubt he'd made the right decision in not having kids of his own. He didn't know how to handle them outside a hospital cubicle.

'I think we should start singing now so he can hear us coming the whole way through the forest.' Freya sidestepped any potential confrontation and took their errant charge's hand without any further fuss.

She was going to make a great mum. Which was exactly why she'd be better off without him weighing her down.

The rousing chorus of 'Jingle Bells' she started finally set them off out the door on a march towards the waiting sleighs. Lucas breathed a sigh of relief once their train of reindeer-drawn carriages was snaking through the lantern-lit woods, temper tantrums averted. It was all thanks to Freya. She was the peacemaker and the calm in any storm. Perhaps if he'd turned to her for guidance and support when the nightmares had begun tormenting him she might've helped quieten the chaos in his head before it had consumed him. Unfortunately his pride was a heavy price he hadn't wanted to pay.

As he watched her inside the dim interior of the log cabin, whispering the relevant info about each child to Santa as they stepped up for their gift, Lucas realised the outcome for their relationship was always going to have resulted in the same tragic ending. She was a ray of light in the shadows, her own excitement almost bubbling to the fore as she tried to keep the children quiet awaiting their turns. Too much of a free spirit, full of love and empathy, to be condemned to a childless lifetime shackled to his issues.

He stood at the back of the room detached from the scene before him, unlike Freya, who was right in the middle of it. The sounds of paper ripping and happy shrieks as the kids unwrapped their presents no longer angered him because he'd missed out on this unparalleled joy as a child but neither could he relate to it the way Freya seemed to. He was just kind of numb to it.

The medication had kept him that way for a time, to quieten his thoughts and help him sleep, but he'd hated that zombielike existence and had been glad when therapy had helped him process what had happened to him so he could gradually be weaned off the antidepressants. He guessed this was his adjustment phase. Not unlike lying in a dark room for any length of time and suddenly having someone switch on a bright light. It had taken time to get used to his surroundings again and adapt accordingly. Life was different now but it simply wasn't the one he preferred because Freya was no longer in it.

'You were so good with them back there.' He made sure to acknowledge Freya's hand in the smooth proceedings as they filed back to the waiting sleighs without incident and watched the compliment pinch her cheeks.

'Similar mindset, I suspect. I was every bit as thrilled as they were to meet Father Christmas. Perhaps I'm not as immune to it all as I thought I was.' That disarming smile he might not have seen again but for this trip made him ache for days gone by and lost for ever. There were some moments from his past he didn't want to erase from memory. All of them including Freya and that smile.

It made him forget everything but what it was to make her happy and the warmth spreading inside him in return. There was no separation, no audience, no cold, when she was glowing at him like this. It was only natural to want to reach out and touch his wife one last time.

'I'm glad you enjoyed yourself,' he said as he framed her face in his hands to capture that look of pure joy he'd thought he'd never see again.

Her lips parted on a gasp and he knew he wasn't the only one struck by that bolt of lightning every time they came into contact. A year ago he wouldn't have hesitated to lean in for the kiss he so desperately wanted but he no longer had claim to that privilege.

She covered his hands with her own and closed her eyes as if she was trying to preserve the moment too.

'Freya, I—' He watched her brow knit into a frown as he spoke and he realised nothing he could say would ever make things right again. He was the cause of that distress written so clearly on her face. Every single time.

'I think we should get back to the village before it gets any later.' He let his hands fall away with the last drop of hope he could ever make her happy again.

For one brief moment Freya had experienced that same contentment Hope seemed to find in her reindeer toy as she hugged it close all the way back to the village. In those few seconds Lucas had held her face cradled in his hands as though he would kiss her at any second, the world around her had shone brightly again. Then he'd let go of her and the shadows had crept once more over her heart to leave her shivering in the dimming light.

She'd been swept up into that optimistic euphoria along with the children. Just as they'd set aside their pain and uncertainty to lose themselves in the excitement, Freya had forgotten Lucas was no longer hers. She would never have relished a stranger's touch the way she had drunk in his. That was what he was now after all this time—a stranger, not her husband—and she'd do well to remember that for her own sake.

She didn't know what had prompted him to reach out when he'd appeared so detached at the cottage, standing at the back and observing rather than getting involved like all the others. Once more she found herself wondering what he'd been like as a child or, indeed, what went on in his head as an adult. That had been half of their problem. She'd never known what he'd been thinking because he would never share his thoughts with her.

As they returned to the village for some last-minute souvenir purchases, she put the last encounter down as an involuntary reaction to the climate. There was every possibility brain freeze had made them re-create some past memory with none of the original sentiment behind it. Or it could have been sympathy, pure and simple. He knew she was an old romantic and a complete sad case wishing this was all real and for the briefest time he'd let her believe they were still together, that she was happy again.

'Can we go on the big slide?' Hope was already running towards the giant ice slide that had been carved out in the centre of the tourist heaven. Judging by the queues lining up and down the hill it was the must-do event before returning home.

'Just once and then we'll have to find the others.' They'd all drifted off to do their own things for the last few minutes. Since the shops and restaurants were all in a circle, there was little chance of anyone getting lost and the bus to take them back to the airport was waiting just around the corner.

'Yay. Rudolph is coming too.' Hope waved her new friend in front of her face and made Freya wish she was that young again when a stuffed toy was enough to make you the happiest person in the world.

They waited as patiently as could be expected for a small child and a reluctant adult in subzero temperatures. Freya found herself watching the skies for those elusive green lights she'd been hoping to see to have made this trip personally worthwhile. So far it looked as though she was going home disappointed.

'I'm sorry you didn't get to see your lights on this trip.' Lucas's voice at her ear had her pulling her scarf tighter to defend against the chills currently rippling along the back of her neck. He picked up her train of thought so easily it was unnerving. Annoying. Inconvenient. Never more so than when she was trying to make sense of her feelings for him.

'It's okay. I think it's been eventful enough.' Managing a group of small children with special medical needs hyped up to meet Father Christmas had been enough of a challenge without throwing in her estranged husband and a lot of unresolved issues. The only thing she wanted to see more than the Northern Lights was her own bed where she could pull the duvet over her head and hide from these emotions which seemed to have reappeared with him.

She thought she saw a blush stain his cheeks but it was probably the cold biting rather than self-awareness of the upset he was causing her by being here. If he'd ever taken her feelings into consideration she wouldn't have spent the worst part of a year wondering what the hell had happened to them.

They moved uphill at an agonisingly slow pace and if it wasn't for the girls she knew they'd both be sitting at opposite ends of that airport bus, desperate to get away from each other as soon as possible. The one good thing to come out of this for her on a personal level was that the mystery of his whereabouts was finally solved, even if the details remained sketchy. It was closure of a kind.

She held Hope's hand, as Lucas did Scarlett's, as they took their positions at the top of the slide and pushed off. There were squeals of delight from the smaller passengers as they slid to the bottom of the hill all too quickly.

'Again!' they chorused.

'Sorry, girls. It's time to go home.' Lucas got to his feet and shot out a hand to help Freya. It would be churlish to refuse it yet she didn't want him touching her and upsetting her equilibrium all over again. She reconciled herself with the fact they were both wearing gloves again and there would be no further skin-on-skin contact.

'Aww.' Scarlett and Hope's sulking began in earnest now they knew this was the end of their snowy fun.

'Just think of all the things you have to tell everyone.' Freya did her best to get them to focus on the positives. At least until they were on the bus and on their way to the airport. She could do without any bad-tempered meltdowns on top of everything else.

'I liked the reindeer.' Hope shrugged, easily distracted with her precious gift still clutched to her chest.

'Well, I like the slide.' Scarlett stuck out her tongue in an uncharacteristic bout of petulance.

Freya supposed they'd had it easy up until now. A busy weekend with small children, and her ex-husband, was always going to have its testing moments and this was shaping up to be one of them.

'We've all enjoyed different things, Scarlett, but it's time to go.' Lucas tried his best to coax her away from the bottom of the slide before the next lot of eager thrill seekers made their way down.

'Yes. We've had a good time. Let's not spoil it now.' As nightmarish as some aspects of this weekend had been for her, he was right—there'd been flashes of true enjoyment for her too. It was a shame the spectre of her dead marriage was always going to haunt any good memories.

Freya tried to take her hand but Scarlett wrapped her arms around her body and shook her head. 'I want to go again!'

Even if they'd had time to join the queue again Freya knew she couldn't give in to this type of behaviour. She didn't want to start a trend amongst the rest of the children when they were about to embark on their long journey home.

Before she had time to put her foot down any further, Scarlett turned on her heel and ran back towards the snaking line waiting to slide.

'Scarlett, wait!' Freya made a grab for her but she dodged out of reach and ran back across the bottom of the slide just as the next group of people came barrelling down.

Scarlett was too busy scowling back to notice the long-legged teen behind her. In painfully slow motion her little legs were swept out from beneath her so she fell back, her head hitting the smooth ice with a blood-curdling crack.

Lucas's cry matched Freya's as they helplessly watched the scene unfold, getting there too late to prevent the fall.

'Scarlett? Scarlett? Talk to me, sweetheart. Are you

okay?' Lucas was on his knees at once, checking her airways were clear and trying to get a response. He placed his hands on either side of her head to stabilise her neck. In circumstances such as these they had to treat the patient as if there'd been a spinal injury.

Freya saw a small trail of blood on the ice and when she parted Scarlett's hair she found a small gash on her scalp.

'I'll treat the head wound.' She grabbed the backpack containing the first-aid kit. That kind of knock to the head could do untold damage and wasn't something either of them would treat lightly. Scarlett's eyes were open but unfocused and her body stiff.

'Scarlett, can you hear me?' Freya covered the wound with a sterile gauze dressing and tried to keep her connected but her blue eyes suddenly rolled back in her head and her limbs began to twitch uncontrollably as a seizure took hold of her body.

'Scarlett, we're going to get some help for you, sweetheart.' Lucas summoned over one of the other nurses, who was passing by, and asked her to take Hope away from the scene and phone for an ambulance.

Freya knew from experience it was better to get one here sooner than later in case they needed oxygen or meds such as benzodiazepines to end the seizure if it went on for longer than five minutes. The head injury was going to need to be treated too.

'Everything's going to be all right, Scarlett. We're right here.' Freya held the gauze to her wound, praying this ended as quickly as it had begun. A prolonged seizure could starve the brain of oxygen, and the longer it lasted, the less likely it was to stop on its own. They'd known this was a possibility, of course, but the whole point of the trip had been to show the children their conditions didn't have to limit their experiences. It was unfortunate they hadn't made it back to the UK before reality had hit.

Lucas checked his watch. 'That's longer than five minutes. I'm going to need to review the protocol sheet and the buccal midazolam.'

As carers for Scarlett during this trip they'd both familiarised themselves with the written protocol provided by the consultant treating her condition should such an emergency arise but the laminate had to be rechecked every time emergency medicine had to be administered. She tossed the bag containing the medication to Lucas then took over the job of trying to keep their patient's head and neck stabilised.

He confirmed all the details were correct on the package before he opened the pre-filled syringe. The sedative, which came in the form of a sugar-free syrup, was supposed to have a calming effect on the brain and was often able to end a seizure.

He opened Scarlett's mouth and made sure the buccal cavity between the cheek and gums was clear before he administered the required dose, then checked his watch again. It was vital they keep an eye on the time to ensure they gave it sufficient time to take effect before they administered a second dose.

'Hopefully the ambulance will get here soon.' There was always a possibility of breathing difficulties with these emergency drugs and only so much they could do out here. If they couldn't stop the fitting she'd need to be put on a ventilator to help her breathe until she recovered.

'We'll be with her until it does.' Lucas stripped off his ski suit and used it to keep Scarlett warm.

Freya saw him shiver as he covered the child with his outerwear. When it came to helping others he always stepped up to the plate without a second thought for himself. That was why it was so hard to reconcile his heartless actions of the past with the man now kneeling in the snow, comforting a sick child.

Freya allowed herself a fleeting pang of self-pity for the husband and father she could've had, should've had by her side for more than one weekend, but she had to snap out of it quickly because she was no longer the one suffering here. Scarlett needed her and Lucas to work together to make this as painless as possible for all of them.

'I'm so sorry you had to come all the way out here.' Freya couldn't apologise enough to the distraught parents who'd arrived at the hospital in the dead of night. This wasn't how any of them had wanted the trip to end.

'We know she's in good hands but we wanted to see her for ourselves.' Scarlett's mother rushed down the corridor with her, understandably anxious to see her daughter.

'Of course.' Freya would've reacted exactly the same way if it had been her child lying hurt in a strange hospital.

The others had flown home hours ago after a brief stop at the hospital for an update and to drop off the luggage, which would now have to be checked onto a later flight. Lucas was the medical lead, so he'd immediately volunteered to stay behind, but Scarlett had been under Freya's care from the start and there was no way she was leaving the country without her. She was feeling bad enough that she'd had to hand over Hope's care to Gillian for the journey home, even though she couldn't possibly be in two places at once.

'How is she? You said on the phone she'd hit her head before the seizure…'

'The doctor is just checking in on her now.' The fitting had ceased before the ambulance had arrived but Scarlett's head injury was still worrying. They'd ordered CT scans on arrival, the results of which might require further investigation or referral to a neurosurgeon if there were signs of any damage. It was a necessary precaution.

On cue, Lucas strode towards them and shook hands with the late-night arrivals. 'Lucas Brodie. You'll be pleased to know all Scarlett's scans came back clear but she needed a couple of stitches to her head wound. They're just keeping her in overnight for observation.'

'Thank goodness she's all right.' Freya's heart lifted as soon as she heard there'd been no long-lasting damage. Without any extra complications, and providing there were no more seizures during the night, Scarlett would most likely be discharged the next day.

'Can we see her?' This time it was the father who was eager for first-hand verification of his daughter's health.

'She's resting now, but the staff said it was fine to sit with her for a few minutes. The doctor in charge of her care is with her now if you'd like to speak to him yourself.' That frown, which had been on Lucas's face since Scarlett's fall, finally evened out as he delivered the good news.

'Thank you, Doctor.' The couple bustled away as soon as Lucas pointed them in the right direction.

'Scarlett's really going to be okay?' Freya wanted clarification he hadn't been sugar-coating anything for her parents' benefit.

'There's still a few tests to run in the morning but all the signs are good.' His hand was cool on hers as he reached out to reassure her and she remembered his earlier sacrifice for his patient.

'You're freezing!' They'd been indoors long enough now that he should've warmed up. It showed how cold he must've been out there in the snow if he was still in the process of defrosting.

'I'm fine.' He tried to snatch his hand away from her grasp, probably embarrassed that she'd discovered he was human after all.

Her inner nurse took over from common sense insisting his discomfort should be of no interest to her.

'You are not. You're practically purple with cold. It's not going to help anyone if you end up with hypothermia, is it?' she scolded, rubbing his palms between both of hers, trying to generate some heat.

Far from blanching at the telling-off, he seemed amused by her fussing over him and her blood boiled that her concern should be a source of entertainment. This whole situation would've been a lot easier if she didn't care whether he froze to death or not. She rubbed his upper arms, hoping to get his circulation going and perhaps give him a friction burn from his sweater. At least her sudden sadistic streak would take her mind off the rounded biceps bunched beneath her sweeping hands and the vivid memories of the body she'd known so well once upon a time.

This was supposed to be about his survival, not her copping a feel.

'If you're *really* worried, I hear that skin-to-skin contact works best at transferring body heat.' The skin crinkled at the corners of his eyes as he teased her and she gave him a playful slap to hide the surge of hormones heating her own body at the suggestion.

'I think you'll live.' She took a step back so she could focus again and watched Lucas run his hand—which was now a healthier pink colour—through his hair, looking every bit as ruffled as he'd made her.

'We're going to stay with Scarlett here tonight. You two should go back to the hotel and get some rest.' Scarlett's father popped his head around the corner and offered them some unexpected respite. As much as every fibre in Freya's body was begging her for rest, she had a responsibility to the little girl that she wasn't ready to abandon.

'We couldn't possibly—'

'I insist. There's no need for all of us to be here. We appreciate everything you've done but go and get some sleep.' He didn't hang around to listen to further argument and Freya was too tired to fight common sense. There was nothing more they could do for Scarlett tonight and Lucas was quick to point out they'd be more help if they got some rest before they accompanied the family on the journey home again. He headed to Reception to use the landline and call the hotel but the heavy sigh on his return didn't fill her full of confidence about their last-minute booking.

'We're here for the night.'

'What do you mean? Surely someone can give us a lift back to the cabins?' This definitely hadn't been on the itinerary but it wouldn't be a hardship to spend another night in Lapland luxury.

'I've just called them. They're booked out. Apparently they had another party arrive straight after we checked out this afternoon.' He shrugged an apology but it wasn't his fault or anyone else's that they'd been stranded here. It was simply bad luck.

'I don't have a problem slumming it in a regular hotel. I could sleep standing up right now. As lovely as the cabin was, I'll settle for four walls and a bed.' She yawned and stretched, her body giving in to tiredness now that they knew Scarlett was safe and sound and her parents were with her.

'Any hotels within trudging distance are booked up too. I guess this isn't the time, or place, for unscheduled overnight stays.' It was obvious he'd done his best to find them accommodation but it wasn't as if they could just check into the nearest bed and breakfast out here in the wintry wilds.

'Thanks for trying. I guess we really are stuck here for the night.' She eyed the mismatched plastic chairs, which were the only apparent visitor accommodation. The local facility didn't have access to a family room, which a bigger hospital in the main town might've had for parents and guardians keeping a vigil.

'As you know, I'm very low-maintenance…' She'd never made outrageous demands of her husband. Only that he honour the vows they'd taken on their wedding day to stay with her, and that had turned out to be too much to ask of him.

There might have been some who'd have screamed and hollered at the prospect of a night sleeping on a chair and stamped their feet until a bed was made available, but she didn't expect anything of anyone any more. She'd do what she'd done for the past year and get on with it. The holdall containing her clothes wouldn't make much of a pillow but she tried to pummel it into submission enough to rest her head on.

'I know you deserve more,' Lucas muttered low enough under his breath she wasn't sure she was supposed to hear.

It didn't matter if he was referring to the sleeping arrangements or her choice of husband when she was stuck with both.

'Are you going to stand there all night?' She had her head turned away from him but she could sense him hovering nearby and that meant there was even less chance of her getting to sleep.

'No, and you're not going to spend the night in that chair either.' The hard edge to his voice and the sound of him stalking back towards Reception had Freya scrambling back to an upright position to see what was going to happen next.

He walked with such purpose and authority it set her pulse skipping after him. It reminded her of the self-assurance that had drawn her to him from the start and with it the sickening realisation she would still follow him to the ends of the earth if he asked her to. Regardless of the fact he'd ripped her heart out once already, she remained a lost cause when it came to Lucas Brodie.

She didn't know what more fate had in store for her

during this trip but she prayed she was going to make it through the next twenty-four hours with the rest of her heart still intact.

CHAPTER FIVE

'THIS IS TOO MUCH, Lucas!' Freya's objection didn't quite gel with her actions as she spun around, arms outstretched, staring up at the sky in wonder like a child seeing snow for the first time.

He knew it was everything she could want here and worth every penny he'd slapped onto his credit card. A glass igloo wasn't merely a step up from crashing on plastic chairs in a corridor; it was a no-expense-spared apology, his attempt to make up for some of the hurt he'd caused her in the past.

With extensive Internet surfing and numerous phone calls courtesy of the receptionist it had turned out there was one last accommodation option available and he'd jumped at this opportunity for Freya's sake. The small igloo village surrounded by pine trees and little else was the ideal place for an Aurora Borealis watch.

'I thought it would be good for you to take back some nice memories of this trip.' And of him. He didn't want her last thoughts of him to be tied to feelings of discomfort and disappointment.

'I'm not going to forget this in a hurry.' She stopped spinning under the glass dome ceiling to give him a bright, unguarded smile and out-twinkled the stars in the dark skies above them. The sight of her just about stopped his heart beating. He'd be content to die right here and now with the thought he'd been able to make her happy again with this one act.

'It's kind of like glamping in the Arctic.' He dumped their bags in the corner of the bedroom/living area. The one downside of his magnanimous gesture was the lack of space. It didn't correlate with the notion of maintaining some distance after their heart-to-heart last night.

As pretty and warm as their little glass bubble was, there was no chance of skulking off to his own room and avoiding her until sunrise. Apart from the separate toilet and shower it was essentially one round bedroom. No TV, no Internet, no distraction from his beautiful companion.

He collapsed down onto one of the beds. At least they weren't expected to share because that really would have been a step too far for both of them. The only thing that stopped it being too claustrophobic was the transparent ceiling and the view above his head of the endless sky. He hoped more than ever that Freya would get her light show and save them from having to make more conversation than he was comfortable with.

'Do you think people can see in?' Freya whispered, as though there was someone eavesdropping on her every word.

'Can you see anyone else?' The only thing in his peripheral vision were snow-covered tree limbs and the orange glow of their distant neighbours. The architects had clearly taken the privacy of their guests into consideration for this experience.

'Well…no,' she conceded, and began to unzip her

ski suit now she was satisfied she wouldn't be giving a peep show.

Although he doubted there were any more interesting sights than her stripping off her Abominable Snowman outfit. More like adorable snowman. Lucas tried to distract his wayward thoughts from the sound of her zip. Not even the spectacle of the Northern Lights would compete with the body he knew intimately beneath that suit.

They both knew that watching her take off her clothes had been one of his favourite pastimes.

'How do they keep the snow and ice off the windows?' she carried on, oblivious to his increasing discomfort.

'Heated glass. Same principle as the underfloor heating, I guess. We've got all the mod cons.' There was a panel by the bed and he couldn't resist pushing the switch to see what other surprises awaited. Although if it turned out it was one of those vibrating beds he might end up having to pitch his own tent outside in the snow. Bar the single beds, this already had all the hallmarks of a honeymoon suite rather than an almost divorced couple forced into spending an awkward night together.

He waited for the seventies' motel jiggling to begin and was almost disappointed by the slow and partial rise of the mattress.

'Is that for a better view?' Freya arched an eyebrow at him as he rose to an almost sitting position in time to see her unpack her night things.

'Probably,' he mumbled, and promptly lowered himself back down again. The idea had been to provide her with a vista to wipe last night's discussion from her mind but he'd inadvertently engineered another sleepless night for himself, having Freya so close. Not only was the thought of her right here next to him a distraction but there was also the worry the nightmares would return.

He hadn't had one for quite some time but there was no absolute cure for the anxiety he still encountered from time to time and there was the possibility all this talk of the past would prey on his subconscious if he drifted off. Since leaving Freya's bed he'd slept alone, but Peter, his flatmate and saviour, had kept him informed of his night terrors at the time. Sometimes his stress manifested while he was sleeping and the sweating, the screaming and crying he'd suffered at the onset of his illness were not attributes he particularly wanted to share with her. They mightn't be together any more but that didn't mean his ego would accept sharing his weakness with her.

As Freya disappeared into the bathroom to change, Lucas plumped his pillows and prepared himself for a long night, thankful his experience of working night shifts had built up his stamina for such occasions.

He couldn't resist a sneak peek as she stole back to bed, or the snort laugh when he saw what she was wearing.

'What? I packed for warmth and comfort, not company.' She dived beneath the covers but it was too late; he'd already witnessed the fleecy reindeer onesie.

'Good.' It came out gruffer than he'd intended, or he'd any right to, at the thought of her having a bed partner. The mere suggestion of another man sharing her bed, or her usual choice of skimpy nightwear, had him frowning. He didn't know how he'd cope if and when their divorce finally went through. They hadn't actually discussed the future, yet he couldn't expect Freya to put her life on hold any longer. It was a real gut punch to finally face up to the fact she could be with someone else. He might just have to flee the country to remain in denial.

'Aren't you going to get ready for bed?'

'I don't wear pyjamas, as you very well know, Freya.' He'd said it with the intention of making her blush, making her imagine him naked in her bed and put all thoughts of any other man out of her head. Of course, she mightn't have the same interest in his love life as he apparently had in hers but she hadn't given him that impression thus far.

Not that he could have his cake and eat it. There was no way he could keep his dark, desperate past to himself and his wife happy at the same time. He'd tried that and failed miserably.

He reached out and flicked the light switch off, plunging them into darkness but for the glittering stars above their heads. He would just lie here uncomfortable and brooding until the sun came up. If he couldn't see her he wouldn't think about her. That was the way it was supposed to work. At least, that was what he'd told himself for the past year.

'There hasn't been anyone else since you, Lucas.' Her admission in the dark reached in past all the bravado to see deep inside his soul. No one else had that ability to expose his vulnerable internal workings and that was what terrified him. She could've listed a whole string of lovers and cut him to the quick but, unlike him, it wasn't in her nature to inflict unnecessary pain or cruelty towards another being.

Lucas got out of bed and walked towards the bathroom, unable to hear any more as the weight of guilt threatened to crush him. Bedcovers rustled behind him as Freya turned onto her side, away from the perfect night and her far-from-perfect husband. He could almost taste the saltiness of her tears on his tongue.

The bathroom mirror mocked him with the younger face of his father. He stripped off his shirt and splashed himself with cold water to take away the sting of his burning shame. Now he was faced with the prospect of having to let her go again, he was questioning if he'd even made the right decision first time around. His anxiety had been so overwhelming then, imagining the worst in every situation, it was possible he'd acted rashly and prematurely thrown their marriage away. If it had been the right course of action surely neither of them should still be in so much agony now?

There was only one way he could attempt to make amends to Freya for the wrong he'd done her, even if he was sweating at the very thought.

The sheets were cool on his naked back as he lay down on his bed and prepared his confession.

'I haven't been with anyone else since you either, Freya.' It was a big confession to make when he knew it would raise all sorts of other questions about their lost year but he owed it to her to return her honesty.

'Then why did you leave me?' Her voice was but a breath in the night, yet he had to close his eyes to steel himself from the blow.

'I was going through some mental health problems. I didn't think you should have to go through them with me and thought I was doing the right thing by leaving. I was so messed up I guess I wasn't thinking about anything clearly.' Silence swallowed him whole.

It really was quiet out here, his painful admission the only sound in the forest. In different circumstances he would've found the setting a tranquil retreat from the daily grind. Not tonight. Not in his head and definitely not in his heart.

'Why couldn't you have told me? I'm a nurse, for goodness' sake. I would've helped you get whatever treatment you needed.' Her frustration at him was justified when he'd recently begun questioning his own decision-making at that time.

'I didn't really know what was going on in my head. The news of my dad's death opened up a Pandora's box of memories and emotions I apparently hadn't dealt with. I didn't want him to be a part of my life with you so I never told you he was a mean drunk who should never have been allowed to look after a dog, never mind raise a child. I think the only reason the authorities never got involved was because I was so good at hiding the bruises. For some reason I thought it was better to have him as a parent than have none at all.' He'd been so desperate to cling on to what had been left of his family he'd accepted daily beatings as normal life. Not to mention the appalling conditions and the empty cupboards of the filthy house he'd been expected to call home.

'Lucas, I'm so, so sorry.'

He didn't take any pleasure in her gasp of horror or any relief in finally sharing the agony of his childhood. It simply brought back that horrible roller-coaster rise and fall of nausea at recalling it, even if he was at least able to discuss it now without breaking down.

He coughed away the ragged ball of emotion threatening to block his airways. 'I left home when I could, moved into a hostel and held down two jobs to put myself through medical school. I mistakenly thought I could escape my father with hard work and determination to make a success of my life, but news of his death brought back a lot of those painful memories and kind of hit me for six.'

'You should have told me. Maybe we could've got through it together.'

'I think I had some sort of breakdown... I couldn't think, or sleep, without images of him rearing in my head. The sound of his drunken ramblings, blaming me for my mum leaving; the smell of his foul breath as he loomed over me and even the shame I felt going to school in dirty, hand-me-down clothes—it all came rushing back at once and refused to leave my thoughts. I was just so full of rage and shame...and wanting to be free of it all.' He let that sink in so he didn't have to spell out that for a moment he'd believed there was only one way of escaping the pain.

'Even me?'

There was a creak as she shifted in her bed. To look at him? To get up and lock herself in the bathroom away from his self-pity? It didn't matter. Now he'd opened the box, there was no way of stuffing all the secrets back inside.

He let out a long sigh. 'I never wanted to be without you but I didn't want to drag you into that darkness. I took it with me. In my head, at least. I know my actions seem selfish but I couldn't see any other way out. His death triggered flashbacks, turned me back into that frightened little boy, afraid of his own shadow. What kind of husband would that have made me?'

'Mine.'

He hadn't heard her cross the room, didn't know she was there until the mattress dipped beside him. He didn't know he'd been crying until she wiped the tears away for him.

That small act of compassion, that comforting physical contact he'd been missing for so long, finally burst the dam, and the emotions he'd thought he'd dealt with came tumbling out once more. This time it wasn't the liquid pain of his childhood pouring down his face; it was grief for his marriage and losing the woman he'd loved.

She slid her arms around him, lifting his torso off the bed and forcing him into a hug. He wanted to resist, to keep hold of what little there was left of his dignity, but he'd forgotten how it felt to be loved. If he'd ever really known it at all until now.

She pressed her warm cheek tightly against his as though she was physically trying to transfer some of his pain to herself. Of course she understood, she was a nurse, but he'd never wanted to be treated as her patient.

'You got the help…the treatment you needed?' Freya swallowed several times before she got the words out, and Lucas could sense her already attempting to find that professional distance again.

He buried his nose in her hair and took a deep breath, wanting to savour her sweet scent before he let go of her in case he never had this chance to be this close to her ever again.

'The strong medication wiped me out for the first

while. They dulled the pain, quietened the memories but they also numbed the world around me, left me unable to function in any emotional capacity. It was the counselling, talking it all out, learning to process what had happened, that finally brought me back to the man I used to be. I'm just sorry it took so long.' Perhaps if he'd fought harder to get back towards the light neither of them would've suffered so much for so long. They might've even saved their marriage or at least found a better way to end it.

'You're here now,' she said, her smile shaky in the moonlight, unable to settle fully on her lips. He could see the steady river of sorrow for him glinting on her face, though she tried to hide it.

'And this was exactly what I'd been trying to avoid.' He brushed away her tears the way she had for him. The weight of his secrets might have finally been lifted from his shoulders but he'd never wanted to dump it on hers. He leaned his forehead against hers, wishing they'd stood a chance from the outset.

If he closed his eyes he could still imagine it.

When his lips found hers he wanted to believe he'd really come home again.

Freya had thought her heart would never ache as much as it had the day he'd left her but knowing now what he'd gone through she was worried it might just break for him. For the little boy, so alone and scared, and for her husband, in so much pain she wanted to take it all away. His hand, still cupping her face, tilted her mouth towards him and kissing him seemed the most natural thing in the world, both giving and taking comfort in the soft exchange.

She rested her palms on his chest, not realising he'd stripped off his top half in the dark. That first touch of his naked skin under her fingertips was electric and her erogenous zones immediately lit up as she reacquainted herself with the smooth undulations of her husband's muscular torso.

She'd intended to offer him support, remind him he didn't have to be alone, yet now all she wanted to do was give in to desire and block out everything except their need for each other.

He teased her lips apart with the tip of his tongue, gently exploring the boundaries. Freya's stronger, more cynical subconscious, which had kept her standing this past year, popped into her mind's eye, wagged a finger and shook its head. Everything in her body language was screaming for her to back away. It was no competition for her soft-hearted inner romantic, who just wanted to love her husband and have him love her in return.

They'd both been through hell and they deserved to take some solace where they could find it. In each other.

She ignored her arm-folding, tutting common sense to get to know her husband intimately again. The tentative kiss grew more confident, more insistent as she met his tongue instead of shying away from his advance. She didn't want to think about the past, not even what the future might hold past this night together. Her thoughts, her body were consumed with the need for this, for him, and the knowledge this chemistry hadn't fizzled out.

His lips were everywhere, setting the skin at her cheeks, her throat, her neck on fire. His breathing was as heavy as hers, full of want and need, and hot enough to melt the glass walls around them.

Committed to the moment, she let her hands travel down his lean torso, every inch of skin as tight as a drum. He'd always been trim but there was more definition, an edge to him she'd never encountered before. It told of hard work and dedication during his struggle to survive.

Lucas sucked in a breath and stilled against her as she reached the waistband of his trousers, casting a shadow of panic over her desire that she'd done the wrong thing by trying to rush this. Her sudden haste had been a combination of pent-up lust, which had been steadily rising since he'd stepped on board the plane, and a need to avoid overthinking this.

She froze, her fingers tangled in his waistband, her pulse racing, as though she'd been caught with her hand in the cookie jar.

'It's, uh, been a while,' he admitted, and she could almost feel him cringing with the confession there was no reason why it should embarrass him.

The thought of him with another woman had been the cause of many sleepless nights and to hear the truth eased part of that associated pain. The separation and subsequent months of abstinence would've made anyone a little nervous, including her, but passion had never been a problem for them.

'Good.' She smoothed her palm over the crotch of his trousers and gave his burgeoning erection a playful squeeze.

His sexy groan made it all the way down to her belly along with her zipper as he peeled her nightwear away as sexily as though she was wearing nothing but the finest silk. He kissed his way confidently across her exposed skin, and her temperature spiked, any theory that their chemistry could be anything other than explosive proving completely unfounded.

With Lucas's assistance her clothes fell to the floor, leaving her naked and exposed to his hungry mouth licking and sucking and leaving her gasping for more. She lay back on the bed, shaking with need and wondering how this had ended up about her, but distraction had always been one of his special skills. Among others.

He moulded her breast easily into the palm of his hand and she fitted there just as perfectly as she always had. Arousal coursed through her body as he plucked one tight bud between his finger and thumb, leaving her content to change the subject on this occasion.

For a short time. There was only so much a girl could take before she was practically pleading for more.

'Lucas…' Okay, a year without him meant she wasn't averse to asking for more.

She'd missed this intimacy, not only since he'd left but also in those last weeks of their marriage when he'd been so emotionally distant. Now that he'd given her some understanding of where his head had been back then, and they'd made that reconnection, she felt as though she'd got back the man she loved. Even if only for tonight.

At one time she'd wanted him to suffer but that had been before she'd discovered the full facts behind his departure and the extent of his true anguish. No one should've had to endure what he'd gone through either as a child or an adult. He deserved peace and a little fun. They both did.

'There isn't much room here,' Lucas said as he manoeuvred his body on top of hers in the tiny single bed built for stargazing, not reuniting past lovers.

The rough, stretched fabric of his crotch rubbed against her sensitive mound, teasing her folds until she was sure she'd climax purely with the memory of what he could do to her.

'Yeah, we need to get rid of these.' Her increased libido was making her brave but also impatient to make the most of what little time they might have together.

He levered himself up off the bed slightly, granting her access to his fly, which she negotiated in record time to liberate him. That perfect, familiar epicentre of his manhood sprang free as she nudged the remainder of his clothes over his backside and down his legs.

She giggled as he wriggled on top, trying to kick his clothes off, their naked bodies accidentally thrusting together at the most intimate of places before they rolled completely off the bed. If anything, this proved neither of them had been perfecting their seduction techniques in their interim. It was a tad more uncoordinated and ungainly now than they'd been that first time when he'd practically swept her off her feet and into his bed but she found it heartening. They were learning together like two inexperienced teens, anxious but eager to reach that first sacred destination together.

Everything about this moment—the fun and the passion—reminded her of that life they'd once had together and everything they'd lost. The tears pricking her eyes told her how much more she was missing Lucas from her life than the family they'd never had together.

CHAPTER SIX

LUCAS HAD NEVER thought he would feel as vulnerable as he had sitting in his counsellor's office, crying and spilling his guts about the punishments his alcoholic father had dished out to him for the purported crime of being born. Acknowledging to Freya it had been a while since he'd *performed* ran a close second.

Thankfully his body's primitive response at the sight of his naked wife had quickly allayed any worries that his masculinity might have somehow been compromised during the course of his recovery.

This night together wasn't something he had planned beyond the logistics of their accommodation but he'd never expected her to give him another chance any more than he'd intended to tell her about the demons that had driven him away. Despite the damage they'd suffered, there was obviously still a special connection between them that refused to be broken.

He mightn't be the smooth operator he'd once been, but being with Freya felt so right nothing else mattered but lying here with her. Those secrets he'd kept had meant holding back a part of himself in the course of their relationship but after baring his soul he now had the freedom to love her the way she'd deserved all along.

As Freya let her hands drift over the trunk of his body, and bit her lip as she dared ever lower, there was no questioning her desire for him either. This wasn't pity over the hard times he'd shared with her, or sleeping with him for old times' sake. She was seeing him as the man he'd never thought he would be again— her husband.

Lucas tangled her hair in his hands and kissed her as though they were the last two people on earth. Tonight, in this glass bubble, they were. Their mouths crashed together and the shadowy recesses of the past faded into insignificance against that need to make love to his wife.

He'd missed her, he loved her, and as their bodies joined together, he knew there would never be anyone else for him.

Those nights he'd spent without her, those vivid dreams when he'd imagined her lying next to him, only to find his bed achingly empty—he channelled it all through his body into hers. He withdrew and plunged back inside her again and again, each time feeling like the first.

The quickening clench and release of her inner muscles around him and the tilt of her hips meeting his started the pressure building inside him too. She was clutching at his back, her head thrown back in ecstasy whilst his every muscle quivered in anticipation of her climax.

Freya's visceral cry of release took him by surprise. Although they'd always been passionate together, he'd never heard her so vocal. It was a primal scream of unleashed pain and passion from a very different woman than the one he'd left behind, and it shook him to his very core. She was stronger, more self-assured than he remembered, which made her sexier than ever and brought his orgasm swiftly. That gunshot intensity reverberated through his body with such force he thought he'd never recover.

Relief and a sense of peace claimed him, body and soul, as he let go. As if the year of emotional turmoil had physically left him, and he'd finally been liberated from the past. He didn't have the energy for anything more than to lie here on the floor, holding Freya close and wishing this could last for ever.

'I've missed this,' she whispered into his chest.

'Me too.' Lucas eventually summoned up enough strength to snag the duvet off the bed and pull it over them for the night. He knew he'd sleep well tonight with her wrapped around him like ivy around a tree trunk. There would be no nightmares or waking up in a cold sweat in a too-empty bed. Tonight he had everything he wanted. For now he was content to believe it could last.

Freya wanted to stretch out every muscle and revel in that glorious post-sex ache winding through her limbs, but that would entail breaking contact with Lucas's warm, familiar body and she wasn't ready to do that yet.

Right now she should be lying like a starfish in her double bed alone, in the home where she'd always imagined their family. This seemed a much nicer place to curl up for the night. Sleeping with her ex hadn't been part of her plan but neither had this whole extended stay.

Would it have happened if he hadn't been honest with her? She couldn't say, but finally opening up to her, exposing that vulnerable side he'd tried to hide throughout their short-lived marriage, had given her the excuse to act on those feelings for him that had never gone away. The husband who'd walked out on her was also a man who'd been in turmoil himself and on the verge of goodness knew what. Seeing and hearing the evidence of that trauma for herself had immediately demanded her forgiveness. It wasn't a time she would ever forget, or easily move forward from, but at least she understood why it had happened.

She could see now how consumed she'd been with her own past to remain so oblivious to his pain. Her grief over losing her baby had driven her to the point of obsession of having another one when she should've been happy she'd found someone special. Both of them had let the unhappy previous lives they'd led contaminate the one they could've had together.

This quiet afterglow was tinged at the edges with a little sadness. If they'd explored this honesty during the course of their relationship they might have avoided the nuclear fallout of their break-up. A year ago this conversation would have swung her into action on his behalf, to save her husband's mental health before things became too much for him. She would've got him the professional help he'd needed, been there when he'd needed to rage or cry, been someone to comfort him for once in his life. Peter had had to step up as his nursemaid, his confidant and apparent bodyguard, fending off hysterical abandoned wives he'd deemed might damage him more. He'd been the one to save him and not her, because Lucas hadn't let her. Whilst she was grateful for those who had intervened on his behalf, it had cost her her place in his life and a year of being in divorce limbo.

Lucas laced his fingers through hers and brought them to his lips. There was no need for words when his love was there in the gentleness of his kiss, his apology for ever causing her pain there in his eyes. Nothing could change what had happened to either of them but she was hoping now that they could start looking forward instead of behind them.

The new chapter of their lives dawned with a strange emerald light as their cosy bubble became bathed in an ethereal glow from above.

'Oh, Lucas!' She sat up, clutching the quilt to her chest as the jewelled skies shifted from midnight blue to green, and back again, with the phenomenon she'd always dreamed of seeing. The dancing arcs of changing light from the Aurora Borealis helped ensure this would be one trip to truly remember.

He rose with her, the heat of his torso at her back. 'You'd think I planned this,' he said with a laugh.

'You didn't?' It all seemed too perfect to have happened by accident. Especially after the year of hell they'd lived through.

He wrapped his arms around her waist and nuzzled into her neck. 'I'll happily take credit for finding your Northern Lights for you but I swear everything tonight has come as much as a surprise to me as it has to you.'

Given his personal revelations tonight, she didn't doubt that. Lucas Brodie was a proud man; there was no greater display of that than when he'd left their marital home rather than admit he was going through a tough time. She didn't know what difference tonight would make to their relationship status, if anything, but for now she simply wanted to sit here and soak up what was left of the magic. The morning and a heavy dose of reality would rear its head soon enough.

A long, leisurely lie-in and breakfast in bed with his wife would've been heavenly but the sunrise brought with it a different list of priorities for Lucas. The first thing he did was to make his way back to the main hotel to phone the hospital and check on their patient. Once he'd been assured she hadn't suffered any more seizures and would be discharged as soon as possible, he started organising the return trip.

Last night had opened a whole new world of possibilities he'd thought no longer available to him and he couldn't wait to get home again. Rather than pack up and move on to pastures new, he'd seen a glimpse of the old life he'd had with Freya and he wanted it back. Now there were no more secrets to keep them apart and they obviously still had feelings for each other, there was a chance they might be able to make their marriage work.

It was the first time since news of his father had triggered his illness that he was actually looking forward to the future. One hopefully with Freya in it. Those early months had been about survival and more recently the recovery of his health and career. Now he wanted to make plans for the married life they should've had together. Including a Christmas free from bleak memories and dark moods. He had a lot of making up to do for last year and now he was beginning to understand the excitement the children had felt leading up to seeing Father Christmas. Suddenly he couldn't wait for all those glitzy trimmings to appear around the house or the smell of turkey and stuffing as he walked through the door if it meant he was spending Christmas with his wife instead of being alone in someone's spare room.

By the time he returned to the igloo with coffee and pastries, Freya was washed, dressed and all evidence of their tryst had been tidied away neatly with the hospital corners of the bedcovers she'd made.

They hadn't discussed what either of them expected to happen after last night but he'd have been more than happy to pick up where they'd left off. It was obvious they still had a fierce need burning for each other. One that went beyond all those barriers they'd both built up during their separation.

'You weren't here when I woke up.' She was still brushing down the already pristine covers, unable to meet his eyes, and it was obvious she'd assumed the worst. That he'd left her again without saying a word.

After everything they'd shared last night that simple lack of trust in him to do the right thing robbed him of some of his earlier euphoria. He'd opened himself up to her completely, probably more than he'd ever dared when they'd been together. Yet she still believed him capable of walking out on her again without a word. It reflected a little of what he'd put her through when she'd opted for that scenario rather than a more logical one. That protective hard shell she'd developed in his absence would take perseverance to break through but he was willing to put in the hard work to make her believe in him again.

'You were asleep. I only went out for this.' He

showed her breakfast before setting it aside to move towards her.

'I, uh, thought you might have gone on without me.' A pair of red-rimmed, pain-filled eyes eventually faced him and ripped his heart in two. She'd been crying over him again, only this time without just cause. In future he was going to have to remember there'd been long-term consequences for his behaviour last year that weren't easily brushed aside simply because he'd finally got his act together. Freya needed time to recover and rebuild her trust exactly the same way he had.

'Hey, I was trying to do something nice for you.' He sighed but in keeping with the spirit of transparency in their relationship he decided to face the reason behind her apparent paranoia rather than leave it as the elephant in the room. 'I would never do that to you again.'

'I just… I couldn't go through that again. If last night was a one-off tell me now and get it over with.' She folded her arms across her chest and he could see her bracing herself for the truth above all else.

'Whatever happens from here on in I promise I'll always be honest with you.' He tugged her interwoven limbs apart, forcing her to open herself up to the possibility he'd changed, and pulled her towards him.

'So, what happens from here?' she muttered into his chest, still resisting as long as she could, but Lucas was determined that these last few private moments together should mark the start of their new beginning. He didn't want them flying back into limbo without having resolved everything once and for all.

'What do you want to happen?' He brushed her hair away from her neck and let his breath tickle the sensitive skin there until she was wriggling against him.

'That's not fair. You're playing dirty...' She was laughing now, a glorious sound after all the serious, often gut-wrenching conversations they'd shared recently.

'That's the idea.' He wanted to put the fun back in their relationship and remind them what they'd had before his dad had managed to ruin his life again.

'Lucas...' She tilted her face up, attempting to scold him, but a flirty half-smile played across her lips, tempting him towards more.

'I love you, Freya. I want to be with you. That's as honest as I can be and as much as I can give you right now.' He didn't want to talk about the practicalities when he'd thought too much about that the last time they'd been together. For once he wanted to live in the here and now, where nothing mattered beyond this little bubble.

She blinked, her eyes closing for a fraction too long, and it was clear she was mulling over what he was telling her. As much as he loved her, he couldn't promise her for ever. They'd both discovered to their cost that was a fallacy.

Then she opened her eyes and said, 'I love you too, Lucas.'

A year of pain and worry evaporated with those words he'd thought he'd never hear again. Love was something he'd taken for granted when they'd been together, but when he'd no longer had it in his life, there had been nothing on this earth capable of filling the void left behind.

He swooped on her lips, eager to reap the rewards of this reconnection and express how he felt about her without worrying about the consequences. They would work it out this time. Somehow.

Freya had instantly thought the worst when she'd realised Lucas had left without waking her and that a night with her had reminded him why he'd left in the first place. Especially when she'd wakened so full of hope that they could make another go at their marriage. In those paranoid moments alone in the igloo she'd considered if it had been better to have had that brief reunion, so full of honesty and passion, and risk her heart again than to have never have had any further knowledge of him at all. Even if he had gone on ahead to the hospital without her and flown home without another word, she could say with her hand on her heart it had been worth every second. Now he was here, reassuring her he wasn't going anywhere for the foreseeable future, all those fears melted away against his lips.

This time there was no holding back as they stripped out of their clothes, eyes feasting on each other's naked flesh in the daylight of their admission as though they were truly seeing one another for the first time. He still loved her, she loved him and she couldn't see any reason why they couldn't be together and start over again.

That ray of hope was all she needed to justify reaching for Lucas again and letting her heart overrule her head. As she wrapped her arms around his neck and cushioned her body against his, he hitched her legs around his waist and carried her to one of the beds. His eyes never leaving hers, he laid her down on the mattress. Then he was kissing her all over so thoroughly she couldn't think beyond where his mouth would land next.

His lips were soft, his mouth demanding, as he

kneaded the tender skin on her inner thigh. That slow ascent towards her inner core left her aching with need for him inside her and that ultimate union of love and trust. He teased her with the tip of his tongue, making her wet with want, until she was arching from the bed and offering herself up to him for more. He filled her with one swift thrust, drawing her arousal straight through the centre of her body to meet him.

'I love you,' she cried out as he lapped her into that first burst of ecstasy so intensely it brought her to the brink of tears. It scared her how much Lucas still affected her body and mind and she only had his word he wouldn't shatter either again.

Then he shifted his body so he was prone against hers, his erection pressing insistently into her soft mound. Even though the evidence of his desire was straining to meet her, he moved slowly at first, answering that call inside her with one satisfying stroke. This was how it was supposed to be—so absorbed in one another it obliterated any of those dark thoughts that had hounded them in the past.

Freya ground her hips to meet Lucas's every thrust, urging him faster, deeper inside to drive out any lingering doubt about rekindling their relationship. That dizzying build-up of impending climax soon consumed her thoughts as well as her body, with Lucas's shallow breaths soon matching her own. They rose and fell together until his final roar of triumph rippled through his limbs and into hers. Freya rode it out with him until she couldn't hold back any longer, all of her pain finally expelled in the cry echoing around the walls.

Lucas didn't care that breakfast was cold or that he'd have one hell of a credit-card bill at the end of the month because this was the happiest he'd been in a long, long time. He and Freya had stayed wrapped in each other's naked limbs until visiting time had started at the hospital and they'd naturally prioritised Scarlett's welfare over their love life. Neither of them would neglect their professional duty in favour of their personal relationship. Once they were all safely home he and Freya would have all the time in the world for lazy mornings in bed, making love and getting to know each other again.

The hotel had arranged a lift for them, during which they'd barely been able to keep their hands off one another. Now they'd let down their emotional barriers it seemed as though they were physically trying to make up for lost time. Not that he was complaining. He'd spent too long without her and didn't want to waste any more time. If she was agreeable he'd move whatever belongings he had out of Pete's and back into the home where he belonged.

When they reached the hospital Freya offered to get Scarlett dressed so her weary parents could go and grab a coffee whilst Lucas checked with the staff that she'd been given her usual AEDs and all her obs were normal before they got their hopes up that she was able to go home.

'How are you feeling today, young lady?'

'I want to go home,' Scarlett insisted when he walked into her room, her forehead puckered into a frown and her lips pinched into a pre-tantrum pout.

'We'll get you there as soon as we can. I promise.' A quick check of her chart put Lucas's mind at ease that she was indeed ready to go so they didn't have a repeat of her last overtired tweenie performance.

'Just wait until you're doing this with your own kids

and then the fun will really begin,' Freya whispered with good humour, but she might as well have jabbed him with a red-hot poker and jolted him out of his love-induced daze. He'd allowed himself to get lost in the fantasy of being with Freya again without considering the long-term consequences of his actions.

They might have faced up to the challenges of the past but ultimately it didn't change who they were as people or what they wanted from life. On that subject they remained poles apart. He still didn't want to take that chance he would follow in his father's footsteps, whilst Freya was born to be a mother.

Oblivious to the cold shower pouring down around them and extinguishing any hope of a future together, she was helping Scarlett into her outdoor clothes and fussing around her like a clucking mother hen. It was at that very moment he knew this was the end.

That mothering instinct blazing brightly in the room was a part of her, no one could deny. Not even him. No doubt that caring, empathetic side had been the key to unlocking that chamber of secrets he'd imprisoned himself in, away from her for so long. It wasn't going to change; she shouldn't *have* to change simply because he'd waltzed back into her life with his daddy issues.

As she buttoned Scarlett up to protect her from the elements and wiggled her boots onto her feet, it was easy to picture Freya doing the same for her own little girl someday. Although he still loved her and wanted to be with her so much it hurt, Lucas wasn't going to change his stance on having children. Not even mind-blowing sex could change the basic flaw in their marriage, which had been there even before his emotional meltdown.

The counselling and endless talking over what had happened might have propelled him through those childhood nightmares but the parenting hangover would last for ever. He wasn't taking the chance that his actions would impact for a lifetime on another small human. Even without his father's dark influences there were plenty of men who inadvertently hurt their children. He was damaged goods with a bad track record with those he loved and there was enough guilt and regret trailing in his shadow without adding more. Freya, her unborn children, and even he, would be better off if this ended here. Regardless of that emptiness already creeping back, eating away at him from the inside out. He knew how unbearable life was without her but it had to be preferable to condemning her to life without the family she obviously still wanted.

'You're a very lucky girl because you got an extra night in Lapland and that means extra Santa gifts.' He swallowed down his new heartache and produced the little snow globe he'd purchased in the hotel gift shop from his pocket.

'That looks just like the snowman at the airport!' Scarlett squealed with delight as she shook the dome and watched the snowflakes swirl around the glass.

'It's beautiful, Lucas.' Freya's appreciation meant he had to work extra-hard to gather his composure.

He'd bought it with her in mind—a token gift of their time together—but how could he possibly be so cruel as to give it to her now, knowing it would be a reminder of the end of their relationship for good? It was a tad traitorous to give it to another girl but he knew Freya would forgive him that, if nothing else.

As for the rest, there was nothing he could do or

say that was going to make up for what he was going to have to do to her for a second time.

Their time together had been a wonderful reunion of two lost souls finally finding one another in the dark again, but he had no more to offer her now than he had a year ago and he didn't want to make her believe otherwise.

Freya hugged her body tight against the cold, even though they'd long left the Arctic Circle behind. The atmosphere between her and Lucas had been decidedly chilly since they'd left the hospital, even though they'd managed to remain professional for Scarlett and her family. Deep down she'd known the magic wouldn't last for ever but she'd imagined they might at least make it home. It could've been that he was trying to maintain a personal distance for appearance's sake but that didn't account for his reluctance to make eye contact, or attempt any meaningful conversation about what was going to happen to them as a couple once they landed back in the real world. He was acting exactly the same way he'd been in those last days of their relationship and suddenly the tension Freya thought she'd rid herself of these past days was back in her body as she activated her self-defence mode once more.

They'd collected their luggage from baggage reclaim, filled in all relevant paperwork required for their unexpected extra night away and waved Scarlett and her much-relieved parents off home. She'd never dreamed this trip would've had such a personal impact. Yet here she was, standing with her husband at the airport, not knowing what route they were taking next.

'I guess it's just us left now.' She had that washing

machine swirling in the pit of her stomach, churning her insides on a speed wash. There hadn't been any semblance of an 'us' for hours now. Perhaps the Northern Lights had added a fairy-tale quality to their tryst that hadn't really been there at all or Lucas had got cold feet at the prospect of being her husband again. Whatever had brought about the sudden change in him, she wanted to be prepared for the fallout this time around. There was no point in living a lie together if he couldn't fully commit to her.

'Thank goodness we all got home in one piece in the end.' He hoisted his backpack onto his shoulder and lifted his overnight bag, leaving hers sitting where it was on the shiny airport floor. If he'd had any intention of leaving here with her, the gentleman in him would've undoubtedly offered to take her luggage too.

Someone opened the washing-machine door mid-cycle and left her slipping and sliding in the mess. Lucas might have made it here unscathed but her heart had definitely been damaged in transit.

He sneaked a glance at the exit and she knew he was getting ready to leave. At least the last time he'd taken the coward's way out he'd had his reasons. Well, she wasn't prepared to stand back and say nothing and spend the rest of her days not putting up some sort of fight.

'Did we? Or are we back to being two very different pieces going their separate ways again?' It took all of the strength she'd built up over the past year to keep the hysteria from her voice. She'd survived being an abandoned wife and she was pretty certain she'd get over being a fling for old times' sake, if this was all it had been to him, but she needed to know. There was no way she was wasting any more of her life waiting for him to make his mind up about what he wanted. She owed herself more than that.

'Freya…last night…this morning… It was a mistake.'

'Way to make a girl feel special,' she muttered as he crushed her last hope with a single word. Through her rose-tinted glasses it had been special, passionate, emotional and all the other positive feelings a woman would want to attach to a night with the man she loved. A *mistake* spoke of regret and remorse and all those negative connotations she didn't want him to associate with her.

He ditched his luggage again so all their baggage lay in a heap between them in the middle of the airport. It wasn't fair. In one of those far-fetched romantic films this should be the part where he declared his undying love for her and they walked off hand in hand. His sigh indicated this was going to be more of a bittersweet goodbye. The kind of heartbreaking tragedy you'd watch in bed with an unending supply of chocolate and tissues.

'It was amazing but does it really change anything between us? We still want different things. For you that's undoubtedly going to include a family and that's simply something I can't entertain. There's no point in either of us pretending this is going to work… In fact, we should probably see about getting a divorce. Then we can both move on.'

He stole her breath away with the blunt truth that she'd been asking for all along. Unfortunately, it wasn't the one she'd wanted to hear.

'Don't you think this is the kind of thing we should

talk over in private?' It was true that desire to have another baby had probably dominated the early days of their marriage but that had been before their split, or Lucas sharing anything of his fears. She wouldn't bring another life into existence unless she was sure her relationship with the father was solid and this proved they were far from that ideal.

'Being with you this weekend and actually talking things through has helped me, it really has, but I think it's come too late for us.'

She wrenched away as he attempted to put his hands on her shoulders. He didn't get to touch her now if he was seriously going to dismiss what they'd had, what they'd shared, as if it had been any run-of-the-mill encounter.

'Well, I'm glad I could fix you and send you on your way.' The few words she managed to get out were dripping with bitterness towards the next woman he'd share his bed with but if he didn't think there was anything worth saving here then she wasn't going to beg him to change his mind. It had taken her long enough to claw back her dignity the last time he'd rejected her and she'd already proved she was strong enough to carry on without him. This was a setback but she'd bounce back again. It was what she did.

'I'm sorry, Freya. I only ever wanted to do the right thing by you.'

His platitudes were muted by the blood suddenly pounding in her ears as she grabbed her stuff and turned away. 'Don't forget those divorce papers. I think you know the address.'

The airport door swished open and she stepped outside with a confident stride. This was it, closure on

Lucas Brodie and her ill-fated marriage. It had come at the cost of another very painful lesson about letting anyone that close enough to hurt her again.

As the cold air hit the tears on her face she swiped them away with the back of her hand. Thankfully she'd developed a thicker skin since last time.

CHAPTER SEVEN

FREYA WET SOME paper towels under the tap and pressed them to her flushed face and neck. It wouldn't be very professional to go back on the wards looking like this when she'd spent the best part of two months pretending to everyone she was fine. After a quick rummage in her purse, she popped a breath mint in her mouth and dabbed on some make-up to try to disguise the redness around her eyes. She stared at the reflection of the stranger in the bathroom mirror. Lapland with Lucas had changed her into someone she didn't recognise any more. She'd clearly underestimated the long-lasting effect spending time with him again would have on her and he'd left her with even more baggage to deal with than before.

The faint sound of Christmas carols filtered in from the wards and made her well up all over again. Whilst everyone else around her was gearing up to celebrate, they only served to remind her she'd been left alone and heartbroken for the season again.

When the wave of grief had passed and the puffiness around her eyes had subsided, she ventured outside into the corridor. Gillian was waiting, propped against the wall with her arms folded and her lips pursed.

'He really doesn't deserve any more of your tears.'

'Tell me something I don't know,' she muttered and kept on walking along the festooned corridor, somehow resisting the urge to rip down garish decorations.

There was no point in lecturing her now when the damage had been done.

'I'm serious. You can't let him get to you now when you'd been making such progress. I thought you'd both managed to get along when we were out there. What the hell happened after I left to have you in such a state?'

'Apparently nothing of any significance to him.' Freya hadn't shared the intimate details with anyone, in the naive belief it would help her forget more easily. She'd been so very, very wrong.

Gillian marched ahead, only to then spin around and force Freya to a complete stop. 'I wish I could get my hands on him. He swans off back to whatever cave he's been hiding in and leaves you picking up the pieces again. It's not right. He obviously must've made some sort of promise to you for you to be so cut up over him a second time.'

Now she thought about it, the only promise he'd actually made to her had been to be honest and not walk out on her again without an explanation. Well, he'd lived up to his word, brutally so. He'd told her he didn't want to be with her or have a family with her. Case closed.

Although Freya was tempted to incite her overprotective friend into bashing Lucas over the head with a bedpan on her behalf. It would be comedy gold if the whole thing wasn't such a disaster. The best of it was neither of them would understand why she was so upset.

'No promises. No blame anywhere except at myself.' It was her prerogative to stay mad at Lucas if she chose, but in the end, she'd had to take responsibility for her epic fail. She really should've known better.

'You can't spend every day crying in the ladies' toilets. You're making yourself ill. Don't think I haven't noticed you're hardly eating anything these days either.' Gillian assumed the role of nagging mother figure since Freya's own parents were happily far enough away they hadn't seen the evidence of her apparent decline for themselves. A tip-off that their only child wasn't eating properly and she'd be whipped back home and force-fed enough carbs to triple her dress size in no time.

At first she'd thought she'd been saved the humiliation of telling them she and Lucas were back together, only to have to admit he'd called it quits again. In another few months her increasing waistline and persistent single status were going to make it painfully clear what had happened anyway.

'I haven't had much of an appetite lately but I'll be fine. You don't need to worry.' The last thing she'd wanted was to draw attention to herself and imagined Gillian had only noticed something was wrong because she'd been looking for the signs. She'd witnessed the fallout from Lucas's unpredictable behaviour once before, so it was no wonder she in particular should be on her guard now.

'Why don't we get you seen by one of the doctors so they can give you something to lift your mood?' Gillian took her by the arm and for a second Freya thought she was actually going to drag her into one of the cubicles.

'There's nothing wrong with my mood. I would just like to get back to work. My break's over and I'm sure we've got a waiting room full of people out there.' There was sufficient drama in the halls of the emergency department every day of the week without adding hers to it. Medication wasn't going to change what had happened anyway.

'Will you stop being so stubborn and please just let me help you? Don't let him ruin your life again.' It was the concern in her friend's voice and that worried frown that finally broke her down. She'd tried to get through this on her own, with limited success, and it was only going to get tougher from here on in. A friend was the one thing she needed right now and that was all Gillian was trying to be for her.

'I won't.' The irony was he'd made her life worth living again after he'd left her with the most precious gift of all. Her guard slipped for a moment and her hands moved to protect the little souvenir growing in her belly.

Fate had brought the two of them together again that night and a lack of contraception had brought her a surprise not long after. Initially she'd put the nausea and unstable emotional state solely down to his rejection too, but she was a nurse; she'd figured it out eventually. As had Gillian apparently as she clocked the subtle movement and let out a shocked gasp.

Freya put her finger to her lips and moved her past the oversized Christmas tree and pile of brightly wrapped presents towards the empty triage room.

'You're pregnant?' Gillian might have done her best to keep the news quiet by mouthing the revelation but she had also grabbed Freya by both arms and was shaking her.

'You're going to make me throw up again if you keep doing that.' Her teeth were rattling but she was finally smiling again. It had been hard, keeping the news to herself, and at least with one confidante she might be able to enjoy this pregnancy. This baby hadn't got off to the easiest start with an absentee dad who'd made it clear a family wasn't in his plans for the future and a weeping mum mourning for her lost love. From here on her focus was going to be on the bundle of joy that would be arriving sometime in the summer.

'Sorry. Oh, come here.' Her friend pulled her into a bear hug and Freya couldn't help getting a tad emotional. The admission had relieved some of the stress from her shoulders now it wasn't a total secret.

'I can't believe I'm actually going to be a mum.' Telling Gillian somehow made it more real than the vomiting or the half-dozen pregnancy tests she'd taken to confirm those first suspicions. With that had come the parenting doubts that she was cut out for this on her own.

'Auntie Gillian will be there for scans and appointments and anywhere else you need me to hold your hand. That's if you want me getting in the way?'

'Of course I do.' Freya clutched her tighter, revelling in the friendship being extended to her and her unborn child. They were going to need all the help they could get. All the exciting stages of pregnancy might seem a tad less daunting as a single parent if she had someone by her side, taking an interest in the little jelly bean growing inside her.

'What about Lucas?' The hug disintegrated as Gillian broached the subject of the unwitting father-to-be and Freya moved back to reclaim her personal space.

'What about him?' Apart from his obvious part in the conception, this baby was nothing to do with her ex-husband. She didn't know how she was going to manage financially or emotionally with parenthood but Lucas not being part of it was the one thing she was sure about.

He'd confirmed it for her with a touching postcard from Lapland a few days after they'd returned, which she liked to look at in those moments of doubt she was doing the right thing by keeping him in the dark. It must've been posted the morning they'd visited the post office, before they'd spent the night together.

I could never be the family man you need me to be...

It would've been prudent if he'd told her that before they'd got married, or indeed before she'd slept with him again. The warning had come too late.

'He has a right to know.' Gillian's tone was much softer than before, probably because she knew she was treading on dangerous ground. Only a minute ago she'd been practically begging that the man be wiped completely from her memory.

'He doesn't have any rights. He wants a divorce.' That word was still a jagged needle piercing her skin every time it was mentioned. It was the legal confirmation her husband no longer wanted her and she had failed as a wife. No one got married thinking this was how it was going to end—living separate lives with a valley full of pain keeping them apart.

'Did he really say that?'

'Yes, he said that. So if you're harbouring any fantasies that a surprise pregnancy is somehow going to fix things you can get it out of your head now.' That had been her initial response too as those two little lines had appeared on the pregnancy test. Until common sense had kicked in and reminded her that married life had never lived up to her dream and it wasn't all going to fall into place now simply because she wanted it to.

The last time she'd seen him, the last words he'd spoken to her had made his position very clear. He didn't want her to be part of his life and a baby would tie them irrevocably together for ever. Neither of them wanted that. She knew she couldn't pretend for the rest of her life that she didn't have feelings for him if he did surprise her and insisted on fulfilling his duty to a child he didn't want. It would kill her to have to see him on a regular basis.

Their relationship had ended nearly a year ago and she'd convinced herself now that night had been a blip, a physical reconnection as a result of high emotions at seeing each other again. A mistake after all. He'd probably assumed she was still on the pill since she hadn't told him otherwise, and if she hadn't been feeling so sorry for herself when she'd got home she might've had time to do something to prevent this.

Except she didn't regret getting pregnant. She gently stroked her invisible bump, grateful for the blessing inside. This was probably her only shot at motherhood after swearing off men for life and she wanted to enjoy every second of it.

'Okay. Okay. You know I don't have any love for the man after everything he's done to you but as your friend it's my duty to ask. From now on I won't say another word about him.' She mimed locking her lips and throwing away the key and managed to make Freya smile again. Something she'd thought she would never do after leaving Lucas at the airport. Even though she'd had weeks of worry, this baby had likely saved her from drowning in a pit of despair over her lost love. She had a different focus now other than herself and her broken heart, and a future to look forward to.

'Thank you. Now can I go and do my job? I can't afford to be fired.' Every penny counted now she was going to be a single parent and with the havoc this pregnancy was already wreaking on her insides she didn't know how long she'd be able to keep working. As if to prove the point, her stomach contracted with a sudden cramp, taking her breath away.

'Are you okay? Do you need to sit down?' Gillian was already pulling a chair over for her but the sharp pain was gone as quickly as it had arrived.

'I know this is early days but it's going to seem like a much longer pregnancy with you fussing all the time.' Freya brushed off the concern so she didn't go down the same line of thought. Cramps and sickness were part of the everyday experience of early pregnancy and she didn't want to stress herself out worrying that every little thing meant she would lose another baby.

'Tough. I'm in this with you.'

Another hug knocked the breath out of her as her new pregnancy partner physically demonstrated the strength of her support. Rather than push her away, Freya embraced the offer of help. For the first time since discovering her own little souvenir from Lapland, she no longer felt alone. Now the secret was out, she could start looking forward to the months ahead and plan her exciting new life as a single mother-to-be.

Lucas had received word that Sam, one of the little boys on the charity trip, had been admitted to the emergency department in Princes Street during the night after a severe asthma attack. Although not strictly one of his patients, he'd called in on his afternoon off to say hello and make sure he was all right. He'd stayed in touch with most of the families from that weekend, concerned with their progress after making a personal connection with those involved. Ironic when he'd been so afraid of committing to a family of his own.

That time with Freya and the children had shown him exactly what he'd been missing in his life but he'd panicked in the face of their strong-as-ever feelings for each other and had run away again rather than talk through his fears. They'd made a good team looking after the girls and they'd had fun together. There was no evidence he would end up anything like his father but he'd let the past take over again and steal Freya from him.

He'd stomped all over her trust by letting her down again and had made it impossible for her to forgive him. Now life seemed emptier than ever he knew the only mistake he'd made had been making a mess of the second chance she'd given him. These weeks apart had been soul-destroying, knowing it had been his own paranoia preventing him from being with her.

He knew he really had lost her for good this time but it didn't stop him lingering in her hospital territory in order to catch a glimpse of her.

He got his wish after he'd paid a visit to Sam on the main wards and he ran into her on the stairs.

'I...er...heard Sam had been admitted. Thought I'd check in on him.' Even though he'd anticipated seeing her again—had been reluctant to leave without doing so—he was a tad tongue-tied when they came face-to-face, as though he'd been caught doing something he shouldn't. After all, he'd been the one to put the brakes on any thoughts of a renewed attachment. If he truly thought they weren't right for each other he shouldn't have felt the need to look for her. He tried to justify his presence here with a valid, professional excuse.

'That's very kind. I was about to pop in myself, but on second thoughts I think I might leave it until later.' She turned and headed back the way she'd come as though she couldn't even bear to breathe the same air as him.

The hostile reception didn't come as a surprise after his recent behaviour but neither did it lessen the burden on his conscience. Every time he thought of how they'd left things at the airport he wanted to punch himself in the face for being so apparently blasé about it all, so it was only natural she wouldn't want to face him now. One night outside his comfort zone and those barriers he'd worked so hard to dismantle had been resurrected in double-quick time because he couldn't shake off that legacy of self-doubt his father had bestowed upon him.

'How are you, Freya?' He chose to ignore the snub and jogged after her in order to attempt a proper conversation. It wasn't merely small talk to ask about her health; she didn't actually look well. The shadows below her once sparkling eyes and paler-than-usual complexion were signs something was amiss. Despite her fiery demeanour there was a weariness surrounding her he could identify with after his own sleepless nights. He wasn't arrogant enough to suggest her thoughts should be entirely consumed by him but he was experienced enough in his own grief to read the telltale signs.

She stopped long enough to acknowledge him with a raised eyebrow, questioning the sincerity of his concern. It smarted as much as the open-palmed slap he'd expected. He still cared about her and that was exactly why he should have left things the way they had been between them. That night together had given them both false hope and caused even more damage than before. She'd told him exactly how much pain he'd put her through after the first break-up and he should never have given her false hope, knowing he couldn't fully commit. By making love to her and backing off he'd hurt her all over again. It was no wonder she could hardly bear to look at him.

'I'm fine,' she spat, taking sufficient time over the reply to warrant doubt.

'I'm not here for a fight, Freya. I just want to make sure you're all right.' He mentally strapped his hands to his sides to prevent him from reaching out to her.

'There's no need,' she insisted, and set off again without him.

It should've been his cue to walk the other way and end his responsibility to her here since she obviously didn't want to see or talk to him again, but he couldn't take his eyes off her when it might be the last time he saw her. He watched her descend quickly to the bottom of the stairs, chin in the air, back ramrod-straight with that same defensive guard back in place she'd had when they'd first met. The one that said, *Trust no one.*

His vigilance meant he saw her stumble when she reached the door, her hands clutching her stomach as she doubled over and had to lean against the wall for support.

'Freya?' He took the steps two at a time to reach her and slipped a hand around her waist to help keep her upright.

'Don't touch me.' She defied the pain she was clearly in to slap his hand away.

'Stop being so stubborn and let me help you.' He might've failed as her husband but he was a doctor too and right now she needed medical assistance.

'I can manage on my own. I don't need…you.' The hiccup in her voice gave way to tears and Lucas's renewed sense of guilt kicked in. He was the reason she wouldn't accept help when she needed it most. Hadn't he done the same thing when his father had repeatedly hurt him until it had been too late? Freya shouldn't have to wait for whatever ailed her to spiral out of control because he'd made her afraid of letting anyone in again.

'I know you don't need me, you're stronger than anyone I know, but at least let me take you to see someone.' If she wasn't going to permit him to give his medical opinion, the least he could do was get her to someone she did trust enough to confide in. It was a pity he wasn't able to offer her the same support she'd provided for him but it was entirely his fault. He'd run out on her twice now, so why should she tell him anything about her life simply because they'd crossed paths now?

She snorted her derision at the apparent idea he knew anything about her now but even that minimal effort had her flinching again. Her legs seemed to buckle beneath her as she let out a sharp cry. Freya wasn't the sort of woman to show any weakness in public, especially not at work. There was something very, very wrong here and he wasn't taking any chances.

'What are you doing?' she gasped as he scooped her up into his arms with little effort.

'It'll be quicker than expecting you and your pride to stagger back to the emergency department.' He wouldn't make any apologies for wanting to keep her safe, although she might not believe he had her best interests at heart.

'Stop it. You're causing a scene.' Even as she was reprimanding him, her face was contorted with pain and he knew he was doing the right thing. He could disappear once he'd got her the help she needed, if that was what she wanted, but he wasn't going to leave her here alone and in pain. Not this time.

'I'm sure they see husbands carrying their sick wives through here every day of the week.' He chose to ignore the small detail that she was in uniform because the only important element of this was to find out what was wrong with her and make her better.

'You're not my husband any more. You made that very clear. Please leave me to deal with this alone.' Her cries echoed in the corridor as she continued to resist his intervention. In the end, he had no choice but to set her back down on her feet before someone did see them and reported him for attempted kidnapping. The thought she hated him so much she would suffer rather than accept his help was a wake-up call to the damage he'd done. He certainly hadn't left her with the feel-good memories of the trip he'd intended by spending the night in that igloo.

At least they weren't too far from their destination and he insisted on accompanying her for the last few steps to get assistance.

'Can we get some help here, please?' he shouted at the staff who were congregated at the nurses' station, and led Freya into the nearest available cubicle. The acute pain in her abdominal region could be anything from appendicitis to a stress-induced ulcer caused by an insensitive ex-husband. In either case, she would need urgent treatment and he doubted she'd be inclined to take it from him.

He helped her onto the bed, and all the while she was crying out and clutching her side. That sense of helplessness he hadn't experienced since his breakdown enveloped him. He wanted to fix everything for her but he didn't know how until they'd run all the tests they needed to diagnose the problem. She wouldn't even let him comfort her, the one thing he should be able to do for his wife.

He stepped out of the cubicle again to yell at the staff, who were already running towards him.

'Lucas?' Freya's shaky voice called him back in time to see a scarlet stain spreading across the centre of the white sheet covering the bed. This time she did reach out for him and he moved quickly to her bedside, willing her to be all right.

'Everything's going to be okay, Freya.' He squeezed her hand to reassure himself as much as her. It was only now, faced with the prospect of something happening to her, he could see what a fool he'd been in not making the most of every precious second he'd had with her.

'Please save my baby.' Her plea plunged straight into his chest cavity and ripped out his heart. She was pregnant? He swallowed down the sudden nausea rising in his belly to focus on comforting her as his brain tried to make sense of what was happening.

'You're in the best place to get help and I'm going to stay here with you.' He moved aside for the team to attend her, his role in supporting her emotionally much more important than trying to interfere in her treatment. She wasn't showing yet and if this was an early miscarriage there was little anyone could do other than keep her calm and make sure she rested.

'How far along are you, Freya?' The senior nurse bustled around, taking Freya's blood pressure, pulse and temperature, and ordered baseline bloods and a urine check in case of water infection. They were being as thorough as anyone could ask in the circumstances.

'About eight weeks…'

The mental calculations almost had Lucas sinking onto the hospital bed beside her. Unless she'd hooked up with someone else immediately before or after their night together, which he highly doubted, this baby was his.

He hadn't given a thought to contraception when they'd been together in Lapland, so this was a possibility he should've considered. Not that it made any difference to what Freya was going through now.

He knew losing a baby would crush her even more than he already had by leaving her. It wasn't her fault, or the baby's, that he'd messed up. He knew what it was to suffer for the mistakes of the parents and he wouldn't inflict the same unjustifiable punishment on another generation.

'I can't go through this again,' she managed to get out between sobs.

He'd barely had time to contemplate being a father and now it seemed as though fate would steal it away from him. Equally horrific, it appeared Freya had gone through this before. Probably alone. It was no wonder she hated the sight of him if he'd caused this to happen twice.

'They're just going to take some blood samples. I know it's hard but try to get some rest.' If he could take her pain or fears away he would, when she'd gone through so much since marrying him. He couldn't hold it against her that she'd kept the news from him when he'd been so vehemently against the idea of a family the last time they'd been together.

Now it was going to be an anxious wait for both of them to find out if this was still a viable pregnancy. The outcome of this day could very well change his life for ever, and while fatherhood mightn't have been something he'd wanted or planned, this baby was a part of him and Freya. Fate had stepped in when he'd made a mess of their relationship and had made the decision for him to be a father. Now they were linked together for the rest of their lives.

He pictured the little bundle of their DNA, with Freya's big brown eyes and warm smile, and he couldn't help but love it already.

Freya wrapped her arms around her stomach, praying that willpower alone could somehow keep her baby safe in there as she was wheeled to the early pregnancy unit. Lucas must've had a hundred questions since she'd dropped the baby bombshell, including asking for confirmation that he was the father, but he'd been calm and supportive so far.

It could've been merely his excellent bedside manner keeping him here with her, but he'd been the one to pull a few strings and get her transferred to the unit for this ultrasound to put her mind at rest that the baby was okay. He'd barely let go of her hand since the cramps had taken hold and she didn't want him to. Even though they'd split in less-than-ideal terms, there was no one else she wanted with her through this. She still loved him and despite all his protestations about becoming a

father she had seen the worry on his face for their unborn child and wanted him to want this baby as much
as she did.

Tears began to pour down her face at the familiar
sight of the tinsel-lined corridors and thoughts of the
last time she'd been wheeled through here on the way
to discover the fate of her unborn child.

After the devastating discovery at the scan of her
first miscarriage they'd told her what would happen
to her body as nature took its course over the follow-
ing weeks but no one had warned her how much she
would mourn the child she had never got to meet. It
had taken her a long time to stop hating those people
who'd told her she was young and could always have
another, as if any loved one was as easily replaced as
an empty milk carton. Or to stop the overwhelming
jealousy and sense of injustice every time someone
else gave birth to a healthy baby when she hadn't. She
wouldn't survive a loss a second time when becoming
a mother was the one thing keeping her going since
she and Lucas had parted ways.

The cramps and bleeding had stopped before she'd
been moved from the emergency department but this
interminable wait for the ultrasound was hell. So much
worse than waiting for those lines to appear on the
pregnancy test in the first place. She knew all too well
what she was in for if the worst happened—sad faces,
apologies and going home without her baby.

Lucas rested his hand on hers and gave her a gentle
squeeze. 'Try and relax. All the tests came back to say
everything was fine.'

'I know but I don't want to go into that room with
false hope, only to see that look on the sonographer's

face that says something's wrong.' Freya would never forget lying on that bed alone, a growing unease when the technician had left the room, and the devastation when she'd brought someone else back to break the bad news that there was no heartbeat. That there would be no baby.

'Do you want me to come in with you?' Lucas made the offer as she waited for her name to be called and she clung to it the same way she was trying to cling to her pregnancy.

'Would you?'

'Of course. This is my baby too. Right?' There was still that air of hesitancy about his role, which could be attributed to the fact neither of them had acknowledged it thus far.

'Right. I'm sorry I didn't tell you but I thought in the circumstances… Your postcard came a few weeks ago…' Until now she'd thought the contents of his note had said everything he thought about the subject of fatherhood. Now, after spending the afternoon taking care of her and fretting with her, she wasn't sure what to believe.

He frowned and she could see him trying to figure out what she was talking about. Then he formed an 'O' with his mouth and shook his head. 'Sorry. I was trying to be honest with you but as usual I've only succeeded in making things worse.'

'Did you mean it?' She had a lot of explaining to do with regard to both pregnancies she'd kept secret from him, but she didn't see the point of putting herself through that if this was all for show. He had to decide once and for all if he was in this with her or not.

'I did. At the time.' The matter no longer seemed so clear cut for Lucas any more.

'And now?'

'I don't want to lose either of you.' The sudden truth hit him as he rested his eyes on the wife he loved so very much and thought of the baby they'd already created. It had taken the shock of potentially having his family taken from him to realise it was what he wanted after all. He just prayed it wasn't too late.

The arrival of the sonographer and the prep for the scan soon concentrated all their fears into one place. The room was silent as they waited for the all-clear and he swore they'd all stopped breathing in order to hear the heartbeat clearly and know beyond doubt the baby was still okay.

'There we go. Normal embryo development for this stage and the lovely strong heartbeat I'm sure you were waiting to hear.' The confirmation that she was still pregnant almost brought him to his knees with gratitude for the chance he'd been given to step up and be a father to this baby.

'Thank you.' His voice cracked with the swell of unexpected emotion at the news.

Huge sobs racked Freya's small frame as she shared his relief and he gathered her into his arms and hugged her close to his chest. As he held her tight and stroked her hair he desperately wanted to make things right. Even if she couldn't bring herself to trust him again she needed someone at her side, supporting her through this pregnancy.

'It's been a long, stressful day for you, Freya. Go home and make sure you get plenty of rest.' The sonographer dished out the same advice she'd been given in the emergency department. She needed to take it easy. It was still early days and they wouldn't want to take any more chances of something going wrong with this pregnancy.

'I'll try,' she promised as she detached herself from his arms, that stubborn streak already rebelling against the idea of help.

'You'll do more than try and I'm going to make sure of it.' He frowned at her, unwilling to let her shut him out when she was going to need him most. That little heartbeat had overridden those fears about becoming a father to make him focus on what was important. The safety of his blossoming family.

'Oh? And how are you going to do that?'

'Easy. I'm moving back home until you've had this baby.'

CHAPTER EIGHT

FREYA TOOK ANOTHER deep breath in and counted to ten as they pulled up outside the house. She was trying to keep calm for the sake of the baby but Lucas wasn't making it easy with this ridiculous plan. It was guilt talking, she knew that, and the only reason she'd let him take it this far was so she could get home quicker. She had to prioritise bed rest over personal feelings when getting into an argument now would only send her blood pressure sky-high.

There was nothing she wanted more than to have him back, raising this baby, with her but not through a sense of duty. If it had been anything more than that, he'd had plenty of opportunity to tell her.

'Thanks for the lift.' All she wanted to do was climb into her bed and alternately thank her lucky stars and feel sorry for herself. Today had brought back a lot of unhappy memories and worry, not to mention the over-whelming relief to still be coming home as a mother-to-be. The effort of it all had left her bone weary.

'I told you, you don't have to go through this on your own.' There was still no sign of any emotional attachment beyond his sense of obligation and even if there had been it would take a lot for her to believe in him again.

By the time she'd got out of the car he'd already opened the front door. She'd forgotten he still had a key. In the naive hope he'd arrive home during those early days of his absence she'd been afraid to change the locks. Now it seemed as though he was quite happy to waltz in as though nothing had happened and take over. She wasn't up for another fight but Lucas pretending he wanted to be part of this was just as bad as not having him in her life, if not worse. It certainly wouldn't make him love her any more—in fact, he'd probably come to resent her for trapping him into a relationship of sorts.

'I am in this on my own. I have been for quite some time in case you've forgotten.' She pushed past him into the house they'd once shared, not really prepared for the sight of him here again in very different circumstances from those she'd ever imagined.

'There's nothing I can do to change the past but I will be here for you and the baby if you'll let me. I know that neither of us planned this, but you still need to take it easy and I'm looking for a place to stay, so this seems like the ideal solution to me.' He tossed his keys onto the table in the hallway just as he always had, so casually an outsider would've sworn he'd never been away. If she'd stockpiled the forest's worth of handkerchiefs she'd cried into, they would tell a different story, but she'd long since picked herself back up and no longer lay around waiting for him to save her from her misery.

'That all sounds very practical but I can manage. This doesn't have to affect you at all.' Today had been a wake-up call. She didn't need stress in her life and that included dealing with an ex who'd never wanted to be a father. The baby came first and she was planning on taking some sick leave until the danger period had passed and even then she might cut back her hours.

Lucas plumped up some of the cushions on the couch and guided her towards a seat, as though he'd just started working in an old people's home. This wasn't the heart-warming return of her husband she'd once dreamed of—it was an act of pity.

'I couldn't be more affected. I'm going to be a father.' He waited until she sat down before he presented his argument. Although he didn't raise his voice, the furrow in his forehead and the careful delivery of his words had her flinching all the same.

In all the scenarios she'd run in her head this wasn't how she'd imagined he would find out either. A threatened miscarriage had barely given him time to get used to the idea of becoming a father before all hell had broken loose. Still, she didn't want the drama to cloud his judgement on the matter when he'd been so adamant he hadn't wanted to start a family with her.

'You don't have to be. I was fully prepared to do this on my own. Just walk away and forget about it. You're good at that.' Now the immediate threat of losing her baby had passed, she was preparing to go into emotional lockdown again. There was no point in letting him get close again, only for him to run when he realised this life wasn't for him. The next time there'd be more than her feelings hurt.

Instead of storming out and slamming the door behind him, which she'd expected and almost hoped for, he sat down on the seat beside her. 'I haven't behaved well towards you, I know that, but I want to make it up to you. I can take you to appointments, help get the house ready for the little one coming, pay the bills, do all the things a partner should do.'

Except love her. That was something that he couldn't seem to force himself to do. She didn't want to play house. It would be too painful when she couldn't have him in her life as more than an obligated father to her baby.

'All the things I can do on my own.' It wasn't going to be easy but she would manage somehow. Time and again she'd found out the hard way she couldn't rely on anyone except herself.

'This house is still half mine, Freya. I could just move back but I want us to work together as a team on this. Look, I'll move out once the baby's safely here if that's what you want. Just let me help.' There was probably a legal argument against it since he'd effectively abandoned her and said 'house' but she knew it was only a matter of time before she caved. Partly because he looked so utterly adorable and sincere but mostly because deep down she knew that was what she wanted.

'I'm tired and I'm scared, Lucas. If I agree to this it's only for the baby's sake. You don't get to interfere in my life. Think of it as a supporting role rather than the lead man.' She needed to protect herself emotionally if they were going to be under the same roof again. They needed clear boundaries so they didn't repeat the mistakes of the past and she could protect what was left of her shattered heart.

'That's fine with me.'

She'd known it would be. After all, it wasn't really her he felt duty-bound to protect. If that had been the case, he would've come back long ago. Her vision blurred with tears and she knew she had to leave before she frightened him off again with actual feelings.

'You know where the spare room is.' He was a lodger now and it was best she start to see him that way. Which might be easier if she moved all his things out of the bedroom they'd once shared. His shirts still hung in the closet for the same reason she'd never changed the locks: she'd still held out that hope for a reconciliation. Just not one like this—where he'd been trapped into it and she was as unhappy and lonely as ever.

'I've made you some vegetable soup and crusty bread. There's even some chocolate cake for dessert.' Lucas balanced the tray on one hand whilst he knocked gently on Freya's door and tried to coax her out with some comfort food.

She needed plenty of bed rest but it wouldn't be healthy for her to confine herself completely to her room if he moved in. He wanted one last chance to prove how much he loved her and to make a go of their marriage, but she was so fragile at the minute, and skittish around him, he didn't want to push her. After everything he'd done she had no reason to trust him but he would be here for her in whatever capacity she would have him. Even if it was only as a chauffeur or home help. Anything was better than spending the rest of his days without her in his life.

'Thanks.' She opened the door wide enough to take the tray and for him to see how pale she was, defying the idea of that mythical pregnancy bloom.

'Are you okay? You're not queasy or having pains again?' He hoped she would tell him if that was the case but since she hadn't seen fit to even confide in him about the pregnancy he wasn't so sure.

'No. Just tired.' It was obvious the attempt at a smile was for his benefit, to get him off her back, but it only managed to deepen his frown. The lack of communication and fractured trust was a side effect, not merely from his illness but also from his continued mishandling of their relationship. In trying to control the situation and prevent the worst from happening, he'd steered them into an even bigger mess. If he didn't want to end up a replica of his father he was going to have to step up and fix things, instead of leaving them to fester out of control.

Which was difficult to do when he was staring at the closed door again, Freya having retreated into her cave with her food like some sort of frightened animal.

He rested his forehead on the cool wood, trying to come up with a solution. As a doctor it was his job to treat the symptoms of an illness but this was about much more than a physical ailment. Freya was unhappy and frightened about the future. He needed something to convince her she could trust him to be there for her and there was one obvious treatment to help get her back to her happy, smiling best. Christmas.

It was only a couple of weeks away, and though he was happy to let the season pass him by without as much as writing a card, Freya in December without tinsel was like Lapland without snow. It simply wasn't the same.

Lucas wrestled the Christmas tree into a bucket in the middle of the living room, sweat running down his back and pine needles pricking every inch of available skin. It had been the biggest, bushiest tree on the lot and he'd picked it specifically because of its close resemblance to those they'd seen in Lapland. Now he'd cut it free of its bindings and the limbs had sprung free, he wondered if he'd been *too* sentimental in his choice. Although Freya had always insisted there could be no such thing as over-enthusiasm at Christmas, it wouldn't come as any surprise if he'd discover a family of woodland animals living in the swaying branches of this majestic beauty. It would certainly make an impact on Freya and that was all he wanted.

His single begrudged contribution during their one Christmas together here had been the heavy lifting of decorations from the attic, so he continued his quest there. One by one he carried the boxes of Freya's treasured baubles down the ladder and into the living room, with a greater deal of optimism than the last time. By that stage he'd already been struggling to come to terms with the news of his father's death and questioning his own suitability as a family man. It was ironic now that impending fatherhood should bring him back.

He didn't know what kind of dad he was going to make, which was why he'd been afraid to take the risk of finding out. That decision had since been taken out of his hands. Even if he was financially supportive, or a physical presence in his child's life, there was no guarantee he'd be able to give that emotional support he'd never received from his parents but he was certainly willing to try. The one thing he was certain of was that Freya would make the best mum. She simply needed a little help to enjoy the pregnancy.

He ripped the tape off the boxes with an enthusiasm he'd never experienced around the season and it was all for her benefit. The amount of glittery fairies and snow-dusted teddy bears surrounding him was quite overwhelming but he vaguely remembered these were the 'room' decorations and set about filling every available furniture space with the oddities. The six-foot artificial pine tree lying in the corner of the attic with its bent branches and the remnants of a few broken ornaments still attached had seen better days. Although it confirmed he'd made the right decision in buying a real tree, images of Freya struggling up the ladder to pack away the decorations alone whilst he had been holed up in his friend's apartment pricked his conscience.

The uncared-for symbol of her emotions last year disturbed him more than the over-the-top nod to a childhood he'd only dreamed of ever could. He'd never understood the whole build-up to one day because he hadn't experienced that excitement himself. It had just been the same as every other day in his house, only perhaps with added disappointment. Freya, on the other hand, craved it, or at least she had until he'd tainted the memory of it. She needed this more than ever.

He was out of his depth in the tangle of fairy lights and tinsel but he draped them around the branches as best he could. It might not win any style awards but as he stood back to admire his handiwork he was quite proud of the display. Even he had to admit it brightened up an otherwise dull December day.

'What on earth are you doing?' a bemused Freya said from behind him.

He stood aside so she could enjoy the full effect of his efforts. 'Christmas isn't far away. I thought we should put a few decorations up to mark the occasion.'

'A few? It looks like an explosion in a tinsel factory.'

The corners of her mouth tilted up as she took in the scene and made it all worth it.

'I thought that was the style you preferred?' He risked a little teasing back, hoping to encourage her back to her usual sparky self.

'Believe it or not, there is some order called for when it comes to Christmas decoration. Symmetry is usually a good place to start.' Freya advanced towards the wonky tree and began to rearrange the ornaments and lights, which even Lucas had to agree he'd chucked on rather than placed with any sort of precision. The criticism didn't bother him when it seemed he'd achieved the purpose of getting her to interact with the world outside her bedroom again.

'You're the expert. I'm still on the beginner's level.' In more areas than just tree decorating.

'I can't believe you went out and bought a real tree. You always complained about the mess they made...'

He'd been in too much turmoil to be bothered with the hassle then but seeing her happy made a valuable argument for going to all the trouble.

'I'm a different man from the one I was then. I wanted you to see that.' Lucas wanted to show her he'd do anything to make her happy, that she could trust him again. More than that, he wanted to convince her this time he was back for good.

As she watched his attempt to decorate the tree, Freya wondered if it wasn't doing her more harm than good to have Lucas here, pretending she could count on him. His gesture was so thoughtful it hurt but she kept asking herself why he would do such a thing if he was only here to save face. No one but the two of them would ever know he'd done this, not even the baby, unless they made it into an anecdote someday. Hope bubbled inside her that this was his way of proving his commitment to her with the one thing she loved almost as much as him.

'You never did this with your mother?' She handed him another box of decorations before she started blubbing again and he wouldn't be able to distinguish her happy tears from all the rest.

Of course she knew now of the strained relationship he'd had with his father but she'd heard nothing about his mother beyond the fact she'd abandoned him when he'd been little. It seemed almost Dickensian that no one should ever have shown him the simple joys of Christmas, such as hanging baubles on a tree or sledding down a hill in the snow, yet he was as awkward in these activities as she was enthusiastic.

He paused as he hung the blue and white snowflake her gran had crocheted for her on his side of the tree.

'I might've done when I was very young but I don't remember much about her at all other than my father's temper and drinking getting worse after she left.' He shrugged his shoulders and continued to upset her sense of visual balance.

It was no wonder she'd had such a hard time persuading him this was fun when the only memories he had associated with the season were probably tied to a sense of loss and gave his actions now more meaning than ever. He was doing this to give her something to look forward to, to take her mind off anything other than happy thoughts, even though it would be a huge personal challenge for him. He was putting her first.

'Is that why you're here now? For the baby?' She

wanted him to spell it out for her so there would be no misunderstanding on either side. If this was about proving himself and abandonment issues he'd never fully explored, she'd rather know upfront instead of waiting to find out eight months down the line and have her heart broken again. It was obvious to her she was still in love with him when it had hurt so much to see him today and that he was still the only one she'd wanted with her when she'd thought she was going to lose the baby. Then again, she'd never actually stopped loving him. She doubted she ever would.

'I'm here for both of you.' He reached over and gave her a half-hug, the first body contact they'd had since he'd comforted her in the hospital. It could've been her hormonal imagination but the gesture seemed to last longer than a mere show of solidarity ought to. There was time for his warmth to seep into her skin and somehow make her feel as though he really could protect her from all the bad stuff. When he did let go he kept his gaze centred on the tree rather than anywhere near her and she wanted to believe it was because he'd felt that connection again too. Just like the one they'd had in the igloo when their world had been each other and nothing else had mattered.

'What's this one? I don't remember seeing this before.' Lucas picked up the little porcelain angel that held so much importance to her.

She could've played down its significance the way she'd done last year when she'd purposely left it in the box. By consigning her heartache to the past and focusing on a future, she'd believed they'd had, she'd thought she'd be able to move past the pain. The ensuing months of misery had shown her otherwise. Lucas had confronted his demons and it was about time she did the same.

'I bought this for the baby I lost.' She took the angel dangling from his index finger and hung it on the front of the tree, where she would see it every day.

Lucas watched it swinging on the tree in a reverent silence that Freya appreciated. Not everyone around her had been as respectful of her loss at the time. As though the early miscarriage somehow hadn't counted as the death of a child. It had felt traumatic enough to a young girl who'd been carrying the much-wanted baby.

'Was it my fault? Did it happen when I left?' he asked finally, clenching his hands into fists as he shared his unwarranted fears over something that had happened long before he'd ever been on the scene.

Freya shook her head. 'No. I was only eighteen when I fell pregnant the first time. We were engaged, I thought we were in love, but he ran out on me the second he found out. I don't know if it was the stress that caused the miscarriage but I guess it was something I never really got over. In hindsight, perhaps my enthusiasm to start a family with you as soon as we were married was my way to get past the tragedy of losing my baby so young. I should never have rushed you into a place you weren't ready to go.'

'I wish you'd told me.' The tenderness in his voice made her question her decision not to tell him from the start, but they'd both made mistakes in those early days of their marriage. With a baby on the way they were going to have to be more mature than ever about how they handled such important issues.

'I should have, I'm sorry, but it was part of my life I simply didn't want to revisit. Everyone told me I was young, I'd get over it in time, and I foolishly believed I really could leave the past behind. It seems we have a lot more in common than we ever realised. Perhaps if we'd both been a bit more honest about our feelings we could've made it through the last year together.' She dared say what she hoped he was thinking. It wasn't the first time she'd wondered where they might be if they'd been able to talk to each other, rather than internalising the baggage they'd brought into the marriage.

'I thought I'd caused you to lose the baby. That you'd never forgive me.' There was a sadness in his eyes as he met hers that made her heart give a little flip. If there was the slightest hope they could still make a go of their marriage, she wanted to seize hold of it and nurture it just like she would their baby.

'Now you know the truth and there's no reason for you to feel guilty, how do you feel about this baby? And me?' There was an involuntary gulp before her last question because she couldn't quite believe she was asking it. She was done pretending if there was a chance of having this for real and they let it slip away for the sake of pride or fear, or whatever reasons they'd had in the past for not coming clean with one another. Whether he wanted to be with her, or he was here for the baby only, she needed to know so she could prepare herself for the future.

'I love you, Freya. I always have. I know it might not have seemed it at times but I've never stopped loving you. Everything I've done... I was trying to protect you.'

'From what?'

'Me.'

'That's the mistake you keep making, Lucas. I'm

not some fragile, defenceless damsel who needs saving and neither are you the villain of the piece. I want to be with you for *you*. I love *you*. All I need to know in return is that you love me and you're going to be here for me. For us.'

'I'm scared I'll turn out like *him*. That I won't be enough.' Finally he let her see inside his soul where those fears were so deep rooted they'd nearly suffocated the life out of him.

'You've always been enough. You just have to believe in yourself.' She took his hand and placed it gently on her midriff and for the first time let herself imagine the three of them as a happy family.

'I might need your help with that.' There was a genuine plea behind the joking facade that Freya couldn't ignore. He was being honest in admitting his fears and asking for her support this time. If she didn't reciprocate that level of trust and believe he'd be there for her in return, they may as well call it quits now. They were both going to have to have faith that they could make it work this time. Although they might have faltered as a couple, they both had to accept the blame for expecting too much the first time around.

'You're going to make the best dad. I know it.' Of that she had no doubt. She'd seen it from the first time they'd worked together on the children's ward and he'd proved it in his continuing care for the youngsters on the Lapland trip. His actions today, and his spontaneous tree purchase, already showed the love he had for her and his unborn child in trying to make Christmas happen.

'I'm really going to be a dad.' He smoothed his hand tenderly over her flat-for-now belly as he came to terms with impending fatherhood, and she knew this baby would finally help love triumph over fear. He was beginning to look towards a future, instead of letting the past keep him chained away from her and everything else that could make him truly happy.

'Yes, you are, and I'm going to be a mum.'

Although there was still a long way to go, that kind of positive thinking and acceptance was exactly what they needed to heal and grow together. Now they'd dealt with the past, this baby was the beginning of a new chapter in their lives—the fresh start they both needed.

She rummaged in the box for a plastic sprig of mistletoe to hold above their heads and seal their new vows to each other in a kiss.

This time she knew love would be enough.

EPILOGUE

One year later

'IF YOU CAN just straighten Reuben's hat, this will be perfect.' Lucas directed his subjects from behind the camera, having become quite the photographer in the months since his son's birth.

'Tell me we're not going to be one of those smug families that sends cheesy Christmas cards of themselves.' Freya adjusted Reuben's green elf hat, which matched her own, but she knew they couldn't hold the pose for ever, no matter how perfect he wanted the shot.

'And why not? I'm very proud of my family.' There was no disputing his claim as the snap-happy father set the timer on his tripod-steadied camera and made a dash into the frame, wearing one of the many ugly Christmas sweaters he'd taken to wearing recently.

The baby, who wasn't to know better, was particularly fond of this particular reindeer jumper with the flashing red nose, but Freya was certain Lucas's sudden enthusiasm for the season wasn't solely for the little one's benefit. He couldn't yet read the embroidered stockings hanging from the mantelpiece, which his daddy had bought for all three of them.

She almost daren't think it but it was possible Lucas was looking forward to Christmas and sharing it with his family as much as she was.

The camera flashed at the exact second their baby elf threw up all over his cute outfit.

'Don't worry, I'll sort it.'

Before she even had to lift a finger, Lucas was there, scooping Reuben into his arms for a much-needed clean-up.

Despite all his fears about becoming a dad, he'd been amazing, doting on his son the way a new father ought to, as well as making up to her for lost time. Their relationship had certainly benefitted from their new honesty policy now there was nothing holding them back from trusting each other, or themselves. They'd both found a certain peace in parenthood, which had gone some way to diluting the pain of the past when they had such a bright future to look forward to together. Starting with their first Christmas at home.

She wanted to make it as special for Lucas as he'd made it for her.

'Any idea what you want Santa to bring this year?' She fished for some gift ideas as he played peeka-boo with the baby on the changing mat. This year she had more reason than ever to go over the top and she couldn't wait to go on a spending spree to show her appreciation for everyone she had in her life.

Lucas paused as he thought about it. Then he turned to her and she recognised that picture of perfect contentment on his face because it was the same expression she saw in the mirror every day. 'I don't need anything else. I have everything I need right here.'

'Me too.' In that second the need for all the fancy

trimmings around her evaporated because she knew
he was right. The sight of her husband playing with her
son was all she needed to make her happy. Family was
the only thing that mattered, and now they had one of
their own, life was complete.

It really was going to be the best Christmas ever.

* * * * *

*If you enjoyed this story, check out
these other great reads from Karin Baine*

*REFORMING THE PLAYBOY
FALLING FOR THE FOSTER MUM
THE COURAGE TO LOVE HER ARMY DOC
THE DOCTOR'S FORBIDDEN FLING*

All available now!

MILLS & BOON®

MEDICAL ROMANCE

THE ULTIMATE IN ROMANTIC MEDICAL DRAMA

---

sneak peek at next month's titles...

In stores from 30th November 2017:

Christmas with the Best Man – Susan Carlisle *and*
Navy Doc on Her Christmas List – Amy Ruttan

Christmas Bride for the Sheikh – Carol Marinelli *and*
Her Knight Under the Mistletoe – Annie O'Neil

The Nurse's Special Delivery – Louisa George *and*
Her New Year Baby Surprise – Sue MacKay

MILLS & BOON®

EXCLUSIVE EXTRACT

He enticed her into one sizzling night… Now notorious sheikh Hazin al-Razim is desperate to claim midwife Flo as his bride!

Read on for a sneak preview of
CHRISTMAS BRIDE FOR THE SHEIKH
the second book in Carol Marinelli's
RUTHLESS ROYAL SHEIHKS *duet*

Hazin lowered his head and their mouths met before he was even fully seated. His lips were warm and Flo's pouted to his.

Soft and sensual, his mouth claimed hers.

She had never known a kiss like it, for it sent a river of shivers through her and the brief bliss of relief faded for she *had* to taste his tongue, yet Hazin made her wait. His hands came to her upper arms and he held her steady when she ached to lean into him.

Then his mouth left hers and she felt its warm drag against her cheek and the scratch of his jaw as his lips found her ear. His breath was warm and he told her his truth. 'I want you so badly.'

For a second she sat, his cheek pressed to hers, his ragged sexy breathing in her ear and his hands firm on her arms and Flo closed her eyes in a vague prayer for common sense to prevail.

It didn't.

Fired on by one kiss, her body crackled like a chip in hot oil and she offered her response to his indecent request. 'Take me to bed.'

Don't miss the scorching duet from Carol Marinelli:

RUTHLESS ROYAL SHEIKHS
*Two royal brothers – bound by duty,
but driven by desire!*

A born leader and a playboy prince… But *nothing* is
more important to Ilyas and Hazin al-Razim than
honouring their royal birth right!

Until their searing passion for two beautiful, fiery women
challenges everything they've ever known – and these
sheikhs won't rest until they've claimed them…

Discover the first part, Ilyas's story
CAPTIVE FOR THE SHEIKH'S PLEASURE

Sheikh Ilyas al-Razim won't let *anything* stand in his
way, especially not the waitress daring to think she can
blackmail him! He'll take the impossibly stunning
Maggie Delaney as his hostage… But once her
innocence is proven, dare she surrender to the pleasure
this desert prince promises?

Available from Mills & Boon Modern

And read the second part, Hazin's story
CHRISTMAS BRIDE FOR THE SHEIKH
*Available from Mills & Boon Medical Romance
Both available December 2017!*
www.millsandboon.co.uk